Return

of the

Wagyl

i

Return of the Wagyl

by *Michael Roses*

Copyright © 2019 Retail Advisory Service

Perth, Western Australia

ISBN 9780975099841

Table of Contents

The eighteenth hole 1

The trip 23

Perth City...29

The fiery election! 40

Going bush 43

The homestead 66

Camping out 79

First night in the bush...96

Wiluna 120

The footy..140

The breakout..149

The DWER 164

Getting hot! 178

Time for action 186

Talawana...198

Thar she blows!...212

Sheep, cattle and crops! 228

Karratha 243

Evening news..261

Jane Wyatt...276

Grand plan 283

The Ministers 297

Gazetted 313

Construction..328

Rain! 350

Back to the bush 354

Dedicated to my great grandmother

Eliza Anne O'Farrell

and to her daughter

Ivy Ellen Skipworth

both of the

Yamatji Community

Carnarvon, Western Australia

Also to the people of

Punmu, Parnngurr, Kunawarritji

and
Jigalong communities.

(and to "Goldie" and "The Tall Man" at Parnpajinya)

The eighteenth hole

The two golfers and their caddies approached the eighteenth tee. They had played the first seventeen holes in this match-play contest and the score was all even – in golfing parlance, all square. It wasn't supposed to be that way as William Piper, the multi-billionaire venture capital financier, had long been a better golfer by several shots. His handicap had been eight or nine for many years. His opponent on this occasion, James Robertson, a successful and wealthy dentist, had long been on a golf handicap of seventeen or eighteen but had cajoled William Piper into a match play contest after a professional golfer had corrected his approach to putting. The professional had noticed that an overwhelming percentage of James' putts that missed the hole did miss to the left, so he had coached James into drawing the putter back slightly inside the line. Now he was putting much straighter – and sinking a lot of putts that he previously would miss. The club professional had also instructed James on how to hit the ball clean off the tee without his usual "dropkick" shot – scuffing the ground which could deflect the direction of the clubhead - so now James was hitting straighter off the tee as well.

The contest may not have happened had William Piper not made a disparaging comment about James in the bar the previous week, after William noticed that James included himself in William's grouping for the club championship rounds that were to start two weeks later. William was sitting at his table in the bar with his two closest friends who were also in his group for the championships, themselves also single figure handicappers. Within the noble game of golf there is a type of hierarchy or pecking order whereby low handicap players regard the higher handicap players as a bit of a burden, as they usually take so many extra shots and tend to scramble a little. Their often-errant sorties into the scrub around the course can rub off onto other players in their group.

"I see you have entered yourself in my group James for the club championships, James. Does that mean we will have to drag you around the course?"

James sought to placate William by stating that he was on the verge of becoming a much better golfer, which drew a crass remark from William.

"No William, I have been taking lessons from Mark this last week and I believe I will be extremely competitive, even on a par with yourself and your friends here."

"Tell me when that's happened James, not that it's going to happen. All three of us are hoping to win the Plate this year you know."

In doing so, James had laid down the challenge.

"Well I am sure you will see what I mean, William. In fact William, I am prepared to take you on here next week William – eighteen holes of match play, off the stick - no shots given. What say for a cool grand – one thousand dollars?"

"Huh, James, really – I wouldn't get out of bed on a Sunday morning for that."

Now James was beginning to feel the insults cutting deeper, especially as William's two friends were listening intently and James detected a slight sardonic smirk from the pair. They too were very wealthy entrepreneurs.

"Okay then! Let's up the ante! I will put my seaside villa in Virginia on the line, if you do the something similar."

William was quick to respond. He knew of James' seaside villa and knew it was worth more than one million dollars but, being as cocky as he was, he arrogantly met the challenge.

"James, if you beat me off the stick, no shots given, here next Sunday, I will hand over to you my cattle station in Western Australia – that's worth tens of millions of dollars. You know you are going to lose James, but a fool and his money go separate ways, so I accept your challenge – on the condition that, should you somehow win my cattle station, you cannot on-sell it within ten years, okay. You need to work it, okay."

William was so certain that he would win this one, as indeed he normally would, but James had analysed how many putts he had usually missed to the left and was confident that he could match it with William.

James didn't disclose to William that his seaside villa had recently been deemed as being at risk from erosion, but William didn't disclose that his cattle station in a remote area of Western Australia had its problems too and was in need of a major restoration of its underground bores that provide water for the cattle.

But in the modern-day world, that's business!

So now they had played seventeen holes of which William had won three holes and James had won three holes.

"We've come all this way for nothing" James said to William.

The eighteenth hole was a long par three of almost two hundred yards with bunkers guarding the green to the left and to the right.

William had the honour. His two iron tee shot landed just short of the green but rolled onto the green to just four feet to the left of the hole. That would be a relatively easy putt for a birdie two on this difficult par three final hole – though he would be putting across the slope of the green. William's caddy gave him the high five, for that was an extraordinarily good outcome for such a long iron shot. Leaving just a four foot putt for a birdie on such a hole was as good as it gets.

James tee shot was with a three iron, as he was younger and somewhat stronger than William Piper and knew he could quite easily reach the green with that club.

It is a strange thing in golf how one player's shot can have a profound impact on another player's shot. William was on the green and ever so close to the hole with what, from the tee, looked like an easy tap in birdie putt. Now James was worried, as he might be about to lose his million dollar beachfront house. How would he explain this to his wife?

James was anxious and his tee shot reflected this. Into the greenside bunker his ball went, about forty feet from the pin, though the face of the bunker before him was not considerable. He really had to get this bunker shot close to the hole for a chance at a par three and hope that somehow William would miss his birdie putt.

James went into the bunker with his trusty sand wedge and feeling quite some trepidation about the shot he was about to play, but also trying also to keep himself composed.

It was probably the last thought he had before swinging the club, but he remembered to avoid hitting too much sand for fear of leaving the ball in the bunker. As he was still several yards from the putting surface James gave an almighty swing, thinking it was better to be long rather than short, as he rarely overshot the hole on a bunker shot.

The worst thing happened! That last thought to hit it a little shallow caused James to skinny the shot straight across the entire green and toward the clubhouse.

William looked at his caddy who once again gave him the high five, as James ball was seemingly about to smash its way into the members' lounge. Except that the American flag was flying atop the flagpole in front of the clubhouse.

Now, the odds of one circular object such as a golf ball impacting with another circular object such as a flagpole would have one believe that such an impact would result in

4

the object in motion ricocheting in any conceivable direction – but not back onto the green, nor into the cup.

But in this wondrous game of golf, such things can and do happen. As if by some form of divine intervention, James' ball rolled up onto the green and slowly trickled down toward the hole. All men watched in virtual disbelief as James' ball rolled closer and closer to the pin – and into the hole for a birdie two. Now it was William who had to negotiate his putt of just four feet, but across the slope of the green. Give it too much borrow or too much speed and it will slide past the hole on the high side. Too little speed or too little borrow and it will miss below the hole. William took an eternity to line up the putt – perhaps even longer than the rules allow. Perhaps even as long as Jack Nicklaus did on the thirteenth green at Augusta in 1986 when he stormed home to win the Masters by one shot!

William calculated he would allow about three ball-widths of borrow to the left and give it the correct speed. He lined up his putt then ever so carefully addressed the ball. He drew the putter back, but ever so gently stubbed his putter on the green on the way through – taking just a smidgin of pace off the putt.

As they say in golf – never up, never in! William's putt finished an infinitesimal half inch short of the cup and slightly on the low side.

James had suddenly become the owner of a cattle station in the east Pilbara region of Western Australia.

William resigned himself to his loss and as golf requires, he was quick to congratulate James and shake hands.

"Congratulations James, you really did play well out there today, I owe you an apology for my comment last week."

William extended his hand for a handshake and the men shook hands before making their way toward the clubhouse.

"Looks like you have an exciting future ahead of you in this club. Unless I am mistaken, I believe we both shot eighty-one off the stick – nine over par. Obviously, you are going to win a few weekend trophies in the next few months before you reach your new true handicap."

"Thank you, William! I do feel a little like a shark over this as I was fully aware of just how beneficial Mark's advice to me was, but I am also surprised that you put so much on the line over this."

James was a little surprised that William's loss did not seem to perturb him very much at all in the moment, though he assumed that William might be concealing some true dismay at losing a cattle station worth more than twenty million dollars – though it would not take long for William to provide an explanation.

"Hey, let's shower and change and talk in the clubhouse over a drink. You won this bet fair and square James."

The men and their caddies made their way into the locker room where they proceeded to shower and to change into clothing that was acceptable to wear within the clubhouse. A lot of members would coalesce at the club on a Sunday morning and stay for lunch to talk business and reflect upon their week in the hustle and bustle of big finance. This club was San Jose's drinking hole for people who were the epitome of the Silicon Valley's high-flyers. There was no paucity of multi-millionaire business people here and standards of presentation and decorum were high. These men were as respected as any at the club and would spend some time talking over a few drinks and then stay for lunch.

While James was still in his shower cubicle William's caddie thought he should make a comment to console his player who had just lost a cattle station of quite some worth. He assumed his golfing friend would be feeling quite despondent about his loss.

"William you played great golf out there today. You've shot just nine over par to play to your handicap and he has had a total day out. There is no way he should have won that match."

"Frank! James told me he had improved a lot from his lessons and I tried to belittle him in front of my friends. I feel pleased for him. He put his money where his mouth is and I fell for it. I do admire gumption in anybody you know. Besides, I have been suffering quite a quandary over the cattle station recently as there are some problems there with the infrastructure. But I will talk to you with James about that when we are in the lounge."

Once the men were changed, they made their way into the clubhouse lounge and took up William's usual table to order drinks – a cocktail for William and his caddie, a beer for James and his caddie. Then the conversation started.

"So James please tell me – what on earth did Mark teach you that has made such a sudden improvement to your game? I mean, I can understand how some lessons can make a modest improvement, but you have played about ten shots better than what you would have just two weeks ago, right."

"Yes I guess that about sizes it up William. Basically, there were two things that he picked up about my game when I played alongside him last month. He approached me to say he could improve my game by several shots so I booked the lessons. The first thing he got me to do was tee the ball up slightly higher and to adjust my swing so that I hit the ball clean off the tee, whereas I had a tendency to do a bit of a dropkick and take some dirt with it – which of course tended to cause some deviation in club head line. It took a while but just by keeping my chin up a little I was able to eliminate the dropkick from my tee shots."

"And the second thing?"

"Putting, William! Mark took note of how many putts I missed that day, as I had never taken lessons with him before and after the game he gave me the sad truth, that I missed seven putts from inside ten feet that all went below the cup. But it wasn't my lining up the putts causing the problem but that I was allowing my right hand to dominate my left in the putting stroke. So Mark got me to place both thumbs straight down the face of the grip and to take the putter back slightly inside the line. You may not have noticed, William, but I sank seven such putts today and missed just one."

"Yes you did sink some putts out there, didn't you! And you picked up your cattle station in Western Australia James. Have you ever been to Western Australia?"

"No! I went to Sydney last year for my son Andrew's wedding but only to Sydney. Andrew married an Australian girl – Rebecca Weston from ... ah ... a place called Little Plains in New South Wales – but no, I did not go to any other places in Australia. Of course, I do know where Western Australia is William but, it is such a big place, can you tell me where your cattle station is?"

"Have you heard of Perth City?"

"Well yes, of course – it's the capital city of Western Australia. I recall they held the defence of the America's Cup there many years ago ..."

"In 1987 James."

"Yes that would be about right – and one thing I do recall from that William, is that – apart from Dennis Connor retrieving the Cup – our man Walter Cronkite went there to cover the story and described Perth City as the world's best kept secret. He showed the city from a hill nearby".

"King's Park, James! It overlooks Perth City and Walter Cronkite's comments are totally understandable. It is quite an enthralling view of Perth City from there, as you will see.

Apart from that Perth is not a small place James – probably about the same size as San Jose. I was last there just a couple of months ago and took a train ride south of the city to a place called Mandurah to see a business associate. He had quite a magnificent house on a canal system complete with a boat mooring, but what did surprise me was the fifty-mile train ride to get there."

"Fifty miles eh!"

"But that is to the south of the city. Your cattle station, James, is in an area known as the east Pilbara."

"The east Pilbara! I haven't heard of that before. So how far is that from Perth City?"

"Oh - only about eight hundred miles."

"Eight hundred miles! Are you kidding me?"

"No James, Western Australia is a big place – more than three times the size of Texas, larger than Alaska and even larger than Greenland. The quickest way to get to your cattle station is to fly into Perth then fly to a mining town called Newman and take a four wheel drive the rest of the way to the homestead. That section is over one hundred miles long on a dirt road, okay. The alternative is to drive there via a town called Wiluna then take the Canning Stock Route north for about two hundred miles, then a deviation track to the homestead."

James was getting the picture and feeling a little apprehensive already about what he was getting into. Perhaps even feeling that he might offer to re-neg the bet and allow William to keep his cattle station.

"So how soon do you think you can make a trip to Western Australia James?"

"Oh I have been contemplating that already and ... ah ... initially I will ask my son Andrew to go there on my behalf to check the place over. Andrew has just graduated from Harvard and completed his doctorate thesis just last month.

He majored in geology and his specialty area is hydro-geology and he completed his thesis on the activities of oil companies involved in fracking in Montana."

"Well, sounds like he is cut out for work in Western Australia James – they have some huge mining operations over there. Don't be too surprised if he stays longer than you expect him to."

"Actually, Andrew is at my residence at the moment William, I really would like him to meet you and to talk a few things over if you don't mind. I could call him now."

"In that case we had better order lunch and give him a little time to get here."

"Well he is just ten minutes away but, great, let's place an order."

James called his son Andrew who was waiting a call from his father but did not have any idea what it was about. He agreed to make his way to the clubhouse forthwith.

"William you said that your cattle station is worth tens of millions of dollars, why would you have put up such an asset as a side bet over a game of golf?"

"James, you know that in this wonderful game of golf most of us only play to our handicap in about one game in every five or six. The rest of the time we are within two, three or four shots of our handicap. Sometimes you play well and you come in two or three shots better than your handicap, but that is not very often. So even on a bad day I will play to a fourteen handicap, right?"

"Right!"

"So being an eighteen handicapper you really needed to have a day out to match me – to play to a fourteen handicap. There was no way you would normally have beaten me out there today, right?"

"Correct - but I did tell you that I had improved."

"Yes, and I was sufficiently arrogant to have paid little heed. Perhaps there is a lesson in that for me to take where I am going – into this new world of education."

A table attendant approached the table.

"Would you gentlemen like another round of drinks?"

The men ordered a second round of drinks.

"You do realise that you gave me odds of almost twenty to one, don't you?"

"James, I know my cattle station is worth almost twenty million, okay. But as you know I deal in venture capital and ... ah ... I am presently working on what could be the latest big thing, which is possibly worth billions of dollars, okay. I have to assess whether the time and energy that I am required to put into presiding over the management of my cattle station in Western Australia might actually cost me even more than it's worth, just from being distracted from the single focus I need to devote to my new venture. It needs all of my time and energy and then some – before somebody else gets there before me."

"Your new venture! Do you mind if I ask what that might be?"

"No I don't mind James. It is on-line education – bringing the best teachers in virtually all mainstream subjects from all over the world, to all students all over the world. Okay!"

"Hmm ... sounds interesting William! Where did that come from?"

"Ironically it came from Western Australia James – the last time I was there I caught a taxi from Perth International Airport to the city and it was the taxi driver who told me that he had just launched an educational website called World of Words. So I checked out his website and I must admit I was duly impressed. It was he who suggested to me that the best teachers in the world should place lesson plans on-line so that anybody can have access to them. I guess I too saw a future in that."

"So I advertised within the private school system here in the States for local teachers who regard themselves as being among the best to come forward and to put their hand up to be involved and I was totally inundated with applications. True, I was offering a substantial increase in remuneration on what they were earning within the school system, but it also seems most of them considered the idea of a year or two out of classroom activities and into something new and different had quite some appeal to them."

"So you know in my situation I have to weigh up the cost of foregone opportunity brought about by any delay caused by all the problems that the cattle station causes me. I really don't have the time to stay caught up in that while I am endeavouring to launch my online education empire. So it's a bit of a relief for me now you know."

"I haven't heard of your project before William so just how far advanced is this concept?"

"No you wouldn't have James as the venture capital system is still in phase one on this and investors are very circumspect about what they invest in, but as much as I am willing to share risk and reward as much as anybody else, if the community does not back this I will be going it alone. There were times I thought Mark Zuckerberg might be interested in something like this but to me this could be bigger than Facebook – you know, from the advertising aspect."

"Bigger than Facebook! That's a bit of a call isn't it?"

"James – how many high school and college students are there in the world who would like to have access to the best lesson plans - online? There are hundreds of millions of them – and not all people are using Facebook you know. My wife does every day but some of the crap that people put up on Facebook, I mean really, do I give a rat's clacker if somebody is having a hamburger at McDonalds? No!"

"Consider also how much corporations spend on advertising at the Super Bowl or the World Series or the NBL. James, they spend billions of dollars every year on advertising and Facebook has tapped into that. But you put something out there that everybody wants to use – like the best lesson plans – and it could be worth much more than Facebook will ever raise."

"Hmmm … I see, yes you could be right William, so why bother going through the usual venture capital community rather than doing this yourself?"

"Oh I will be the major shareholder but I need others involved for the expertise in getting this out to the market. We will need to bring in teachers and lecturers from every country James. Apart from that the organisational hierarchy within every country will need to be very specialised so this has to involve some top organisational executives from the outset. My own executives are not up to this – they are very good at what they do but this kettle of fish is vastly different to anything we have dabbled in previously. It … ah … gets me very excited James."

James looked to his left to notice that his son Andrew had just signed in as a visitor to the clubhouse.

"Oh, Andrew is here now. William I would like you to meet my son Andrew. Andrew meet Mr. William Piper."

"Good morning Andrew."

"Good morning Mr. Piper."

"Call me William please and congratulations on graduating from Harvard Andrew. You must be relieved to know that is behind you now – all those years of study."

"Thank you, William, yes I guess I can take the foot off the pedal just a little now but it is an ongoing aspect of life really isn't it – keeping up with the latest in change and the technology in particular. Even in my field of hydro-geology the outpouring of new software is mind-blowing."

"Yes we've been discussing that here this morning Andrew and I have been telling your father about my own foray into education which we are working on at the moment. But your father has something important to tell you."

"Andrew ... ah ... William and I would like you to go to Western Australia for a while to oversee the management of a cattle station that William owns ..."

William glanced at James. He wasn't sure what James was thinking but he thought that perhaps James wanted to break the real news to William with some circumspection.

"... which should be quite an adventure for yourself and Rebecca and ... ah ... you can stay there as long as you want to ..."

"A cattle station! I don't know a lot about cattle William."

"No but there are some issues pertaining to the subterranean water supply which, you must admit, is right up your alley Andrew."

"Well, what can I say, thank you William, I have been contemplating my immediate future and ... ah ... I am already finding that things are pretty competitive out there in relation to job prospects, so I guess I can do that for a while. I did complete some electives in business management because it, kind of, permeates everything in the professional realm you know."

"Yes Andrew and your father has procured a type of shareholding in the cattle station, so you will be working for your father too."

"Really! Wow that is great! A bit of a change from fillings and extractions eh father?"

"Yes so I am very pleased that you are available to leave sometime soon if you think that is possible."

"Oh I am sure that Rebecca will be very pleased to travel to Australia again as she hasn't been there to see her family in over twelve months now."

"So you could go to Sydney first before proceeding on to Perth. Sure! Just take a few days in Sydney Andrew but I would like you to be at the station within two weeks if you can manage that."

"Oh sure, no problem, three or four days in Sydney then ... ah ... Perth eh! How far is the cattle station from Perth?"

"You will need to fly north from Perth then take a four-wheel drive to the station Andrew, which is quite some way from Perth City. It is rather remote but it is also very self-sufficient. They grow their own vegetables and fruit and we have some dairy cattle for milk, we have chickens, sheep and a fishpond. So there's no paucity of good food and, of course, plenty of beef."

"Where does the beef come from?"

"Beef cattle, Andrew - but don't worry the staff take care of that. We need somebody there to oversee the renovation of the underground water supply. From what your father has told me, you could be just the right person for this."

The table attendant returned with drinks and asked if they would like to order their lunch.

William ordered a fillet mignon with mushroom sauce and roast vegetables, James ordered the fish of the day with creamy tartare sauce and a side salad and Andrew ordered lamb shanks with garlic sauce, fries and a garden salad.

"So how often do you visit your cattle station William and can you tell me about the landscape?"

"I have made a point of being there twice every year for one week at a time for the last ten years. The workers know that I will be there and that keeps them in shape. It's a very arid landscape, semi-desert, very hot in summer – which, of course, is between December and February in that part of the world – and that is also their wet season when the monsoons and occasional cyclone activity has a bearing on everything. Apart from that, it has its own unique beauty – a lot of red dirt, sand dunes and clear blue skies. Oh and make sure that you carry a sat phone everywhere you go – people have perished out there from time to time by being ill-prepared. So that is an absolute imperative, Andrew, that you always have a sat phone with you at all times."

"And William you mentioned a stock route in that part of the country - can you tell Andrew what you know about that."

"Ah yes the Canning Stock Route which is about fifteen hundred miles long, it goes from the town of Wiluna to somewhere in the north of Australia, but I'm not sure where. We do have contact occasionally with people who are stranded or in some form of trouble and we've taken more than a few in until they are well enough to return to Perth City."

"You mean they don't continue their journey?"

"No, if they are under-prepared they usually become disillusioned with the whole experience and want to return to civilisation as quickly as possible. It's not uncommon for people to be out there on the trail for two or three weeks. Then they have to contemplate the long journey back to Perth or on to Darwin – and that's a long way from anywhere."

"So William you said you would like Andrew to be there within about two weeks. Is that to take over the management from somebody who is leaving?"

"The managing couple will be leaving next week actually as they have suffered some misfortune, but, the other staff can keep the place ticking over for a while in most respects. The water infrastructure is probably beyond their capability, so Andrew will certainly be worth his weight in that respect."

"So what type of misfortune beset the managing couple? Did they suffer an accident or something?"

"I was hoping you wouldn't ask. Yes, Frank and Diane have been good for me there but she suffered from a snake bite and was very fortunate to survive the ordeal. We flew her to Newman by helicopter then the Royal Flying Doctor flew her to Perth where she was in intensive care for several days."

"Snake bite! So there are some deadly snakes in the area?"

"Andrew! Western Australia is the world's capital of things that can bite you, sting you or eat you. Yes there are many species of deadly snake there – brown snakes, death adders, the gwardar, the dugite and even tiger snakes in some wetter areas of the Pilbara region."

"Hmm ... not sure I should let Rebecca in on that straight away. Perhaps when we arrive at the station I will caution her a little."

The men's luncheon dinners arrived at the table and they continued to chat further as they enjoyed their lunch.

"So where is your wife Rebecca now Andrew?"

"Oh she is here with me in San Jose and I know she has been planning to make a move according to my job prospects but, I'm not sure she was planning to move that far away."

"Well, being Australian herself she will be an asset for you in acclimatising to the particular sub-culture over there. Your father mentioned that Rebecca's mother is from a small town in the east."

"Yes William, Rebecca's mother is an Aboriginal lady named Eunice Atkins, an Aboriginal artist who goes by the name of Rima. She has many works on display in various parts of the country. Oh and Rebecca has been to Perth several times for friends' weddings I believe and possibly for a football final too."

"Hmm ... she won't be far away from Aboriginal people at the station Andrew. In fact I believe there are still some desert dwellers out there at times. My workers have come across families in the desert who were in a spot of bother more than once."

"Why would they be out there if that put their lives in peril William?"

"Just think of the land as their church Andrew and you will be on the right track, okay. The Australian Aboriginal people have a profound affinity with the land that people of other cultures cannot fully understand, perhaps excepting our own Indian population."

"Hmm ... okay I will keep that in mind William thank you."

"So William, if you don't mind me asking, when my son Andrew arrives at the station, what are the accommodation arrangements for Andrew and Rebecca and will they be living in the shadows of other workers there?"

"No James there is a separate house for the managing couple and the workers have their own bungalows in a communal type of situation, which seems to suit them because they coalesce in the evening around a barbeque or a campfire or just to drink some beer. But the manager's house is some hundred yards away from the commune, as we call it."

"Well that is encouraging Andrew, Rebecca and yourself will be able to live as a married couple just as you are here. I was a little concerned about the setup out there you know."

"No there's no shortage of anything out there William, we have to be as self-sufficient as possible. You can't simply run down to the corner store for a loaf of bread or a pint of milk. The station has its own fully equipped workshop with almost all engineering and mechanical facilities you will ever need. We have a tradesman there named Jack who is a welder by trade but has turned his hand to mechanical fitting and he can do just about anything, so he can fix whatever breaks down."

"Great!"

"Yes, in fact we lease him out at times to neighbouring stations when they need him."

"So how do you … ah … get your cattle to the market William?"

"Well after mustering by helicopter, trailbike and cattle dog we load them into trucks and they make the journey to the port at Geraldton – that's the nearest big town on the coast Andrew."

"Cattle dog?"

"Oh yes the Aussie healer! It is a distinctive pure breed of working dog well suited to the conditions and the task they are assigned rounding in those cattle. Sturdy little devils they are, not as affectionate toward humans as most other breeds but they are totally obsessed with cattle. We have red and blue healers and they keep the dingoes at bay too."

"Dingoes?"

"Oh absolutely Andrew the dingoes are all over the place and they are vermin, of course, so we cull them occasionally but they always bounce back in numbers."

"Do they feed on the cattle?"

"No they like to eat sheep – of course sheep can't defend themselves but the cattle can see them off. But their main staple diet is the natural fauna – the lizards, snakes, wallabies, small kangaroos and roadkill too."

"Are the dingoes aggressive?"

"Dingoes! No way, they are in fact one of the most timid species of dog on the planet. The only time to be wary of dingoes is when they have pups."

"And ... ah ... there is another breed of cattle dog over there isn't there William ... ah ... that red dog they made a film about?"

"The kelpie! That's strictly a sheep dog Andrew. No you won't see any kelpies in our neck of the woods, they are specifically for sheep farming in the grain growing areas. They grow a lot of wheat out there but further south where there is more rainfall in winter. I have seen them of course and they are an extremely intelligent breed of dog – even comparable to a border collie really - but not quite as affectionate toward humans. Too obsessed with sheep to care about anything else! Legend has it the kelpie was actually bred from the dingo by an Irish scallywag who crossed a dingo with a Scottish Collie just to see what he came up with. But if you need a dog that can run all day, don't look past that kelpie. Oh we also have a couple of kangaroo dogs that the workers take out when they are on horseback to keep the wild boars at bay."

"Kangaroo dogs! I have never heard of a kangaroo dog before."

"No you wouldn't have - they are not very common but apparently they are a cross breed, most likely between a Greyhound and a Scottish Deerhound or an Irish Wolfhound so they are a very large dog and very fast and agile too. Apart from being sufficiently aggressive if wild boars do get too close."

"You seem to have picked up on quite a bit of Aussie lore there William."

"It's a different world there Andrew and it is rather infectious, so be prepared to be slightly adjusted yourself, okay."

The men ordered another round of drinks.

"But they are really a lot like us aren't they, those Aussie people, we ... ah ... seem to have a lot in common."

"Oh sure and you know the last time I was there I was talking to Jack and he explained to me that when he was a young boy and television first came to Australia in the early sixties, most of the programs worth watching were from here in the States. He mentioned ... ah ... Rin Tin Tin, Fury, Sea Hunt, Leave it to Beaver, Highway Patrol, Seventy Seven Sunset Strip, Disneyland and, of course, the Micky Mouse Club. In fact Jack recalled that in watching Leave it to Beaver they first learned of so many things that we enjoyed here in the States that they had never heard of before – like donuts and hotdogs, milkshakes and hamburgers. Jack says when he was a boy and went to Scarborough beach on a hot summer day in Perth City he could buy a pie or a toasted sandwich and that was it."

"So they developed a type of cultural affinity with us through television before the world became a small place through the internet?"

"Yes exactly Andrew and they eventually managed to play catch up with respect to white goods too. Jack recalls that even as a boy in the late fifties his parents did not have a refrigerator or a washing machine. Nowadays, of course, most of what they buy comes in from China, Japan or South Korea so they are not short on anything. But the station is not short on technology Andrew - we have a satellite dish, the helicopter, an airfield and a small plane and a generous supply of all parts that might be required should something break down."

"So Andrew, has William been able to whet the appetite for Australia a little?"

"Oh look I was blown away by my short stay in Sydney, sure, it reminded me so much of San Francisco with the harbour, the bridge, the beaches and the weather. Yes I am looking forward to this change, so thank you William."

"No, thank your father Andrew, he will have more to tell you about this when the time is right I am sure, don't you think James?"

"Yes I guess so! Perhaps we will spend the rest of the day together son and just work through a few issues to get you ready for the trip."

With their luncheon completed the men stood and shook hands to go their separate ways.

"James I will have my attorney contact yours to make the arrangements for the documentation to be signed but my word is as good as a contract. James Robertson, on this day, Sunday the sixth of October 2024 you have become the owner of a cattle station in Western Australia. Andrew, I wish you the best and I am sure this will be a great experience for you."

"Thank you, William - and good luck with the internet education project. I really do hope you succeed with that William - it sounds like something the entire world needs."

"Yes thank you James and once again, I do apologise for treating you with the disdain that I did here last weekend. Goodbye now, I am going into the office to discuss some issues with the club captain."

"Goodbye for now William but I will see you next week for the championships."

James and Andrew turned to leave the clubhouse.

The trip

James and Andrew went to Andrew's house to inform Rebecca of the news that would bring about a profound change to their lives for their immediate future – though they had no idea at that time just for how long their lives would be completely upturned. They entered the house together and Rebecca greeted her father in law.

"Hi darl! Hello James, how are you?"

"I'm fine thank you Rebecca - busy as usual and have just been to the golf club to negotiate a new deal with a very fine and wealthy man, actually."

"Great! What kind of deal is that?"

Andrew answered for his father.

"Ah ... it's a deal that requires you and I to move to Australia for a while to work, actually, Bec."

"Australia, wow, will that be Sydney?"

"Ah ... no not exactly, in fact the other side of Australia ... ah ... Western Australia if you don't mind that."

"Oh Perth, great, I've been there several times. It's a very beautiful place you know. Great weather too."

"Yes well we will start from Perth but father has something to tell you about his new venture and where we will be required to move to."

"Ah ... yes, well, Rebecca I have bought into a cattle station in the east Pilbara area and the station is in need of a major renovation of a complex watering system that provides drinking water for the cattle, as it sometimes doesn't rain out that way for several weeks or even months at a time. So Andrew is aptly suited to being involved in the project as the water will be drawn from the water table, so from below the ground."

"The east Pilbara eh? Hmm ... that would seem to take up a fairly big area? So just which part of the east Pilbara are we talking about here?"

"Okay its east of a town called Newman and west of a large lake called Lake Disappointment."

"So it's way out in the sticks then! And just how long are we expected to go for?"

"That's indefinite at this stage Rebecca, but I would envisage that Andrew could be required there for at least six to twelve months. But don't worry William Piper who is arranging this has assured us that the station has all the mod cons, you know, television, internet, a fully furnished house with a home theatre, a swimming pool and even has its own airplane and airstrip."

"Yes well way out there you would need your own plane just to go shopping. But, hey, great that's going to be quite a change from what we have been doing and I will be much closer to my family. Perhaps they could come visit me occasionally."

"Yes I'm sure they will and we will certainly encourage them to do so – even pick them up from Perth City."

"So how soon do we leave?"

"Well we do need Andrew there as soon as he can be so without causing too much inconvenience to you both, can you tell me how soon you could leave."

Andrew looked at Rebecca and shrugged his shoulders as he wanted to give her the space she needed to bring some loose ends together before setting out on such a momentous sojourn. He knew she would want to say goodbye to all of her friends with a luncheon or two and to pack suitcases and arrange for some furniture removals. The rest she would place into storage so they could rent out their house in San Jose for at least six months.

"Okay just give me three days if that is alright with you two. I need to do a few things and say goodbye to people."

"Sure, so shall we say, let's see, today is Sunday, why don't we book flights out of San Jose this coming Thursday or Friday."

Andrew thought that Rebecca would opt for Friday but she surprised him.

"Thursday will be fine. I can manage that. So do we fly to L.A. or San Francisco?"

"We could spend a night in San Francisco if you would like to. Apparently its quite a long flight to ... ah ... Brisbane from there, so we could break up the trip a little that way."

"Excellent! I love San Francisco. So it's Brisbane to Sydney for a couple of days to see my family and then on to Perth?"

"Right!"

"And from Perth how do we get to the station?"

"We will fly north to Newman then go by four wheel drive to the station. The staff will arrange to be there for us."

"Okay so, I had better start packing and work out what we are taking and what we are leaving behind. Well congratulations my husband."

Rebecca gave Andrew a small kiss on the cheek.

"Oh and is the salary package up to standard with what you might have earned here in the States?"

James responded.

"Oh Andrew will earn a lot more there in Australia and there will be a package for yourself too, Rebecca, as there will always be something to do. William informed me that his managing couple were grossing over four hundred thousand."

"Geeze that's a lot – four hundred thousand!"

"Yes well it's not a nine to five job you know, in fact it is very much a twenty four seven situation – be on call at all hours every day. Of course, most of it involves managing the other workers to ensure their efficiency. The managing couple are preparing comprehensive notes and files covering the entire situation. You might need to meet them in Perth to go over things."

"So they won't be there when we arrive at the station?"

"No they have already moved on to Perth ... ah ... she had a small accident and needed medical treatment."

"Oh that's no good. What type of accident?"

They were hoping she wouldn't ask.

"Ah ... she had a bit of a run in with a king brown."

"A king brown eh? Hmm ... I do know something about Australia's snakes, of course and the king brown is probably the second or third deadliest snake in the entire world, so she is very fortunate not to lose her life."

Andrew decided to attenuate any possible reticence this might cause by acknowledging Rebecca's knowledge of Australia's snakes.

"Really, so what are the other two deadliest snakes?"

Andrew and James looked at each other and exuded a slight giggle.

"They would be the fierce snake and the coastal taipan - although the eastern brown or the western brown or the death adder or the tiger snake would all be almost as deadly. Most Australian snakes are pretty deadly!"

James and Andrew were impressed with Rebecca's knowledge of snakes as William had mentioned the same, but James was keen to alleviate any concerns she might have.

"They were able to administer an anti-venin there at the homestead as they always keep a supply for just such an emergency."

Rebecca shook her finger at James.

"I've heard that line before ... that was Foghorn Leghorn."

James and William laughed.

"Okay so let's get moving boys … today Crosby, today! I will call the travel agent to book the flights and the property manager to rent the house out and also arrange storage of the furniture Andrew, okay."

"Yep, fine darl, I will contact the banks and the utilities and Inland Revenue. Oh and I might sell the cars before we go, I can do that through an agency."

"I'd be interested in the Jeep Andrew if you don't mind."

"Oh sure, done deal father thank you, that is one problem I won't have to contend with."

"Okay I will leave you two to get on with making your arrangements, oh and thank you Rebecca for being so positive about this. I realise it is probably quite a shock to you."

"Oh don't worry James, life here in the Silicon Valley can be just a tad plastic you know."

"Yes I know what you mean – it's all about money, money, money here isn't it."

"Yes you could say that – perhaps the fresh air of outback Western Australia will clean our brains a little."

"Okay I will be off now. We will catch up later today or tomorrow."

James and Andrew shook hands and Rebecca stepped forward to give James a small kiss on the cheek. They said their goodbyes and James left. Andrew was uncertain whether Rebecca would react any differently in James' absence but he didn't have to wait long. He saw his father to the door and returned to the kitchen.

"So … ah … what do you think?"

"Well it's so very sudden but, hey, Australia, what can I say, it's my homeland. I have never been to the Pilbara but I do know it has its own unique beauty, I mean, you see plenty of images on television through all of the touristy type programs. It is also very hot."

"Hot eh?"

"Yes there is a town up there somewhere called Marble Bar that holds the world record for the most number of consecutive days above one hundred degrees Fahrenheit. I heard once before that it was about one hundred and sixty days in succession."

"So good thing they have a swimming pool then eh!"

"Should make good use of the pool alright! Actually I can't wait to get there and see the place – a cattle station – sounds like an adventure for sure. Could be hard work but it should be interesting. Did they say how many staff they have there?"

"Yes William said they have about ten, most of them involved in mustering the cattle on horseback once they are located by the helicopter. It's a very large station, about one hundred thousand acres."

"Hmm ... that could be about forty thousand hectares. And how many cattle do they have?"

"Thousands! Not sure exactly, but thousands."

"And your father has become a shareholder?"

"Yeah that's a bit of a mystery to me at the moment, they were both a little coy about the arrangement, but James said he would fill me in on the details later."

Perth City

Rebecca and Andrew took a flight from San Jose to San Francisco and stayed there for one night. Their flight from San Francisco on a Qantas A380 took about sixteen hours and they arrived in Sydney about eight o'clock in the morning. Rebecca had booked the flight to Sydney rather than to Brisbane so she could spend a couple of days with family and friends. She had told Andrew once they had arrived at the airport.

Andrew was pleased to be in Sydney again as he had been there just once and was keen to take in more of the sights, as he had not visited the Opera House previously nor taken in the view from the Sydney Tower. On their final day in Sydney Rebecca's sister and brother-in-law took them to see the Blue Mountains near Katoomba. Andrew was impressed for although these mountains are not as high as the Sierra Nevada Mountains in California, he appreciated the mystique of the blue haze and the Blue Mountain's relative elevation by Australian standards.

After spending three days in Sydney Rebecca and Andrew took a Virgin flight to Perth City.

Upon landing at Perth Domestic Airport and collecting their luggage Rebecca and Andrew caught a taxi into the city. The taxi driver seemed quite an affable character.

"Good morning – welcome to Perth."

"Good morning, thank you."

"And where would you good people like to go this morning?"

"Driver we need to go to a central hotel please – one that is quite reputable. We haven't actually booked into any hotel yet."

"Okay if you wish to stay in the centre of the city in a five-star hotel I would recommend ... ah ... perhaps the Westin Hotel sir or the new Ritz-Carlton."

"Sounds good, thank you!"

"I believe you are from the States sir! Have you been to Perth before?"

"No but my wife Rebecca has been a few times."

"Do you mind if I ask which state you come from."

"We are from San Jose in California."

"Ah ... the Silicon Valley. I advertised a few times in the Mercury News for an investor for my educational website – World of Words - but I didn't get any takers. I think there are a lot of small-minded people in the venture capital industry."

The taxi was heading toward the city and the driver intended to go via the Farmer Freeway but Rebecca wanted to take a different route.

"Excuse me driver can you please go straight ahead and take us into the city via the causeway please."

"Certainly madam."

"What is that complex we just went passed?"

"The casino at Burswood."

"What is this, a lake?"

Rebecca answered her husband.

"No, it's the Swan River dear. Perth has a very beautiful river."

"The Swan River! Looks like quite a scenic little spot."

"Is this a lake?"

"No this is still the river – we just went over an island in the middle of the river."

The taxi driver took the left exit to travel via Riverside Drive from where his passengers could have a good view of the river.

"So this is the Swan River. Seems like a very wide river!"

"Yes, it is but here the river is virtually an estuary and is only about five metres deep. This section is known as Perth Water."

"I see! So driver can you tell us what are the must see places in Perth?"

"Kings Park!"

"Kings Park – what is Kings Park?"

"Several hundred hectares of pristine natural bushland just on the western side of the city and overlooking the city and the river. It does provide quite an amazing view of the city. There is a restaurant there and the war memorial too."

"Sounds interesting!"

"Elizabeth Quay on the waterfront is a must. The South Perth Zoo is certainly worth a visit. It has all the large cats, elephants, giraffe, a very large crocodile, bears and a lot of Australian fauna too. The casino that we drove passed … ah … a river cruise to the Swan Valley where the wineries are and to Fremantle too of course and the museum and Art Gallery. And depending on how long you are here for, a trip to Rotto would be a good idea."

"Do you mean Rottnest Island?"

"Yes miss."

"How far is that from the mainland?"

"Only about twenty kilometres sir. It only takes about thirty to forty minutes to make the journey by ferry."

"No, we will be here for just two nights so we might put that off for another time. Perhaps when we are returning to the States we could spend a little more time here."

"Or we could come back to Perth for a few days while we are still managing the station. Particularly if my family want to make a trip to see me."

"Yes that is certainly a possibility darl so let's wait and see. Driver you mentioned Fremantle, isn't that where they held the defence of the America's Cup many years ago?"

"Yes sir that was in the summer of 1987 when Dennis Connor's 'Stars and Stripes' took the cup back to the U.S. - and when your Walter Cronkite described Perth City as 'the world's best-kept secret'."

"Yes I was just a young boy then but I do remember that. Is this the main street of Perth?"

"Not exactly! This is Adelaide Terrace which virtually becomes St. George's Terrace just a little further on, but literally it is the same roadway."

"Okay so now we are entering the main street of Perth – this is St. George's Terrace."

"What is that building to the left?"

"That is the Perth Concert Hall and just a little further on you will see Government House."

"Government House? I believe you people had a change of government recently Michael."

"No that was the federal government that changed dear. This Government House is for the state government of Western Australia. It's the official residence of the state governor."

"Yes that's right, the federal government has changed – the Labor Party was elected back into office just three months ago and Mr. Anthony Albury became our new Prime Minister, but back in March of this year we retained the same Labor government here in Western Australia."

"Hmm ... seems like a busy place. So what is the population of Perth now?"

"The city and suburbs? Probably about two point two million people now. But suburban Perth does cover a very large area, extending from about fifty kilometres north to about seventy kilometres south along the coastline – as the crow flies."

"Gee that really is quite a vast expanse alright – much larger than San Jose by population and by area! What was that you said about the raven?"

Rebecca laughed.

"That was a crow not a raven. Haven't you heard that saying 'as the crow flies'? The people of South Australia would take offence at that. It means in a straight line rather than by roadway."

"No I have never heard that expression before. Is that a little Aussie colloquial?"

"Yes dear!"

"And why would the people of South Australian take offence?"

"Because they are the crow eaters dear."

"Ah ha! And what are you West Aussies called driver?"

"Sandgropers! That's because so much of the coastal plain here is comprised of sand."

"Do all you Aussies have a nickname like that?"

"No, but the Queenslanders do – they are the banana benders because they grow so many bananas, but I'm not sure about the others. Apart from the New Zealanders – they are Kiwis of course. Although half of them live over here now."

Rebecca giggled.

"So we are now approaching Barrack Street where the Ritz-Carlton is sir."

"Actually we don't need to go to the hotel straight away – driver do you mind taking us to King's Park please, I would like my husband to view the city from there."

"Certainly miss, it will take just two minutes to get there."

The taxi proceeded along St. George's Terrace to Malcolm Street and then Fraser Avenue until the driver stopped at the end of Fraser Avenue, from where tourists view the city.

Even from the vehicle Andrew could see that this was going to be quite an impressive viewing of the city.

"Driver we will be just a couple of minutes so keep your meter running."

The taxi driver turned to respond.

"Well your fare to here is fifty one dollars so we will call that an even fifty and I will turn the meter off so please just take your time. I am in no hurry to go anywhere. I suggest you walk over to the war memorial also. I cannot park here so I will go behind the restaurant over there and come back in, say, fifteen or twenty minutes. Would that be okay?"

Rebecca responded.

"That's very good of you, thank you. I know you understand the significance of this moment for my husband."

"Absolutely miss!"

Rebecca and Andrew walked across to the lookout platform from where they had a clear view of the city, the freeway interchange, Perth Water and the Narrows Bridge.

"Geeze, I see what you mean Bec, this really is an extraordinary view of the city. I haven't seen anything like this in the States apart from, maybe, San Francisco."

"No and it does have some similarities with Sydney doesn't it, with the river, the bridge and the quay – well in contrast to Melbourne, Brisbane and Adelaide I mean."

"Well I haven't seen those cities yet either, but I know what you mean. I can see what Walter Cronkite meant about the world's best kept secret. Most cities back in the States are just so banal compared to this."

Rebecca and Andrew walked to the war memorial and spent some minutes perusing the thousands of names of Australian soldiers who perished in World War 1. They then walked further away from the first viewing platform and toward the Narrows Bridge from where they had a better view of the Swan River to the west of the bridge and the vast expanse of Melville Water. They were duly impressed with the extraordinary beauty of Perth City and the Swan River, as all tourists are. After several minutes of taking in the view, they started their walk back the same way toward the taxi. Upon arriving at the taxi they noticed that the driver was resting in his seat that he had laid back, which appeased any feelings they had that they might have taken too long for him, as he seemed to be resting. They got back into the rear of the taxi and the driver set off back toward the city.

"So what did you think?"

"Yeah wow - that sure is really impressive eh! You people are so fortunate to have such a beautiful city to live in. I noticed the train crossing the bridge, it seemed to be travelling quite fast."

"Oh sure, the train cranks it up to about one hundred and thirty kilometres per hour in between stations. Fortunately, there are not many stations either so the people living in Mandurah about eighty kilometres south of Perth can be in the city in about fifty minutes."

"Mandurah?"

"Yes, if you have time Mandurah is also well worth a visit. It's on the coastline where a large estuary adjoins the ocean. It's a very beautiful seaside town and very oceanic. A great place for a picnic or a barbeque! I go there occasionally to enjoy fish and chips for dinner. We have some great fish varieties here – dhufish, whiting, cobbler, snapper and gummy shark."

"Shark eh! I've heard about your sharks over here in Western Australia. There seem to be more shark attacks here than anywhere else in the world."

"That's probably true but when I was a young lad growing up in Perth there were no shark attacks anywhere. One man was taken by a great white at a place called Jurien Bay which is about one hundred kilometres north of Perth in 1967 but he was a scuba diver. The next shark attack, to the best of my knowledge, was at Cottesloe Beach here in Perth about 2005. Since then we have had a spate of shark attacks and we have lost six or seven people in as many years."

"Geeze that really is quite a turnaround. What do people put that down to?"

"Overfishing!"

"Ah ha! That makes sense. This building to the left reminds me of something."

"Dumas House! It is colloquially known as the Weetbix Box. All of our government Ministers work from there."

Rebecca giggled, for she knew that Andrew knew nothing about the famous Aussie breakfast cereal.

"And this small residential tower to the right is known as the thermos flask!"

"Huh! I can see where that comes from."

"So driver we could actually take the train all the way to that seaside resort you mentioned?"

"Mandurah – yes but when you arrive there you will need a bus or taxi to get to the foreshore which is about five kilometres away."

"That might be worth a sortie tomorrow dear – fish and chips for dinner, I like the idea of that!"

"Yes well that could be on for sure if we can set aside three hours in the afternoon and into the evening."

"So we are now turning into Barrack Street where your hotel is. This is the Ritz-Carlton on the right."

Hmm ... well thank you driver for all of the information you have given us. Do you have a card so we can call you whenever we need a taxi?"

"Yes sir this is my direct line and my email address via my website."

As they were removing the luggage from the taxi Andrew perused the driver's business card.

"World of words dot com eh! What is that about?"

"Advanced English vocabulary written in short stories."

"Call me Andrew. I'll have to look that up. So your name is Michael. It's been good to meet you Michael."

"Thank you Andrew, I hope yourself and Rebecca have a wonderful time in West Oz. Goodbye and see you next time!"

"For sure, goodbye Michael."

Rebecca and Andrew checked in to the hotel. They would spend two nights in Perth and spend the remainder of the first day taking in the attractions mentioned by the taxi driver Michael, including a river cruise to Maylands and then to Fremantle. On the way to Maylands the hostess made some commentary about the developments at Burswood and East Perth.

"What you see here to the east is the Burswood complex which includes the casino and several five-star hotels and now the new Perth Stadium, which hosts Australian Rules Football and test cricket. A rather controversial development, Perth Stadium, but it will undoubtedly add something very special to the city, especially as people will have access via the new footbridge and the parklands surrounding the complex. You might be surprised to learn that until about the mid nineteen eighties this entire area where the casino, hotels and stadium are now was a rubbish tip and an industrial area."

The ferry did an about turn to set off for the port city of Fremantle.

"Now over here to the west again you have a great view of the East Perth residential area with its very beautiful new buildings and the waterway that was once just a drain. This area too was an industrial area until about the mid nineteen nineties when the state government decided to relocate all of the grotty old rusty factories to new industrial zones away from the city. So now thousands of people live here with close proximity to the city centre."

"Oh and the waterway that was previously reduced to a drain but has now been restored was called Claise Brook and is actually part of the drainage system of a large lake to the north-west of the city – Lake Monger. Aboriginal folklore has it that Claise Brook was a water serpent the Aboriginal people referred to as the Wagyl."

The ferry took them to Fremantle where they walked the streets for about four hours taking in the sights of all the old buildings, St. John's Square, the Fremantle Prison, the Roundhouse and the Maritime Museum. They enjoyed a kebab in the café strip for lunch after which they became aware of Cicerello's seafood restaurant where they might have enjoyed a fishy luncheon, but this simply set their minds on the taxi driver's suggestion for the second day.

On the afternoon of the second day Rebecca and Andrew did, in fact, take the train from the Esplanade train station to Mandurah and were completely enamoured by the ambience of the seaside town – enjoying fish and chips for dinner by the estuary.

"You know that taxi driver was right Bec. That was one of the most enjoyable days of my entire life, taking that train ride to Mandurah and being able to absorb the ambience of the town, that delicious fish and chip lunch we had. That was an afternoon of magic for me."

"Yes I know what you mean. These people certainly do have it lucky eh? Perhaps we might move to this area one day Andrew. I like the look of those canal homes with their private boat moorings."

They returned to the city for their second night and prepared to leave early the next morning.

They were totally unaware that, ironically, the taxi driver they had met was the very same taxi driver who had given William Piper the idea of the on-line education venture that led them on their own venture to Western Australia.

Would they become aware of this one day?

The following evening Andrew sent Michael a text asking if he could take them to the airport the following morning, but unfortunately Michael's reply was that he had already booked a regular passenger for that morning from Rockingham to the airport. They might, however, meet again in the future.

The fiery election!

The bushfire tragedies that raged through the States of Queensland and New South Wales from November 2019 through to March of 2020 had changed Australia's political landscape. Vast sections of both states had become a virtual tinderbox over a period of several years and after numerous houses were burnt down and many lives lost, Australia's former emergency services commissioners were unanimous in attributing the problem to climate change. They had seen the gradual decline of rainfall in most parts of Australia over a period of more than thirty years and knew this to be the main cause. They knew that no amount of hazard reduction could possibly change that situation – with the size of the continent being as it is. They were also widely regarded within the Australian community as people who were above the politics of either the shareholders of the energy companies or our community of tree-kissing vegans.

When the fires began to rage again in the summer of 2020/21 the political blame game became even more vehement with conservative politicians once again being unduly branded by some as 'virtual arsonists' – such rationale being based on the chasm between Liberal Party and Labor Party policies pertaining to the emission of greenhouse gases. The Liberal Party had surprisingly won the Federal election of May 2019 by scare-mongering too many Australians into believing that the Labor Party's policies would cost them jobs - the strings of the puppet being typically pulled by the shareholders of Australia's energy companies.

In this they were following the footsteps of their former Prime Minister Mr. John Howard, who had previously won a virtually unwinnable election with the typically deceptive 'baby overboard' saga. That forlorn, sordid refugee who was holding up his baby to show the child to his drowning wife in her final moments, had virtually been branded by the Prime Minister of Australia as a potential child murderer. With the most despicable utterance in Australian political history, Mr. Howard told the electorate that he did not want such people coming here to Australia and in doing so had successfully wooed the racist vote away from the One Nation Party. With almost every Australian election being so close as to be determined by just one or two percent of the adult population, his exhortations to that small percentage of racist Australians achieved the desired outcome.

At the election of May 2019, the people of Queensland and New South Wales had reacted with the hip-pocket nerve – the Queenslanders, in particular, fearing their Adani coal mine might not see the light of day under a federal Labor government. They wanted their well paid jobs that would emanate from this new mine site. Any repercussions pertaining to climate change would not be their problem – or so they thought. The Liberal Party of Australia had typically acceded to the demands of Australia's energy providers who wanted their golden ten percent return on investment. They would pull the strings of the puppet, no matter at what cost. They were constantly aware that they could take refuge within Australia's other ruling-class bastions - the shares of Australia's four major banks, or insurance companies – or retail property developers.

The bushfires in the summer of 2024/25 would be even worse, with hundreds of homes being lost in the bush and even dozens of homes on the outskirts of Brisbane and Sydney also being destroyed. More than fifty people perished in the fires of that summer. The rainfall of the previous year had fallen to an all-time low in outback Australia.

Now the people were beginning to understand the truth. There was a new realisation that the policies of the Labor Party – the party of rectitude - were what Australia really needed to avert such threats from climate change in the future. When Prime Minister Scott Morrison used this acrimonious blame game to call a snap election in May 2022 out of electoral expediency and seeking an endorsement of his party's policies, the Labor Party won a landslide victory and Mr. Anthony Albury became the Prime Minister of Australia. For the first time in Australian political history, the hip pocket nerve had taken a back seat and the electorate had become more cognizant of some critical issues that were affecting our only planet – rather than being so flippant about the same. The Labor government would be returned to office in the following election of 2026, following a wave of massive investment in renewable energy.

Going bush

After spending one day in Perth and Fremantle, the following day Andrew and Rebecca took a chauffeur-driven limousine from the Ritz-Carlton to the airport for a flight to Newman in the Pilbara. Due to a weather warning the pilot decided to take the coastline route and as Andrew had never seen Australia before Rebecca allowed him to occupy the window seat 'A'. As such, just a short distance from Perth he was able to view the wind farm between Lancelin and Jurien Bay.

"Looks like a substantial wind farm down there. Quite a few turbines – twenty-four I think."

The flight to Newman would normally be just over an hour and a half but mid-flight the captain made an announcement.

"Attention please passengers, I regret to inform you that due to adverse weather conditions at Newman we have a need to deviate this flight to Karratha where you will be accommodated if necessary at the Best Western motel complex until we can fly you on to Newman. We do apologise for the inconvenience this will cause but as you will undoubtedly understand when there is a severe thunderstorm at your destination, as there is at Newman at present, we regard your safety as our major priority."

"Karratha! Where is that from Newman dear?"

"Karratha is on the coast but probably only a half hour flight from Newman. Sounds like we might have to stay there overnight though."

"Ah not to worry! See a little more of Western Australia I guess."

They did indeed spend that night in Karratha, booking in to the Best Western just before six o'clock in the evening.

43

Once they were settled in the room Andrew turned on the television to get the six o'clock news. Just as the news commenced Rebecca asked Andrew if he would like to go shopping. Despite being slightly miffed he did notice that the first news item was about a car that ran off the road somewhere in Perth and crashed into someone's house. He took the opportunity to respond to Rebecca.

"No I think I'll just catch up on the news of the world while I have the chance dear."

"Is there anything you would like me to buy for you?"

"Oh yes some Listerine please and a new toothbrush – an Oral B please, large and soft."

The news coverage was interviewing a witness to this momentous event in Perth.

"Anything else?"

"No that's all thanks darl."

Rebecca went back into the kitchen for a moment. The second news item came on – this one about how the fire brigade rescued a kitten that was stuck in between two rows of bricks of a new house under construction. Again an eyewitness to this shocking event was being interviewed. Rebecca returned to the room and asked a further question.

"Andrew I don't know what access we are going to have to shops once we are there so you might need some new socks or jocks or deodorant, all that kind of personal stuff, you know."

Andrew dropped the volume of the television down quite some way.

"Yeah okay, point taken, if you get me a five pack of socks and the same of jocks and a couple of cans of that Blue Stratos deodorant from the pharmacy, that should suffice for now."

The third news bulletin had started so Andrew turned his attention back to the television to catch the bulletin and turned up the volume to catch somebody talking.

"... my grandfather established this property and we have lived here for more than half a century so to see it blowing away like this is just so soul-destroying. Our next property neighbour, old Jim McPherson, just couldn't take it any longer and his whole family is understandably still in shock at his passing but with what the bank was doing to him he just couldn't take it any longer, you know. We really, really feel for his family, his wife and his children."

The reporter turned to the camera.

"Karl that is a very typical story out here in outback Queensland and the same terrible situation prevails in most of New South Wales with this prolonged drought now in its second year. Some properties here have had absolutely no rainfall whatsoever since the beginning of March last year and there is no telling if this drought will be as bad as the six year drought from 2006 to 2011. If it is, a lot of families are going to be totally destroyed. Back to you in the studio."

Andrew turned the volume down again.

"Geeze, did you hear that? I had no idea that was happening. There was no mention of this drought when we were in Sydney."

"As I recall we didn't catch any news while in Sydney dear."

"But no mention of this from your family either Bec!"

"Sounds like they have been hearing of it for quite some time – must be a case of complacency I'd say."

Rebecca left the room to go out to do her shopping at K-Mart, as the Best Western is only about a two-minute walk from the Karratha shopping centre.

Andrew sat there in stunned silence at the news of the drought, contemplating how absolutely terrible the situation must be for hundreds of families in the affected areas. He had seen quite some devastation back in the States and he was aware of how critical the farming sector was to Australians and their economy. He was overcome with feelings of helplessness but had no idea of just how this news story would become his primary motivation in the not-too-distant future.

Having been informed by the airline that the flight to Newman would not leave Karratha until early afternoon, Andrew successfully made a call to book a charter flight to Newman for the next day that would have them in the Newman early the next morning. This would allow them to travel to the cattle station the same day rather than having to spend a night in Newman.

The charter flight would leave Karratha at seven in the morning. From where he was seated in the jet, Andrew was able to talk to the pilot.

"Good morning madam, good morning sir, thank you for flying with me today. My name is Phillip."

"Good morning Phillip. I am Andrew and my wife is Rebecca."

"So you people are flying to Newman and is that where you will be staying or working?"

"No we are going on from there to a cattle station east of Newman."

"Really! Which cattle station?"

"Jennifer Downs!"

"Oh William Piper's station – and what will you be doing there?"

"I'm a hydro-geologist and the watering infrastructure there is in need of a major overhaul, so we could be there for six to twelve months. So you do know of Mr. Piper?"

"Oh sure, he purchased that station probably ten years ago when the beef prices were low and I took him there a few times. He saw it as a long-term investment believing the prices would rebound – as they have. He seems like a very astute businessman."

"Astute, hopefully – shrewd, hopefully not!"

James' comment educed a wry smile from the pilot. Perhaps he knew something.

"Okay let's buckle up? Here we go!"

The plane completed its taxi to the runway, got the all clear from the control tower, proceeded down the runway then ascended abruptly. Once they had reached altitude their conversation resumed.

"I believe you had to spend the night in Karratha due to the storm at Newman?"

"Yes but that's fine - it did allow us to do some shopping so that was okay. Did you hear about the storm?"

"Yep! They copped the tail end of the cyclone that hit Broome the day before. Wind gusts up to one fifty kilometres per hour and over seventy millimetres of rain. How was the flight from Perth – was that a little rough?"

"Just a little but one thing I did like, I was able to see the turbines on the wind farm not long after we left Perth."

"Yeah, those turbines provide electric power to the desalination plant south of Perth. So you are from the United States Andrew! Do you intend to stay long?"

"I envisage that we will be managing the cattle station for at least six months, perhaps twelve, so we will just see how that pans out. I have never been here before."

"In that case I will take you inland a little so you can view the mines – perhaps Pannawonica or Tom Price. That will give you some idea of the scale of the mining operations. Some of these mines in the Pilbara have been operating for almost fifty years. Certainly Tom Price and Newman have been."

"So they transport the ore to port by rail?"

"Yes! Every mine has its own line to the point of convergence and some of the rail systems are over four hundred and fifty kilometres long."

"The mine site at Newman – Mt Whaleback – holds the world record for the longest train in history."

"And how long was that?"

"Seven point three kilometres!"

"Geeze!"

"Yeah most of the trains are almost two point five kilometres long so they hitched three of them together to set the world record. When you get to Newman you can see an aerial view of that train on top of Radio Hill."

"Is this a type of mountain range down here?"

"Yes that's the Hamersley Ranges. The highest twenty peaks in Western Australia are in the Hamersley Ranges. These iron ore mines are part of a mineral deposit that starts near the coast just south of Onslow and extends in a south-easterly direction for about five hundred kilometres.

"You gotta be kidding me! Five hundred kilometres, that's over three hundred miles."

"If you look down now you will see the town of Pannawonica and a clear view of the mine. I am staying at this altitude to give you a good view of the operations here."

"Well I appreciate that Phillip, thank you! And the weather at Newman has cleared up since yesterday I believe."

"Yeah that happens quite often in fact. So many days up here are perfectly fine in the morning until about mid-afternoon and then the rain comes in. Sometimes that brings strong winds and electrical activity. We do get some cracker thunderstorms up here – must be due to the extent of iron in the ground."

"Uh huh ... that makes sense. So the ground up here could virtually be an electrical rod then."

"You could put it that way yes. The workers reckon they can weld two rocks together. Your wife seems to be dozing off back there Andrew."

"She didn't sleep that well, probably due to the excitement. As they said in the film - 'must be a chick thing'. She hails from New South Wales so the last couple of days in Sydney to see her family were a real buzz for her."

"Which film was that?"

"Alien Resurrection!"

"Could also be the jet lag, of course. The flight from the States to Sydney took sixteen hours. Could take a few days to get over that."

"Hey what's this down here, some type of agriculture?"

"Oh yeah, that's the Nammuldi Agricultural Project where they grow hay for the cattle. The surrounding terrain is suitably flat and you can see the very substantial watering system they have there. Those pivots are eight hundred metres wide and some of those individual spans are over eighty metres long. Actually the hay cultivation is really an adjunct activity – the real purpose of the project is to draw water out of the mines, as they have dug down below the water table, so they extract the water and it has to go somewhere."

"So the ground up here is sufficiently fertile to grow the hay?"

"Oh sure, people say that in this red dirt if you have water you can grow virtually anything."

"So why don't they?"

"Well most of what we need is grown further south in the Gascoyne area closer to the large markets, so the town of Carnarvon grows fruit and vegetables virtually all year round. Although now there is talk of Western Australia becoming a food bowl for south-east Asia. Which just might have quite some merit in more ways than one."

"How's that?"

"Oh, politically! We are part of south-east Asia, together with Indonesia, Malaysia, Vietnam, Thailand and others."

"Uh huh!"

"There's a similar drive now to expand our aquaculture industries, especially in the Kimberley region further north. There's no paucity of water up there – in fact it is said that Lake Argyle holds about seven times the quantity of Sydney Harbour. So they are now dabbling in artificial lakes and ponds for all types of sea creature – prawns, crabs, several varieties of fish and so on. Not sure about lobster though, they are probably too fussy about where they live."

"I believe our cattle station has some type of fishpond – I think my father called it marron?"

"Marron! Yeah marron, which really is quite a delicacy, rather like a freshwater lobster just smaller. Although the largest marron ever caught is larger than any lobster."

"Really?"

"Yeah! I believe that one is on display at the Western Australian Museum in Perth. Bloody huge thing it is – about three feet long."

"Hey we almost went there to the museum but my wife chose the art gallery instead. So we must do that the next time we are in Perth."

"Yeah, you could grow marron virtually anywhere if you have water and some meat to feed them."

"Like on a cattle station hey!"

"Plenty of meat out there mate, for sure. Of course you wouldn't feed your cattle to the marron when you've got far too many kangaroos, goats, camels, horses, emus, pigs, dingoes and donkeys all over the place. Just shoot some of those bastards and feed them to your marron. Most of them are not native to the place."

"Really! All over the place eh?"

"Oh, shit yeah. Bloody nuisance they are, most of them. Only good for shooting! Do you shoot?"

Andrew paused for just a moment to give a considered response.

"Ah ... no I go to church instead."

"Each to his own! You probably will when you get there. Especially if those razorback come at you."

"Razorback?"

"Yeah the large feral pig! You didn't see that film then did you – Gregory Harrison, Judy Morris!"

"No I must have missed that one. How large do the boars grow?"

"Oh bloody huge up here mate! Kill you in ten seconds flat they will. Worst thing is they will then eat you – all of you. Make sure you do take a gun with you out there. Never know what might come at you."

"Okay thank you for the advice. I'm sure the station will have suitable ordnance. So what else do I need to be wary of out here?"

"Spiders! The redback evolved here in the Pilbara. The little beggars are everywhere and get into everything. Be sure to check anything before you pick it up. I was bitten years ago but didn't realise until the doctor told me what it was. Then I remembered the pinprick on my finger and killing the redback sometime later."

"I think I saw that on an Attenborough program. That is very similar to our black widow spider in the States isn't it?"

"Yeah but far more pervasive, especially out here. It's only a matter of time before they get into the U.S. – they are already in New Zealand, Japan, Germany and now, apparently, in parts of England too. Of course they get into everything so they travel overseas on old cars, furniture, sea containers ..."

Andrew interrupted Phillip.

"Are they deadly?"

"Well yeah they are! In fact a young child was bitten by a redback spider just within the last couple of years and passed away. It really was a terrible tragedy for the young parents because they didn't know what was happening. The spider was in the young girl's bedroom. But prior to that I believe the previous death from a redback bite was about 1958, when the anti-venom was developed. But you have to be pretty damn unlucky to be seriously affected by a redback bite because most people have access to medical treatment fairly quickly. Just remember, the first treatment is an application of ice if you have access to some."

"Ice, okay I will remember that, thank you. So you think there will be redback spiders at the station?"

"Huh - bloody well for sure mate!"

"And anything else we need to be wary of?"

"Yep – kangaroo tick! Nasty little bastards those things are. You don't even know they are on your body until you start to feel unwell. People have died from those too. Sometimes they will get onto a person's scalp so nobody can see them there. There's also a trapdoor spider that will typically rear up on its hind legs and protrude its fangs toward you but it's likely to then run away – pretty bloody fast runner too mate."

"Kangaroo tick eh?"

"Okay over to your left is the Tom Price mining operation and the town of Tom Price. The ore at Tom Price is running low now after fifty years but they have mined the deposits not far from the town at Western Turner and Brockman One which they transport by rail through the town. Some people think the town will die but it won't die completely, of course."

"Looks like a bit of a mountain up ahead of us there."

"Yeah that's Mt. Bruce – the second highest peak in the state. Until about 1967 it was believed to be the highest peak, but the Surveyor General found another peak further south was about fifteen metres higher."

"Why did it take so long to ascertain that?"

"Well nobody had reason to go near Mt. Meharry until the iron ore was discovered. Even the Great Northern Highway was a dirt road back then."

"I see a mine over here to the left."

"Another BHP site, Area C, and then a little further south you will see West Angelas which is a Rio Tinto site and then further south the Hope Downs sites."

"So despite that downturn a few years ago, the mines were still putting out volume?"

"Oh sure, the price went south for a couple of years but the output was still as high as it has ever been. It just meant that the Chinese were able to purchase their ore at a lower price during that period. Which is fair enough – the general assessment is that they were paying too high a price during the boom times. The big miners were making a fortune. Now the price has bounced back quite a way."

"And what are the Chinese doing with the ore?"

"Oh there's no doubt the Chinese are huge of infrastructure development – all the usual stuff, bridges, apartments, railways."

"Hopefully they haven't been covertly building aircraft carriers!"

"Ah ... that's definitely the American in you talking now. How many carriers do you guys have now?"

"Eleven! Ten Nimitz class and just one of the new George Bush class! That was commissioned recently and the plans for subsequent carriers may have been placed on hold but with our new President who knows – they might be constructed in the next few years."

53

"Well the cost is astronomical isn't it?"

"Yes but the technology has replaced a lot of the manpower requirements – I think they need less than three thousand personnel now rather than five thousand."

"Can he afford to build more carriers?"

"Probably not but he will. Our Presidents don't seem to have a handle on the budget situation. We just keep borrowing from future generations."

"And what's the answer to that?"

"Nobody knows – it's a case of kick the can down the road. I think there is probably just one answer really – a wealth tax! Wealthy people slip through the tax net one way or another, usually with artificially contrived schemes or by playing the international monetary game – locating their headquarters offshore where they pay little tax. Some of our largest wealthiest corporations have based themselves in Ireland for that very reason. And now the bitcoin currency has changed everything even more-so. Nobody seems sure what can be taxed."

"Perhaps you should go into politics Andrew. You seem to have some answers there."

"Yeah maybe one day – in the States, of course."

"So now we are approaching Newman airport you can see the mining operations down there at Mt. Whaleback, which is a BHP mine. That mine is the largest open-cut iron ore mine in the world. Okay buckle up for the landing people. How will you get to the station from here?"

"My father has arranged for somebody from the station to meet us here. Apparently, we have a drive of about three hours to the station, so we should be there by mid-afternoon."

"Hopefully the track is not too wet. There's been a lot of rain here lately."

Andrew aroused Rebecca for the landing. The jet landed at Newman airport and Andrew and Rebecca said their goodbyes to Phillip and waited at the carousel for their luggage.

That was when an elderly gentleman approached them to introduce himself.

"Gidday! You must be Rebecca and Andrew."

"Yes!"

"My name is Jack, Jack Lambert – better known as Anne's father. I'm from the station and I am here to take you to your new home."

"Ah ... Jack, I have been told a little about you. It's great to meet you Jack! So this is Newman airport. How far are we from the town here?"

"Seven miles for you – eleven kilometres for me! We do need to go into Newman before we leave to pick up some parts for a vehicle and our chopper. They will be arriving by truck about midday."

"And I believe we are almost two hundred miles from the station."

"One hundred and seventy two miles to be exact. It's a good thing you have arrived early because it's quite a long trip. We can only average about fifty miles an hour on the dirt road."

"I thought William Piper said it was about one hundred miles."

"It might have been for him – old William usually slept all the way".

The luggage arrived and they made their way to the four-wheel drive – a Nissan Patrol four-door ute with a canopy over the rear well. Jack headed north toward Newman and parked in the car park at the shopping centre.

"Now I need to go into the hardware store and I could be about half an hour so you guys could do some shopping in the supermarket if you want to. I need to pick up some welding rods, some nuts and bolts, some grease and a few other things. You might want a snack or a coffee perhaps? There's a Dome Café just over there. Also that new supermarket, the I.G.A. does sell some great hot foods like casseroles and such."

"Hmm ... a cappuccino would be good Andrew – and perhaps a toasted ham and cheese sandwich."

After almost half an hour they met back at the vehicle. Old Jack had loaded some new bore caps and the other items he needed.

"Okay here we go folks!"

"Perhaps we could go to the top of Radio Hill to see that aerial pic of the longest train?"

"Yeah no worries!"

Jack took the couple to Radio Hill where they were astonished at the photograph of the longest train in history. It seemed there were four triple-sets of locomotives and more than seven hundred cars. From there they also had a view of the Mt. Whaleback mine site. They then left Newman and headed north along the Marble bar road before turning west at the Jigalong Community turnoff. From the Jigalong road Jack would normally take a deviation toward the south-east to take a different road toward the station but whilst in Newman he had picked up some things for the community.

"I'm just going to drop this compressor for a Land Cruiser off at the community. We won't be there long – they don't accept a lot of visitors here. Of course, I have approval to come here because they know we make this trip occasionally. Apart from that my grandmother was Aboriginal."

"Are you Aboriginal Jack?"

"No, I have never identified as Aboriginal and being raised in Perth I had little contact with Aboriginal people so I would never have been accepted by the Aboriginal people as being an Aboriginal person. They are the two requirements in the legal sense. No, my grandmother was the last of that family lineage to identify as such."

"Do you have any siblings?"

"I have two sisters but they never identified as Aboriginal either. My father was a very successful businessman so my sisters went to Iona College – a private school and I attended Marist Brothers College in Churchlands. So we both had little contact with Aboriginal people. They would come to our house occasionally to see my mother but not very often. But we always knew the Aboriginal blood was there in the family."

"And how do you feel about that?"

"It's a great privilege to me Rebecca – the way I see it, I have ancestry that dates back in this country for tens of thousands of years – about sixty thousand is the latest estimate. Australia is a very special homeland to me."

"I'm so pleased you said that Jack because you may not realise this, but I am Aboriginal."

"Really! I wouldn't have thought so but now that you mention it, yes I can see that."

"Yes, I was born at Little Plains in New South Wales but my mother was very young so I was adopted out. She was only fifteen when I was born. My father was white and much older but I never knew him of course."

The drive to the Jigalong community would take approximately one hour so they occasionally discussed various issues along the way.

"Hey that would be a kangaroo! And another!"

"Yep! You will see plenty of them out here."

"I have never seen one before outside of an American zoo. They sure do move along eh?"

"Is that a dingo?"

"Sure is! He might be after those roos."

Suddenly a loud crack rang out – what seemed very much like a gunshot.

"Was that a gunshot we just heard?"

"Sure was! That would be somebody from the community up ahead taking out some roos or even the dingo. They will eat the roo and cull the dingoes any chance they get."

"Eat the kangaroo eh!"

"Oh shit yeah – good meat that kangaroo. Very high in protein and vitamins! They'll make a kangaroo tail soup too."

"This would not be a good place to break down would it – I mean, further out past the community you would be lucky to see anybody right?"

"Correct – but that's exactly why we have the satellite phone and forty litres of water in the back. You just never know when you might be stuck out here for a night and into the next day too, before help arrives."

"So if that was to happen would you just sleep in the vehicle Jack?"

"Nah! We've got some swags in the back of this wagon too."

"Swags?"

"Yeah, a bit like a cross between a small tent and a sleeping bag."

"You wouldn't want a wild boar to disturb you in the middle of the night if you are in one of those Jack."

"No but that did happen to me once. Fortunately I had my two dogs with me and I just managed to get out of my swag before he attacked. The dogs held him at bay long enough for me to grab my gun. Luckily I had the kangaroo dogs with me."

"Kangaroo dogs?"

"Yep, Brewster and Casey! They've both gone now but we have two more."

"So you shot the boar?"

"Shit yeah! Made some good tucker for me dogs."

"So if you didn't have a gun what would you have done?"

"I must admit the incident has made me think about that and I reckon if ever I was attacked by a boar I would grab something like a shirt or even a sock and be ready to shove it down his throat, if that would be at all possible. Or even a rock or a stick might do the job."

"Why do you think that Jack?"

"Well think about it this way. A wild boar attacking will be belching air pretty much and he has to breathe right. So ram that piece of cloth into his mouth and shove it down his throat to block his windpipe and I reckon he is going to pretty soon move his attention from attacking anything, to trying to get some air."

"Yes, good point Jack."

"He doesn't have hands to grab hold of a shirt or a sock blocking his throat now does he? That would also take his attention away from trying to bite anybody with those tusks. He'd run out of breath pretty quickly too I reckon. He'd probably go down within one minute and croak it within two."

"Well hopefully we never come across that situation, eh? So the community is not far up ahead of us."

"Only about another six miles. We won't be there long – just long enough to drop in the compressor and have a brief chat to the administrators. They might want something else done next time we come though, perhaps place an order for beef or something."

As they approached the community and some dwellings became visible Andrew and Rebecca sat with stunned silence at the sight of the very simple dwellings that the people of the community had to live in. Then some children ran out from a decrepit old car wreck adorning the front yard of a house, waving their arms and cheering, for they knew Jack's vehicle.

"Gee the ... ah ... houses are pretty basic eh. At least they have solar hot water on every roof and a satellite dish."

"Yes, but the water here is poor quality – very high in calcium content and the hot water systems need to be re-conditioned every couple of years."

"Seem to be a lot of wrecked cars lying around."

"Ah ... yes they actually have an entirely different cultural approach to things like that. They don't regard the front yard of the house as being any different to the back yard really. They don't have to impress the neighbours because they all do the same. It's just a matter of being practical to them."

Jack drove to the workshop and handed over the parts he had brought from Newman to the workshop foreman Blake. Andrew and Rebecca got out to stretch their legs. Rebecca started to take some photographs.

"Thanks Jack, it's one of the school vehicles that broke down, or at least the air conditioning did. You got some visitors for the station eh?"

"The new managers actually! Dunno how long they're gonna stay for. He's from the U.S. so might be a bit rugged for him eh."

"What about his missus?"

"She's Oz! From Sydney apparently but she has seen some parts of the country."

"Oh well, wish them luck. At least you got a good home for them."

"How are Jimmy and Travis going out there?"

"Yeah, good mate – though I think the Parnngurr people miss them a bit. Still, it's a great opportunity for them. At least old man Piper paid good money – not like some of them around here. Maybe Jimmy's missus will be ready to take him back sometime soon."

"Yeah, I hope so! You can't really blame the guy for wanting the odd drink eh, considering everybody around him was drinking at the mine when he did his apprenticeship. So does Trav look like getting through his apprenticeship too?"

"Not sure really! He likes the cattle work too much. You know old man Piper was seriously considering just handing over the whole box and dice to the Jigalong mob eh."

"Yeah I heard something about that. Hope he does one day. Be a great thing for the Martu if they had ownership and control. Good thing that Jimmy and Trav are there eh!"

"Blood oath mate! Maybe this new guy can get some more Parnngurr kids in there. Here comes the administrator now."

"Gidday Jack, thanks for dropping those parts in. The kids will appreciate having air conditioning in their vehicle again."

"No worries mate. I'm taking Andrew and Rebecca over there out to the station. They are going to manage it for a while."

"Well I might have to delay meeting them till later, I have to duck out now to a bit of an emergency. Somebody seems to have had an accident with a firearm. I had better get going. Blake I am taking that ambulance vehicle over there in case we need it."

"Okay Malcolm, see you next time."

"Oh Jack the Talawana Track might be a bit boggy in parts, we had some rain here yesterday. If you get stuck give us a hoy."

"Yeah thanks Blake, I had better keep moving with these two so they can arrive before nightfall then. Andrew, Rebecca, we better hit the track."

They got back into their four-wheel drive and headed out the same way they came in back to a turnoff, from where they would head due east toward the Karlamilyi National Park.

"So the population here Jack would be just a couple of hundred people."

"Yeah just over four hundred I believe. But it does fluctuate a lot because they go walkabout to Nullagine or Newman or Wiluna, especially when a relative dies. That happens a lot because they are all relatives really. Somebody might pass away in Port Hedland and they head off up there for up to a week at a time."

"Some of them would seem to be ... ah ... would you call them full-blood Aboriginal?"

"No you wouldn't actually – a person is either Aboriginal or they are not. It doesn't come down to percentages of blood like it might have years ago. If they have ancestry and identify and are accepted by the community, they are Aboriginal."

"Well pardon my ignorance on that Jack, it's just back in the States a person can only claim to be American Indian if their parents are both full blooded Indian."

"Oh I do know what you mean and yes, there are some people here at Jigalong whose family bloodline has never been attenuated with non-Aboriginal blood. If you want to put it candidly, yes, some of them sure are dark-skinned. But you might have perceived that they don't seem to differentiate that way. We have two Aboriginal people at the station from the Parnngurr community which is just to the north-east of the homestead by about sixty miles – Jimmy and Travis. Jimmy completed his apprenticeship at

Whaleback a couple of years ago. Travis got started but came in for some rough treatment so he didn't persevere past his second year. They are bloody good workers though!"

"So Jack how many people live at that community where Jimmy and Travis come from?"

"Not really sure miss but not half as many as at Jigalong."

"Hey mules!"

"No they are donkeys in fact, although there are some wild brumbies around here too so there could be the odd mule."

"Brumbies?"

"Yes wild horses!"

"Now you two might like to get some rest because this section of the track is about a four-hour drive and there's not a lot to see on the way."

"Ah ... quite the contrary Jack, I find this landscape absolutely fascinating. I have never seen anything like this before. It's so harsh and rugged and that red dirt really is quite unique eh. Holy shit that dirt is red! I mean, apart from the fact that there is vegetation here, this landscape could quite easily pass for being on Mars."

"Yep it sure could! The rocks around here are among the oldest on the planet. Many are over two billion years old."

"That old eh!"

"Yes, in fact in recent years the oldest mineral on earth was found here. I think it was dated at more than three billion years old."

"That's definitely fascinating boys but I think I'll take Jack's advice and go to sleep, so please wake me when we get there okay."

"Okay, I will put some soft, relaxing music on for you Rebecca."

Jack selected a compact disc from his centre console and popped it into the player. The music started.

"Hey that really is beautiful music. What is that?"

"The Celtic Orchestra's 'Celtic Moods'. It's one of my favourite albums."

"Hmm ... so what are your other favourite albums Jack?"

"I'd have to say the Celtic Orchestra's 'Celtic Inspiration' cos it's just as good."

"So there could be some Irish in your family Jack."

"My great grandparents came from Tipperary in 1870 so yes the Celtic blood is certainly there. But you can't beat the Irish for a powerful melody."

"So apart from the Celtic link, your favourite music is what Jack?"

"Oh look I grew up in the best years of rock and roll. I remember as a boy seeing the Beatles on television for the first time in 1963. I really loved their first couple of years but then I swung over more towards groups like the Searchers, the Kinks, the Animals, the Troggs, the Easybeats here in Australia, then the Doors and Creedence Clearwater. And those Motown girls like the Supremes and Ronettes and Crystals and so on. They were fantastic too."

"I've got all that music on USB stick now of course."

"Hmm ... you've certainly got some good music favourites there Jack. I've heard of most of them but not those Easybeats you mentioned. You'll have to educate me on that Jack."

"The Easybeats were virtually Australia's version of the Beatles at the time – 1965 to 1966. The Beatles first appeared on the Ed Sullivan Show in New York in February 1964. The Easybeats released their first hit singles and first album in 1965 but their concerts had all the hysteria of a Beatles concert, which was surprising considering that at the time the guys were only about eighteen years old. Girls were screaming and rushing the stage and fainting, it was pandemonium for the police. Yeah, they had some good music, mainly boy girl stuff. Their biggest hit was 'Friday On My Mind' which made it to number one in the U.K. but wouldn't have in the U.S. Quite a strange thing that - the difference in musical taste between the U.K. and Australia and the U.S.!"

"So what would be your favourite number one hit of all time Jack?"

"Hmm ... that's a difficult one. It would be close between ... ah ... 'Light My Fire', 'Proud Mary', 'Satisfaction', 'Heart of Glass' and 'That's When I Think of You' by 1927. I should be biased toward Proud Mary because when Creedence Clearwater came to Perth in February 1972 I actually met John Fogerty at the hotel where they stayed at Scarborough Beach."

"You met John Fogerty?"

"Sure did! He was the biggest star in the world then – the Beatles had disbanded and Jim Morrison had passed away. Myself and a mate, Steve Whinnen, nabbed John Fogerty when he left his room on the first floor to go downstairs to where Doug and Stu where. Of course by then John's brother Tom had left the band. So we ran up to him and I said, 'hey mister are you John Fogerty' and he looked at us and smiled and said, 'yeah sometimes'. It was him alright, so he shook our hands and had a chat for just a minute then went his own way toward the room. So that was the biggest thrill for us. But if I had to select just one song, I would say The Beatles' 'I Want To Hold Your Hand'. After all, it was their biggest selling single. I watch their first performance on Ed Sullivan occasionally."

"Really – their biggest seller eh! I didn't know that Jack. You mentioned one there that I have never heard before."

"Ah ... 'That's When I Think of You' by a group that called itself '1927'. Not surprising that you've never heard of it because they are an Australian group. Bloody great song though – won the ARIA for the best hit single here in 1988. You can hear it now if you want to – I've got the CD here."

"Great, yes I would like to hear that if it's one of your favourites."

Jack removed the Celtic Orchestra CD from the player and took the 1927 CD from the console and popped it into the player. As soon as the music started Rebecca spoke up.

"Hey yeah I remember this song – it's fantastic."

"You're supposed to be asleep!"

"Yeah soon enough!"

"Don't worry Rebecca I will pop that CD back in as soon as this song finishes okay."

After the song finished Jack replaced the Celtic orchestra CD and started it again from the first track 'Easy and Slow'.

It didn't take long for Rebecca to fall asleep.

The homestead

After almost four hours they arrived at the homestead.

"Well, this is it – your new home."

"Wow looks great – like a little oasis in a desert, eh. Lots of beautiful garden surrounding the house! And those palm trees - fantastic."

"Yes they do provide some important shade at various times of the day depending on where the sun is, but the house is also very well insulated. You'll find it quite cool in there even without the air conditioning on. I believe the house was built sometime around 1947 but old William had new insulation installed within the roof to keep the heat out. Of course out here in winter it does get pretty bloody cold at night so that's when you want to keep the heat in."

They alighted from the vehicle and were pleased to be able stretch their legs. They could see some buildings in the distance and a couple of people moving, then they removed their luggage from the vehicle. Some white corellas flew overhead making their typical squawking noise, causing Rebecca and Andrew to look skywards.

"What's that bird way up there?"

"That's a wedgy Andrew – a wedge-tailed eagle. It's the largest eagle in the world. You'll see plenty of them out here too. The biggest ones stand about three feet tall."

"Are they dangerous?"

"Oh, if you went near their nest they would probably give you a bit of a fright. Years ago one unlucky bloke was actually held down on the ground by a large wedgy that proceeded to bite chunks from him, but that is the only case I know of like that. Not sure why he couldn't free himself or break the bird's neck. That's what I would have bloody well done. There's no sense being eaten by an eagle I always say."

Jack was becoming increasingly aware of Andrew's ignorance of the Aussie fauna and was now playing some trifling games on that – even though his story of the man suppressed by the wedge-tailed eagle was actually quite true.

Rebecca and Andrew proceeded to take their luggage into the main house. They were surprised at the stately home, adorned with prime Jarrah furniture, lush leather lounge suites and artworks of famous cricket players and thoroughbred horses. Jack suggested they make themselves at home so they started their first tour of the house. It was a large house with six bedrooms and three bathrooms. Already they were aware of the aroma of some food cooking in the kitchen and found two large slow cookers full of a meat dish, a large pot of boiled vegetables and a smaller pot of boiled rice.

"Hmm ... someone's been busy already. Smells great!"

Rebecca looked through the kitchen cupboards and pantry and made Andrew and herself a cup of tea, while Jack went to round up some of the workers – the ones who had worked there the longest.

"Perhaps I will give you good folk about half an hour to settle in then I will ask the workers to gather outside to meet you, okay?"

"Yes half an hour should be fine Jack thank you."

Rebecca took time to look through the kitchen cupboards and found they were short of nothing but was surprised to see so many sachets of flavouring – there were dozens of them, beef burgundy, Moroccan lamb, Thai, Indian curries, Vietnamese, chilli con carne, beef stroganoff and many others. There was also no paucity of top quality cooking implements, two catering size pressure cookers and two bread makers. Andrew had made his way into the main bedroom and was surprised to see how spacious the room was, the vast walk in robe that was virtually a room itself and the king size water bed they would sleep well on. It was quite apparent that the managers had made this into a good home. Being so far from anywhere, that was quite understandable – no sense making a good woman feel as though she was camping out.

Rebecca opened a new packet of Lipton Red tea and proceeded to make a pot of tea. She boiled the kettle, half-filled the ceramic teapot with boiling water then let it stand for over a minute to ensure that the teapot was hot before emptying the teapot to make the tea. Both she and Andrew detested shabby tea making, though being American Andrew was quite partial to a cup of coffee also. Rebecca also found some home-made biscuits and cake which Andrew thought were very special – rather like Sister Margaret used to make at his local Sunday school. They were already starting to like this new home of theirs.

"Gee that tea is nice, I hope there is enough for another cup."

"Yes, it is nice isn't it? I've never had that brand of tea before. Better make sure we keep the stock levels up on that one. But I did notice there is also some Madura tea, some Dilmah tea and some Yorkshire tea in the pantry. Must be some fussy tea drinkers up here."

Jack gave them more time than he said he would because he knew they take a good look around the house and he didn't want to rush them. After almost one hour he knocked on the front door.

"Hello Rebecca, Andrew, the staff are here."

The workers were gathered around outside the manager's house to greet the new managers and to introduce themselves. Rebecca and Andrew walked out of their front door to meet them. It was now about four thirty in the afternoon. As they walked forward toward the group there were smiles all round. Andrew commenced the proceedings.

"Good afternoon everybody!"

"Good afternoon!"

"My name is Andrew and this is my lovely wife Rebecca. We ... ah ... will be managing the station for the next few months ... ah ... not really sure yet just how long we will be here but, very much looking forward to learning the ropes of the cattle industry and getting to know all of you very well too. Mr. Piper and my own father have sent me here for a very specific role to do with the watering system that needs a major overhaul and I must admit we really do not know very much at all about the cattle industry, so I expect that all of you will put us in the loop on quite a lot of it and that you will continue to perform your roles without interference from us, because you people are the experts here".

"Now don't expect us to remember all of your names straight away but I would like you to introduce yourselves and in just a few words let us know what you do here, okay. We have met Jack of course who kindly met us at the airport."

Andrew motioned toward the man standing to his left.

"Robbie! I am an ex jockey so I lead the horse team sir."

"Hello my name is Jill and I am with Robbie in the horse team."

"Karen! I tend the gardens, the vegie patch, the fishponds and assist the horse team too when I get time."

"Jimmy! I am the tradie so all mechanical repairs to the vehicles, welding, fencing and all that kind of stuff."

"Frankie! I am the pilot and I also maintain and repair the plane and the chopper. That doesn't tie me down for a lot of time so I mount a horse or a trailbike whenever we are rousing the cattle too."

"Narelle! I am in the house, do all the cooking, cleaning, general sort of chores, keep the house operating."

"She's a bloody good cook too."

"Is that so? That's good."

"Yep, she always gets us off to a good start and we can always look forward to a great meal after work. Plus a couple of beers of course."

"Goldie! I am a horseman too boss. But I double up as the slaughterman when we need beef."

"Travis! Ah ... horseman, rouse-about, help Jimmy with the cars and whatever."

"Okay thanks for that people, we will try to remember all of your names as quickly as we can."

Rebecca spoke up.

"So what time does your day finish here?"

Jack responded.

"Early start, early finish! We get out and about at sunrise cos it gets pretty hot here late in the day, but our day never really finishes cos if we need to do something, we get out there and do it, you know. Narelle starts earlier than us to give us a good brekky plus our tucker for later in the day."

Andrew turned to look around the area and noticed that not very far outside the cleared area that contained the buildings there were trees and shrubs, as if the bushland was not too far from the homestead. He was a little perplexed by something.

"So ... ah ... where are the cattle?"

Andrew's ignorance educed a boisterous laughter from the group.

"Did I ... ah ... say something funny?"

Jill was the first to speak up.

"There's no cattle around here boss. You see that hill over there."

She pointed toward a hill on the distant horizon.

"Them cattle will be on the other side of that hill."

"Right! I see!"

"Yeah but only about fifty kilometres on the other side of that hill. But by tomorrow they might have moved quite some way. They tend to move around a lot. They'd also be spread out a lot too."

Jack spoke up again.

"That's why we need the chopper. We've got over ten thousand cattle here on the station. Frankie will do the flyover and radio in where some large groups of cattle are so we can get out there and muster them toward the nearest pen. Them cattle know where the pens are so they know what's going on – except they don't know what happens to the ones we load onto the trucks."

"And they get trucked off to where?"

"The port at Geraldton, then to the middle-east or Indonesia, most of them."

"Yeah so we will all get cleaned up now and have a beer or two while Narelle prepares our dinner. She'll bring ours over to the mess room over there next to the bungalows."

"Seems like a great little setup you have here. Okay we will let you do your own thing and we might catch up again in the morning."

"Nice to meet you two."

The workers turned to walk toward their quarters and Rebecca and Andrew returned to their house. Narelle followed them.

"If you two are ready for dinner I will serve yours and then take the dishes to the mess room."

"Thank you, Narelle, we will have a quick shower and be out in a few minutes. You could just leave our plates in the oven, that would be fine."

"And you will find some sweets in the refrigerator."

Narelle had prepared a dish of Moroccan lamb with mashed potato, peas, corn, onion and mushroom flavoured gravy. She served the plates for Rebecca and Andrew then left the house with the trolley of pots for the workers' mess.

Rebecca and Andrew sat at their dining table and proceeded to dine.

"Wow this sure is a delicious dish she's made up here. They weren't wrong about her cooking eh."

"You can say that again. I must get her to teach me how to cook up this dish."

"Yes, I hope she has some leftovers – I might sneak out here during the night for a snack."

Following their main course Rebecca found two plates of dessert in the refrigerator – sherry trifle sponge cake with cream and ice-cream. She also noticed two empty sachets in the kitchen litter bin – McCormick's 'Moroccan Lamb'.

"Ha ... I believe I have found the flavouring that Narelle has used on our dinner tonight – McCormick's 'Moroccan Lamb'. Hmm ... must ensure we have plenty of this in store eh Andrew?"

"I reckon ... I don't believe I have ever tasted anything as nice as that."

Following their dinner Rebecca proceeded to clean their dishes but Narelle had returned to do the same.

"No need to do that miss, that's part of my role here. The managers always had some bookwork to do in the evenings so you can leave that for me. But may I suggest that you two might go see what the workers are getting up to over there."

Rebecca and Andrew looked at each other then walked toward the front window of the house from where they had a good view of the outside area.

"Looks like they have lit up a fire over there near the bungalows."

"Oh yeah – I wonder what that is about. Perhaps we had better go over there and see."

"Yes good idea – we don't want a fire getting out of control around here."

Rebecca and Andrew left their house to commence the walk toward the bungalows, which were about one hundred metres from the house. As they approached, they could see the fire more clearly and could see people sitting around the fire.

The workers were sitting around the campfire drinking beer and other pre-mixed drinks when Andrew and Rebecca approached them.

"Hello again. We hope you don't mind us visiting your little bonfire gathering here. Narelle suggested we come and see so we thought we might as well get acquainted with what happens around here. But don't let us change anything you do okay."

"The boss man never visit us here boss! But take a seat and grab a beer."

Andrew took a stubby of beer from the esky and handed Rebecca a can of bourbon and Coca Cola. They sat on a rock with a cushion atop.

"So the boss man, as you call him, never visited you here eh?"

"No boss, he always too busy in the night doing his books and being on the internet. He reckon he have to watch the stock market whenever he could."

Rebecca and Andrew looked around at the workers who seemed to be enjoying a rather romantic moment sitting in the open by the fire, indulging in chat.

"Nah he was just a bit too snobby to come and sit with us."

"Just as well too cos he seemed so up himself – you couldn't be yourself while old William was around."

"You guys seem more down to earth already."

"Well Rebecca is Australian so what do you expect?"

74

"You can call me Bec okay!"

"Well thank you for that, we will try to stay down to earth then. Hey that's not a bad drop of beer. Swan Draught eh, hmm! I will have to get you to buy a few cartons for me next time you visit that town. Is it Wiluna?"

"Yeah, it's what everybody in Western Australia drank back in the day. Now there's all that girly cats piss on the market – what is it, some blonde or corolla or that shit?"

"Corona! So Jimmy and Travis are up to something else!"

"They'll be here soon – they're getting themselves ready."

"Ready?"

Just at that moment Jimmy and Travis exited a bungalow and started walking toward the campfire. That is when Rebecca and Andrew could see that they had adorned themselves in paint and were wearing a skimpy crude pair of jocks. They were each carrying a spear and Travis also had a didgeridoo. Travis handed the didgeridoo to Robbie who was not Aboriginal himself but had learnt to play the instrument.

"Well what do we have here?"

"The boys thought they might treat you to a corroboree boss, as a welcome gesture."

"Hey fantastic, we've never seen a corroboree before."

Jimmy and Travis moved a few metres away from the fire and Robbie started to play the didgeridoo. Jimmy and Travis started their dance while Jill provided some commentary on the meaning of the dance, which lasted for several minutes.

"The young boy was sent out alone into the bushland to hunt for a kangaroo or a wallaby as a test to enter his manhood. He had only a spear and a boomerang but no container of liquid. He would have to find his own water and was not able to return to his people until he had made a kill. With his boomerang he could bring down a bird for food.

The boy walked for half a day before he came across some kangaroos. He tried to stalk the kangaroos but they were alarmed by five dingoes that attacked them. Now he had to wait for the dingoes to wander off, because he knew they could be a danger to him. He had no food yet that day and was getting hungry. When he was sure the dingoes had gone, he walked in the opposite direction away from where the roos were. Later in the afternoon he still had not succeeded in finding any food, apart from some berries and coconut from the base of a grass tree. Then he saw something move in the scrub nearby. He stood still to observe what caught his attention. Nothing moved so he thought that he too had been seen so he slowly backed away to be out of view of whatever had moved. He peered through the branches of a bush, then saw something move again. He thought this might be a large snake but rushed forward to tackle whatever this animal was, to see it was a large bungarra. He used his boomerang to send the bungarra into the dreamtime and held it up to allow it to bleed. The boy was pleased with himself for now he had some food to keep him going into the next day. He found a clear spot in the bushes where he could light a fire to cook his bungarra. The fire would also protect him through the night from dingo and wild pig. He gathered rocks and formed them into a circle then gathered some dry twigs and branches. He used a crooked stick and some spinifex leaves to make a bow with which he turned a stick on some wood to create a spark and within a few minutes he had made a fire. He got some bigger pieces of wood to burn for he knew he would need some hot coals on which to cook the lizard. He stoked the fire gently to keep some coals burning without much flame and he placed the lizard onto the coals. He knew he would have some good food within an hour. Just as his dinner was ready a single dingo appeared out of the bushes and stood there looking at the boy and at the bungarra on the fire. The dingo was looking very hungry for its ribs were showing through its skin. The boy knew this dingo would not harm him, for this dingo was a good dingo and the boy, too, was dingo. His parents had told him that he was dingo in the dreamtime. The boy removed the head of the lizard and held it out and the dingo came forward to take the food. The boy used a stick to pierce the lizard and held it up for himself to eat. The dingo ate the lizard's head then looked at the boy again. The boy removed the tail from the lizard and held that out for the dingo to take. The boy continued to eat the lizard's legs cos they were the best part of the lizard. Then the boy handed the dingo part of the lizard's body and the dingo ate what he was given. The boy knew the dingo was very hungry. When the dingo had eaten enough food, he lay down by the fire to stay with the boy. He too fell asleep by the fire knowing that the dingo would alert him to any wild pig. In the morning the dingo had gone and had taken the rest of the lizard, just as the boy was hoping he would. Then the boy walked toward a water hole by watching birds flying up and down from the ground and he drank water. Then he heard a noise and thought it might be a kangaroo so he walked and stalked toward the noise with his spear. He found some kangaroo feeding on grass so keeping some bushes between himself and the mob he slowly got behind one small male. The boy threw a rock over the mob that landed in the bushes and made them stand up and look in the other direction. He carefully came out from behind his bush and with his spear he sent the young kangaroo to the dreamtime. The boy would drag the kangaroo back to his people with pride to be welcomed by all his people into his manhood and the tribal elders were very pleased with the boy."

This was obviously the end of the corroboree and the group clapped and thanked Jimmy and Travis for their rendition, but it was Rebecca and Andrew who were totally enthralled by the performance. They felt totally privileged by what they had seen. They really could not believe it.

"Hey boys that was bloody fantastic – I have never seen anything like that before in my life."

"No nor have I" said Rebecca. "That was just so amazing and thanks, guys, for getting yourselves decked out the way you have. All that paint all over you, wow."

"Yeah guys I can't believe what I just saw, I mean, I've seen some American Indian dances before but, geeze, that was so totally awesome what you guys just did for us. Your leg movements were just so captivating. So you boys must be experienced corroboree dancers eh!"

"The boys go down to town every few weeks during winter for the corroboree when there's a bit of a crowd there getting ready to hit the track."

"Town! What town?"

"Wiluna – where the pub is! That's when they bring back our supplies of grog."

"So that track would be the stock route!"

"Yeah the people usually leave in groups for safety reasons so they fork out quite a few dollars to watch the corroboree."

"Andrew you said the word 'bloody'- where did you pick that up from?"

"Ah ... probably from the pilot, why, is that a privilege for Aussies only?"

"Nah you're okay, just took me by surprise that's all."

"So Andrew when do you plan to get into the job looking at the wells and bores out there?"

"Hmm ... can't think of any reason to wait Jack. Perhaps we head out in the morning, but where would we need to go to?"

"Our first stop will be out at Lake McDonald cos we have a couple of bores there, so we should head off at sunrise but we won't be back till the following day."

"Really! So we will have to sleep in the swags eh? Better take a couple of dogs eh?"

"You getting' worried about those wild pigs already Andrew? Don't blame ya but yeah, the two big dogs will keep us safe."

Rebecca spoke up.

"Well I'm pleased to hear that – don't want to lose me hubby quite yet. So what are the dogs' names?"

"Buster and Princess. But don't worry miss they are good dogs. Your hubby will be quite safe."

Travis spoke up.

"Them pigs are shit scared of Buster. He's a big boy as you'll see tomorrow when you get packed up."

"And on that note I suppose we had better retire to get some shuteye – could be a long day tomorrow. Thank you once again Jimmy and Travis for the corroboree, it's something I will never forget."

"Goodnight guys. Oh Jack what time should I be up and ready?"

"We should be on the road by seven, okay, so I will be packing the ute around six thirty."

"Okay see you tomorrow."

Camping out

The next morning Narelle had made Andrew and Jack a full breakfast of bacon, eggs, a beef sausage, fried tomato and mushrooms.

Jack was outside loading the four-door ute, which had a canopy over the tray section. As Andrew approached Jack threw a couple of swags onto the back seat of the ute then picked up an esky to place onto the rear floor. Jack had a bag of clothing with him.

"Shall I put this into the rear section Jack?"

"You can if you want to but the dogs might chew it up."

That is when Andrew realised the two kangaroo dogs were in the back tray section of the ute, so he walked around to view them. A steel mesh grid isolated the dogs to the inside of the ute and Andrew had his first view of these substantial kangaroo dogs.

"Wow they sure are big dogs. Hello Buster, hello Princess."

Both dogs were lying down and gave a slight wag of their tails. This placated Andrew into knowing they were friendly toward him.

"Andrew I will just place your bag here. Oh and this is for you too."

"What's this?"

"Your sanitation kit – soap and water and a hand towel, for when you have got to go. Yours is the blue one, mine is the green okay."

"Are there toilet facilities out there?"

"Yeah sure – behind any bush! There's no ablution block out there mate. You'll just have to take the shovel, duck behind a bush and kangaroo it."

"Kangaroo it?"

"You'll work it out."

"We also scrub up before handling any food, okay. That's something I insist on. I worked in the food industry for many years."

Rebecca had come out to say goodbye and to give her husband a kiss, for he would be away for a couple of days.

"Now take care you two and keep an eye open for snakes. Are you sure you have the sat phones?"

"Don't worry Rebecca I have gone right through my check list as I always do before going bush, right down to the fly repellent. Your husband will be fine."

Just then one of the dogs made a noise so Rebecca walked to the rear of the ute to view the dogs.

"Geeze they sure are a size eh! I've heard about these kangaroo dogs – never seen one though. Hello doggies!"

Princess and Buster were lying down but endeavoured to wag their tales. This made Rebecca feel good about these large canines. She had been so worried about her Andrew mixing it in the bush with wild boars and dingoes.

"Okay let's hit the track Andrew."

It was now just after seven o'clock and Jack got into the driver's seat and Andrew the passenger's side. They said their final goodbyes and Jack started the ute moving.

"Okay Lake McDonald here we come."

Along the way in this first leg to Lake McDonald they would occasionally engage in discussion.

"How far away is Lake McDonald?"

"About fifty clicks but it will take about an hour to get there. Probably take a couple of hours to sort that first well. Then we'll head south from there and check the other wells and pumps. The last of them is way down near the boundary of this station."

"We've got enough water then?"

"Enough for about four days! You just never know when you might get stranded in a bog after a heavy shower, but we're never too far from help. The sat phone solves that problem. We won't be roughing it too much though. Natalie has made us both a couple of rounds of sandwiches for lunch and a frozen pack of Chinese food for dinner tonight. Tomorrow morning we will make a good breakfast with cereal and then bacon and eggs, knock up some sandwiches for lunch then for dinner we will do a steak on the gas cooker."

"What will the dogs eat?"

"Oh they'll catch something out there – maybe a rabbit or a bungarra. Whatever they catch we'll cook it up on a spit for them. Oh and we've got plenty of milk. I like to give the dogs a drink of milk to start the day and before they go down at night too. It's good for their bones. Buster likes banana milk and Princess the spearmint milk."

"You flavour the milk for the dogs?"

"Yep – gotta keep them happy! They might cross a big buck roo out there."

Andrew looked at Jack and pondered the moment – almost too afraid to ask.

"How big?"

"Phew – biggest one I ever saw would have stood more than seven feet tall at the head. Had muscle on him too – looked a bit like a weightlifter on steroids."

"Seven feet, geeze that's a tall roo eh."

"Yeah the dogs were about to go him but I called them back – not for their sake but I thought a roo that had reached that size deserved to live on. Would have been a shame to have ended such an eminent life like that."

"There's a soft side to you then Jack!"

"Should be a soft side in every man Andrew."

"Agreed!"

"You strike me as being a type of new-age male Andrew."

"Yeah my father was always a good talker when I was a boy, having lost my mother at such a young age I suppose he showed a lot of affection to ensure I wasn't missing anything my mother might have provided me with. He would always tell me that he loved me and praised me a lot for anything I did well. I will be the same with my children when we start a family."

"You got plans to start soon?"

"Probably this year depending on what happens here, of course. We could be here for longer than we planned. Just have to see what happens I suppose."

"Well, there are worse places in the world than the east Pilbara – might take a bit of getting used to though with the weather the way it is. It can get into your blood system though."

"Oh I can appreciate that. There are similarities with many places I have seen back in the States - New Mexico, Arizona, Nevada – they all have quite extensive arid, desert-like areas not totally dissimilar to this topography. I was totally enthralled by those places when I went there with my father. Of course, out here you have you own unique flora and fauna to complement the landscape. Yes this really is quite extraordinary. But so remote too, geeze, you wouldn't want to be stranded out here without any way of calling for help eh."

"That happens too often unfortunately. People come here from overseas to do the Canning Stock Route and have absolutely no idea of what this terrain is like or what they are in for. If they don't take adequate precautions and wander off somewhere, they can perish out here."

"I'll have to pick your brains on all of this so that I take the same precautions that you do Jack, in case I ever need to come out here alone."

"You should never come out here alone Andrew. That's the first thing I will tell you – always have someone with you. You just never know when you might be bitten by a snake or break a leg or whatever. So another person to provide first aid is a must out here."

"Okay I will remember that Jack thank you. So how long do you expect to stay on here in your capacity Jack?"

"To be honest I will probably move on later this year. I have a lady in Perth who wants to spend some time travelling, fishing and all that. She is really looking forward to spending quite some time in Tasmania and then New Zealand. I must admit that does have quite some appeal to me too – a bit of a change from this hot place. The plan is to buy a caravan in Tassie, spend several months over there then sell it before we move on to New Zealand and do the same over there. We spent a couple of months on the east coast of Australia years ago in a camper trailer, but as you get older I suppose you look for a better way of doing things – you know, less muscle required setting up a caravan for a night."

After almost an hour Jack and Andrew arrived at the first well and drinking trough on the perimeter of Lake McDonald – a flat and dry salt lake - and noticed the drinking trough was dry. The cap on top of the bore was so old and had not been serviced for such a long time that it had seized with calcium deposit, which was quite a significant problem with the underground water. Jack had brought six new well caps with him that he had sent up through a hotshot courier from Perth, for he suspected the caps on some other bores further east might be the same. He had mentioned the need to service the caps to the former manager who was rather too complacent about many problems. Jack was unaware that this cap he was about to fit and another one had been dropped in the factory from a height and was fractured. This would later cause a significant problem.

Jack let the dogs out from the back of the ute. They immediately headed into the scrub for a run and to see what fauna might be in the vicinity. Andrew was duly impressed by the dogs massive loping stride.

"They won't get lost, will they?"

"Nah ... they won't go too far and they do know their way around here. They can smell their way back to the trough."

"Hmm ... so this is a salt lake eh? I must admit I expected something quite different. It's so bright and so flat."

"There are thousands of lakes like this in Western Australia Andrew. This is one of the smaller ones."

"Really! How big are the larger ones?"

"Lake Disappointment not far south-east from here is a big one – that's about sixty by thirty clicks."

Jack and Andrew walked to the trough to see that it was empty as Jack had closed the valve on his last visit as the trough had cracks in the lower sections. Jack set about preparing some resin to repair the cracks so that the trough would once again hold water for the cattle to drink. Jack explained the apparatus to Andrew.

"So this is the bore, this is the shut off valve which we closed last time we were here and the cap on top. The float behind the trough controls the flow just like it does in your toilet cistern. So to replace this cap we first shut the valve off. This particular cap is now over ten years old so we are going to replace it before it deteriorates any further. We need to do the same on the bore at the other end of this lake."

"Are there just the two bores on Lake McDonald?"

"No there is another about midway but that one should be fine. But we do need to repair a trough or two way down near the boundary, so we won't get there until tomorrow and we will check them all as we go."

"How many bores are there?"

"On your entire property, about twenty all up, but we will only check about half of them today and tomorrow. The others are back toward the south west from here. This resin will take a couple of hours to set so we need to stay here until we can open the valve again. We might stoke up the gas cooker to boil a billy for a cuppa eh. Natalie has packed some home-made biscuits and cake for us too. So in the meantime we could go to the top of that hill over there to give you a look around."

"Okay that would be great. What would I expect to see from there Jack?"

"Oh, pretty much more of the same really – just from three hundred feet higher that's all. Still, it will be worth the look."

Andrew set up the gas cooker and filled the billy to make both Jack and himself a cuppa while Jack was finishing the application of resin.

"Make it with one litre of water and four teaspoons of tea leaves. That will give us two cups each mate. I'm pretty fussy about me cuppa."

"Will do!"

"The biscuits are in the Tupperware bowl."

The men sat down for half an hour and enjoyed their cup of tea and biscuits. The dogs came back without a catch but Jack knew they would find something later. Jack threw them both a few biscuits.

"Okay we will pack up and go up the hill then check this resin on the way back before we head to the next well."

Jack took Andrew to the top of the hill from where he had a panoramic view of exactly what Jack had said – more of the same. The area was surrounded by semi-forest and scrub as far as he could see.

"Hmm ... sure is a desolate sort of place, but also very beautiful. I believe people say you could grow anything out here if you had enough water."

"Well yes you probably could but there could be a significant problem with pests – just as they had up north at the Lake Argyle cotton project decades ago. We do get locust plague out here occasionally you know."

"So a mesh or a net covering a crop would be the go eh?"

"Huh! That would cost a fortune for such a large area that you would need to make it viable. But perhaps that depends on what you would be trying to grow. There would be a big market from south-east Asia for some crops – perhaps capsicum, cucumber, celery, broccoli – who knows."

"Spring onions?"

"Yeah them too eh! I suppose someone could give it a shot but, you know, everyone wants a financial return without losing too much money in the process eh."

"Well we just might have to give it a shot one day. Maybe bring some Asian tourists out here to eat the vegetables."

"Yeah, good idea but what would you do to bring that on Andrew?"

"Well a bloody great golf course, of course! Just choose the right location and make it something different and special and they will come here. Perhaps with fairways being bordered by some of those fantastic rock formations that I saw on the way. I've seen some very radical golf holes back in the States and the aura of this place would be enthralling to Asian tourists if you were to build the golf course in the right place. Who knows – grow some fruit and make it a health farm resort where people who are obese could spend a few weeks to lose a lot of weight."

"Yeah well keep that concept in mind Andrew and we might try to find that special location one day."

"Where would they fly into here Jack — would it be Perth City?"

"No the airport at Port Hedland is an international airport, so you would fly them to there then to Newman I suppose."

"Or to a dedicated airport at the actual location. On the way here I noticed that there are several airports servicing the mines, right?"

"Yes, that's right there are dedicated runways at, let's see, Area C, Yandi, West Angelas, Brockman, Marandoo and one shared runway between Christmas Creek and Cloudbreak. I believe they can fly in an aircraft the size of a Boeing 737 and those aircraft carry perhaps over one hundred and fifty passengers."

"Hmm ... worth a thought for sure! But it would depend entirely on the course design and that would depend entirely on the location. I had an idea once before that a resort course could feature a clubhouse atop a hill and every three holes went away from the clubhouse and back to it again — so that there were six greens around the clubhouse. Or even double that for a thirty-six hole golf course."

"Why would you do that Andrew?"

"So they can drink more on the way around!"

Jack burst into laughter at Andrew's facetious response.

"You want them to drink while they are trying to hit a golf ball? Have you ever tried to hit a golf ball while intoxicated Andrew? It's bloody well impossible."

"Yes I know but the fun side of it would be far more important than their golf score. And the ambience of the surroundings is what it would be all about Jack. This really is an extraordinary place. I am sure a lot of very wealthy Asian people would make a trip to a place like this just for that experience alone. Besides, with the layout I have suggested those Asian tourists would be spoiled every third hole with condiments as well as drinks. There could be a small catering facility at every third or sixth green. I mean, you could have some of the very best chefs in the world serving aperitifs and that alone could be a feature of such a resort."

"But not here Andrew, not at this spot, I mean it just doesn't have the right topography for such a thing. Perhaps somewhere where there are some more prominent hills."

"Yeah well we might have to go on a search in the plane one day Jack – just for that purpose. But there's no harm in dreaming about it. It just seems to me this place has so much potential that remains untapped."

"Oh shit yeah but, to build a runway and a golf resort – those mining companies have a lot of money you know. Their runways are fully fenced off from your kangaroos, emus, camels, donkeys, goats, pigs, rabbits and dingoes – you can't have those little buggers getting in the way of a plane landing or taking off. The cost of operating such a facility could be prohibitive."

"Well I've seen just how much money wealthy people are prepared to part with if you look after them properly Jack – spoil them that is. If you ever get to Las Vegas you will see what I mean. Try five thousand per night for a room at some of the top resorts."

"That much eh! That might include women though too, Andrew."

"No they will pay even more for access to women. I mean, some men in particular are making hundreds of thousands of dollars in profits every day Jack, so they will pay well for a good time. They rationalise by convincing themselves they need some quality time out to keep themselves motivated to make good decisions and stay fresh and sharp for their business interests."

"Okay well let's keep all that in mind but we better be heading back to that bore now."

"So is this the highest point around here?"

"Yeah probably for about twenty clicks. You will see some more hills like this as we go south."

Jack and Andrew returned to the bore where Princess was proudly holding a rabbit between her jaws.

"Huh! I told you they would catch their own supper."

The rabbit was still kicking so Jack took hold of it and twisted the body to break its neck. Then he placed the carcass into a hessian bag and threw it into the back of the ute.

"Do you think the resin is set now Jack?"

Jack pressed into the resin and gave it the all clear. He opened the valve and the water started to flow into the trough. Andrew was quite impressed with the water flow, at the rate the water was gushing out into the trough. It certainly would not take long to fill the trough which held over three hundred litres of water. As the trough filled the float shut down the valve to stop the water flow.

"That's all good so we really need to make our way south to check the next one before nightfall, but we will check on this one on the way back Andrew. Now, we both need to drink about a litre of water after climbing that hill."

Jack passed Andrew a container of water. He knew the dangers of dehydration.

"Buzz, Tiges ... in the back!"

The dogs ran over to the ute and jumped into the back section as ordered. Jack packed up his tools and the billy and gas stove and the men headed south. They would continue discussion about a range of topics on the way, as both men had quite some fascination with the world as it is.

"Well I have to hand it to you Andrew, you certainly have some fresh ideas there and I hope you can put them into practice."

"I like to be innovative, you know, give things a crack. You just never know when you might strike a goldmine – or make the world a better place. I mean – take the people who developed the spreadsheet and HTML for example. Look how a simple idea has changed the world forever. A lot of people would have been doing their household budget on a manila folder with rows and columns but not seeing the computer applications for that and then somebody got the idea of allowing people to be connected via the internet. And then came electronic mail, hey, you can send a document to the other side of the world in a faction of a second. Nobody would have believed that thirty years ago."

"True! My camera blows me away. My first digital camera was a massive three megapixel and at that time I recall that five megapixels was considered to be professional level. Now my new camera has a twenty-four megapixel capacity. I saw a guy from IBM on television and he stated that they could now fit thirteen thousand transistors across the width of a human hair. That is just so mind-blowing it's unbelievable. So I looked into that and found he was referring to the four nanometre transistor. Now a company claims to have developed the one nanometre transistor."

"Yes, I know what you mean but where will it all take us Jack? Perhaps one day you will be wearing your PC on your wrist eh. Just talk into it and it connects to a central cloud system that does whatever you want it to - transfer funds, email somebody."

"I thought that was a reality already."

"Not quite!"

"What blows my mind away is just how some things developed in such a short period of time, you know, like from the first motor car in 1885 to the T model Ford in 1908 - or from the Wright brothers' first flight in 1903 to the first jet fighters in World War II. Or the development of radio in the late nineteenth century, then television after the war and then computers. Makes you wonder where we will be in say, one hundred years from now, or one thousand years from now."

"Really! What about in a million years from now Jack, or in fifty million years or in one billion years from now."

"Yeah the mind just boggles eh. That's if we survive that long Andrew."

"Oh I believe we will. I have a pet theory that the universe is the Garden of Eden and it is there for us to explore and to colonise. I was totally blown away when I became aware of the Hubble Telescope's first images of deep space. In fact even NASA was blown away because they had absolutely no idea what they would find out there."

"Really! I haven't heard of that one Andrew. Tell me about it."

"The deep space view - geeze! They really did not have any idea what was out there in deep space so they pointed the Hubble at an empty hole in the sky and took about eleven minutes of exposure time with more than one hundred and fifty orbits of the earth and found thousands of galaxies that they had no prior knowledge of. Then they found the same result by looking through another hole in the sky in the southern hemisphere so concluded that it was virtually homogenous – the same everywhere. Even NASA had difficulty believing what they found. So next year the James Webb telescope will look even deeper into space because it will detect infra-red light which is something the Hubble cannot do. Any galaxies further out will only be detectable in infra-red."

"Hmm ... makes you wonder why all those galaxies are there eh."

"Well Jack, I personally believe that if there is a God in heaven, he would not have created all those galaxies just for to peer at through the Hubble telescope. So I hold hope that we eventually crack the code for space travel. In fact, I believe that some of these alien visitors who have been coming here for some time now might actually be us from our future – you know, from a point of time in the future when we can travel backwards in time to revisit the Earth."

"Yeah, well, that sounds like quite a plausible possibility there Andrew but how long will it take for mankind to develop the technology for space travel or time travel?"

"Well believe it or not Jack, NASA is working on that as we speak. A French mathematician published a paper about a decade ago where he put forth an equation that allowed for space-time travel without contravening Einstein's fundamentals within general relativity theory, but that allows for travel faster than the speed of light."

"Hmm ... I thought Einstein's theory stated that was impossible."

"It does but the new theory is based on the expansion and contraction of space-time before and after a spaceship because apparently space-time can do whatever it wants to do. So it's like taking a shortcut through space as would happen with the folding of space-time."

"Ah yes I have seen a theory like that illustrated somewhere – also one pertaining to worm holes or even, perhaps, black holes being doorways between universes or some shit."

"Yeah well that just might turn out to be more than shit one day Jack, you just never know. I tend to believe that God would not create such things if they served no purpose for us."

"And parallel universes eh?"

"Perhaps an infinite number of universes Jack! After all, if there is a God in heaven surely his power would be infinite – I mean, nothing whatsoever could limit what he would be capable of creating, right?"

"Yeah I suppose that's a fairly compelling line of logic Andrew. But do you really believe it?"

"I believe that absolutely Jack!"

"What – the part that he could or the part that he did?"

"I believe he has and that we are supposed to go there. According to the latest mathematical modelling the propulsion system would not be limited – a spacecraft could travel at any speed and so reach the farthest parts of the universe in a very short time."

"So rather like that wormhole in Stargate eh?"

"You saw the film Jack?"

"Yes I saw that when I was in Perth years ago. I must admit I was duly impressed by the theme of the film so it would be one of my favourites for sure. Kurt Russell was always one of my favourite actors ever since boyhood. Russell and James MacArthur were in everything Disney."

"So what is your favourite film of all time Jack?"

"Oh I don't have much doubt about that, particularly relevant to its era and the impact it had on, well, not only myself but on my sisters too and that was "Swiss Family Robinson" from circa 1960 or 1961. James MacArthur featured in that film too."

"Yes I know the one – I first saw that film with some nieces and nephews while attending a family function. I must admit it sure was a bit of an adventure, eh? I mean, throwing coconut bombs at pirates and that tiger fighting the two dogs."

"Don't forget the race with the ostrich and the baby elephant."

"Ah ... now you're starting to re-live that Jack!"

"Definitely have to watch that again someday."

"Don't tell me you haven't seen it since Jack?"

"I'm afraid that is the case Andrew, yes."

"But Jack you can download that film through Netflix now – straight to your living room."

"Yeah well I wouldn't know how to do that but, Narelle probably does. Must put that on top of the to-do list for when I get home."

"So you have a to-do list Jack?"

"You pick up on everything I say don't you Andrew?"

"Oh I completed an intensive listening course as part of my business studies. The lecturer admitted it was all about money, you know, to be a good businessperson you've got to be prepared to listen to people."

"Yeah, sounds like good advice to me! Not many people do though!"

"So tell me about your to-do list Jack – what do you have on there at the moment?"

"What after this sortie! Ah ... my tax return, sell off the four-wheel drive to buy a later model, then prepare a comprehensive description of what is involved in operating the station for you and your wife so I can take some time off and travel with the missus. Buy a caravan and head for Tassie for a few months."

"Then New Zealand eh?"

"Yep! That's the plan."

"You might be tempted to stay in New Zealand Jack. That happened to some friends of mine and they've been there for more than ten years now. Apparently, it's the beauty of the place that captivated them."

After about one hour they arrived at the second well and Jack let the dogs loose once again. Jack checked the bore cap and decided to replace it. Andrew observed as Jack shut off the valve and used his tools to unscrew the retaining bolts that held the cap in place, fitted the new cap then bolted it back together. He opened the valve and the water started to flow again – the entire process taking just thirty minutes. Andrew was duly impressed.

"That didn't take long."

"Some of them take longer, especially when the nuts are seized, you need to apply some heat to free them. That's why we have those portable gas burners. Got to be very careful not to start a fire out here though – the scrub is so dry a fire will take off and there'd be no way of stopping it."

"Actually I thought I saw some burnt out areas on the way Jack."

"Yes you would have, during the wet season there are lightning strikes and virtually no way of preventing the fires so the bush just burns until it stops. Sometimes the next downpour extinguishes the fire."

"And this trough is okay eh?"

"Yeah, I did some work on this one last time, just a few months back. There'll be a couple of others that might need some work though. The next one is about forty kilometres south of here and we will stay there for the night but we had better head off now."

The men packed up the tools, the dogs jumped into the rear of the vehicle and the men headed south again. Once on the track Jack handed Andrew a plastic bottle of water and opened one for himself.

First night in the bush

Upon arrival at the third site Jack iterated that they would spend the night at this site so he set the dogs loose again then commenced setting up the swags and the campfire. Jack advised Andrew to drink some more water as he knew they would partake of a beer or two with their dinner. Jack had a rock fireplace set up at several sites and this was one of them. There was no paucity of kindling and firewood about the place, so he and Andrew gathered enough to keep the fire burning through the night. They had eaten their sandwiches on the way to the second well so by now they were starting to feel peckish. Jack started the fire as the sun was setting in the west and the ambience of the evening was setting in. There was no wind so everything was eerily still and silent – the only noises being what the men were making themselves as they went about their chores. The crackle of the fire was only interspersed by the odd clanging of the frying pan that Jack was positioning onto the rocks.

Andrew was awestruck by the sense of isolation, as he had never been in such a situation before.

Jack took out the containers that Narelle had prepared and emptied the contents into the frying pan.

"Looks like the casserole has thawed out okay! Sure looks like good tucker too actually – lots of good meat and a variety of vege's in there. That woman would make any man a great wife."

"Narelle, yes she certainly cooked all of us a great dinner last night."

Jack opened another container and emptied rice into the mix, then gave it a bit of a stir.

"Better make sure we stir that up every five minutes or so I reckon, just to make sure it doesn't burn on the bottom.

Those wild dogs will be starting to smell this by now if there are any nearby."

"Do you think there will be Jack?"

"Oh they won't be too far away, but what I mean is apparently those dingoes can detect a smell like this from about six miles. Only take them twenty minutes to cover that distance, but don't worry by then our dogs will be back here. Of course, I do have the rifle in the truck so if any get too smart, we just might have to shoot the bastards eh."

"So are they a native dog to Australia?"

"Not really! They migrated here from south-east Asia a long time ago, possibly when the indigenous people did. Their arrival virtually wiped out a lot of the megafauna that did exist here – like that wombat that was the size of a small cow and so on and the thylacine too."

"Thylacine?"

"Yeah, also known as the Tasmanian Tiger where it survived until Europeans exterminated it. But it did live here on the mainland too. It was a marsupial like the kangaroo and the koala with a pouch for its young. Occasionally there's a purported or reputed sighting in Tasmania or at Nannup in the south-west of WA too but nobody ever produces a photograph."

"Nobody knows if the dingo arrived before the people or vice versa. But they still survive in parts of south-east Asia."

Just then Buster and Princess returned to the camping area so Jack prepared the rabbit they had caught earlier. Andrew watch as Jack skinned the rabbit and skewered it with a metal skewer then positioned it on hot coals on the fringe of the fire where it would cook slowly.

"My father told me, whenever you eat rabbit, make sure it has long ears and a short tail – not short ears and a long tail."

Jack then served the dogs some biscuits to keep them happy until their dinner was ready, then washed his hands before returning his attention to the men's meal.

"Andrew, our dinner will be ready soon so let's break out a stubby or two beforehand."

Jack opened the esky cooler and took out two stubbies of beer – Swan Draught again.

"Get that into ya son! Won't take long for it to go down."

Jack was right! Within a minute both he and Andrew were reaching for a second stubby of beer.

"Sure does taste good when you are thirsty, eh Jack?"

"Shit yeah, that's the best time for a beer, providing you've had sufficient water first though. That's why I got you to drink that water earlier today Andrew. People don't always realise when they are becoming dehydrated out here. That can be a big mistake. No, to really enjoy a good cold beer you need to make sure that your body has sufficient fluid or the beer will go straight to you brain."

"You're going through that second one nicely Jack."

"Oh yeah, I will need three or four before it satisfies my thirst – after that I can settle down to one every hour or so. You not doing too badly yourself there Andrew."

Jack took his third stubby from the cooler but thought it best to let Andrew finish his second, which didn't take long.

"Certainly is peaceful out here Jack. Be a good place to clear out the old brain eh? A good place for a person to meditate for example, should one so choose to. Think I'll have that third beer now if you don't mind."

"That's the way! I usually find that three beers are sufficient to take the yearning away then you feel strangely peaceful in whatever you do next – like cooking, dining, washing the dishes etc."

Jack reached over and turned the dogs' rabbit.

"Give that ten minutes on that side and they will be happy. I'll just rest our frypan on those two hot rocks."

Suddenly both dogs leapt to their feet and growled, then raced into the scrub, startling both men. A few seconds later they heard the dogs bark then a yelp.

"What the ... "

"That was a dingo Andrew, that yelp, so the dogs would have seen him off."

"Do you think they would have killed the dingo?"

"No if that happened there would be a lot of growling and snarling so I suspect the dingo did a runner. But that will keep him at bay for the rest of the night. He will probably tell his mates too!"

Just then the dogs returned wagging their tails and took up there position again.

"What have you dogs been up to eh? You got that bloody dingo didn't you Buzz eh? Tiges, what did you do about it eh? Did you get the dingo too Tiges? Good dogs!"

They were intelligent dogs and understood everything that Jack said to them. Andrew was duly impressed with what he had just witnessed.

Jack removed the rabbit from the fire and cut it across the middle then placed it into a metal dish to cool off before feeding the dogs. Then he served Andrew his dinner of casserole and rice and then his own.

"Hmm ... good tucker eh mate?"

"Sure is!"

"Better break out another beer to wash it down cos it seems pretty spicy eh."

"Yeah she's got some chilli or satay in there, or both, so better have another beer!"

"That's the spirit! Beer number four coming up."

The men were so grateful that they were able to consume such a delicious meal way out in the sticks and enjoy a beer as well. Jack placed some newspaper on the ground and gave the dogs their rabbit meal.

"Wow this sure is something very special out here Jack. I have never experienced anything quite like this before."

"I suppose it's what we call 'roughing it' – a lot of the exploratory people in the mining industry would do this regularly. Of course once they set up a camp, they have a mess and all but those drill rig boys would quite often just have to rough it this way."

Jack recalled many of his forays into the mining industry for Andrew – the sites he had worked, the types of jobs he had done, how lucrative it was back in the days when the ore prices were high, how the Pilbara properties had fluctuated so much during the boom then the downturn and back again.

Andrew told Jack about his research into fracking in the U.S.A. and how destructive it was how the ecology lobby was taking action through the courts to prevent its expansion. He recalled his days at college, the sport, the girls, the interest groups he got involved in – orienteering, theatre and pilates.

After half an hour the darkness had set in and Andrew peered skywards.

"Sure are a lot of stars visible from here Jack. Geeze, I've never seen anything like it."

"Take a look through my binoculars Andrew - that will blow your mind away. This is the best place on the planet to view the Milky Way."

"Is that what we are looking at? Looks a bit cloudy to me Jack."

"That's not cloud Andrew – they are stars of the Milky Way forming that cloudy appearance. That is why it is called the Milky Way. Here, take a look through these. You see the Southern Cross over there? Take a look at that now."

Andrew put Jack's binoculars up to his eyes to view the Milky Way Galaxy.

"Holy shit! I don't believe it! You mean they are all stars surrounding the Southern Cross?"

"Yep – they sure are!"

Andrew scoured the night sky with the binoculars and his mind was indeed blown away with what he could see. He spent a few minutes peering at various parts of the galaxy. He had been following NASA for some time but had never actually seen the galaxy like this before.

"I've seen the Hubble Deep Space View of the galaxies on the NASA website but I wasn't aware that we could see so many stars in our own galaxy like this."

Just then Princess raised her head and looked around out at the dark bush. Buster was asleep. Princess stared into the darkness for several seconds then let out a muffled snarl. This aroused Buster who also raised his head to stare into the darkness. Then her snarl turned into a growl and she rose to her feet and stepped forward, with Buster close behind her. Jack reached for his rifle for he knew the dogs had been alerted to either dingoes or pigs. Princess let out an angry bark, then another. Buster leapt to his feet and trotted toward the dark bush. Princess followed not far behind him, for neither dog was afraid of anything that might be lurking in the dark bush that night. The dogs would actually enjoy a stoush with a feral boar more than anything. The two dogs stood at the edge of the clearing a few metres from the bushes. Suddenly it came charging out – a large boar with tusks, grunting and squealing. Buster dodged a hit from the boar then made his move, grabbing the boar around the neck and bringing it down. The boar might have been big but Buster was a good sixty kilograms himself and the boar stood no chance. Jack and Andrew were surprised and impressed that Buster had managed to bring the boar down so quickly without any assistance from his mate, but it was what came naturally to this huge canine.

Jack took his rifle and put a single bullet into the head of the boar to end its suffering. He slit the boar's throat to bleed it then after a few minutes he slung it by the foot to a hook on the side of the vehicle. The boar would provide some good meat for the dogs the next day.

Andrew's heart was racing, for he had never seen anything like that either. He was duly impressed with the dogs and experienced a feeling of being protected by them. No doubt they would make it known if any other boars or dingoes came near the campsite.

"Well on that note Andrew, I think I will get a good night's sleep."

Andrew watched as Jack set himself into his swag then did the same.

The next morning, Andrew was awakened by noise before five o'clock just as the night was giving way to the light of day. He lay there a moment thinking about his experiences the day before then after a few minutes he realised what had awoken him. It was a constant sound of chirping birds – an absolute cacophony of dozens of birds. This, too, was a new experience for him. There were so many varied calls he realised there must be several different species of birds chirping. He decided not to move but to lay there taking it in. There was no other discernible noise at the time, so he realised that Jack must have still been sound asleep, as if this cacophony of birdsong was quite familiar to the old timer. No doubt to the dogs too. Andrew looked at his sat phone and the clock had just ticked past five in the morning. He decided it was best to lay there for the moment contemplating what might be in store for him in the day ahead. No doubt they would have time to service the remaining nine bores, he would probably see some more

Australian fauna, the dogs would catch something - and Jack might have to shoot something then he would knock up a decent meal or two. It was all in a day's life in the Aussie outback. The occurrences of the previous day seemed somewhat surreal to Andrew but it seemed to him that these Aussie bastards just do this sort of thing as a matter of course – catch a rabbit, chase a dingo, shoot a pig! Yep, that seems to be just life down here in Oz.

Andrew turned onto his right side then he heard a noise. He looked at his sat phone again and the time read ten minutes past six. He had fallen asleep to the birdsong and now it was Jack who was up and about. Then he heard the dogs drinking so he decided it was time to rise. Old Jack was stoking the fire to get some flame happening and had set up two cereal plates and a container of milk on the fold up table. He had just given the dogs a drink of their flavoured milk – one whole litre of each, but he would then provide them with water to drink as they wished. This time Buster was drinking spearmint milk and Princess the banana milk. The dogs loved this flavoured treat so much they would consume the whole litre before turning to drink water.

"Morning Andrew!"

"Morning Jack, dogs, birds!"

"Huh! You heard the birds no doubt."

"Yeah you could say that Jack – just before five it was."

"Best part of the day Andrew – take it in son."

"Yes, I must admit I can appreciate that Jack, never heard anything like it though."

"Tell you something Andrew – there are more species of vertebrate animal here in Australia, than there are in the entire rest of the world combined. Birds are a big part of that Andrew – there are hundreds of them … species … here, in different parts of the country of course. But even just up here, yep, dozens of them."

"I think I heard all of those Jack."

"Well you don't need an alarm clock up here, now, what type of cereal would you like, we have Weeties and Corn Flakes."

"I'm familiar with the Corn Flakes of course so I'll give the Weeties a crack Jack. Is that an Aussie cereal?"

"Yep, sure is – one of the most popular too. I'll get some bacon and eggs happening then we can have cereal while that is cooking up."

At that the kettle sounded its whistle so Jack put two mugs on the table and measured some tea into each mug then poured boiling water into the mugs. He then placed two frying pans onto the fire and put bacon into one and bacon and eggs into the other. Then he sliced two tomatoes in half and placed them in with the eggs.

"Give that a minute to brew Andrew and get some good tea inside you. Make sure you have two cups this morning – gets your hydration levels off to a flyer."

While Jack was doing that Andrew filled his cereal plate with Weeties then poured a generous amount of milk onto his cereal, sprinkled on some sugar and let it sit until the flakes absorbed some of the milk. Jack turned the bacon then placed some large slices of bread into a metal holder, placed a metal frame over fire and placed the bread on top of the frame – obviously how he does toast in the morning. Andrew started to drink his tea and consumed his first cup in just a minute then commenced eating his cereal. Jack sat down to his cup of tea.

"That bread is straight from the Engel so it is still frozen but that's okay, the fire will thaw it then toast it for us. Before we leave here, I will take our ingredients for lunch out of the Engel so they thaw in time – a couple of rounds of ham or silverside with pickles or chutney. We'll knock up a flask of coffee for each of us too before we pack up here. How's the cereal?"

"Bloody well delicious cereal Jack that's for sure – Weeties eh? Would go well in the States."

Jack had chosen the Corn Flakes for his cereal so he drank his tea then started his breakfast. Midway through his cereal he got up to turn the toast and the bacon. He was very careful not to let anything burn – they couldn't afford to waste time cooking it all over again. Jack got their plates ready and after a minute he removed the toast and placed it onto the plates.

"You can butter your own toast there Andrew and I will do mine."

"I see you like butter on your toast Jack."

"Worth every penny of it, as my father used to say."

Jack brought the frying pan over and gave Andrew two eggs and a generous serve of bacon – four bacon rashers plus a fried tomato. Jack had the same. He topped up the kettle and placed it back onto the fire before sitting down to his bacon and eggs. It seemed he had this ritual of cooking down pat. The dogs were munching on biscuits Jack had placed into their milk bowls. When they had finished dining, Jack made the flasks of coffee then mixed the remainder of the boiling water with some cold water to wash the plates and the frying pans. The men then packed up their swags and loaded the vehicle ready to set off down the track. Jack put the boar into a hessian bag and slung it from a side rail of the vehicle with a hook on each end so that it wouldn't bounce around too much. Then he took out his sanitation kit and opened his plastic water bowl and soap container and placed the soap into the water. Andrew was watching on. Then Jack grabbed a shovel from the ute tray and a roll of toilet tissue and walked off into the bush.

"Just going for a quick crap mate."

He had his sanitation kit ready to wash his hands as soon as he returned, rather deliberately indicating to Andrew that this was the way it is done. After completing your private business, you wash your hands immediately, for the sake of everybody's hygiene.

Jack was gone for about five minutes and on his return, he indeed thoroughly washed his hands then proceeded to load everything into the vehicle. He started the ute and let it run for five minutes before heading off toward the south. Once on the road again, Andrew had time to reflect on the morning's activities.

"Thank you for cooking that breakfast for me Jack, that was fantastic. I must say I have never seen anyone do that in such a well organised manner before. I suppose you need a good brekky to start the day out here."

"Thanks Andrew, yeah that's for sure, it's important to avoid feeling drowsy later in the day – get some good tucker into ya. We'll stop for smoko about nine then for lunch about one o'clock."

"So how far do we go now before the next bore?"

"Each one of these following bores are about five to ten kilometres apart, so that's three miles and six miles in your lingo, which gives the cattle plenty of drinking holes as they graze without having to walk too far. They come to know where the troughs are of course. They are not stupid animals, not as smart as dogs or even horses but they do have a brain to the point that they are socially structured, you know. They have a hierarchy of seniority – at least they have a leader and those who aspire to be and you will see the head cow keep those aspirants in check occasionally."

"Yes I did see that once before on a dairy farm in the States."

"There's a small herd of cows now – say fifteen, perhaps twenty. You see they have some newly born calves too, frolicking as they do."

"Why only that many if you have thousands here Jack?"

"Well they do tend to form clans that way but this would be just a small part of this clan. There could be a hundred in total here. Yep quite a few newborns there eh."

"So where are the bulls Jack?"

"You've got three bulls Andrew but they are territorial so you won't see them together and it's best to steer clear of them okay. They can be nasty."

"Steer clear of the steer eh Jack?"

"Yeah Andrew that's it mate, well said."

After five kilometres they reached another bore. Jack and Andrew inspected the bore and everything seemed to be working well so they left that bore and continued south.

The next bore was nine kilometres further south and they replaced the bore cap in the same way they had done earlier. Then they stopped for their sandwich lunch, drinking coffee from their flasks, before checking several more bores. By the time they reached the last bore Jack had just one cap left and he used it. By now it was getting close to six o'clock so Jack decided it was best to camp out for the second night. In the morning they would drive back the same way and check all the bore caps and troughs again.

"This is our home for the night Andrew so we will gather some wood and set up the fire. Just get some of that light stuff over there for kindling to get it started and I'll get some branches."

Jack let the dogs out of the ute and set off to gather wood he could see about fifty metres away in a clear area. The dogs had gone in their own direction. Andrew gathered some kindling and got the fire started while Jack had collected a large dry branch that he would cut up with his saw. Then Andrew saw something move among the bushes. To his horror a large bull came out of the scrub and started in Jack's direction.

"Jack!"

Jack turned around and saw the bull heading his way and gathering speed. The dogs were not aware of what was happening. Andrew watched in horror as the bull closed in on Jack. Suddenly Jack hit the ground lying on his back and totally prostrate on the ground as the bull approached him. Andrew assumed that Jack was going to play dead, but he was wrong. Jack stretched out both his arms sideways and clenched his fists. Andrew by now had jumped into the ute and started it, engaging the gears to drive toward Jack but the bull was now virtually upon Jack.

Then Andrew saw something quite peculiar happen. As the bull put its head down to possibly attack, Jack's arms swung in and hit the bull to the face. The bull reared up and jumped backwards then started kicking its rear legs up as it moved away from Jack. Andrew drove in between Jack and the bull and Jack wasted no time jumping into the passenger's seat. Now the dogs came rushing out of the scrub and saw the bull off.

"Thanks Andrew!"

"Shit Jack that was close. For a moment there I thought you were in real trouble, geeze, I've never seen anything like it."

"Yeah but it's happened before, different bull though."

"Ah ... what did you do to ward him off Jack - looked like you gave him a double punch to his face?"

"Only one thing you can do really – gotta go for the eyes mate – they are very sensitive of course. The animal needs his eyes to see and they don't like having a handful of dirt splashed into their eyes. I was able to grab a handful in each hand and give him a double dose. So, no, I didn't actually punch him in the face I gave both his eyes a decent cover of dirt."

"Shit, that's one for the books! Do you think he will come back?"

"No - now that he knows the dogs are here, he will keep his distance."

"Bloody hell Jack that was a fright."

"Yeah, good thing I went bush earlier eh. You might be due to go soon, so if you do, I suggest you duck over there behind that windmill in case some nasty dingo visits you. But look out for snakes too Andrew. Now let's get this fire going. I'll take the dogs with me to recover that large branch over there. That should keep the fire going all night. Buzz, Tiges ... here!"

Andrew watched as old Jack went to retrieve his large branch of firewood with the dogs trotting alongside him and had to admire the old mate for what he had just witnessed. He felt so relieved that Jack had survived the charge of the bull. That night the cooking procedure went just as it did the night before and the casserole had a distinctly Indian flavour to it.

"Hmm ... beef vindaloo tonight from Narelle, plus some more rice to go with it. Great choice Narry."

The men broke out some stubbies of beer, completed their dinner and made a cup of tea then did the clean up before settling down to have a couple more beers before retiring.

"That sure was an eventful day for you Jack - my own pulse rate is still up there even these two hours later."

"Oh I'm okay, that bull probably would have just had a bit of a sniff then taken off, but you can't be sure so best to do what I did. He might think twice about approaching a man again. Taught him a lesson today, we did. Just means this beer goes down much better Andrew – good to be alive! Pass me my number four will ya."

The dogs got into the legs of the boar that Jack had cooked up for them – the rest of it he had buried. They had also caught two more rabbits that Jack had skinned and was cooking up for the dogs to eat the next day. After consuming their own dinner, the dogs then enjoyed their drink of milk before lying down to rest.

Despite Buster's impressive performance of the previous night in bringing down the boar, there was to be something quite different on this second night. As the night progressed the two dogs were sleeping as Jack and Andrew sat talking after eating their dinner. The two rabbits were still cooking on the spit when Princess once again raised her head to stare into the darkness. She stared for several minutes before letting out a muffled snarl. This aroused Buster who also stared into the night. Both dogs were looking around and making an occasional whimpering sound, as if something was bothering them but they didn't know what. Could this be another large boar, or an entire pack of dingoes that might test the two kangaroo dogs? Princess got to her feet and walked tentatively toward the bushes as she had done the night before, only this time occasionally lowering her head to sniff the ground and looking up into the bushes. Buster was still lying down, not sure what to make of his mate's antics. Princess looked up into the darkness and stared as if frozen. Jack and Andrew were watching and just waiting for Buster to join the fray or to do anything, but he just lay there staring at Princess, for he had never seen her like this before.

Then Princess let loose a yelp. Buster arose and trotted forward to be by her side. Jack had never seen the dogs act this way before, so he reached for his rifle. He was sure this would be either a parcel of pigs or a pack of dingoes. Andrew reached for his camera, for whatever was about to happen would be very interesting. Princess and Buster stood still for several minutes without making any noise or moving. Jack was totally perplexed.

"Jack what is it?"

"I'm stuffed if I know mate – I have never seen the dogs act like this before."

Then quite suddenly, Princess turned and trotted back to where she had been lying beside the men and assumed a sitting position. Once again, she made a whimpering sound, as if she was frightened. Buster lowered his head to the ground and took a couple of very tentative steps forward. Then he looked up again and simply stared straight ahead. Now Jack was really worried, for Buster feared nothing and would normally be letting out an angry snarl if he thought he was being challenged. Then Buster did something very strange that Jack had never seen him do before. He started walking backwards toward the men while still maintaining a focus on the bushes ahead of him and again lowering his head to sniff the ground. Buster maintained his very slow rearward action until he was almost alongside the men, then he turned and trotted back to be beside his mate. Now Jack was even more worried, for whatever was lurking in the bushes had virtually persuaded his two fearless dogs to retreat to safety. Jack cocked his rifle, ready to fire at whatever.

After about two minutes of the men staring into the darkness, Jack saw something – a pair of eyes.

"Andrew – do you see what I see?"

"No I can't see anything. Where?"

Jack pointed the gun barrel toward the bushes.

"Look! Look along the gun barrel and tell me what you see."

"I don't see anything Jack."

"Well I see a pair of eyes – a pair of dim yellow eyes."

"Oh yeah now I see it – but I think they just did a slow blink."

"Yeah I saw that too – but what the hell is it?"

"Could it be a camel?"

"No! Whatever that is its eyes are too high off the ground to be a camel. Shit, they must be eight bloody feet off the ground."

"That's impossible Jack!"

"Yes I know – but we are looking at it."

Then there was some movement. A shadow of a figure was only just discernible but it made its way out of the trees. The dogs whimpered again. The tall dark figure slowly moved further forward. It was huge but the men still had no idea what they were looking at. They too were both frozen still. Then Jack seemed to experience a rude awakening, as the huge figure took another step forward toward the fire. Jack muttered in a low voice.

"My God! I don't believe it!"

Andrew responded with a whisper.

"What is it Jack? Please, tell me what that is."

"I don't believe it Andrew."

"The hell is it Jack?"

"I don't believe this – it's a yowie."

"A what?"

Jack turned his head towards Andrew and very softly muttered.

"A yowie."

"The hell is a yowie Jack?"

Jack whispered .

"Bigfoot!"

"Holy shit you gotta be kidding me Jack. But geeze he must be over seven feet tall."

"Eight!"

The yowie stepped forward to where the men had a better view of him and he reached down to grab the rabbits off the fire. He looked up to see that the men were still seated.

"Quickly Andrew – your camera, take a shot."

Andrew pointed his camera and waited for the yowie to look up, then snapped a pic. The flashlight startled the big yowie and it turned and took a few giant steps to disappear into the bushes.

"I don't believe it Andrew – we have just seen a yowie. And you have just become the first person in human history to have taken a photograph of a yowie."

"You mean these creatures are so rarely seen Jack."

"Almost never seen Andrew – it's been just a piece of mythical Aboriginal folklore, until now. I still cannot believe this has just happened. Though I do know an old bloke from Newman, old Wally, who reckons he saw a yowie one night at the camping ground at Mount Robinson, north of Newman. But nobody ever believed him. Shit this will be world news."

"Well there are plenty of people in the States who claim to have seen the Bigfoot, but nobody has ever produced a verifiable photograph of one. So he was never going to harm us eh, Jack?"

"No, the dogs seemed to know that Andrew. If they thought he was going to cause any harm I'm sure the dogs would have stood their ground – even though they have never seen a yowie before. That was really strange – the dogs seemed to show him respect and gave him his space."

"Yeah, they did, didn't they Jack?"

"Well I don't think we will ever see him again, but shit, what a huge privilege that he came here to visit us."

"Do you think there are more out there in the darkness?"

"No way of telling – they obviously don't occur in large numbers and nobody knows where they hide out, if I can put it that way. Somebody might claim to have seen one every five or ten years, though I suppose not everybody would speak up for fear of being ridiculed."

"Well we've got him on film now – or should I say ensconced in pixels now."

"Can you rig up that camera to the sat phone and email it to Rebecca? We need to ensure that is preserved as soon as we can."

"Yeah probably!"

Andrew succeeded in using a mini cable to link the camera to the sat phone and emailed the pic to his email address, though Rebecca was asleep and would not see the photograph until the next morning.

The men were so mesmerised by what they had witnessed that they sat there for quite some time talking about their encounter with the yowie. They thought it would be best to drink a few more beers to remain calm. Fortunately they had a good supply of Swan Draught, for Jack knew they would be out in the bush for two nights and you just never know – once a man or two get drinking there's no telling where it stops.

"So Jack is there anything else within the Aboriginal folklore that you understand about this yowie?"

"Only that he appears so infrequently because something extraordinary is about to happen. They say he comes out to change something in a big way. I still can't believe what just happened. But what I am trying to comprehend, Andrew, is why us and why now? Can't have a lot to do with me Andrew! I've been here for years. You're the newcomer here - must be to do with you I'd say. So what's in your background that might have enticed the yowie to grace us with his presence today?"

"Why would a yowie want to visit an American?"

Jack waited a minute after he remembered something that Wally had told him before putting the question to Andrew.

"Andrew, tell me the most significant thing that has happened to you in your entire life."

Andrew took a deep breath and contemplated.

"That's a big question Jack – maybe completing my PhD thesis, meeting Rebecca, being born to the parents I was. My father has always been very wealthy – I've never had to want for anything."

Then Andrew thought some more.

"Though I did lose my mother when I was a young boy. I was just four years old when she died of cervical cancer. I still remember her though. I will never forget her face. She was very beautiful. My father didn't tell me until I was about fourteen years of age that my mother was Navaho."

"American Indian?"

"Yep – full blooded Navaho Indian was my mother."

"Hmm ... could be some melding of the blood happening here if you two ever have kids."

"My father met my mother in New Mexico when he was there one time on a business trip working for a drilling company. He got stuck out in the desert for a day and then some and she just happened to come by on a horse and rescued him. Got him back to a place where he could get assistance. So he went back to reward her and they seemed to double click you know. She certainly was a very beautiful woman. Most people don't lose their mother at such a young age, but I can't say that she would be the reason for this happening tonight."

"You never know! My mate I told you about – Wally. He lost his mother at age four. That's a bit more than a coincidence Andrew. So you are part American Indian and your wife is Australian Aboriginal. Hmm ... could be!"

"Could be what Jack?"

"Well the Aboriginal people say the yowie will only visit people with a very special purpose in this life, so it could be. That's all I can say to you Andrew."

"Well I don't doubt that mothers do watch over us from heaven."

"You believe in heaven?"

"Ever since Sunday school!"

"We better get some sleep – if we can get to sleep after that experience. We could be in for a long day tomorrow. We have to make it all the way back to the station and check those bores on the way."

"Perhaps we could track that yowie?"

"No chance Andrew! They have never been tracked. Our Aboriginal people are good trackers. They've saved many lives finding people who were lost out bush somewhere. So a yowie would surely know how not to leave tracks. Nup! We will never see him again. So your mother was Navaho eh?"

"Yeah I reckon she'd be up there in those stars somewhere. Best we turn in now eh."

"Just before we do, try this nightcap."

Jack took out two small wine glasses and a bottle, opened the bottle and poured Andrew a small nightcap. Andrew took a sip.

"Hmm ... that's good stuff. What is that Jack?"

"Port, Andrew – Penfolds Club port. Best value port in the world. It's not cheap shit but not expensive either ... up here about fifteen dollars for a bottle. And on that note, it's goodnight."

The next morning the men were once again awoken by the cacophony of birdsong. Jack went through the same breakfast ritual as the previous morning except that this time he gave Andrew a glass of orange juice before making the tea.   Then Andrew had the Corn Flakes and Jack had Weeties.

"That made a pleasant change Jack."

"Yep, sure did. By the way I had a look for yowie tracks over there ..."

"And ... "

"Nothing! It's just as the indigenous people have always said – he never leaves a track. Did you send that pic to Rebecca?"

"I didn't mention this to you Jack but there is no image there – just the fire."

"But he had the rabbits in his hand!"

"Yes, they seem to be in suspended animation, if you know what I mean. He just doesn't show in the image Jack. Perhaps he was too dark to show."

"Yeah that must be it, of course. Maybe that's why they only appear at night."

"Okay let's get this show on the road – it will be getting on dusk by the time we arrive."

"Just in time for one of Narelle's dinners then Jack."

Jack smiled and nodded.

"Probably a roast bloody turkey or something!"

The dogs finished drinking their milk and their biscuits, so Jack ordered them into the rear of the ute and headed north. The trip home was very straightforward but for a few goats that stood their ground on the track near the fifth bore. All of the bores and troughs were fully functional, so Jack felt greatly relieved that he would be able to leave with his woman for Tasmania in the near future. Within a couple of weeks Andrew would be pretty handy around the station – at least he had seen how to mend the troughs with resin and replace the bore caps. On the journey back to the station Jack gave Andrew some verbal information about the entire process of raising the cattle from their calving to the point where they are sent off to the beef market – of how they select the breeders including a young bull occasionally.

Upon arrival at the house Rebecca came out to greet the men.

"Hah ... the boys are back in town!"

"You sound like an advertisement for the West Coast Eagles Rebecca."

"Who are they Jack?"

"Just a local West Aussie football team Andrew. The season doesn't start for a couple of months yet though."

"I've seen some games on television – looks like a really fast game Jack. Is that your team the ... ah ... Eagles?"

"No! I'm a Fremantle man Andrew".

"Do they do alright?"

"Yeah!"

"Okay if you boys get yourselves cleaned up Narelle has a really fantastic dinner cooking in the oven – a roast turkey!"

"You know her too well Jack!"

"After dinner Andrew we'll take a look at the inventory on the computer system and we'll update the records for the plant we've modified. And I don't know if anyone has let you know yet but tomorrow around mid-day we are all heading off to Wiluna. The boys have a monthly corroboree performance they need to take part in. Quite a big show this one - there will be several dozens of tourists and others there and the boys join a larger group of other dancers from around the region. Apparently, they are going to film this one and send it off to London for the King to view."

"Okay, can't wait!"

Andrew and Rebecca went into the house and the men to their respective quarters, so they could all prepare for dinner.

"So how was your first sortie out bush dear?"

Andrew contemplated for a few seconds.

"Well quite an enthralling experience actually - I saw a few things that I had never seen before, very interesting too!"

"Tell me!"

"Well first of all the dogs caught a rabbit which Jack cooked up for them to eat, then they chased off a dingo that came in too close to the camp that first night, then on the same night they brought down a boar that came screaming out of the scrub and ... ah ... Jack shot that one ..."

"You saw him shoot a boar?"

"Single shot to the head. Then on the second night we ... ah ... did you receive that pic I sent to you?"

"The one with the fire yes."

"Did you notice anything peculiar about that pic?"

"Only that I could see two rabbits you were cooking above the fire but couldn't see how you had them set in place."

"Okay well I might have to tell you about that later – for now we had just better get ready for dinner."

"How were the well caps?"

"Yes, we replaced six of them, repaired some troughs and checked it all on the way back. I really appreciate old Jack for taking me out there. He was attacked by a bull but he managed to fend it off by laying low then shoving dirt into its eyes."

"Shit, that sounds serious Andrew."

"It sure was, but I am just so relieved that it was him and not me ... I reckon I would have just frozen. That was one bloody large bull too."

"Well any bull that attacks my man is going to end up in the meat factory. Now, I will jump into the shower first because I take longer to get ready, okay."

"Please do, I will just duck into the kitchen for a quick beer. You can build up quite a thirst out there."

Rebecca showered then served dinner as Andrew was taking his shower. The roast turkey came with an abundance of roast potato, peas, corn, onion and gravy. Narelle had excelled yet again. After they had cleaned up Jack and Andrew went into the office for half an hour so that Jack could instruct Andrew on how to update the plant inventory and to peruse all of the other files the station kept on computer. By ten o'clock they had all retired for the night.

Wiluna

The next morning Rebecca assisted Narelle in preparing some food for the sojourn to Wiluna as they would be on the track for about six hours and they would need some sustenance along the way. Old Jack showed Andrew through some more of the inventory records on the computer system and how to operate the radio and the satellite communications system. Then they both went with Jimmy and Travis in an old beat up Land Cruiser to inspect some fence damage that was caused by lamebrain donkeys a few days earlier. Andrew was duly impressed as Jimmy and Travis went about their role of repairing the fence. Travis had a fire extinguisher handy as Jimmy used oxy-acetylene equipment to weld some wires together. A wayward spark did land on some old grass and caught fire but Travis soon had that extinguished.

"Pretty to watch boys!"

"Ah that's nothin' boss, we doin' that all the time out here. Might need to cull some of them stupid donkeys soon though, they're causing more damage than they used to. Make good tucker for the marron eh – turn 'em into good tucker for us that way eh boss."

"So the marron are good tucker eh?"

"Bloody good tucker boss! Should do another dam to grow more of them, that way we could eat marron every day yeah."

"Hmm ... food for thought! No sense in not growing your own food I suppose. You boys will have to show me the ropes to do with the marron farm – I haven't seen that yet."

Jack responded.

"We can show you that as soon as we get back to the homestead Andrew – the dam is behind the staff quarters.

There's enough marron in there to give us all a feed about once or twice every month. You'd have to build ten of them to feed marron to the boys every day Andrew. Then they'd probably get sick of the stuff ... nah ... they need their beef and lamb intake too. Plus the occasional chook and fish of course. But Narelle has all that pretty well sorted. They all get good variety in their meals. Perhaps one more dam would be a good idea."

"What time are we leaving for Wiluna Jack?"

"Should hit the road by midday I reckon, that's why we need to head back soon – let you boys get ready for the big show. We'll just check that fence down the west flank on the way in – see how that's holding up since last week."

"I checked it yesterday boss it's all good."

"Nice work Jimmy! Perhaps we can head off a little earlier and show Andrew and Rebecca the sights of Wiluna."

Jimmy and Travis both laughed quite vociferously at that suggestion by old Jack and Jack knew why, but Andrew was a little perplexed. Travis said it all.

"The sights of Wiluna eh boss?"

"Ah ... where will we be staying in Wiluna Jack?"

"Rebecca and yourself will stay in the hotel Andrew – the rest of us will just pitch our swag in the camping ground where the tourists stay. We have booked your room for you."

"Why don't we stay with you guys?"

"Old man Piper wouldn't so we figured you might want to follow suit. Perhaps next time you might stay where we do but on this occasion, you might be best to check it all out first. You got to think of your missus too eh."

"Did old man Piper have a missus?"

"Huh ... did he what? A different one every time. They came up from Kal and met him there. Quite a bit younger than him too they were. Always top lookin' sheilas too - if you get the drift!"

"Oh ... I see ... hmm ... well he may not have had a woman back in the States and he was here for a few weeks at a time was he not? A man can get pretty lonely you know."

"Yeah well, good for him – you can't hold that against a bloke now can you? He probably deserved a good time occasionally. Don't know if he did have a woman back home though. He certainly never spoke of a lady in his life. Not our business either really. Okay boys let's head for home and we'll go via the herd track to the east of that ridge and just check for calves that might have been taken out."

"Taken out?"

"By dingoes Andrew."

"I see!"

The men set off for the eastern ridge as Jack said but found all was well – no calves lost to dingoes in that area lately. They arrived at the homestead just before eleven o'clock and the girls were busy preparing everything to be loaded into the vehicles. The men went to their respective quarters to shower and get cleaned up for the trip and to prepare their personal belongings, including their corroboree dress. Andrew and Jack did the same and both prepared their movie cameras. Within the hour they had all gathered outside the homestead, said farewell to Frankie and Jill and prepared to hit the road.

Andrew and Rebecca would go with Jack and Narelle in the Nissan Patrol. Jimmy, Travis, Karen, Robbie and Goldie would all go together in the Land Cruiser. They were all looking forward to this corroboree because it was touted as being the culmination of several others that had been performed in recent months in a continuing theme about the rainbow serpent.

Frankie and Jill would remain at the homestead.

The journey south did take almost six hours and when they arrived in Wiluna, they could see a convoy of four-wheel-drive vehicles, most with caravans, parked up along the main roadway. There were six in one group and another group of five further down the road and another group of four down a side street. Other groups were already within the caravan park.

"They'll be here for tonight's corroboree then they'll hit the trail tomorrow no doubt."

"Which trail will that be Jack?"

"The Canning Stock Route Andrew. Wiluna is the starting point so they will stock up on fuel and food from here for the long journey north."

"And how long will that be Jack?"

"Oh only about a thousand miles."

"You got to be kidding me Jack."

"Nup! To be quite precise, Andrew, the Canning Stock Route is one thousand one hundred and fifty miles long – so eighteen fifty kilometres in Aussie speak. From here all the way to Hall's Creek mate. Gonna take this mob over a week to make it, probably more than two weeks. You might want to try that someday yourself Andrew. They usually go in winter so must be a hardy lot this mob – probably ex-miners."

"Aw dunno Jack … I can think of a few things I'd rather be doing with two weeks of my time Jack, to be quite honest. These guys must be bloody mad. Lot of women there among them."

"Hey make no mistake mate – you'll find that women are more into this type of activity than we mere males are. Maybe they've been kooked up for too long. Anyway we will get you two checked in to the hotel over there and get the rest of us set up in the caravan park. This pub actually closed down back in 2017 but a young couple have taken it over and done a great refurbishment since the gold price went through the roof, so you should be comfortable staying there. We will set up back there in the caravan park then meet you in the hotel dining room. What say in thirty minutes? The corroboree will start about eight o'clock."

"Roger that Jack."

Jack parked outside the hotel and took Andrew and Rebecca in to check in. Once they had been provided with their room key Jack went back outside. Rebecca and Andrew checked their room.

"Hmm ... bit of an old looking place eh Bec?"

"It's been here for a long time Andy. It will suffice. The bed seems soft enough."

"Hey don't get me wrong – it has a romantic feel about it. Like what I might expect in an old western town back in the States. I could just about expect Mr. Matt Dillon and Miss Kitty Russell to be next door."

"Who are they?"

"Ah ... don't worry about it!"

Rebecca and Andrew showered and changed then went downstairs to meet Jack and the others in the hotel restaurant. They arranged for two tables to be set aside for them and their friends, then took a seat to wait for the others. After just five minutes the others arrived together and the table attendant proceeded to take their orders.

"Hello would you like to start with drinks?"

"Yes can we please have a bundy and coke for Rebecca and a jug of Swan draught at this table for starters and two jugs of the same for that table and I believe Narelle and Karen there will have bourbon and coke. The table attendant organised the drinks within just a couple of minutes.

"Bec this one is for you. You will notice I did not touch the top of the glass. Women can be pretty fussy about that so just letting you know I am onto it. Here we go Andrew – a well-deserved beer. Hope you've had enough water in these last few hours."

"Thanks Jack, yes I am definitely learning from you mate."

The table attendant then proceeded to take their dinner orders. As she was doing so a large group of people then walked in and took up their tables alongside – six tables.

"What will you have dear?"

"Hmm ... think I will have the soup followed by the surf 'n turf. Looks good – squid, Moreton Bay bugs, crumbed prawns, barramundi and a scotch fillet. How about you?"

"Better start with one dozen Oysters Kilpatrick then the fillet mignon. Jack what will you have?"

"Same as always – the soup of the day then the lobster platter, thanks Andrew. The others will have steak, chips and vege's with a truckload of gravy and onions."

"How do you know?"

"Cos they aren't paying for it, you are."

Andrew looked over at the other table. They were all sitting there smiling toward him.

"Oh ... I see, well yes that's fine Jack."

"Andrew, every time we come here, they just all order the same shit so they ain't about to change now. It's one of the few constant re-assurances in life out here you know."

"You guys don't want soup or entrée?"

"Nah boss we just want to tuck into the steak and chips, that's good for us. Will have dessert though!"

Narelle spoke up.

"Chips is one thing I don't do Andrew, so they make the most of it whenever they come here."

"Sounds good - whatever!"

"Old Jack!" bellowed a familiar voice.

"Pistol Pete, how are they hangin' mate?"

The men shook hands.

"Loose and full of juice, as always! You got new company Jack I see."

"Rebecca, Andrew meet pistol Pete Stewart – he runs Walkabout Tours up the stock route."

Andrew and Pete shook hands and Pete discerned Andrew's American accent.

"Andrew and Rebecca are taking over management of the station Pete so you'll see them from time to time around these parts."

"Pleased to meet you good folk! Hope you've got some fly repellent – and some snake anti-venom and redback anti-venom! Place is full of things that want to kill ya."

"Yes we seem to have everything we need, thanks Pete."

"You seem to have a good contingent of independent travellers to accompany you on this trek Pete."

"Yeah, about twenty vans all going together – safety in numbers you know, from snakes, spiders, razorback and all that eh! Not meaning to scare you folk now."

"Oh I've had more than one fright already Pete. Jack here had to fend off a large bull yesterday."

"Not the same bull as last time Jack?"

"Afraid so mate – might be time to send him off to the knackery."

Andrew looked surprised for Jack had told him of the previous occasion that he was attacked by a bull but not that it was the same bull. Jack glanced at Andrew and perceived Andrew's querying gaze. For he respected that Andrew was his employer and would be concerned about something like that.

"Was no sense getting you too worried Andrew. I know now that I need to put that bull down. Maybe next time we cross paths."

Jack caught the attention of the table attendant and ordered another round of drinks for both tables.

"Well Pete good luck on this trip and we'll have to catch up for a beer before I leave the station."

"Sure thing Jack, I'll let you know when I am next back in town."

"Might have to be down in Perth Pete."

"Okay I'll wait to hear from you Jack, all the best to you and your wife Andrew. Hope I haven't deterred you too much with talk of snakes and spiders, but watch out for stonefish while you are up here."

"Thanks Pete goodbye now."

Pistol Pete Stewart re-joined his groups who were busy ordering drinks and meals at their tables.

"Quite a character Jack, is your mate Pistol Pete. He mentioned stonefish."

Jack burst out laughing.

"No bloody stonefish up here mate. He's having a go at ya - messing with your head."

"Oh, I see. Well I'll ... ah ... put that one in the bank."

Their dinner plates arrived and Rebecca and Andrew were somewhat taken aback at the generous portions they had been served.

"Hmm ... thank you miss - looks great. I should take a photograph of this dish. That's a fine looking lobster dinner you've got there Jack."

"Should be – costs about a hundred bucks."

"Well I hope you enjoy it Jack but I've got to say, you have certainly deserved it. I don't mind telling you that I ... ah ... woke up several times through the night thinking about what happened out there those last two days. That really was quite an experience for me Jack."

"Thanks Andrew but once I go make sure you take Jimmy or Travis or both okay – and don't forget to take the rifle. Never know what might happen out there."

The group enjoyed their dinner then ordered sweets, apart from Jimmy and Travis who had departed to prepare for the corroboree that was due to start at nine o'clock.

"The boys have left to get themselves painted."

"How many dancers do you think there will be Jack?"

"Be more than a dozen I reckon. This is the big one – some boys and girls have come down from Parnngurr which is quite some way north from our station – up near the Karlamilyi National Park and just off the Talawana Track. Jimmy and Travis are from there. It's a smaller community than Jigalong and very remote. The elders there know all the old dreamtime stories."

"Somebody said something about it being filmed for the King of England."

"Yes there' a film crew in town from the technical college at Rockingham outside of Perth. Apparently, the King watched a corroboree in Alice decades ago and was really taken by it but never got the chance to see another. So he has requested that a genuine corroboree be sent to him to view. Might have taken a while to find a group that could fit the bill, but this Parnngurr mob are still very tribal in their rituals, so they got the nod."

"Hope they are getting well paid for it. The King of England wouldn't be short of a dollar."

"A pound, Andrew!

"Oh yeah!"

"Yes, the King has made a generous offer - the funds will go into their community trust account and cover the cost of installing solar infrastructure. Should provide them with free electricity forever."

"And your boys Jimmy and Travis are a part of this?"

"Oh yeah we've had a couple of other Parnngurr boys and girls come through the station for work but they invariably return to the community after a stint with us – some do a few weeks others stay a lot longer. They all learn something – welding, fencing, horse skills, cattle mustering. They love to get out there on horseback but even more-so on trail bike of course."

"Well that certainly was a great dinner, look forward to that again in a couple of months from now."

"Yes but we had better be heading off now towards the community centre where they will hold the corroboree. They have a kind of amphitheatre out back behind the building. Come on you lot, finish your drinks."

All six of the adults arose and headed for the exit, with Andrew covering the tab on the way out. They made their way to the community centre which was only about two hundred metres down the road and entered via the front gate. A sign read "$20 adults $5 children 10-18, under 10 free".

"Six adults mate" said Jack as he drew notes from his pocket to cover the cost. Rebecca and Andrew were impressed at Jack generously offering to cover the cost without even consulting them.

Dusk was turning into darkness, so the group took up seats in the front row, just before a large group came in from the caravan mob. The seating was soon occupied so Rebecca and Narelle surrendered their seats to two elderly women and, as Narelle had a small blanket, they took up a seating position on the ground, with their legs crossed. Rebecca was able to lean backwards against Andrew's knees. Both Rebecca and Andrew were starting to feel really excited about this, as they could detect movement behind the curtain that had been slung across a crude metal pole setup. The brief corroboree by Jimmy and Andrew a few nights earlier had really whet their expectation for this.

But they had no idea how their lives were about to change forever.

The surrounding lights dimmed and for a moment there was near total darkness, which drew some faint murmurs from some of the ladies who were present. Then some red and yellow lights came on that lit up the stage area. The expectation grew.

Suddenly the sound of clanging sticks rang out to a two-four beat and indigenous people came through the curtain onto the stage area. There were four tall men, four shorter men or boys and four women or girls. All were adorned with the most extraordinary painted costume that covered their bodies, three of the men holding spears, one a didgeridoo and the women holding and playing the clanging sticks. Three boys were adorned with a red headband and one with a yellow headband. The boy with the didgeridoo took up a seated position to the side of the stage and proceeded to bellow out a continuous drone of notes, as they do. The men and the boys commenced their dance routine, but only to the sound of the clanging sticks and the didgeridoo, stomping their feet, turning in circles and moving their arms and spears in different directions. Then the men began to chant in their indigenous language, the boys silently continuing the dance. A female person would begin the commentary soon thereafter. The men had danced for about three minutes when she came in.

"A long, long time ago, in the dreamtime, a boy had reached the age of manhood so his people required him to go into the bush to prove himself worthy of the circumcision that would bring him across. He knew how this was, for all of the elders in his tribe had done the same. No boy could enter manhood without going through this timeless ritual. He would need to be alone in the bush and the desert for many days and could not return until he had hunted a dingo and a wallaby and returned these to his home. He would need to find his own water in the bush or he would perish."

As they danced an elder with two spears handed the boy with the yellow headband one of his spears and pointed toward the distance. The boy took his spear and turned to look directly ahead above the audience. As the drone of the didgeridoo and the clanging of the sticks continued, the boy stood there for a minute, seemingly contemplating his assignment, perhaps with some trepidation, for it was known that not all boys would return. Then the boy started to move, bending as if searching as he stomped his feet and went from left to right across the stage and back again.

"That's Travis Andrew!"

"Hey yeah, you're right. Wow he's fantastic!"

Travis had a small white birthmark on the outside of his left thigh.

"Is that Jimmy who gave him the spear?"

"I don't know it's so hard to tell."

The commentary continued.

"The boy searched and searched for his first day but never saw a single wallaby or a dingo. He was becoming really thirsty and needed water, so he looked to the sky to see where the birds were flying to".

The boy looked skywards and from side to side.

"The boy saw many galah diving down to a rock below a hill, so he knew he would find water there. He went to the water hole and kneeled down to drink."

The boy on the stage got down on hands and knees and motioned to sip water off the ground. Then a small child came onto the stage with her arms outstretched in front of her and moving her hands and her hips from side to side. She was adorned in red, yellow and ochre paint.

"Suddenly, the boy seen a large snake come toward him, he jumped up and stepped backward. The boy was going to spear the snake, but the snake moved very slowly to the water and took a drink, so he watched the snake and let it drink. Then the snake turned away and went back to where it came from. The boy was getting tired and it would soon be dark so he climbed the rock to sleep in a cave at the top."

The boy lay on the ground for a minute with eyes shut.

"The next morning the boy went back to the water hole at the bottom of the big rock to drink. He took a drink then he wait in the bush to see what would come to the water hole. He not have to wait long."

Another young child came onto the stage on all fours bounding around as if to imitate a rabbit. Then the child stopped and put its lips onto the floor.

"The rabbit came to drink and the boy knew this rabbit would give him good tucker for days, so he let the rabbit drink and he very slowly creep up behind the rabbit and he spear the rabbit."

The boy cast his spear into the rabbit between the child's arm and chest, then he picked up the child and placed her down to the side of the stage.

"The boy skinned the rabbit and lit a fire to cook it up."

The boy squatted on the stage and took some sticks and straw to light up a fire.

"Now the boy had good food and water he knew he could stay at the water hole until he catch a wallaby and a dingo. He cook his dinner then he notice the snake come back out from the rocks."

The first child came back onto the stage once again motioning like a snake.

"The snake went to the water hole again and took a drink. Then the snake look at the boy cooking his rabbit. The snake moved closer to the boy. The boy broke some meat off the rabbit and threw it to the snake. The snake took the meat and went back to its hole."

"Then the boy see a small wallaby come near the clearing so he cover his fire with a kangaroo skin. The wallaby came to the water hole for a drink. The boy waited until the wallaby was drinking then he threw his spear but it missed the wallaby, so the wallaby jumped away. The boy knew he would have to do something different. The boy cut some branches off a bush and he strap them to his chest and his back and he stand at the water hole where the wallaby drink from, holding his spear."

Another young child bounded onto the stage adorned in red colours.

"A dingo came to the water hole and the boy stood very still with his spear ready and while the dingo was drinking the boy speared the dingo. Now he just need a wallaby but no wallaby came for the rest of the day so the boy went back to his cave to sleep through the night. The next day the boy had some rabbit for his morning tucker then he put his bush dress on again for he thought the wallaby could come back again. The boy stood waiting at the water hole. The boy heard a noise and hoped it was the wallaby but a group of seven pigs came to the water hole to drink."

Seven more children came onto the stage, adorned in kangaroo skin. They circled the boy.

"The boar was a big pig with big tusks and the boy was frightened for he knew the pigs could kill him and if they did they would eat him. He stood very still and the pigs thought he was a tree. Then the boy saw the big snake come out of her hole and quickly move toward the pigs."

The snake child came back onto the stage.

"The big boar saw the snake and let out a loud squeal for he knew the snake would kill him, so the pigs all turned and they ran away."

The seven children who played the role of pigs ran from the stage.

"The snake looked at the boy then went back into her hole. The boy was no more frightened but felt safe with the snake near him. As it was getting late in the afternoon the boy returned to his fire and ate some more rabbit. Once again the snake came out to get some food and the boy threw the snake some rabbit. As it was getting very hot the boy went back to his cave where it was very cool to sleep for the night. He knew the wallaby would come back in the morning so he would be ready this time dressed up as a bush."

The boy lay down to sleep.

"In the morning the boy returned to his fire, ate some tucker and put his bushes back on to wait for the wallaby."

The wallaby child came onto the stage again.

"The boy stood motionless and then the wallaby came to drink and the boy speared the wallaby. The boy cut off some wallaby tail and cooked it on the fire. The snake came out to get some wallaby and the boy give the snake some more food. Then the boy see a baby snake come out behind the mother snake so he feed the baby snake too. Now the boy could return to his home and take the dingo and the wallaby and they would make him a man. The boy walk all next day to his home."

The boy walked around the stage carrying two kangaroo skins.

"When his people see him coming, they ran to the boy. They hugged him and kissed him. Then they held a big feast, for the boy had returned. His elder brother was very happy for him. Then they did the corroboree to induct the boy into his manhood. The elder men then took the boy aside and slit the boy's penis to make him a man."

The men and women on stage commenced an elaborate dance with the boy in the centre and everybody dancing around him that totally enthralled the audience and lasted for a full ten minutes.

Then everything changed.

Another woman came onto the stage carrying a long stick that was adorned at the top by a snake carving. She assumed the central position among the four adult male dancers as the didgeridoo and clanging sticks became even louder. She did a peculiar dance around the boy, turning and swirling, sometimes quite rapidly as she bowed to the boy and continued to dance around him. For the boy had chosen the snake as his identity. The entire rendition was becoming quite loud but then as the woman suddenly turned the snake carving atop her stick flew off. All of the dancers noticed this, as did the boy playing the didgeridoo and the women clanging their sticks and the noise came to an abrupt halt. The snake carving flew through the air for what seemed a long time and was heading toward the audience.

Everybody on stage stood there stunned and motionless as the snake carving landed between Rebecca's folded legs.

Rebecca looked down at the snake carving for a few seconds while there was total silence, then she looked up at the stage where everybody was standing still also in total silence and staring at her with mouths agape. For they knew there was some significance in this, that to others would seem to be just an aberration of their ritual. Rebecca picked up the snake carving and stretched out her hand for someone to collect it but nobody did. They just stood there staring at her for several seconds, then as she still had her arm outstretched, every person on the stage turned and walked toward the rear curtain. They had all exited the stage.

The audience sensed that the corroboree was over, despite its abrupt ending, so they all applauded.

"Well that was a rather sudden end to the show. Looks like you won a prize dear."

"Oh, I'm sure they will want this returned to them – perhaps we can give it to Travis later."

137

Jack intervened.

"Well we can all head back to the hotel for a couple more drinks before we turn in eh? It's only nine thirty."

"Yeah sure Jack let's do that."

They all set off back to the hotel as did several of the caravan trekkers so when they arrived there were about fifty people in the public bar. Rebecca, Andrew, Narelle and Jack took up a table and Jack ordered drinks. There were six other tables occupied in the public bar – one of the tables was in a corner at which three very elderly Aboriginal women were seated. Rebecca looked up and noticed them then commenced to sip her drink. She still had the snake carving in her hand.

"What will you do with the carving?" asked Narelle.

"I'm sure they will want it returned."

Rebecca glanced once again at the three elderly women who seemed to be staring at her. She then looked away.

"I think I will hand it over to Jimmy or Trav tomorrow. They should know who to hand it to."

"That might be quite a privilege for you Rebecca, being handed the baby snake from the story."

"Is that what you think this is, the baby snake?"

"I'd say so – I mean, look where it landed!" as Narelle gave Rebecca a small affectionate nudge. Narelle was just starting to come out of her shell with Rebecca.

"Rebecca looked up again at the three women and this time their stares had become so totally transfixed she started to feel a little uncomfortable about it.

"Narelle don't look now but have you noticed those three elder women sitting over there in the corner looking our way. Take a look when you get a chance and just tell me what you think."

"Okay!"

Narelle took a sip of her drink and moving her eyes around the room she looked up at the women. It was distinctly noticeable that they were staring at Bec.

"Definitely got you in their sights Bec – I'd be a worried woman if I were you. Perhaps they want their baby snake back."

"You know you might be right. I'll just go to the bathroom and take it to them on the way."

Rebecca arose and walked toward the table of the three indigenous elder women, taking the snake carving with her. She stopped at their table as they continued to stare at her.

"Hello ladies, perhaps you can return this beautiful carving to its rightful owner because it landed on me during the corroboree, okay."

The women sat there motionless and without a whisper, just staring at Rebecca, for they knew the implications of what had occurred at the corroboree.

"I hope you don't mind, but can you do that for me please?"

Then Rebecca placed the carving onto the table and walked toward the ablution area. As she was about to go through the first door she looked to her left. The hotel public bar had an 'l-cove' shape and the narrow, shorter section had no chairs, nor were there any people in that section, just a painting that was affixed to the far wall. She noticed it before she turned to walk through the door. As she exited the door Rebecca stood a moment and looked again at the painting – a brown, ochre coloured painting with circles and three black hands. Now she was intrigued. She walked toward the painting and as she got closer and closer more detail came into view. There was a lizard in a circle, a kangaroo and an indigenous hunter with a spear sitting on a rock. Rebecca walked up close to the painting and checked the fine detail. Now she could make out a number of other animals – a goanna in a circle, the lizard, a turtle in a circle, a snake in a circle with a face within the snake and the kangaroo. But she failed to notice the second snake in the circle with the lizard.

There were three black hands on the painting – a left hand, a right hand and another left hand. The snake in the circle with the lizard was between the left and right hands. At that moment a total compulsion came over Rebecca to place her hands onto the pair of hands on the lower left section of the painting. She raised her hands and placed them exactly onto the pair of hands. Rebecca closed her eyes and stood there for a moment in that position. Without knowing it, she fell asleep. The three elderly women could see this happening from where they were seated and simply watched in stunned silence. For they knew what was happening – they had witnessed what happened at the corroboree. They had been waiting for this moment. Rebecca did not know that she was already pregnant from the night before, to her husband Andrew, but she was now being impregnated by the spirit of the Wagyl who would provide this child with its identity – the rainbow serpent.

Narelle had noticed Bec go into the l-cove so went to see what she was doing. Rebecca was still literally attached to the painting as Narelle called for her.

"Bec? Bec!"

Narelle approached Bec and stood alongside her but Bec was standing with eyes closed as if totally asleep. Narelle gently took Rebecca by the arm.

"Bec" she whispered.

Rebecca snapped out of her trance, looked at the painting, took a deep breath and turned to look at Narelle.

"Oh ... Narelle, sorry, I didn't mean to ... ah... are we all still here?"

"Yes but you've been standing here for almost ten minutes. What are you doing?"

"Ah ... I don't know ... ah ... just looking at the painting here. I haven't seen anything quite like it, it's so beautiful. I wonder who painted it."

"Yes, it is beautiful but they may not appreciate us touching it. Look there is a name here ... 'Rima' is the artist. Now come back to the table please – those elderly women have gone now."

Rebecca and Narelle returned to the table and, indeed, the three elderly women had left. The men were still drinking their beer so Rebecca decided to turn in for the night.

"I think I'll go off to bed now dear but you can stay here with Jack. I'll see you both in the morning."

"Oh we've just learned there's a football match here in the morning between two local teams starting at eight o'clock so we might take that in before we head back. I've never seen an Aussie Rules match before as you know."

"Sounds great dear, I will see you in the morning."

Rebecca headed off up the stairs to her room but Narelle stayed with Jack until he was ready to leave as they had to walk to the caravan park in the dark. The boys had a couple more beers before turning in.

The footy

The next morning all were up and about before six o'clock due to the light and the heat. The hotel started serving breakfast at six thirty so they all gathered once again in the lounge. When Jimmy and Travis walked in the others had a chance to congratulate them.

"Hey guys, well done, that was really something special you boys did there last night, Rebecca and myself were totally blown away. That must have taken quite some preparation."

"Thanks boss yeah it went okay until ..."

"Until what?"

Jimmy looked at Rebecca then thought he should explain.

"Ah ... until the snake came off the pole boss, we still had some ways to go but ... we never seen that happen before. Then the old women signal us to go off the stage."

"Oh, well ah... I suppose King Charles will just have to believe that's how the story ended. Now you fellas make sure you get a good brekky okay. Then we are all going for a walk around this town before the footy match gets underway – check those sights of Wiluna I mentioned the other day."

The breakfast menu was a typical full on menu with a good selection of fruit juices then cereal from Weeties, Corn Flakes, Weet Bix, muesli, Rice Bubbles, Coco Pops and oatmeal. Then a serve of bacon, eggs - fried, poached or scrambled - sausages, fried tomato, mushroom, onion, hash browns, lamb's fry and a selection of fruit salad. This all came with heaps of toast from home baked bread plus strawberry, raspberry and apricot jam spreads available too. Everybody enjoyed a hearty breakfast then recovered their belongings from their room, loaded them into the vehicle then took the short drive down Wotton Street to the football oval.

A crowd had already gathered, mainly indigenous people for both teams were comprised only of indigenous young men and boys. The players were running about on the field limbering up before the game, kicking a few footballs around. One team was wearing a white guernsey with two red v's and the other team a blue guernsey with a yellow sash. Travis was playing for the white team and Robbie for the blue team. Suddenly a loud whistle sounded and it was the local umpire Mr. Richard Brown, the chief executive officer of the Ngangganawili Aboriginal Health Service, assisted by local health worker Ms June Ralston and the Wiluna Shire CEO Mr Colin Barclay as goal umpires. The boundaries were manned by two local young police officers, Ted and Fred, who were fit enough to run the boundary and keep up with the play. Due to the heat, each quarter would be of just ten minutes duration with a ten-minute break in between to allow for consumption of water – and whatever the umpires were drinking.

Play got underway when somebody rang a bell and the boys got straight into it. Andrew was quite taken by the gusto and keenness of the players who displayed exemplary skills. There was quite a lot of talk noise coming from the field as players called instructions to their team-mates and even more coming from the crowd. There were dozens of very young indigenous children standing around the boundary cheering for their players. Andrew looked at the children for several minutes with utmost admiration for they were such beautiful little people, adorned in vivid and stark colours of green, blue, yellow, red and black. He noticed the elder women, too, were very colourful with their dress. Within four minutes the first goal had been scored and a loud cheer went up – the ball was raced back to the centre and the game restarted. Rebecca, too, was captivated by the spectacle, for though she had been to football matches before she had witnessed nothing like this – and these were her own people. Within another minute a second goal had been scored by the same team and just before quarter time that team had dominated and kicked four goals. Jack had ensured that Rebecca, Narelle and Andrew were positioned on the boundary alongside a woman named Eunice Atkins – the most vocal spectator in AFL history. Eunice wasted no time in voicing her take on the first quarter. The white team kicked the first goal then the second and third goals.

"That's that boy Cyril doing that, he gonna play for the Dockers next year. His uncle is Cyril Rioli – played for Richmond, he did."

"Yeah not bloody fair having him in their team he too good a player. See that mark he took over there and he's kicked two of their goals already."

"That blue team better get that Nicky Winmar onto him – his uncle Nicky played for Saint Kilda, he'll cut that Cyril down a bit."

"Oh bloody great mark Shaun! That's Shaun Michael, his uncle Steven played for South Fremantle - and Western Australia too against them bloody Vics. He always cut that Michael Tuck out of the game he did, that Steven Michael. Won the Sandover Medal too he did!"

"Ya see that boy there who made that tackle – that's Nicky Matera he's a nephew of them Matera boys who played for the Eagles. His uncle Peter Matera was the best bloody tackler in the AFL - he'd run blokes down like nobody else did."

"So which team do you barrack for Eunice?"

"I go for the Dockers, they did well this year eh Jack!"

The second quarter commenced and the dominant team kicked a goal within the first thirty seconds then another after just another minute. This was shaping up as a bit of a thrashing but then the umpire awarded the other team two free kicks and a fifty metre penalty to realise the blue teams first goal. At the bouncedown he awarded another free kick to the blue team's ruckman who gave the ball a roost with a torpedo kick and the umpire spotted an infringement against the full forward. Another goal to the blue team. Now the score was six goals to two goals. After the next bouncedown there was a bit of a scrap and Richard Brown awarded another free kick indicating a player was being held without the ball. The crowd became a tad vocal, particularly Eunice.

"Eh that's wasn't a free kick he was holding the bloody ball!"

"All over his back umpire!"

"That's a high tackle umpire!"

The umpire missed a few then gave the blue team another free kick.

"That's bloody bullshit umpire!"

Jack whispered to Rebecca and Andrew to explain that Mr Brown always tried to even things up a little because the white and red team always won these games. It was important to give each side a fair go. At three quarter time all players got a quarter of an orange to consume. There seemed to be some kind of magic power in a quarter of an orange.

The game ended with the white team running out winners by just three goals – Mr Brown was always going to ensure that they did win but not by too much. The players left the field and headed for the changerooms while the umpires got together for bit of a chat about some local issues.

"Well, we'll get the boys into their ute soon as they change and head off back to the station."

"That was great Jack, thank you for suggesting that we stay to watch. These people have a ... ah ... strong little community here."

"They've got some issues - the alcohol, domestic violence, nutrition, education, but there are a lot of good people are working on it, most of them indigenous people of course, as they should be."

"So when the pub was closed, did they still manage to get alcohol?"

"They would drive to Meekatharra to procure alcohol when the pub was shut. The community workers reckon the social problems here got worse then because there was even more alcohol available to them. Since then the hotel and the police can monitor what is going on – they actually banned walk in sales for a while there. Lack of opportunity here is the main problem but the local mines are giving quite a few people a go now. We try to do our bit as do the other station owners in this region."

"Will it be okay if I go back with you Jack?"

"Please do Narelle – seems like you and Bec are bonding there just a little."

The boys were still in the changerooms when Jack suggested they take a quick sortie down to the mine, which they did. He knew that Rebecca and Andrew had never seen a gold mine up close like this.

"Looks like a pretty crude place!"

"Yeah true, but it matters not how the place looks - they dig up plenty of precious gold from here."

"Shit they are big trucks over there – look at the size of the ute against them."

"Yep they are 793 Cats – the biggest in W.A. The tyres are eleven feet in diameter. They'll take about two hundred and fifty tonnes in a load."

"Is that a girl driving that truck?"

146

"That's Shelley Winmar – her son was playing for the blue team out there today. Good player – bloody good player. He'll go all the way to the AFL that kid will."

"Now best we get back to the boys and girls cos they should be just about ready."

The two vehicles would make the return journey up the track together for safety reasons. When they arrived back at the station it was getting on toward dusk and they were met by Karen and Frankie.

"How was the trip?"

"Same as really, but for the corroboree, that was bloody good."

"Hmm ... bit of an incident here yesterday, Karen was in the garden and I was servicing the chopper when a parcel of pigs came through. Must have been twenty of them. They might have bailed up Karen but we had let the dogs out for a run so the dogs took to 'em. Should have seen them scatter!"

"Hmm ... means we'll need to do a bit of a cull soon if there's that many in one parcel. See any big boys?"

"Two! That big razorback would be the biggest I've seen around here Jack. They don't come any bigger. Had one broken tusk – been in a fight with something."

"Hmm ... means there must be another one out there too somewhere. We'll get up there in the chopper tomorrow and see if we can find them – I'll take them out from the chopper. Hopefully we'll find those big bastards before Andrew is here managing, without me. I'm looking into a new type of trap that's come onto the market – it gets them in with bait then the fence drops down around them. Can take out the entire parcel that way but I'd still like to get those big boys while they are in this vicinity."

"When do you expect to leave?"

"Probably another two weeks max, I'd say."

"Okay I'll have the chopper ready for the morning Jack. You must be ready for a beer."

"Yep bloody good idea, thanks. Andrew, Frankie has a beer here for us. Goldie, Trav get a couple of these into ya – you boys deserve a coldie."

Andrew took up the offer, cracked the top off his first stubby and was then put in the loop about the pigs.

"Shit that goes down well."

"Yeah sure does but Frankie has just let me know about a few too many feral pigs that came through so we are gonna take to them in the morning with the chopper."

"You want me to go along?"

"The chopper only seats two Andrew, but tomorrow after we return, I'll give you some instruction with the rifles okay. Do you shoot?"

"No I go to church instead. You got more than one gun?"

"We've got a twenty two, a three oh three and a seven six two. You need to learn all of them. Couple of big razorbacks will need the seven six two."

"What you mean you don't have a Browning point five zero calibre out here?"

Jack smiled! Andrew was being a tad facetious as he realised the station had a good selection of suitable rifles.

"What do you use the twenty two for?"

"Snakes!"

"Oh!"

"Tomorrow I will show you the pig trap I have enquired about from the States – it's the "Boar Buster", can catch a whole parcel at once and be activated remotely."

The boys cracked a second stubby as Narelle had rushed inside to heat the food dishes she had already prepared for everybody's dinner. Rebecca had gone to their room to get cleaned up. Andrew would follow as soon as the beer drinking ritual had demolished a couple. Once Andrew was showered, he entered the kitchen to find that Bec has served his dinner – beef vindaloo with broccoli, cauliflower and champignons. Just another excellent dish from Narelle, who had by now also served the workers in their own mess room.

The next morning Andrew had a full breakfast again but Rebecca had just cereal, as she had a low appetite from eating vindaloo the night before. Jack and Frankie took off in the chopper to hunt the feral pigs while Andrew checked the net for details of the Boar Buster that Jack had alerted him to. He was duly impressed and decided they would procure one immediately. He had already seen enough of wild boars to concern him and did not want any of his staff being injured or even killed. There was no guarantee that Jack and Frankie would locate the feral pigs on this sortie with the chopper. Andrew also looked at tracking devices thinking he might be able to use the dogs to track the pigs and identify where the dogs were. He also thought he might construct a pen and use baits to lure the pigs into the pen on a regular basis then employ the Boar Buster within the pen. Andrew was intent on exterminating wild boar from the station property. He wondered whether the Boar Buster might be used for other wild vermin, like donkeys or goats and would consider trialling it for that purpose.

After a short time, he heard Rebecca making some noises and went to see what she was doing. He found her in the bathroom.

"Are you okay Bec?"

"Oh, Andrew I have just been sick ... aw ... that was terrible. Must have been something I ate."

"Hey, lie down and try to take a nap, I'll get you a glass of milk. My grandmother used to say that was the best thing to put some lining back onto your stomach wall."

"Okay thanks."

They would find in a few weeks' time that Rebecca was suffering morning sickness.

Jack and Frankie returned about an hour later to report they had taken out two large boars and about four other large pigs but that there were, indeed, about another twenty pigs in the parcel. Andrew showed Jack the Boar Buster on the internet then immediately ordered a unit from an Australian supplier. It would arrive in Newman in about one week's time. Jack then took Andrew and the dogs out to a clearing a few hundred metres from the dwellings where he had a rifle range set up. He gave Andrew his first lessons in riflery. But unbeknown to the men, two of the bore caps that Jack and Andrew had placed on bores that previous Monday on Lake McDonald were about to collapse under the pressure exerted by the aquifer, as they had been fractured in the factory.

The breakout

It was late on a Thursday afternoon when the breakout occurred – one bore cap releasing about four o'clock in the afternoon, the other within an hour. Water gushed effusively from the bore caps and quickly spread to the surrounding area around the trough. The force of gravity being what it is, the water had just one way to go – into the nearby Lake McDonald. As the water started to flow onto the salt lake it carried with it some surface soil to create an area that was covered with quite dirty water but as the flow spread across the lake the dirty appearance attenuated to become clear. The water flowed onto the lake spanning outwards in a gradual semi-circular encroachment upon the lake – initially at a rate approximating one metre per minute but decreasing as time went by as the water flow covered a wider expanse. Within a couple of hours the water coverage of the salt pan had extended to a distance of about two hundred metres from the bore.

That may not seem like such a vast section of the lake for the water to cover in a couple of hours, given that Lake McDonald is about four kilometres long and about half as wide, but it was going to be a long night. Apart from that, there were two bores pumping water out onto the lake. By sunrise the water coverage of the lake – albeit a very shallow coverage – was almost total.

Now, the Pilbara region of Western Australia is a very hot place in summer. The town of Marble Bar to the north holds a world record for the longest consecutive number of days above one hundred degrees Fahrenheit, almost thirty-eight degrees on the centigrade scale – one hundred and sixty consecutive days above one hundred Fahrenheit. It is one of the hottest regions on the planet and on the previous day

Marble Bar had recorded forty-three degrees. By eight o'clock in the morning, the ambient temperature at Lake McDonald had already hit the mid-thirties and by ten o'clock it had reached forty degrees and would stay that high until late in the afternoon.

By ten o'clock the entire lake had been covered with more than one millimetre of water – and the evaporation had started. The mist was rising and as quickly as the bores kept pouring water onto the lake and it was dispersing uniformly across the lake, it was evaporating into the atmosphere. All through Friday the water evaporated and by nightfall the salt pan was completely dry. Hundreds of thousands of litres of water had evaporated into the atmosphere through the course of the day, a day when a low-pressure trough off the coast near Exmouth would ensure the prevailing wind at Lake McDonald was heading in an easterly direction. Though the water had evaporated completely, the following night the water gushing from the bores completely filled the lake again and by mid-morning on Saturday the evaporation process recommenced.

"Good morning Alison, bright and early start I see. How was your weekend?"

"Hi Glenda ... ah ... yep got here at seven this morning. My weekend? Same as for a typical Aussie wife - washing, ironing, frigging etcetera. How was yours?"

"Huh ... I know what you mean. Mine, yep, pretty much same as without the frigging – think he might be past it actually, my Grant. Had a good workout at the gym though. Is that Saturday's satellite image you are looking at there?"

"No, this is today's image."

"Today's image? But I am sure I saw that cloud formation on Saturday morning when I came in for a short time. Show me Sunday's image please."

"There it is, same type of cloud formation – only today it is more extensive as you can see. Saturday morning it was crossing the West Australian border now it's ... ah ... approaching the centre."

"That's so unusual, we didn't expect any dense cloud activity like that this weekend. Look at all four of those images. Why does that cloud formation seem to be originating from that very precise position in Western Australia?"

"Yes and it is also gaining in intensity isn't it. Could be a drop of rain in that. Might bring some relief to a few farmers somewhere."

"Hmm ... but we haven't forecast any rain to anywhere in the Territory. That could become an issue for us Alison. We had better put out a revised weather alert – and we had also better contact the satellite boys to home in on whatever that source of precipitation is. I have never seen anything like it. Geeze look at that – that small section just turned red."

It was a beautiful fine, sunny morning at Uluru!

The weather forecast was so totally unequivocal in predicting a glorious fine summer day with clear blue skies and a maximum temperature of a modest thirty-four degrees. The forecast range was for fine weather for the next five days, with absolutely no prospect of rain in sight.

"Welcome everybody to Red Rock Tours and thank you all for gathering here this morning as we requested. We hope you have all enjoyed a good night's sleep after yesterday's arduous trek. It seems like everyone is here. Are we all ready for our first walk around Uluru?"

"Yeah" shouted a contingent of about twenty tourists, all decked out in cool summer gear. People were wearing singlets, t-shirts, shorts even bathing jocks. A couple of interpreters were with the Korean and Japanese tourists present to convey the instructions.

"Thank you for all wearing your hats too, as instructed, as our hot Aussie sun can cause some damage out there. Our boys Matt and Chris will be carrying backpacks with adequate water for everybody so sing out if you need a drink. Now once we arrive at the base of the rock we will do a final roll call before we set off. It is important not to go too quickly for your own abilities – some people here are obviously quite fit – and then there are the rest of us. You don't have to race anybody and most of you will take about two hours to walk around the rock, okay. So we will now board the bus for the short drive to the base of the rock."

The tourists boarded the bus in an orderly manner and took up their seats. The bus arrived at the base of the rock within five minutes and they alighted. Brian Mansfield, the tour director, conducted a final roll call and everybody was present.

"Okay good people, here we go!"

A couple of very fit Kiwi trekkers hit the trail hard and were quickly out of sight. Seems they do this sort of thing quite regularly over there across the ditch. Most of the tourists just set off on a rather leisurely stroll as suggested. About forty minutes later they were all at the far end of the rock and really enjoying the view of the harsh red landscape.

"Looks like a bit of cloud heading this way Brian."

"Yeah Matt but we checked the forecast this morning and it ain't gonna rain here today, that's for sure and certain. Make sure everyone is hydrated."

"Water for anyone?"

Several people came forward to collect a bottle of spring water. Brian continued his rendition to the tourists.

"Now to the west you have a clear view of Kata Tjuta - the Olgas – an extremely ancient rock formation dating from the pre-Cambrian era, created by vertical block lifting of the sandstone formation that goes below the surface from here to a depth of approximately two hundred kilometres. You can see how the elevation of the Olgas, which are much higher than this rock, is sufficient to have a modest effect on the localised weather, with that light grey cloud formation accumulating directly above the actual range."

"Shit! Lightning! Holy hells bells that wasn't supposed to happen today."

"What time did you check that weather forecast boss?"

"Natalie did about seven this morning Chris – buggar me I hope she didn't get that wrong."

Just then Brian's mobile phone rang. It was Natalie."

"Brian you won't believe it, we have just received a weather alert from the weather bureau, there's an anomaly they don't understand, it's coming your way and it's going to piss down. Get those people out of there."

"You're telling me – I'm staring at the bloody thing! It's already pissing down over there at the Olgas love and we are at the far end of the rock right now. Holy shit did you see that?"

Three bolts of fork lightning had jolted the Olga's within a fraction of a second.

"See what? How can I see anything where you are from here?"

"No Nat, I said that to the boys – that lightning has just gone up ten notches of the post – boys get them out of here quick as. Nat that bloody anomaly they mentioned is a magnificent bloody thunderstorm and it's coming our way. We are getting out of here straight away. And when you get time to do it check with the bloody bureau what's happened and call me back. They might have some explaining to do cos these people here are about to get thoroughly drenched. There's no way we are gonna get back to that bus before this shit hits us."

He was right! The tourists were more than halfway around the pathway on the rock – but still several minutes away from the bus when she came down – as heavy as rain ever gets out there. Needless to say, they were all completely saturated by this anomalous downpour. A few women ran screaming as they went but others ran lapping it up, for they had never experienced anything like this ripper of an Aussie outback downpour. Good thing for them that it was actually quite a hot day. When they got to the bus and boarded it was still pouring down and Brian addressed the group.

"Ladies and gentlemen, I am so sorry, I do apologise on behalf of Red Rock Tours from the depth of my heart for what you have just experienced but there was no way that we were going to have any rain here today. The weather forecast was for fine weather for many days but my wife called me to say the weather bureau in Darwin called her just about thirty minutes ago to alert her to an inexplicable change that even the bureau could not understand, so ... ah ... all I can say to you all is, once again, we are very sorry and we hope you can all get dry pretty quickly."

Brian looked at the group and was somewhat perplexed by the sight that many of them were actually smiling, until one Kiwi spoke up.

"Don't worry mate that was bloody great!"

"Yeah fantastic!

"Best experience since we landed here from the U.K. Brian. We don't get that over there – just a shitload of drizzle actually."

"The lightning show was awesome Brian."

Everybody laughed so Brian eased up on himself.

"Well actually I will tell you a story – years ago our somewhat famous Leyland Brothers came here and copped a violent storm and the rain was so heavy that it formed a moat that completely surrounded the rock. So one of them rode a motor bike around the rock then claimed to be the very first person to go around Uluru as an island."

That brought out a few laughs too.

"Now Matt and Chris have some dry towels here for you good people to dry yourselves with, okay!"

Privately, Brian was still quite perturbed with the whole situation and was keen to ask questions and get some answers. His business relied heavily on his reputation and word-of-mouth advertising and he knew that somebody would mention this in a feedback website sometime.

"Now what we are going to do is take you all by bus to the changerooms at the caravan park okay and everybody will have a chance to change into some dry clothing, but, once again I do apologise, my wife has informed me that the weather bureau believes this is a freak occurrence okay and they do not understand why this has happened."

The bus drove to the caravan park as Brian had indicated and all of the tourists were quite relieved to change their clothing. Brian called Natalie again.

"So what's the go love, have you spoken to anyone?"

"Yes Brian, Glenda Tyrie from the bureau in Darwin has said that an unusual source of precipitation has occurred in Western Australia and they are looking into it. She said this is beyond the comprehension of any weather bureau experts and they have alerted people from Monash and Murdoch universities about what happened here today."

"Oh maybe it was a bloody U.F.O. with aliens on board. What will they think of next?"

"Now Brian you know that they are very good and expert people at the Darwin bureau - but Glenda reiterated that from their satellite imagery the source is very specific and localised to an area of the east Pilbara."

"The east Pilbara – that's a bloody long way from here."

"So they are all looking into it now."

"You realise we could go under from this – it will only take one of these people to give us an adverse rating then who knows!"

"Now that's not likely to happen, in fact it just might be a blessing for us – perhaps some free marketing of our tour."

"Yeah, maybe, we'll see!"

Meanwhile back at the weather bureau some information was starting to filter through from those satellite boys.

"Glenda, hello, it's Jacob here from Aussat."

"Hello Jacob, what do you have for us?"

"Yeah, well, ah ... seems like all this precipitation is emanating from just one comparatively small salt lake in Western Australia, which means that for some obscure reason that salt lake has been given a good coverage of water in just these last two days. There hasn't been any rain there for a while so it's all a bit of a mystery to us here, too, at the moment. It's not a huge lake, only about five kilometres by two. We've alerted the local shire and the DWER – the Department of Water and Environmental Regulation - in Perth..."

"The DWER?"

"Yes the DWER will want to look into whatever has caused this to happen – save for an earthquake or a volcano it can't just happen naturally so there's got to be some kind of human intervention involved."

"What type of intervention?"

"Oh, probably somebody stuffing around with a mining project as they do over there in the west – you know what they are like over there!"

"Yes, everybody does! Over there they dig up dirt and make a fortune and over this way we bend bananas or shoot crocodiles or some shit. Which area of the east Pilbara are we talking about here Jacob – it's a pretty big place you know and I know that because I used to work at the bureau in Perth? It's the biggest shire in the world, in fact!"

"Yeah, the world's largest shire in fact. The salt lake in question is east of Newman by nearly two hundred clicks so they haven't had any rain at all in that area for a couple of months ... ah ... Lake McDonald south-east of Jigalong is what we are dealing with here. The initial sat pics show water flow from two separate sources about three kilometres apart."

"Lake McDonald, okay I will look that one up, so keep me informed will you please. People are already trying to put egg on our face up here. The tourists at Uluru got caught up in a downpour."

"Now Glenda you know I still want to take you out for a pizza dinner at Tippy's, so yes I will keep you totally in the loop okay."

"Yeah thanks Jacob!"

"So a salt lake in the east Pilbara region Alison. Now what do you suppose those boys could be doing over there this time?"

"Salt lake! There wouldn't be any water on a salt lake at this time – there hasn't been any monsoon rain there for weeks. Did I hear you say Lake Macdonald which is that large lake near the Northern Territory border?"

"No this one is a small lake on a pastoral station about two hundred kilometres from the town of Newman. The lake has been covered with water somehow."

"Why would such a small lake cause this effect Glenda?"

"Because there is plenty of moisture in the atmosphere at most times, just not sufficient to cause rain to form, so this additional precipitation from the lake was just the trigger factor that brought the ambient moisture to coalesce into rain. It's similar to what occurs with cloud seeding using silver iodide."

"All that from such a small lake!"

"Yes but don't forget Alison that it gets pretty bloody hot over there during the day, so whatever water hit that lake would virtually evaporate instantly and it was really the effect of the Olgas and Uluru causing the moist air to rise that has led this to happen. That storm was localised to both so the direction of airflow must have been highly conducive as well. Apart from all that, that Jacob still wants me to go out with him."

"You going to?"

"I'm not a huge fan of pizza."

"Hey, big spender, get real!"

The girls had a bit of a giggle.

"Doesn't he realise there is decent restaurant or ten up here in Darwin!"

"He's probably never been to any of them."

"That wouldn't surprise me! Last week Ray took me to Lazy Susan's for my birthday – the seafood was really good."

"Well hopefully Jacob will call back with some more info soon – I'd like to pacify everyone at the rock as soon as I can."

The storm had been very localised at Uluru but weather watchers all over the country had seen this extraordinary occurrence, where satellite images had shown red over the Olgas and Uluru. It was a known fact that landforms of high elevation could cause a sudden downpour in remote areas, but it was assumed there would be no further rainfall activity. It was assumed that the moisture levels depicted in red would soon dissipate to become green and yellow.

It was assumed!

Into the night that stream of moist air was flowing into New South Wales toward the back of Bourke, which was in the centre of the drought effected areas of Queensland and New South Wales. The drought was in its third year and locals were worried about a repeat of the six-year drought from 2006 to 2011 occurring.

It was a bright sunny Tuesday morning in Bourke. Life was going on as normal with a few locals walking the main drag doing some light shopping at the IGA and Spar supermarkets, but things were really tight. The local economy relied quite heavily on the sheep industry and the only grazers doing okay were the thousands of kangaroos in the area. Then it started! The telephone rang at the local post office. Cheryl answered the phone.

"Cheryl it's Lisa from Louth, you wouldn't believe it, it's just started pissing down here."

"You're kidding me!"

"No it just came down out of nowhere, a few clouds came across then a few minutes later the sky went dark and ... well, listen to it ... that noise is the rain on the roof of the pub."

"But the forecast was for hot and dry weather for the next week, as usual."

"I know, well they got that wrong and I'd say it's coming your way. We've got people dancing in the street here."

"Really! Ah ... just how expansive does it look to you Lisa?"

"It seems it's only about ... say ... seven or eight kilometres wide but it went straight over us so we really copped it."

"Okay thanks Lisa, I'll let people know. Have you got onto Facebook yet?"

"No, will do soon as ... and you'll cover the Bourke community eh?"

"You betcha! This could be a bloody life saver."

The rainstorm took three hours to reach the Bourke district and by then the whole town was waiting for it. They hadn't seen any rain at all in more than four months and that was just one millimetre of rain. The weather bureau in

Sydney had been alerted and was checking the satellite images already. It seemed the moisture from Uluru was melding with moisture coming in from the north from a high pressure system off the coast of Queensland. But it was heading in a south-easterly direction toward Bourke, but nowhere to the north of Bourke. The pastoralists and farmers of Queensland, too, were watching anxiously and expectantly. Would they, too, receive some rain for the first time in many months? Their livelihoods depended on it. By the time this weather anomaly reached Bourke hours later, the people of Bourke were standing in the streets watching for it. Sure enough, they watched a cloud-band form on the horizon and slowly and gradually move closer to their town. Lisa from the Louth hotel was pretty accurate – the cloud-band seemed to be about ten kilometres wide and it was heading straight for the town of Bourke. Again, as it started to rain in Bourke, people were dancing in the streets.

That Tuesday night Andrew and Rebecca were watching the ABC News telecast when this extraordinary sequence of events first hit the national news. The downpour at Uluru might have been largely dismissed as an aberration but for this weather system anomaly to reach Bourke the following day was big news.

Rebecca and Andrew were chatting while the news covered an incident involving the United States President, but their attention was drawn to the story about Bourke.

"... and the President claimed that after his discussions with Kim Jong-un the world would be a far safer place."

"The town of Bourke in outback New South Wales which is presently caught up in the middle of one of the regions worst droughts received some unexpected rainfall today as a peculiar weather system drenched the town in the early afternoon. Weather experts are still endeavouring to explain the exact cause of a localised system that was also responsible for an electrical storm at Uluru yesterday morning that took tour operators by surprise, resulting in dozens of tourists also being thoroughly drenched. Preliminary analyses seem to indicate an unlikely source of precipitation emanating from the east Pilbara region of Western Australia. The town of Bourke received five millimetres of rain in only about twenty minutes. The rain has brought some hope to pastoralists that a change may not be too far away. Sheep grazier Randolph Blewett said the rainfall across his property would realise some feed growth in the next week and supplement his need to provide stock with fodder brought in from the west, but that a lot more rain was needed to overcome the drought conditions that prevail."

"Huh, fancy that Andrew, we got a mention on the national news – the east Pilbara."

Rebecca had no idea that it was actually they, themselves, who were anonymously mentioned in the news bulletin, but they would learn something the following day.

The next morning the telephone rang. It was the CEO of the East Pilbara Shire.

"Good morning Andrew Robertson speaking."

"Mr. Robertson this is Robert McPharlin of the East Pilbara Shire calling to speak with Mr William Piper if he is available."

"Good morning Robert, how are you? Ah … no William Piper is in the States and he won't be here again – he is in the process of transferring this property to my father James who is also in the States, but I am here to take over management of the ranch … ah … station. Can I be of any assistance?"

"I hope so Andrew, we have been contacted by the weather bureau in Perth City and also by the Environmental Protection Authority regarding an unusual weather occurrence that has affected parts of the Northern territory and New South Wales that seems, anecdotally at least, to have originated from your property – specifically from Lake McDonald. So what are you boys doing out there? Just why would your Lake McDonald now be flooded with water?"

"Lake McDonald!"

"Yes – your Lake McDonald."

"Hey we saw that on the news last night but we had no idea it was coming from here, I mean our property … ah … we were out there at the lake just last week, my man Jack and myself and we replaced some bore caps that were perishing, but we fitted new caps so I find it surprising that something could have gone wrong on our property."

"Well it has and you need to get out there and check out what is going on – the people at Uluru are not happy Jan."

"Ah … Jan who?"

"Never mind that – do you have any idea what might have happened to cause this?"

"No, but I will talk to my man Jack and he can take the chopper out there soon as to inspect the place and … ah … he can call me from there and I will call you back today, okay."

"Okay please get onto this straight away we have a few people on our backs already."

"Which people?"

"The DWER!"

"The DWER?"

"The Department of Water and Environmental Regulation down in Perth. They closely monitor any human activity that might cause a disruption of any kind to the environment. We do get more than our share of enquiries from the DWER because of the mining industry so they are extremely vigilant. Unfortunately, not everybody in the industry has a proclivity for protecting the environment. The DWER can levy substantial fines on anyone who doesn't do the right thing. Now, I need to call them back as promptly so please call me back soon as you ascertain the nature of the problem."

"Okay will do!"

"What was that about dear?"

"You remember last night we were watching the news and there was that item about the weather at Uluru and that town of Bourke."

"Yes!"

"Well that unusual source of precipitation they mentioned is actually coming from the salt lake on our property that Jack and I went to last week. It seems that something has gone awry and water is gushing onto the lake."

"You mean we caused that downpour at Uluru and Bourke. Good Lord, well, I hope they can see something positive in this."

"Yes one would hope so. But the shire CEO mentioned that the DWER in Perth is seeking an explanation."

"So what are we going to do?"

"Only one thing I can do – send Jack back out there with Frankie in the chopper today to see what's happened."

The DWER

"Jack would you be able to come in here please we need to talk – and ask Frankie to prepare the chopper for take-off as soon as possible please."

"Okay, sounds serious! I'll be there in two shakes of the dog's tail."

"Frankie! You need to get the chopper ready a.s.a.p. please. Sounds like you and Andrew are going somewhere in a hurry."

"I'll need to refuel first. Take about twenty minutes."

"Okay you do that and I'll see what gives."

Jack walked over to the main house and Andrew and Rebecca were waiting in the front office.

"Jack come in please. Would you like a glass of lemonade?"

"That would be wonderful Bec thank you. Andrew!"

"Hello Jack, thank you for coming in so promptly. We've had a call from the shire, there is a problem out there at the lake – McDonald."

"What kind of a problem?"

"It's flooded – seems the entire lake is covered with water and they say our lake has caused a substantial downpour at Uluru on Monday morning and in Bourke, New South Wales, on Tuesday morning."

"You're shittin' me Andrew! I saw the news about the storm but, geeze, to say that came from here, that's a bit of a tall one."

"The weather bureau has been tracking it. It wasn't all from here Jack – the Uluru storm was but the Bourke precipitation picked up some moisture from a high pressure system in Queensland and together they caused the problem at Bourke."

"Problem? Isn't that what they need right now – more rainfall?"

"Well you and I and almost everybody else might think so Jack but we are not the government."

"No and thank God for that Andrew. We get things done – they don't!"

"I'm sure a lot of people would share your cynicism of the government Jack but for now we need to ascertain what has happened and report to the shire today. So I need you and Frankie to get out there in the chopper and call me on the sat phone please. Ah ... we did everything right didn't we Jack? I mean, the way we went about the installation of the bore caps and all, it seems strange that something like this could happen."

"Did it all the same as we always do Andrew. Could be one of the older ones that we didn't replace has given up on us. While I am gone it might be worthwhile getting straight onto Newman Hardware and order enough extra caps to replace the others."

"Yes I will do that. Now how soon can you boys leave?"

"Frankie is refuelling as we speak so we will be gone within ten minutes. It will only take about half an hour to get there so you should hear from us within the hour."

"Great, thanks Jack. Oh and you will take some supplies with you eh?"

"Here you are Jack - lemonade!"

"Thanks Bec! Yes, we will take water, food, the phone and the guns Andrew."

"Oh yes, the guns – might run into your mate out there again. You know what to do if he shows up, right!"

"Yep! Good thing we've got that young buck coming of age now."

"He is?"

"Yep – saw hm practising the other day."

"Practising? Oh ... ah ... never mind!"

"He'll need to sort out his own patch though! Big Rudolf won't want him too close.

"Rudolf?"

"Yeah Rudolf is the other big boy. The soon to be terminated bull is Rambo."

"So what name has the young bull got?"

"Scomo – in honour of our then Prime Minister."

"You could have named him "Ant" in honour of your new Prime Minister, Jack."

"We did consider that Bec but Scomo seems to have a nice ring to it."

"So if you do take out Rambo Jack, what will you do with the carcass?"

"Oh the dingos and pigs will take care of him Andrew, after the crows peck his eyes out. Cattle do die out there from time to time. That's the chopper starting up. Okay we'll be off and call you soon as I get there Andrew."

"Thanks Jack, good luck!"

Rebecca and Andrew went outside to watch Jack and Frankie leaving in the chopper. By now it was after midday, so they went inside for lunch knowing they would receive the call from Jack within the hour. Andrew called the hardware store in Newman and ordered another four bore caps. Bruce informed Andrew the bore caps would arrive within three days on the Toll triple road train – that he would be able to collect them on Saturday.

"Thank you Bruce I will send Jack in to collect them so would appreciate a call to confirm their arrival if that is okay with you."

"Will do, look forward to seeing old Jack again – missed him last time."

As Frankie and Jack approached the lake they could very readily identify what was happening. Water was gushing from the top of one of the new bore caps that Jack had installed just five days before. The spray was fanning outwards away from the lake but the water had accumulated around the bore and was flowing into the lake about forty metres away.

"Holy shit Frankie, look at that. That's a bloody new bore cap pissing out that spray."

"Why do you think it would it do that Jack?"

"Only one possible reason Frank – they've served us a dud."

Frankie set the chopper down on a flat surface near the lake and the two men went to inspect – Jack took the precaution of taking the rifle in case that rogue bull was in the vicinity.

"That water could have been flowing ever since last Friday. No bloody wonder the lake is covered."

"That water coverage is only a couple of mill Jack."

"Yes but it starts to evaporate as soon as the temperature gets up. Probably from eight in the morning right through to six or even seven it would be evaporating. I'll get in there and shut off that valve. You hold the gun – and don't point it in my direction, keep it pointed to the ground."

Jack waded through knee-high water for several metres to shut off the valve. He inspected the bore cap and detected a fracture around the top of the moulded section from where the water was gushing.

"Yep it's cracked! Copped a dud all right. Bloody brand new bore cap. The hardware wouldn't have known though – the water pressure would have forced it."

As Jack was wading out Frankie noticed old Rambo the bull coming out of the scrub.

"There's your old mate Rambo Jack."

"Well spotted Frankie! I'll take the gun thanks."

"You gonna take him out?"

169

"Worst thing he could do right now is charge the chopper while we are trying to leave. You know what that would mean. Apart from being stuck out here for too long it would be a salvage job, that would. Besides, he had a go at me the other day and we've got young Scomo coming through to service the cows."

Jack flicked the safety switch and took aim at Rambo. The old bull was motionless and staring at the men when Jack put a single bullet between his eyes. The bull dropped like a ton of flesh – his reign as head bull was over.

"Okay we'll call Andrew and let him know what has been going on out here but we need to check the other bore caps as well."

The men returned to the chopper and Jack phoned Andrew.

"Hello Jack, what did you find?"

"One of the new ones gave way Andrew – the very first one we fitted in fact. It had fractured near the top so would have been faulty before we took it. I've closed the valve to stop the flow and while we were here we took out old Rambo too, by the way, so we'll head off down south to check the others now."

"Okay thanks for that Jack. I'll call the shire and if there are any other problems please call me back."

"Will do!"

Jack got his tools and removed the faulty bore cap. The men got back into the chopper and as they were ascending Jack looked back and noticed two dingoes that had already approached the carcass of old Rambo.

"Couple of dingoes onto old mate Rambo already."

"Geeze that didn't take long!"

"A mate up at Whaleback – old Dicko White – told me that one day he was alone up there at the Pondy in his ute and a large male dingo attacked his vehicle and jumped at his driver's side door while the ute was still moving. Old Dicko reckons he must have had pups nearby for him to do that. Scared the shit out of him it did, but luckily he was in the ute not out of it."

The men headed south checking the bores as they went by doing a low hover and everything was in order with the second bore cap but the third one at the south end of Lake McDonald had also given way and was gushing water just as the first was. From the chopper the men could see that the water was also flowing out of that lake and had started to flow down a creek bed into another lake. This second lake was now approximately half covered with water and the men could detect that it was still spanning outward across the lake. They knew that by the end of the day it, too, would be covered with water so they set the chopper down again. Jack got onto the telephone.

"Jack how's it going?"

"Number two was okay but the third one has given way too and looking at it from the chopper it's a dead ringer for the first."

"Dead ringer?"

"Yeah a dead ringer – it's pissing out water the same way. We are at the bore now so I'm about to shut it off but the water has flowed from McDonald into the lake south from here."

"Shit! Ah ... how bad does that look Jack?"

"It's only reached that second lake sometime in the last few hours I'd say – it would have started flowing through the night - but it is spanning out across the lake as we speak. It flowed down the creek bed of course! We checked it from the chopper before landing and from up there, Andrew, that water flow looks like a bloody long snake. You might have the return of the Wagyl happening here mate."

"Wagyl?"

"Yeah that rainbow serpent the dancers were on about at the corroboree. Bloody long snake that presides over the waterways here in the west."

"Oh yeah that snake! Okay now I will call the shire and let old mate McPharlin know what's happened. So we've stopped the flow and the water covering the lake will evaporate away over the next ... how long?"

"Oh up here it's so bloody hot that what is in the lake will be gone within a few hours Andrew. But you do understand that what has evaporated over the last couple of days will still be on its way to the east, eh!"

"Yes, of course! Hopefully we won't have any more tourists getting totally saturated."

"Well like I said before, Andrew, those farmers around back of Bourke wouldn't be too upset. They might even be really thankful for what they about to receive – this is gonna be like manna from heaven to them mate."

"Hmm ... that moisture could go anywhere over the next few days Jack. Hope it doesn't upset too many people."

"Be a good job if we could leave this flowing for a while I reckon. Fill the second lake for the rest of today and see what happens."

"Jack, that could put me in serious trouble with authorities. McPharlin has to report back to the DWER."

"The DWER won't need to know Andrew if Frankie and I just stay here until dusk – let the water flow from this bore for the rest of the day to fill that second lake. Frankie has his night-flying ticket so returning to base after dark won't be an issue."

"Are you being serious Jack?"

"Blood oath mate! Andrew, you saw the news about all those farmers over there who are being ruined by the drought Andrew. Shit - this might be the only hope they have of saving their farms, their homes, their cattle, their livelihood, their businesses, their marriages – even their lives Andrew. A lot of them won't make it mate. We've seen it happen so many times before and nobody does anything about it. Those droughts have been ruining families ever since we crossed the Blue Mountains in 1813."

"In 1813?"

"Yeah 1813! Look Andrew, people have suggested piping water from the Kimberley for decades. There's enough water up there to solve all of Australia's water problems. I believe you looked down on the Nammuldi project from the plane on the way over. Why haven't they replicated that type of massive hay production throughout many parts of Australia already? We have enough water to do it. People are trucking hay over to the eastern states from W.A. Andrew. You saw the people in Bourke dancing in the streets. That downpour we caused last week has never happened before, Andrew, so we have a chance to really do something about this, the drought."

Jack sent Andrew into deep contemplation.

"I've told old mate McPharlin that we are onto it Jack. If I was to allow you to do what you are proposing here Jack, what would I tell him?"

"You tell him we've got it under control Andrew – he doesn't need to know the euphemistic nuances of that comment. You could save many lives if you do this Andrew. Nobody needs to know."

"The weather bureau is tracking it."

"They won't have any idea that we let this water flow for another seven or eight hours Andrew. Then tomorrow it will evaporate and the lakes will be dry again."

"You mean *the* lake – lake two Jack."

"Yeah of course. So we need to do this Andrew, I mean, what's the worst that can happen?"

173

"Don't know they haven't said anything about and repercussions till now. Okay Jack, you boys stay there till dusk okay and check out the coverage of that lake before you return."

"Thanks Andrew! God bless ya mate!"

Jack terminated the call then got his tools to remove the faulty bore cap.

"Okay Frankie I'm going to turn this valve on again and we are going to shut it down tonight. We need to fill this lake."

"Why?"

"To help those poor bastards in the east who are hurting."

Jack turned on the valve and the water gushed.

"Okay let's get the chopper up there."

"Where to?"

"Back to the first bore – we're gonna turn that one back on too."

"Did Andrew say to?"

Jack looked at Frankie as they got into the chopper.

"Trust me!"

By now it was about two o'clock and the men arrived back at the first bore and Jack opened the valve. The water coverage of the lake had been reduced to about one millimetre, so Jack was so pleased that he had taken the initiative to replenish the water in Lake McDonald. He would close the valve just before dusk and head back to the second bore. In the meantime that would give the men time to check all of the other bores and ensure they were all in order. Andrew called the shire CEO.

"East Pilbara Shire Jackie speaking how may I help you?"

"Andrew Robertson calling for Robert McPharlin please."

"Ah yes ... Mr Robertson, Mr McPharlin is expecting your call. I'll put you through. Mr Robertson on the line for you sir."

"Andrew it's Robert here, how did you go?"

"Robert our men are out there now – for some reason two of the new bore caps we fitted fractured so my man Jack is out there taking care of that now. It seems they must have been faulty when we purchased them last week so Jack will bring them back in."

"Okay that's good, you must take that up with the supplier – they might be responsible for anything that comes down the line."

"Down the line?"

"Yes I need to call the DWER poste-haste to explain so they will probably be in touch with you."

"Really?"

"Yes I assume your man Jack took some photographs."

"Ah … yes I believe he did yes."

Andrew would call Jack back to take some pics as soon as he got off the line.

"Now there could be some repercussions for you in this from the DWER in the form of an infringement notice being issued okay – just letting you know."

"Infringement?"

"Yes and that usually involves a penalty."

"Penalty?"

"A fine! Could be a few thousand, who knows! The big boys get hit for millions sometimes."

"What big boys?"

"The mines! There was an oil spill on a site here last year – the DWER hit them for two million. But that was a sizeable oil spill Andrew and you are a small fry okay. So don't worry too much."

"Okay I will let you know if anything transpires."

"Thank you for calling me Andrew, goodbye."

"Goodbye Robert."

Andrew called Jack who was on his way back to the first bore.

"Jack can you please get some pics while you are there – the shire wants them for the DWER. Are you boys checking the other bores?"

"Yes we've just done that and they are all good. So we will see you about nine tonight."

"Okay thanks Jack."

"So is everything okay love?"

"Two of our new bores were fractured but Jack will bring them in and we will send them back. The shire CEO informed me that the DWER might issue an infringement which could involve a financial penalty."

"For what?"

"Seems they refer to it as environmental vandalism or something like that. Obviously, they exercise pretty strict control up here. Seems to be a lesson learned though eh."

The shire CEO called the DWER as soon as he was off the telephone to Andrew. About four o'clock Andrew's phone rang.

"Andrew Robertson, good afternoon."

"Good afternoon Andrew my name is Jane Wyatt and I am calling you from the Department of Water and Environmental Regulation - Environmental Service Division. How are you this afternoon?"

"The DWER ... oh ... ah ... good afternoon Jane, yes everything is fine with me. I assume your call relates to the matter of the lake."

"Yes Andrew but for now all I am seeking is your approval to forward correspondence to you from the DWER by email, rather than you having to collect it from Newman. The snail mail process would take at least three days whereas we could communicate via email within a short time."

"Ah yes that would be fine Ms. Wyatt. I will give you our email address."

"We do have an address for the station if that is still the same."

"Well yes it will be, we haven't changed anything like that – only been here about a week."

"Fine thank you for that, I will forward an email to you directly. Goodbye Mr Robertson."

"Call me Andrew. Goodbye Ms. Wyatt."

Andrew went to the station computer and opened incoming mail. The correspondence from the DWER was already there.

"That DWER email is here already Bec. That Jane Wyatt must have had it ready to go while she was talking to me."

Andrew printed the correspondence and read it to Bec.

"Dear Mr Robertson. I understand that you are now the manager of Jennifer Downs formerly managed by Mr William Piper, who, I am led to believe, will no longer be in a management capacity of the Jennifer Downs station."

"I am writing to you as it has been brought to the attention of the Department of Water and Environmental Regulation that a recent transgression of environmental protection has occurred on your property, in the form of excess water being expelled onto a salt lake – specifically in this instance, Lake McDonald – without an Environmental Impact Assessment having been conducted."

"It is believed that this expulsion of excess water has covered the surface of Lake McDonald for a period of days resulting in abnormal evaporation entering the surrounding atmosphere. It is also believed that, based on information provided by weather authorities, the excess precipitation may have, or was likely to have, caused unexpected weather activity in various parts of the eastern states and/or the Northern Territory. The Department of Water and

Environmental Regulation regards such transgressions as serious and, on this occasion, cautions you to ensure that the situation is remedied as quickly as possible and that there are no ongoing incidents of this nature."

"Should there be any further incidents of this nature emanating from Jennifer Downs station the Department of Water and Environmental Regulation will have no option but to levy a substantial penalty – in this case approximating $100,000. I am sure you will appreciate that such a penalty is substantial and undesirable and I expect you will do everything to comply with all environmental protections."

"If you have any further queries please contact me on the number above or by email."

"Regards, Jane Wyatt, Manager – Department of Water and Environmental Regulation."

Andrew saved the correspondence into an appropriate documents folder.

"Undesirable? That's a bit of an understatement love."

"Hmm … well I hope they don't find out that we are going to continue flooding the second lake until nightfall. That was Jack's idea to help farmers in the east overcome the drought. Still, what's $100,000 to us when we just might save those people hundreds of millions eh Bec."

"Jack suggested that? Are you really going to do that Andrew? You surprise me!"

"Why is that dear?"

"Well I have always known you are a really good person but to put that kind of money on the line in endeavouring to assist the farmers over east … um … that is quite exceptional really, my good man."

Rebecca sidled up to her good man and put her arms around him.

"Well listening to Jack talk about it Bec, I realised that he is really so passionate about the whole situation and he also mentioned a few ideas that sounded so compelling really, so I acceded to what he was asking of me – just to let the water run until nightfall and see if that makes a bit of a difference – because nobody else will."

Getting hot!

Frankie and Jack arrived back at the first bore and Jack turned on the valve. Without the bore cap the water flowed freely from the bore and gushed over the ground. The men then took refuge from the sun by sitting in the chopper which Frankie had positioned so they were not in direct sunlight. A gentle breeze was blowing, which made the situation bearable. The temperature had peaked at forty five degrees in the shade on this day.

"So we gonna sit here for the next five or six hours Jack?"

Jack reached back into his backpack.

"Here ya go mate – get that into ya."

Jack handed Frankie a stubby of Swan Draught. He had brought two six packs with him in a chiller bag that also contained a bottle of frozen cordial, specifically for the purpose of keeping the stubbies cold.

"Bloody hell Jack, you think of everything mate."

"I was planning on being out here for a while Frank. We need some action going on around here."

"Jennifer Downs?"

"No mate – bloody Australia! Shit! Did you see the news this last couple of days? You know – what we did in causing that storm!"

"Oh, yeah Jack – you caused a bloody storm over there mate. Should be more of it eh?"

"Gonna be too late for a lot of people Frankie. At least a couple of blokes have ended everything for themselves already. Don't know what their families will do eh? Just hand it all over to the bloody banks. Then who's going to take it on?"

"Have another stubby Frank – and don't worry we've got plenty of water for the rest of today and Narelle prepared a couple of meatball and spaghetti dishes for us. They will thaw out long before dusk."

Jack and Frankie sat there for the rest of the afternoon enjoying the beer and Narelle's dinner, then just before nightfall Jack shut down the valve of the first bore, then they flew to the second to shut that down also. By the time they headed back toward the homestead darkness had fallen. They arrived back at the homestead after nine o'clock. The lights of the main house were off so Jack figured that Rebecca and Andrew must have been asleep, so he and Frankie showered and turned in. They would have to be up by five in the morning.

The next morning Andrew was up early also, so he took the short walk to see Jack.

"Morning Jack! How did it go?"

"All good boss! We shut the bores off just before nightfall and ..."

"Bores? I thought you were only going to continue flooding the smaller lake."

"Well we did then we sat there for a bit so I thought I would have time to get some extra water onto McDonald as well, because I knew that would almost be dry, so we went back there to the first bore Andrew and I opened that up again. You know out there a couple of millimetres of water will evaporate pretty quickly."

"Hmm ... but that water will still be on the lake tomorrow morning Jack and the weather bureau will know that it should have evaporated."

"Andrew, those people are experts, yes, but they won't be that diligent to spot the difference, you know what I mean. They don't know there were just three mills of water on the lake."

"I hope you're right – they've threatened me with a substantial fine if it happens again, though I'm not totally averse to paying out for a good cause."

"Well it bloody well should happen again. But I suspect the wheels will be in motion on that part of it already."

"What do you mean Jack?"

"Andrew there are thousands of farmers over there – if some of them get rain to alleviate their immediate problem and they know where it came from, the rest of them will call out for some respite as well. Just watch it happen."

"You mean we repeat what we have already done but with approval from the Department of Water and Environmental Regulation?"

"Nup! Those two lakes are not big enough! I was thinking about this on the way back Andrew. If you want to provide rainfall to those drought affected areas you're gonna have to flood Lake Disappointment."

"Lake Disappointment?"

"East of the Canning Stock Route. She'd be about fifty clicks by forty I reckon. You put water on that lake at the right time Andrew and you will be number one national hero. Of course ... um ... to flood Disappointment you would need to sink about a dozen bores, let them flow during the night to get coverage and then keep it flowing during the day to replenish the evaporation."

"So virtually whatever quantity of water we would pour onto Lake Disappointment would be going straight into the atmosphere."

"That's the way I see it Andrew! But you're not going to make an impact unless you establish at least a dozen bores around the western side of the lake."

"Hmm ... could be worth a shot, but you know what the DWER said about what I've done already. They will be none too pleased if I flood Lake Disappointment. They will come down on me like a ton of bricks – who knows how much they would fine me for implementing that idea."

"Yes, I know, but you've really got to feel for those farmers over east, you know. Sometimes people just need to take action Andrew. If you leave it up to those bureaucrats nothing would ever get done. And you've heard the reliable predictions yourself – this drought is likely to last at least another three or four years. That will ruin a lot of people's lives – permanently. And there may never be another chance for those properties – I mean, who in their right mind would ever try to resurrect a cattle station that has been blown away by drought? So it's the kind of thing that I would do. By now things should be getting hot over there Andrew and those farmers will be demanding some action. They'll be onto their local reps like a swarm of blowies will be at old mate Rambo by now."

"Oh yeah ... how did that go?"

"He went down like a sack of spuds. A couple of dogs were at him pretty quickly too. The pigs will get most of him though, a couple of crows to peck his eyes out ... then the blowies will finish him off. You know how it goes up here Andrew."

"Yeah ... I'm learning! Bit of a change from Las Vegas."

"Well, Andrew, mark my words, once you've got this red dirt in your blood, you won't want to be anywhere else in the world mate."

"We'll see! Just on that Jack, is there ... ah ... is there a golf course up here anywhere?"

"Of course there is! There's a very good golf course in Newman. You just have to scrape before you putt, that's all."

"Scrape?"

"You'll see!"

The men retreated from their chat to enjoy another satisfying breakfast prepared by Narelle that included both

Corn Flakes and Weeties, for Andrew had now developed a liking for both. By seven o'clock the temperature had already risen to the mid-thirties and the evaporation process on the lakes had commenced. The experts in the weather bureau in Darwin and Sydney were onto it. By now it was after ten o'clock in Sydney.

"I just had a call from Sydney - that lake still has water in it Alison."

"Must have been sufficiently deep to have lasted through yesterday Glenda."

"Hmm ... I suppose you're right. We'll keep an eye on it today – might have to pacify Red Rock Tours again."

But what was happening in the east was all important. The weather system that had given Bourke its first rainfall in many months had widened it path as it went on a south-east trajectory and was now providing similar relief to farming areas to the west of Tamworth and Orange. Some areas received five millimetres of rainfall overnight, Dubbo received even more and some areas up to ten millimetres. By the time the system hit Mount Canobolas it was pelting down. The mountain received over thirty millimetres of rain in less than an hour. The weather bureau had issued the updated forecasts for all of these areas in due course and as experts in their field they understood what had happened. But it still bewildered all persons concerned that such an anomaly could actually occur – and be caused by a little salt lake in Western Australia. Especially two very significant politicians named Chris Minehan and Anna Pellizzari – the respective state Premiers of New South Wales and Queensland.

Things were getting hot! The Minister for Regional New South Wales had briefed his Cabinet colleagues that morning about the anomaly and its positive effect on communities that were locked in the drought. This included his own property west of Dubbo and he had received calls from the largest private employer in his region – Fletcher International Exports, who were keenly interested in ending this drought for the sake of their sheep industry. Ms. Beresford requested her Minister to contact his counterpart in the west to ascertain if there was any plan to extend this aberration – although it was recognised that the confluence of this modest precipitation from the lakes with the greater weather system moving south from Queensland was a contributing factor. They knew that weather conditions would not always be conducive to achieving this type of result. The salt lake anomaly in the west might have to be turned on at an appropriate juncture according to weather patterns.

The Minister returned to his office and consulted his research assistant, Janice Brown.

"Jan could you please contact the relevant Minister in Western Australia once they have arrived at their office and establish a conference for me. I need to discuss this weather situation with them. It seems they in the west have the capacity to influence what happens over here."

"Yes sir will do. They should be there soon. Remember that with daylight saving we are three hours ahead of them now. They have a Minister for the Environment and a Minister for Water, Forests and Fisheries, sir."

"Hmm ... better speak to both of them I suppose. Perhaps a conference call to bring them both in Jan if you can arrange that please."

"Will try sir."

"And we also need to consult our own Minister for the Environment Gabrielle Downton to make sure she is onside with us on this."

"Yes, of course sir."

A short time later Ms Brown had arranged a call to the Western Australian Minister for the Environment Steven Dolsen, but the Ministers for Water and Agriculture were overseas. The two men engaged in conversation.

"Good morning Minister, I am calling in relation to the recent revelation that water flooding a salt lake in Western Australia has brought about much needed rainfall here in New South Wales. I assume you are aware of that occurring."

"Oh, I did see something about that in passing."

"In passing? The entire situation is very big news over here – many areas of the outback New South Wales received their first rains in many months. It has been given very wide coverage in the news here. Has it not been well covered in the west?"

"Ah ... well ... not really, we did see that the tourists got a bit of a drenching but that's about it really. I don't recall seeing anything these last few days. I'm not responsible for what the media here presents to the public."

"Well we are in the middle of a substantial drought and it has come to light that this drought just might be brought to an end should Western Australia come to the party and flood the odd salt lake. So could you please take up this issue on our behalf and implement an action strategy that might bring some relief to the east?"

"Action strategy?"

"Yes, I suggest that you have your department consult with, perhaps, the geography department people at the universities and with the weather bureau, you know, all the usual stuff. We need to get some water onto some strategically located salt pans over there. I have been to the Pilbara many times and I know there are literally thousands of salt lakes in Western Australia. Well if one small salt lake can produce the result we had here this week it would seem that we could possibly end the drought. There are some very large salt lakes in Western Australia as you would undoubtedly know – Lake Disappointment for one and that Lake Mackay near the border."

"Hmm ... does sound a bit far-fetched to me – that one tiny salt lake could bring that about but if that's what the weather people are saying we'll have to accept that for now."

"It happened because there was a confluence of the precipitation caused by your tiny salt lake with a weather system that came down from Queensland – that is what caused so much rainfall. The Queensland precipitation itself was insufficient to reach the critical point to manifest into rainfall. Moisture from the west raised the level above that critical threshold – that's what happened. We've been talking about it over here for the last two days."

"Well I suppose there could be some merit in it so ... ah ... leave it with me and I will make a few calls and get back to you. Could take a couple of days, though. I would need to consult quite a few people over here."

"Please remember that every day is critical for our farmers now. I will await your call."

Time for action

Meanwhile Andrew had taken the opportunity to check the details of Lake Disappointment via the internet. Jack's words resonated in his mind – the old timer had an empathy for the farmers who were in dire straits and possibly losing everything. He called Jack into his office.

"So Jack tell me ... how would we go about flooding Lake Disappointment?"

"You would get the equipment up to Newman on a triple and send a three man team out there to do the job. That Dicko White fella I told you about. He's picked up an eight wheel Tatra 813 that will carry up to one hundred tonnes - that will get you out there. Bloody thing will go anywhere. Plus if needed he's got a tandem axle trailer that can carry a thirteen tonne load, but you won't need that. That rig and the bores you need would probably come in at fifty tonne load I reckon."

"A Tatra 813 eh? Why would he buy something like that?"

"To get urgent freight out to Telfer and to the Newmont Mine in the Tanami Desert. Shit they pay huge dollars when they need something urgently and his truck is the only vehicle this side of the black stump that can make that trip when the rains come."

"What black stump?"

Jack took the opportunity to be a tad facetious with Andrew's innocent ignorance of Aussie colloquialism.

"The one out back of Bourke."

"Oh, over there!"

"Yeah old mate Dicko was out there at Tanami just a couple of weeks ago after that cyclone hit."

"So how soon could we have those parts up here?"

"Get them onto a Toll triple within a day, they would be in Newman inside of three days Andrew. It's only a fifteen hour drive from Welshpool or Kewdale to Newman but they have to load the stuff. Once it arrives in Newman the Toll yard will offload it from the trailers then load it onto Dicko's Tatra as soon as he's ready. That will only take an hour so if Dicko is all go you could be on your way via the Talawana Track within four days easy."

"And how long will it take to get there – to the lake?"

"Buggar all! The Tatra will only do about forty or fifty clicks on that track with the load, but even so it's still only an eight hour trip. The boys would be drilling the next day."

"Okay we had better check with your mate Dicko – see if he's up to it. Can you call him for me please - I'd like you to speak to him first, maybe butter him up a little, you know."

"Got his number in my contact list Andrew."

Jack phoned Dicko White, who immediately recognised it was Jack calling.

"Jack you old bastard, how are they hangin'?"

"Gidday Dicko, same as mate, how's things at your end - excuse the pun."

"Can't complain – had a few good jobs lately because of the cyclone. Worth a few bob."

"Yeah well that's why I am calling Dicko – we've got a job for you too."

"What's that mate?"

"Gotta get some bores out to Lake Disappointment soon as – get some water flowing onto the lake."

"Disappointment? That's an Indigenous Protected Area."

"Yeah but me boss wants it done so we're gonna do it right! We caused a bit of a downpour over east when Lake McDonald got slightly flooded last week."

"Yeah I saw that on the news. Word went around the town here that it came from Lake McDonald."

189

"So if you are good for the job me boss Andrew wants to order the parts. They could be in Newman within two days. You might have to fit a drill to the back of the truck."

"Already done Jack. I sank a bore for the Parnngurr community last week. So is your boss dinkum about this?"

"Yeah mate he is. I'll put him on okay."

"Hello Dicko this is Andrew Robertson, how are you?"

"Yeah good Andrew but I have to tell you I have got some reservations about this job Jack has mentioned. I mean, if I sink those bores on or near Disappointment the Department of Water and Environmental Regulation will probably hit me with a massive fine. Shit, mate! That could be half a million! Apart from that you need approval from the Water Corporation to sink any bores."

"Yes well there's quite some political pressure being brought down on the DWER Dicko but if it does penalise you, I will cover your fine whatever that might be and remunerate you one hundred thousand for this job, okay? I just want to get this done as soon as possible. Got it?"

"One hundred thousand, yeah okay – I was about to quote fifty but I'll take a hundred. Suit yourself - if you want to cover it and reward me the amount you just said, I will get the rig set up by tomorrow night."

"Thank you Dicko. Now I need to know - how long will it take you to complete the job? There will be twelve bores, each about five kilometres apart."

"Twelve eh? Well the water is accessible enough so, including travelling time and the distance they are apart, we could probably sink twelve bores in two days."

"So you could do one dozen wells within just three days starting in two days from now?"

"Yeah that would be the plan, yeah!"

"Okay! I want you to get cracking as soon as the parts arrive. If you invoice me I will deposit twenty thousand into your account today and then I will deposit funds into your bank account each day as you go. My man Jimmy will be out there to monitor the progress and report to me, okay."

"So what's it all about really? Why would you do something like this to try to end a drought in the east? Nobody else has ever bothered too."

"Because somebody needs to! Those pastoralists over there in the east are Australians aren't they?"

"Don't get me wrong Andrew if you are intent on doing this to end the drought for the sake of those people then I take my hat off to you mate. Perhaps this could have been done fifty bloody years ago. I just find it quite perplexing but totally admirable that an American should come in with such conviction when we Aussie bastards might have been far too complacent about all of this. It really upsets me like a lot of people to see those farmers go under that way."

"Well perhaps an outsider like myself can take a clear look at things. Now tell me something - after you have sunk a bore you cap it right? Then we can turn it on when we want to."

"That's it, yeah! The final segment has the valve in place with a solar powered solenoid and electronic control box and you can programme it to turn on and off whenever you need to from your sat phone using a code that is provided."

"Right that's exactly what we need. The wind patterns have to be right before we turn the system on. I am going to order the freight now so please keep the next week free for this job."

"Okay, if you make that deposit today, you're in charge. By the way – I reckon a better idea would be to flood the Percival Lakes."

"Percival Lakes?"

Andrew looked at Jack who nodded his head seemingly in concurrence, for he surmised that old mate Dicko White was suggesting the Percival Lakes as an alternative.

"Yeah they are north-east of Disappointment and won't cause as much controversy. I could get there down the Marble Bar to Telfer road through Punmu and onto Wapet Road or I could go via the Talawana Track through Parnngurr. You see, Lake Disappointment is right on the Canning Stock Route and ... ah ... a lot of people see that lake Andrew, maybe not so many at this time of the year but what you are proposing to do, setting up bores, would be evident during the winter busy season too of course. Besides, the Percival Lakes cover a much wider expanse so would probably pick up a wider air stream. You might leave Tobin lake out of it because the stock route covers that and maybe a couple of smaller lakes in the national park too. But the main Percival Lakes are huge mate – much bigger than Disappointment."

"You got any idea just how big those lakes are?"

"Yeah! The main lakes are over two hundred clicks long ..."

"Over two hundred kilometres?"

Jack nodded again – he knew of Percival lakes and he was getting the drift.

"You've got Lake Auld pretty close too, so you could string that one in and that's about half as long again. All up well over two hundred clicks."

"Lake Auld?"

Jack was smiling, for he knew what Dicko was proposing and he was now getting excited about this.

"Do you think one dozen bores could do the job?"

"Yeah start with that and see what happens – we can always duck out there again within a few days if needs be. Might have to wait for the DWER to show its hand on this one before you go any further though. Of course, if they don't kick your butt and this plan works you might want to cover Lake Disappointment then give some thought as to whether you want to venture further south to Lake Burnside then Carnegie and Wells."

"Burnside, Carnegie and Wells?"

Andrew looked at Jack again. Now Jack was really dancing because his mind was racing about the prospects of developing an evaporation area larger than Tasmania.

"Yeah, Carnegie would be well over one hundred clicks long and Wells would be sixty or seventy – just depends on whether you could string some sections together, you know, with the topography or pumping water to a hilltop then using the drainage basin to allow the flow as it does."

"Hmm ... okay one step at a time as you said Dicko. I'll check for your email and deposit funds today okay, so I will email you the receipt."

"Yeah thanks Andrew. I will send you the details of the supplier so you can call them and order the equipment. Make sure you order stand-alone equipment – it has got to have the solar pack and solenoid etc. so you don't need a dozen generators. They might want to invoice you so that you can email a receipt to them before they supply the equipment to Toll. Oh and I'll need to take a trailer load of rock to place around the base of the bores to catch the flow, otherwise she's just going to gouge a bloody big hole around each bore. I can supply the rock so that will be in my invoice okay. I reckon one tonne of rock for each bore and we'll supply a flow pipe from the bore to the rock bed."

"Oh yes of course, we will need something there to prevent erosion around the bore, thank you for that."

"See ya later mate and I better say goodbye to Jack."

Andrew handed the phone to Jack.

"Dicko what have you done? You've got me boss thinking about this but, shit, what a great idea – put those useless lakes to some good work for a change eh?"

"Just thought I would put him in the loop you know cos he's never been out there and those lakes are bloody huge as you know."

"I've seen Percival and Burnside Dicko but never been that far south to Carnegie. Bloody fantastic idea mate, it's a good thing you get around the way you do."

"Well we'll see what happens and what kind of shit comes down the line but as you know, Jack, there are still more salt pans even further south. If this plan works then everybody is gonna have to think about it."

"So you okay to take Jimmy and Trav out there with you?"

"Yeah plus one of my own boys, Nathan, who knows what to do. Be a good learning experience for your guys of course. Who knows, young Trav might want to get into drilling eh!"

"Okay I'll drop them into town to be there the night before you are ready to go. We'll put them up at the Purple Pub."

"Okay, old timer, look forward to seeing you again and sinking a few ales at the Purple. You be staying the night too?"

"Dunno mate will check with the boss, see what he's got planned for the next day. Hope so if we get drinking a few, be a good idea. See you then."

Jack handed the phone back to Andrew but Dicko had hung up.

"Hmm ... your mate Dicko seems to have a few ideas of his own Jack."

"I suppose he's just covering some possibilities. Sinking bores is one of his lines of work now so he can only benefit from this if it goes that way. Now they won't waste any time getting that equipment up here Andrew so you can expect that to leave Perth tomorrow and be here the day after. I had better get Jimmy and Travis all set for the trip to Newman the day after tomorrow. If they spend one night in Newman, I reckon Dicko will want to be on the road before sunrise. They'll be gone for about four days so they'll need to be well prepared with the gear they take."

"Yes and as Dicko said, it should be a good experience for them too Jack. Will Dicko provide all their food and fluid needs?"

"Yeah they'll all have a swag and Dicko has a good fridge in the Tatra so he'll be well prepared. They'll have more than enough food for the trip."

Dicko White emailed all details to Andrew who promptly called the bore supplier then made the payment. He emailed a copy of his receipt to the supplier, to Toll and to Dicko. Now Dicko knew that the supplier would be compiling a consignment and that the following day Toll would be on its way to the supplier's yard to load it. Things move pretty quickly in Western Australia due to the mining activity. When the big boys – BHP, Rio, Fortescue and Roy Hill – order equipment people get onto it straight away. There are always double road trains ready to go from the Toll yard which pick up a third trailer from the haulage yard at Wubin for the journey north. The supplier emailed Andrew a copy of the Toll consignment note which Andrew sent on to Dicko. Now Dicko could track the consignment and know exactly when it would arrive in town. He would load his Tatra 813 the same day and be ready to head off up bush the following morning. Jack knew he had to leave the homestead the next morning with Jimmy and Travis if he was to return in daylight, so he called Jimmy and Travis in.

"Boys we are off to Newman first thing in the morning. You two will be staying overnight then going out bush with Dicko White to sink some bores – probably take a couple of days. So you need to get some clean clothes together, your jocks and socks, your hygiene pack to clean your teeth and anything else you want. Dicko will provide all your tucker."

"Where are we going to Jack?"

"You'll be heading off up the Talawana to Percival Lakes – give you a chance to call in at home too for a short while. I'm sure Dicko won't mind if you stop at Parnngurr for a bit. You boys will need to help Dicko and his mate to sink the bores – be a good learning curve for you too. So make sure you wind up your work by four o'clock today and get a good night of sleep. I need you up at five so we can leave by six in the morning."

Jimmy and Travis did what Jack required and the next morning they were on the road before Andrew and Rebecca had arisen. That same day the Western Australian Minister for the Environment decided to consult his departmental advisers who were typically conservatively pessimistic about the whole idea of flooding salt lakes in Western Australia as an attempt to end the drought in the east.

"That idea has Buckley's chance of working, surely. You'd never get a sufficient amount of water into the atmosphere from a few salt lakes to end the drought."

"I agree, look at just how vast that drought area is – it must be about half the size of Western Australia."

"What impact is this going to have on the ground water levels of the basin?"

The Minister decided to make his first call to the head of the geography department at Curtin University – Mr. Alan Pilgrim. He was keenly aware of what had transpired the previous few days as were his fellow geographers at Murdoch University, Edith Cowan University and the University of Western Australia. They had all been to a meeting the previous day and the topic was discussed at length and, as such, Mr. Pilgrim was able to cover the narrow range of views the lecturers had expressed. Narrow because they concurred with each other that there were reasons the concept would probably be of benefit but it was all contingent upon water quantities and the prevailing weather patterns. The weather that caused the storm at Uluru and Bourke was conducive to the outcome it caused. Mr. Pilgrim expressed the view that such a system would need to be turned on at an appropriate time and this would require input from the weather experts. If this was not adhered to, there could be consequences – such as flooding in areas that were not targeted.

"You wouldn't want to cause a massive downpour at the Adelaide Oval during the AFL showdown or an Ashes test match now would you? Even worse – the MCG on Grand Final day or at Flemington on the first Tuesday in November. If you do that some people might get a bit upset."

"Hmm ... point taken! So we would need to stipulate that such a system can only be activated with endorsement from the weather authorities."

"That would be an absolute imperative, yes."

"Okay Alan thank you for your input."

"Well you heard the man – could be all systems go but with strict guidelines in place. Marcia could you get onto legals at the Attorney General's office and submit a brief please. We are probably going to need a legal charter of operation of some kind with something like this. As I recall from my high school days that is what happened with the Snowy Mountains Scheme – because it was going to affect four different states. Oh and touch base with the Environmental Protection Authority too – sound them out with what we've heard from Curtin please."

"Will do sir. I believe we will also need to involve the Federal Minister of the Environment and Water sir."

"Yes, please touch base with Terri Butler and include her in all communications."

Marcia emailed the Attorney General's office to outline what type of legal opinion was required in order to draft a charter of cooperation for the various states. Then she called the Environmental Services Division of DWER in Perth.

"Jane Wyatt speaking."

"Jane its Marcia Hines from the Minister's office, how are you?"

"Hello Marcia, what's news?"

"Jane, we've had calls from the Ministry of Regional New South Wales requesting that our state government consider extending the coverage of water onto our vast and numerous salt lakes as an attempt to bring about additional precipitation the likes of which occurred recently at Uluru and in Bourke, hoping to have a positive effect on drought areas. My Minister has had me email the Attorney General for an opinion about what a charter between the states might involve, but obviously, the EPA will need to have considerable input to this proposal also. We have checked with the universities and the word is there could be some merit in this providing the synoptic charts are favourable. But obviously there is going to be some environmental impact so the Minister has instructed me to consider a referral to the EPA."

"Hmm ... I spoke to that station owner just the other day about this – or was that yesterday – ah ... the normal course of action would be to reprove any such environmental vandalism, which is why I decided to castigate him myself actually."

"Well perhaps what comes down in the rain will vindicate what that man has done, in the end."

"Okay I will have our environmental scientists work on that for a few days and get back to you as soon as we have something. I assume they may want to utilise more lakes than just the one that was flooded last week because that comparatively small lake wouldn't necessarily make a difference under other circumstances."

"Yes the Minister for Regional New South Wales has been to the Pilbara and he did refer to Lake Disappointment. But there are numerous other, much larger lakes of course."

"Hmm ... as if my staff aren't busy enough already. Okay I appreciate the call Marcia, leave it with us, we will suspend other ongoing matters to get on with this – I do realise the significance I assure you."

"Jane, just imagine if we ended the bloody drought in the east, holy shit, that would be a feather in the old cap eh!"

"Be worth a few votes that's for sure. By the way how are you and Jason coming along?"

"All over red rover! I told him last week to piss off after he was caught out again with that English floosy, Chantelle. His loss – my gain."

"What do you mean Marcia?"

"Oh I didn't waste too much time Jane – got straight onto a few sites, had a ball or two last night actually."

"Huh – half your rotten luck and good luck to you. He never was good enough for you. Hey catch up for after work drinks soon."

"Okay Jane look forward to that, bye."

Talawana

Jack and the boys arrived in Newman after spending half an hour at Jigalong to check what supplies they might need to be dropped in on the return journey and Jack booked all three of them into the Purple Pub. Andrew had given Jack permission to stay overnight himself, so he took the boys to the Dome café for some refreshment then to the local IGA supermarket to buy some extras they might need for three or four days out in the desert – including the mandatory sunscreen and Aeroguard. Then Jack took the boys to the local Martumili art centre to meet some of the local artists. After almost an hour at the art centre the boys went to the top of Radio Hill where they had wanted to see the aerial photograph of the longest train in history.

"There she is boys – eight loco's and over seven hundred cars - seven point three kilometres long that train."

"Far out Jack it looks like a bloody long snake eh."

"Yeah wow! Hey, pretty good view of the town from up here Jack."

"Yep! Sure is. There's Dicko White's yard over there in the industrial area. You can see the yellow roof on his Tatra."

"Why has he got a yellow roof Jack?"

"Dicko thought it would be a good idea if ever anyone had to try to spot him out in the desert from a plane or a chopper or something. You never can be too careful out there eh boys."

"Hey, I just saw that Tatra move – maybe Dicko is going to collect that equipment. The Toll yard is in Whaleback Drive so we'll see if he heads in that direction."

Sure enough, Dicko's Tatra headed towards the mine site where the Toll yard was in Whaleback Drive so Jack knew they could catch him there as soon as he had loaded, which would take the best part of an hour. The Toll triple had just pulled in meaning it had left Perth by early afternoon the previous day.

Jack drove the boys around the industrial area so they could see which businesses were operating from Newman, the largest town in the east Pilbara. Jimmy had been to Newman previously but not the younger Travis. There seemed to be a lot happening.

"All three of the major companies have new mines under construction at the moment, so some of that activity rubs off onto the smaller businesses here boys. BHP is doing South Flank, Rio doing Koodaideri and Fortescue doing Eliwana. There's going to be a lot of construction jobs going up here in the Pilbara for the next couple of years boys. Might be a chance for you to complete your apprenticeship Trav."

"Yeah that'd be good."

"Okay we better head on over to see Dicko and get you boys in the loop for a start tomorrow."

Jack headed off along Welsh Drive which took them around the back of Radio Hill toward the Whaleback mine site. Sure enough, there was Dicko and his truck at the Toll yard and his Tatra was already being loaded. They stayed out of the yard but did catch Dicko's eye and he acknowledged their presence. It took the forkie another twenty minutes to complete the loading process then Dicko strapped it all down. Jack could see that Dicko had his trailer attached.

"He'd have those rocks in that trailer. Bloody good truck eh boys."

"Never seen nuthin' like that before Jack."

"Nah me neither!"

Dicko finally got the load sorted and started his truck to leave the yard.

"We'll just go over there to that spot I'm sure Dicko will catch us there."

He did. Dicko parked up the Tatra as the boys checked it over.

"Hey old timer how's it going?"

"Yeah good Dicko, good to see you again. This is Jimmy and young Travis who'll be going with you tomorrow. We've done some shopping so they've got sunscreen and repellent so they are all set. We are at the Purple so I'll make sure the boys are up and had a cup of tea and brekky on time for you."

"Good stuff, Jack, be leaving about six I reckon so I'll cruise by the Purple. Can't make it out for a beer tonight mate cos the missus is a bit crook so we better duck over there now for a quick one eh."

'Yeah we'll be in that. Nice rig you got here Dicko – I heard about it but looks even better."

"Yeah set me back a bit but shit, those hot shots are paying for it. They love me Jack, cos there's no way they would get a lot of that freight out there without this baby. Bloody thing will go anywhere thanks to the Czech army."

"What kind of donk is in it?"

"An almost eighteen litre vee-twelve injected diesel Jack. Just shy of two hundred kilowatts of power, four independent diffs, only weighs just over fourteen tonnes but apparently, she can pull loads of nearly one hundred tonnes. Bloody ripper eh."

"Yep, she's a gooden alright. And you picked up the trailer with it too."

"Yeah! When we get out on the track, I'll give your boys a crack at driving it Jack. That'll be good for them. They can toss a coin to see who drives it into Parnngurr, that should impress a few people. So see you at the Purple in five eh."

"Yep a couple of quickies won't hurt. Trav is only seventeen but they won't know that. Be a good education for him. He's had a few stubbies back home but never been into a pub before."

Jack and Dicko and the boys met at the Purple Pub and sank a couple of beers then Dicko said goodbye after arranging to see them in the morning. Jack and the boys showered and changed then dined at the restaurant.

"We'll turn in straight after dinner boys – got to make sure you get a good sleep. I will bang on your door at five and we'll have a good brekky. Dicko should be outside around quarter to six so you guys need to be waiting there for him okay."

Dicko was there next morning on cue and handed Jack a carton for Andrew.

"Jack can you please give this is to Andrew - it's the remote control with all of his instructions so he can activate the system. It's pretty straightforward so he'll manage this okay."

"Will do!"

The boys said goodbye to Jack and they all headed off up the Nullagine Road toward Marble Bar and turned toward the Parnngurr community. As soon as they hit the dirt Dicko engaged all-wheel drive and the Tatra was eating kilometres. Jack left them at the Jigalong turnoff and Dicko proceeded toward Talawana along the track. About twenty clicks up the track Dicko showed Jimmy and Travis the controls then allowed Jimmy to drive the Tatra for one hundred kilometres but Trav had won the toss to take it into Parnngurr, which he did. He was welcomed by about fifty kids running out to greet them. That was a real buzz for the young man as they all knew him well and they were ecstatic to see young Travis behind the wheel of this monster all-wheel drive. Dicko broke out the billy to make himself and his mate a cup of tea to allow Jimmy and Travis time to see their families which they did for two hours. It had been several months since they were last home. Then Travis insisted that Jimmy take the controls again to drive the Tatra out of the community which he did, for Travis wanted Jimmy to feel the same excitement that he had. By now, all of the adults too, were there to see them off.

They were still over one hundred kilometres from the Percival Lakes when they left Parnngurr so Jimmy drove the Tatra for fifty kilometres then Nathan took over the driving, for they had to turn to the north-east along the Canning Stock Route to reach Lake Auld at well twenty eight. When they reached Lake Auld the boys were amazed that they could see into the distance and the lake just didn't seem to stop. Dicko had decided to sink four bores along Lake Auld, six at the main Percival Lake and the other two on the smaller lake between. By now it was mid-afternoon and though the boys were a little weary from the long trip Dicko thought it best to sink at least one bore that day. He selected a spot at the southern end of Lake Auld then he and Nathan removed the trailer, set up the rotary drill and started drilling. Dicko gave a running commentary of instruction to Jimmy and Travis as they went, for he intended to have the boys set up a bore the next day. Travis was taking pictures as they went on his mobile phone.

Within an hour they had struck water at a depth of just fifteen metres. Dicko and Nathan inserted a screen then prepared the casing and sank it. Due to the natural pressure water was flowing freely from the bore so they men installed the bore cap and shut the valve. Dicko installed the solenoid which would keep the valve closed until Andrew opened the valve remotely with the satellite control unit. The entire installation process took about two hours and Jimmy and Travis had observed keenly, for they knew they would assist the following day. Finally, the men constructed the flow pipe and covered the output area with rock from the trailer. The first bore had been set up that same day and Dicko then bypassed the solenoid unit and allowed water to flow onto the lake for a few minutes.

"There you go boys – the first water onto Lake Auld and you guys were here to see it."

Travis was video recording this part of it and at the time had no idea just how significant his recording would become, for this was the beginning of the end of Australia's persistent drought and his recording would be retained in the national archives in Canberra.

"Okay that's a good job done for today boys, we'll set up camp over there and get some tucker going. Hope you young blokes don't mind a beer or two – just make sure you drink some water first okay. Now on the passenger's side of the truck we have got a shower setup so you can get clean for the night and don't worry, there's a screen so you can have your privacy. There's sufficient water in the tank for a five minute shower each okay, and a rubber mat to stand on until you are dry and clothed. So that will be a daily ritual out here – gotta be clean for a good night's sleep."

Nathan was setting up a large open tent so they had respite from the sun. He then set up a barbeque and after washing his hands put on a dozen sausages and four large pieces of steak. While the meat was cooking, he set up a table and fold up chairs. Then he tipped a container of onions onto the hotplate and opened several cans of vegetables – beetroot, asparagus, bean mix and peeled tomato. As the meat was nearly ready he broke out eight eggs. The boys would eat well at the end of each day.

"Here you go boys – get some of these stubbies inside ya. Got enough there for four each night for each one of us okay."

The Tatra had a large storage compartment and Dicko had two eighty litre Engel fridge/freezers on board – one for the steak, bacon and chicken, the other for bread, water and the beer. The dinner procedure would essentially be the same for the next two nights, as would the morning breakfast procedure, with Nathan serving fruit juice, cereal then cooking bacon or sausages and eggs. Nathan would then make up some rolls with meat and salad for lunch.

The next morning the boys packed up the camp and headed north along Lake Auld where they would install three more bores that day, before reaching the small lake before Percival Lake where they established two bores. By the end of the second day they had completed seven bores including the first at the southern end of Percival Lake. While they were there setting up camp a parcel of pigs came out of the scrub to the edge of the lake.

"Dicko – boars!" said Nathan.

"Yeah a bloody big boy there too eh."

"You gonna take him out? They can't breed without him."

"Nah there'll be some young codger to take his place. He's an old one for sure eh. He might keep the young blokes away from his women."

The next day the boys installed the remaining five bores on Percival Lake by about three o'clock and Dicko called Andrew to let him know.

"Gidday Andrew, all done mate, we are at the final bore at the top of Percival lake so whenever you are ready give it a shot and we'll see how she goes."

"Good work Dicko thank you. I'll just put the phone down on speaker and flick the switch."

Andrew flicked the switch as Rebecca looked on with a beaming smile across her face. She was really impressed with how her husband had acted so quickly on this, for it was just three days earlier that Andrew had first spoken with

Dicko White. Within a couple of seconds Dicko's voice came back over the phone.

"Thar she blows boys! Andrew, you have just sent your first water onto Percival lake. She's running down the rock bed onto the salt pan right now."

Rebecca placed her arm around Andrew and kissed him on the cheek.

"How does it look Dicko?"

"Bloody fantastic mate, but young Trav will show you because he is recording this on video."

"Okay well why don't we let it run for five minutes and then I will flick the switch off so you can make sure that works."

"Okay and we'll check the other eleven on the way back. Those switches are all set up so they will all come on at the same time of course. We will camp out again tonight because it will be getting on dark by the time we reach number eleven and we won't drive back in the dark, so your boys will be back in Newman by midday tomorrow. They did a good job assisting us to drill and insert the screens and the casings Andrew. Make a good couple of offsiders they will."

"I appreciate that Dicko – we will encourage them in any way we can."

"By the way they both drove the Tatra – Trav drove it in to Talawana and Jimmy drove it out of Talawana. Yeah they did really well."

"Okay Dicko I will turn off the valve now so check that please and I will leave it up to you as to whether or not you need to call when you reach the other bores."

"Okay Andrew, we will certainly know if the water flowed but I might get you to flick it on again from the last bore just to double check everything. Catch you then mate."

"Goodbye Dicko."

Dicko and the boys set off back down Percival Lake toward the other bores, checking each one as they went. The journey back to the first bore only took two hours as the Tatra could get up speed across the salt pan. They arrived at the final bore and Dicko got Andrew to flick the switch and it was all in order with the water flowing onto the lake.

"All good Andrew now we are going to set up camp down near Talawana so the boys can be with their families tonight okay. Catch you some other time."

Dicko and the boys got back into the Tatra and headed off.

"Oh Andrew there is an email just in from the EPA and they have advised they are looking into a proposal from the east and will be in touch."

Andrew went into the office to read the email as he was a little worried but also hopeful and optimistic that sense would prevail and his substantial outlay was not in vain.

But he forgot to flick off the switch.

Andrew read the email which indeed referred to the request from the eastern states and that the state Minister for the Environment, Steven Dolsen, was seeking legal advice regarding cooperation between states for the purpose of intervention into weather systems. The email stated this had never been considered previously and will require a cautious response and possibly federal legislation prior to any party proceeding to implement any form of operation that might cause interference with weather systems.

"What do you think you will do dear now that we have already set up our watering system of Percival Lakes?"

"Well the first thing we need to do is upload all weather details from the last week and do some kind of analysis of the synoptic charts so that we know why the winds were conducive to carrying the precipitation to Uluru and then on to Bourke last week. I suppose I should call the weather bureau in Perth and Sydney tomorrow and have a chat to them – ask them some pertinent questions. Obviously, I would tell them who I am and that I caused the previous situation to develop and just want to know how it all unfolded. Hopefully they will divulge specific details about the air flow and moisture content levels and so on. I mean, I know that I would need to be cognizant of what a likely outcome would be if I do flick the switch, now that we have the capacity to flood such a large lake system. I don't want to cause a huge downpour where it's not required but it already seems that these pollies are not going to do anything until legislation goes through the federal government ... where is it ... Canberra."

"Yes that could take six months."

"Exactly so if I can identify a favourable weather pattern, I just might be prepared to turn the system on without approval. I sure do hope they offer sufficient information tomorrow. Well best we prepare for dinner then I will do some research tonight on the internet. Good thing they've got that satellite dish out here eh."

Meanwhile the Tatra was on its way back to Talawana with Dicko at the wheel as it was starting to get dark. Dicko knew he would be driving for at least thirty minutes in darkness. A number of kangaroos jumped across the track then several goats. Dicko was oblivious to the fact that Andrew had left the bore system flowing. During the night, the entire Percival Lake system would be completely flooded to a depth of five millimetres and the next day was going to be a stinker – forty six degrees in the shade. That night Andrew checked the weather system patterns at the Bureau of Meteorology's website, where interactive prognostic weather maps were detailed for the next week. He was also able to check recent weather maps for the last week and could see why the rather modest amount of precipitation caused by his inadvertent flooding of Lake McDonald had caused the rain at Uluru then Bourke. The low pressure trough off the coast between Karratha and Exmouth with its clockwise airflow had been deflected toward inland Australia by a high pressure system in the Great Australian Bight. Another high pressure system off the coast of Queensland had caused southerly winds from the Gulf of Carpentaria toward southern Australia. With the detailed prognostic charts Andrew was now confident that he could keep an eye out for favourable conditions and he was determined to flick the switch, for something had to be done.

The following day Jack would drive back to Newman to collect the boys and the new bore caps that Andrew had ordered to replace the faulty bore caps.

"Gidday Bruce, how's it going?"

"Good Jack but I believe you've had a bit of drama out your way."

"Yeah but we are working on something positive and my new man Andrew is getting on with quite some action. I've got those two faulty bore caps in the back of the ute so I'll bring them in."

"I'll get the boys to carry your new caps out and they can bring the other ones in. Guys can you take Jack's bore caps out please and bring in the other two. So ... ah ... what kind of action?"

"Well I'm back in town already to pick up Jimmy and young Travis who went out with Dicko White to Percival Lakes a couple of days ago."

"Oh yeah ... what for?"

"We've sunk a dozen bores out there Bruce. Andrew reckons he might flood those bloody big lakes to end the drought over east."

"Strewth! Noble ambition Jack but that's Crown land - he'll get his arse kicked. I mean, I hope he does succeed but

I wouldn't like to be in his shoes when the truth comes down."

"Well it was actually my idea to start with cos I suggested he leave the bore running on Lake McDonald for a while but geeze, he's picked it up and is racing with it already. I've never seen a bloke move so fast. It's less than four days ago he first spoke to Dicko, now they are on their way back already, got all twelve bores done in just two days."

"Yeah Dicko doesn't stuff around does he. He took a shitload of stuff from here out to Tanami the week before last. Good thing he bought that bloody huge truck – that thing would cross the Sahara Desert."

"It's an impressive piece of machinery alright. Andrew told me that he gave Jimmy and Travis a drive for about an hour each. Gave them some instruction then got them to assist on sinking the bores too. They were able to stay at Talawana last night on the way back."

"Good old Dicko eh!"

"Yeah so they should be back in town soon. Might give them a counter meal at the Purple before we head back. Gonna be close to nightfall when we reach the homestead."

"So ... ah ... when do you guys plan to flood the lake?"

"I will have to leave that up to Andrew. He's completed a PhD in hydrogeology so he's pretty cluey. Of course, the pollies are on the trail now so hopefully it gets the green light and we'll see what happens. Dicko suggested that if this goes well, we might have to get the government to flood Carnegie and Wells ... oh ... and Burnside."

"That's a bloody big area Jack – bigger than Texas as they say."

"Yeah but Bruce, just imagine if we can turn this on at the right time and prevent drought in the east from ever occurring again. What would that be worth to the country – billions Bruce."

"Yeah you're right about that. Good luck with it all!"

Just then the Tatra arrived back in the carpark outside the Newman Hardware.

"Your boys are here now, so we'll catch you next time Jack."

"Thanks Bruce - see you later."

Jack went out to greet the boys.

"Gidday boys, how did it go?"

"Yeah good boss we drove the truck."

"And we sank some bores too."

"Dicko - well done mate!"

The men shook hands.

"No worries Jack the boys did really well. We got the job completed on time and we actually watched the water flow from bore twelve up the top end and from bore one on the way back. Now it's a case of wait and see. I hope your man Andrew can work out when to flick that switch."

"Yeah I reckon he'll be onto it. Okay boys we'll go for a quick lunch at the Purple then head back okay."

"Catch you later Dicko, thanks again mate."

"See you Jack."

Jack and the boys headed back after lunch on the four hour trip to the homestead. All concerned were still oblivious to the water already pouring onto the Percival Lakes system, which had been flowing all through the previous night and right through this day. Nobody would realise until the next morning when Jack got a chance to speak with Andrew.

"Morning Jack, welcome back, I trust the boys are okay."

"Yeah better let them sleep until they wake naturally Andrew – that trip would have taken quite a bit out of them. They were telling me all about it on the way back, how they drove the Tatra, set up the bores, watched as you turned the water on ..."

"Holy shit!"

Andrew started running toward the house. Jack yelled out.

"What's the matter?"

"Not sure I turned the bloody thing off."

He hadn't! Andrew looked at the satellite control unit and to his immediate horror saw "system running". He immediately switched it off but started to ponder what might be the situation out at the lakes. Jack wasn't far behind Andrew. He didn't need to ask. The look on Andrew's face told the story.

"So you left it running by mistake Andrew."

"Yep, sure did. All this time. Right through two nights and an entire day."

"Good chance the lakes will be partially flooded then Andrew."

"Yeah – how much bigger are those lakes than Lake McDonald Jack?"

Jack, laughed. "Oh only about one hundred times bigger Andrew, but let's see, two bores at McDonald, twelve at Percival, six times as many bores running for three times longer. According to my arithmetic what you've done would only just cover those lakes with about one mill of water. Of course it would have been evaporating all day today and will do the same tomorrow, so you won't know the outcome for at least a day or two."

"Hmm ... I wonder what kind of outcome that will bring about Jack."

Thar she blows!

It was a bright and sunny day in Adelaide – in the morning! Being the first week of December it was all happening at the Adelaide Oval – the fifth day of the Ashes Test match between Australia and England. There would definitely be a result in the game, as Australia had been bundled out in its second innings for just two hundred runs, after trailing on the first innings by forty runs. Now with England comfortably situated at two for eighty seven at lunch and needing just another seventy four runs for victory with eight wickets in hand, the English side were in a commanding position.

Not a good number that – eighty seven!

Adelaide Oval was packed to the rafters with an ambience of expectation for an English victory. The television audience, too, both in Australia and in England was at its peak – for England had lost the Ashes in Australia in 2017 and this home series gave Australia a real chance of retaining the tiny urn. Now, in Adelaide the weather is relatively predictable. It is not like Melbourne which gets all four seasons in one day. An old adage is that Adelaide gets Perth's weather - after we here in Perth have taken the best parts of course – and the weather in Perth had been fine for several days. The forecast for Adelaide was, earlier in the day, for fine weather for the next five days. The English commentators were in fine form.

"If Bairstow and Jennings can add even just another twenty or thirty I dare say that England will win this test match and go one up in the series and they will be very difficult to overhaul from there."

"Yes, Joe Root and Ben Stokes are certainly in fine form too having both scored half centuries in the first innings and centuries in the lead up match against Victoria, so I would expect them to take England very close toward victory even if a wicket or two does fall."

"And they now have two complete sessions in which to score the runs, so we will definitely see a result here today – hopefully in England's favour."

"We should all be enjoying an ale at the Sheraton well before dinner tonight Alastair."

"Yes, I'd say so Tristan – just one for you but a few for me!"

"I say there are some clouds moving in from the north – there was no prediction of rain here today – correct?"

"Oh absolutely correct Alastair, it can't possibly rain here today – I checked all of the weather information this morning."

"So Jonny Bairstow and Keaton Jennings are now walking onto the ground preparing to take England to victory here over Australia with Joe Root and Ben Stokes padded up in the dressing room should they be needed, after the English opener Rory Burns and the nightwatchman Ben Foakes were dismissed in the morning session. But one would fully expect the English cricketers to clean up this seventy four runs before the tea interval. And now we are joined by Ian Chappell for his commentary in this what should be the final session Ian."

"You would expect so Alastair - I cannot conceive of any way that Australia can take these last eight wickets for less than seventy four runs but I have just entered the grandstand from the practise area and I have got to tell you that those clouds coming in from the north are getting somewhat darker by the minute. I wouldn't be prepared to call them rain clouds at the moment considering the weather forecast was for fine and sunny conditions all day, but, geeze I have seen some strange things happen in Melbourne over the years and this is starting to look ominously like a Melbourne day to me."

"But surely the weather bureau could not possibly get the forecast so horribly wrong Ian. That just does not happen here in Australia."

Just then play got underway after the luncheon interval and Mitchell Starc opened the bowling.

"Now for the first ball after lunch and Starc bowls to Bairstow who lets one go outside the off stump and it goes through to the keeper."

"Normally Jonny Bairstow might have tried to cut that wide ball through the gully for four but, let's face it, they have plenty of time up their sleeve so there's absolutely no need for our boys to take any risks whatsoever."

"Why have they just turned the lights on?"

"Well the light has faded a little but not to the point where we would need lights, surely!"

"But why is the light fading?"

Just then there was a knock on the door of the commentary box. It was Bill Lawry putting his head in to draw the commentators' attention to something.

"Ah ... excuse me fellas but we've just received an updated weather report and there is a bit of a weather system heading towards Adelaide coming in from the north."

"What kind of a weather system?"

"Seems to be electrical!"

"Lightning? You have got to kidding us - there is no rain this side of Hadrian's Wall."

"No but there is this side of the black stump and it's heading this way."

"Where is it coming from?"

"Back of Bourke!"

"Where's Bourke?"

"Never mind that – they've turned the lights on because if any rain does fall here it could be several minutes away and the lights do take that long to crank up. Just thought I would let you all know."

Mitchell Starc completed his over and Josh Hazlewood took the ball to commence the next over. His first delivery was clipped down the leg side for four runs. As everybody was watching the ball race toward the boundary to the west, a minor flash of lightning occurred to the north.

"Was that lightning?"

"I'd say so – looks like Bill might have been right. Hopefully it doesn't come down this far."

But almost as Ian Chappell spoke a bolt of fork lightning struck near the clock tower at the Elizabeth City Shopping Centre, about twenty five kilometres to the north. Bill Lawry came back in.

"The weather bureau has just informed us that it received a report from Clare that it started pelting down there about twenty minutes ago."

"Clare who?"

"The town of Clare north of Adelaide. It started as a bit of a sprinkle but it was really heavy within half an hour. Looks like we could be drenched in the next hour or so."

"I don't believe it – how can this possibly happen? England is going to be robbed of a victory here today."

"No, the weather doesn't rob anybody Tristan – it's what we call the rub of the green here in Oz."

"Yes, thank you Ian, I will have to remember that for next time."

"Well the rain hasn't got here yet and perhaps it won't ..."

Another flash of lightning, this time brighter and evidently closer – the players started running from the ground.

"Now the umpires have removed the bails and the players are leaving the ground."

"Well it certainly looks as though the players have seen something that we can't see ..."

Then there was an enormous clap of thunder.

"Ah ... that was only about a ten second delay so that lightning was only about two miles away."

"You mean three kilometres!"

"Whatever! This weather is totally unexpected and we are now in peril of this match being delayed or even washed out as now the ground staff are preparing to cover the wicket area."

The ground staff were racing onto the oval with their tractor and trolleys with canvas covers to protect the pitch. No sooner had they covered the pitch, when down it came.

"This is a totally unexpected downpour we have here at the moment having been informed earlier in the day that we would have fine weather, so hopefully the bureau can explain where this has come from, but for now it's fair to say we won't see any play here for a while. Let's hope we can still get a result to this match."

Bill came back into the room. He had been outside calling the weather bureau.

"Sorry boys the bureau's latest update is for rain continuing for the rest of the day and into the evening. She's going to be washed out for sure and certain."

Needless to say the Bureau of Meteorology in Canberra was onto this to provide an explanation of what had caused such an extraordinary event. The precipitation had reached a high altitude but condensed as it reached the cooler areas north of Adelaide, with the elevation of the Flinders Ranges coming into play.

"What the heck is that?"

"A lake system in the west again – just like last week, only this time more expansive and further to the north."

"What the heck is going on over there? They've just washed out the Ashes Test match. Call the B.O.M. in Perth, see what they have to say."

"Bureau of Meteorology Perth office Glenda Cork speaking, how may I help you?"

"Good afternoon Glenda its Barbara Temple from Canberra calling, are you people up to speed with what has just happened in Adelaide?"

"Yes of course, the source of the precipitation is the Percival Lakes system which is approximately two hundred kilometres north-east of Newman in the east Pilbara. We suspect that some of the same people who caused last week's downpour are somehow involved in this again, so we have referred the matter to the Department of Water and Environmental Regulation which is going to investigate. The DWER was prompt to issue warnings to the station owner involved in that saga last week. So I wouldn't want to be in his shoes when Jane Wyatt telephones him."

"Okay can you please c.c. us in on any email communications you have in relation to last week's event and today's too please. The South Australian government and Cricket Australia are asking questions already, though it seems this might have saved the Aussie team's arse on this occasion. We might have the King of England on the phone next."

"Now wouldn't that be something! By the way the Western Australian Minister for the Environment has received calls from fellow Ministers in the east who want an enquiry into the viability of using the salt lakes in our state to influence the weather over there, so he has requested the EPA make a report. I suppose what has happened today will also be referred to, even though it did come down on the Adelaide Oval at the wrong time."

"Okay please keep us in the loop on all developments Barbara thank you."

By now the post-match interviews with respective captains are taking place at the Adelaide Oval.

"Pat Cummins, a very lucky escape for Australia in the first Test match."

"You can say that again Ian, we were cooked until that storm broke out but even during the lunch break the weather forecast was for a bright and sunny afternoon, so we were expecting to go one down here today."

"Yes Pat, I would say that you definitely would have gone one down, now for your information that weather system has taken everybody by surprise, even the weather forecasters at the B.O.M. so it seems to be an act of God really."

"Well praise the Lord Ian, we'll move on to Perth next week then to the MCG for the Boxing Day test."

"And what will you change if anything for the Perth test, just the two hundred out there yesterday, not good enough really is it from the batsmen?"

"No it's not good enough so we will give consideration to the young bloke from Queensland who has been knocking on the door for the number five or six position. He seems to have a bulletproof technique and Steve Smith becomes available too which will be a welcome return for him."

"Pat Cummins, thank you for your time."

"And now Jonny Bairstow is getting himself into position here, so this will be interesting to say the least, the Englishmen will be feeling totally robbed of a victory here today even though it was inclement weather that has brought this down. Jonny thank you for joining us, what an absolutely extraordinary change in the weather, you must be feeling this one got away, but we don't yet know how."

"Well what can I say Ian, I have never seen anything like it, even just ten minutes earlier the sky was looking reasonable with just some cloud in the distance and then that came over in a hurry and then down she came. Is there a problem with the weather forecasting here in Adelaide?"

"No and the forecasters are actually in Canberra and are among the world's best but something similar happened last week in Bourke in New South Wales. So sudden changes in the weather can occur in the Australian summer and we actually did receive a call about fifteen minutes before it hit so they were onto it. It does seem that the Flinders Ranges north of Adelaide may have been the precipitating factor."

"Well I hope this doesn't happen in Perth next week, my boys are feeling totally perplexed and dejected by this, but I told them the weather is nobody's fault, so we will just move on."

"Well good luck in Perth Jonny, perhaps you can peg back this one that got away."

Jane Wyatt telephoned Andrew Robertson.

"Andrew Robertson good morning."

"Andrew this is Jane Wyatt calling. I am just wondering if you people there have anything to do with an anomalous weather event that is rather similar to what happened last week, that has just washed out the Ashes Test match at the Adelaide Oval."

There was a brief period of silence.

"Ah ... Jane thank you for calling, I can explain what has happened yes ... ah ...it wasn't supposed to happen this way ..."

"Sounds to me already like you are involved Andrew."

"Well yes, you see the other night after we installed some bores and the remote system was activated so that we could test it, I was distracted and ... ah ... my man left the area thinking that I would definitely turn the system off, but I as I say I was distracted and as the whole thing is very new to me and I overlooked it and ... ah ... it ran water onto the lakes for about forty hours, so the lake was flooded, yes."

"So you installed bores at the Percival Lakes within three days of my previous telephone call Mr. Robertson. May I ask how many bores you installed and why."

"Ah ... twelve, twelve bores Ms. Wyatt."

"Twelve bloody bores! Why?"

"Because ... somebody has to do something."

"About what?"

"About the terrible situation in the eastern states where farmers are losing their cattle, their sheep, their farms, their crops and their livelihood Ms. Wyatt – that is why."

"So you took it upon yourself without any environmental impact research to sink twelve bores then you left it running overnight, all the next day, then all of the next night until when, may I ask."

"Until this morning actually, I didn't realise what I had done until my man arrived back here and mentioned it. Ms. Wyatt the plan was to carefully monitor the prognostic charts available through the B.O.M. website and to wait for favourable conditions before activating the system. I just failed due to my lack of attention this first time."

"I dare say this could be the last time Mr. Robertson. Now the DWER is probably going to levy a substantial fine on you and you are not to activate that system without approval from the state government, do you understand?"

"Well yes, of course I will abide by your instruction, but I will make a formal submission to the federal government advocating that this system be given the chance it needs to prove itself. We believe quite fervently in this here, I mean, even looking at what occurred today, it was not the right place nor the right time Ms. Wyatt but, shit it worked! If we can direct that rainfall to the east where they need it, we can save many lives from destruction."

"That may be so but I am manager of the Environmental Services Division of the Department of Water and Environmental Regulation and we don't do this type of thing willy-nilly so you send your submission to the feds but until they get involved you need to comply with my instruction – do not turn it on again. What you don't seem to understand in this Mr. Robertson is that we cannot allow people to draw copious amounts of water from the water table without consideration of environmental impact. It is not an infinite resource and is something that all pastoralists, like yourself, rely upon to maintain their cattle stocks, so that is something for me to consider."

"I understand yes, but if you don't mind me saying so, I did read a report in the press recently where one of the major miners in this area – I believe it was Christmas Creek – announced that the reserves of underground water are far more extensive than was previously believed."

"I am aware of that yes, even so that has not been fully assessed. Now I am going to report to the state Minister for the Environment so there will be a lot of discussion taking place today so whatever you do send to the feds send me a copy please, if you don't mind."

"Yes I will do thank you Ms. Wyatt."

She was right! Now the Federal Minister for the Environment and Water Terri Butler was getting involved. She had been watching the cricket when it happened and was aware of the similar occurrence the previous week.

"Prime Minister's Office good afternoon, Barbara Wilkinson speaking."

"Oh good afternoon it's Terri Butler the Minister for Environment and Water, can I speak to Anthony please if he is available."

"Yes, of course Minister. Prime Minister I have Ms Terri Butler on the telephone for you."

"Yes put her through please Barbara. Hello Terri, how are you today?"

"I'm fine Anthony but the English cricket team isn't. Have you seen what happened there today?"

"Ah ... too busy to watch but I did hear something, why?"

"Well the B.O.M. has informed me that those boys in the west have done it again, only this time it has dumped on Adelaide during the cricket. I am still awaiting info from my counterpart in the state government but, Anthony, this is the second time in a week that unexpected rainfall has occurred because of the lake systems in the west. It's a shame that this lot didn't happen last week because it was far more substantial but it's only a matter of time before the conditions will be favourable again. Imagine if we can end the drought Anthony, there'll be massive votes in it for sure."

"Hmm ... you're not wrong about that Terri, providing it is seen as coming from federal and state Labor governments."

"The next state election in W.A. is only twelve months away Anthony but to get this up legally we are going to have to introduce legislation into Parliament a.s.a.p."

"And if we proceed without an accord some cretin will sue for damages."

"Probably, but we should just wear it – they will make themselves so very unpopular if they do and we succeed with this. The short cut would be to call the state Ministers together for a conference – you know, show some unilateral unity on this and a written accord prior to legislation. Just call it a trial."

"Hmm ... okay I will call a Caucus meeting for tomorrow morning, say eleven o'clock, that might give the Attorney General some time to consider the validity of an accord. I think they did something like that years ago for the Snowy

Mountains Scheme. Was way before my time though, yours too Terri."

"Okay see you tomorrow morning Anthony."

Having torn a strip off Andrew Robertson and laying down the law to him Ms. Wyatt telephoned her Minister to put him in the loop. She had aspirations to enter politics herself at the next state election and become the Minister for the Environment, but not through the Labor Party.

"Good morning Minister for the Environment's Office."

"Yes good morning this is Jane Wyatt may I speak to Steven please."

"Putting you through. Minister I have Jane Wyatt on the telephone."

"Good morning Jane, now I wonder why you would be calling – not."

"Morning Steven, yes I don't believe what that guy Robertson has done up there this time, you know he sank twelve bores around the Percival Lakes then inadvertently left the bloody thing running for best part of two days and washed out the cricket."

"Yes it's the talk of the town here – revenge for what happened over there in England some time ago."

"What happened over there?"

"The glucose fiasco – they won the Ashes with it."

"Oh, I don't know anything about that I'm afraid, but I do know that he has pumped a shitload of water from the water table and it has dumped on Adelaide."

"So when did he set this up? He didn't mention it to you last week."

"No apparently he has gone from go to whoa in just four days ..."

"Four days! Maybe we need this guy."

"Not funny Steven, we can't have people doing this kind of shit you know that. I have informed him that he will be fined for this and I suggest we throw the book at the guy."

"So you did say inadvertently Jane, how could this be inadvertent?"

"He stated that he was testing the remote system while his men were there to observe but as they were leaving he was distracted and he overlooked turning it off, so the water flowed right through the night, all through the entire next day and all of the next night until about seven in the morning when his man had returned and he realised then that he had not turned the system off. That's how! So the evaporation went right through two complete days Steven."

"So if the rain that was dumped on the cricket was from the first day of evaporation, where is the second lot?"

"There was just one complete day of evaporation in between the two nights."

"No, the water that poured onto the lake through the second night would be on the salt pan for the next day Jane - and evaporating. That's today!"

"Holy shit you are right ... um ... I had better get back to the B.O.M. to see if they can track it."

Too late! There had been a change in the weather and a vast change in the Australian political system. This was now a time for action, as exemplified by one Mr. Andrew Robertson – a bloody American! And the Australian Labor Party would follow suite.

Meanwhile, back at the ranch, Jack had come to the main house to check on Andrew. Rebecca greeted Jack.

"Come in Jack, Andrew is in the front office."

"Jack – I left it running, right through two nights and one day. Flooded the bloody lakes and caused the downpour at the cricket. Washed out the game. The DWER has called already and I will be fined, quite substantially too I might add, but I was always prepared to wear that Jack, so let it be."

"Andrew, I feel for you mate but geeze, I take my hat off to you for what you've done and ... ah ... you just never know Andrew, your blooper just might be the one single thing that snitches this for us."

"How so Jack?"

"Well you washed out the cricket in Adelaide, so a lot of people are going to take notice, aren't they?"

"Yeah, well, they are already but it's not all good. I have been castigated by the DWER for sinking those bores without approval. Apart from that she has instructed me to leave the system off while they look into everything. Said that the ground water supply is finite and all cattle stations need it, which they do of course."

"So the DWER has cautioned against drawing water from the water table. You might want to talk to Rio and Roy Hill about the possibility of running a pipeline from the Hamersley Agricultural Project near Marandoo, down their access roads to Roy Hill then pipe it in from there. They have an access road that goes all the way along the rail line to Port Hedland. You could put it to them that it wouldn't do any harm to run a pipeline outside the road – at least that way your teams would have road access to the route.

"Another option if you can't access Hamersley Ag water would be to bring water in from the ocean. There's no shortage of water there. If the state comes on board with this the best solution would be to run a pipeline from Hedland down the Nullagine Road through Marble Bar to Nullagine then inland from there. That way the Percival Lakes could be flooded at any time without having to draw on the aquifer."

"It's saltwater!"

"It won't be saltwater when it evaporates."

"No of course not but what I mean is, you would be putting additional residual salt onto the lakes."

"Well they are totally bloody salty already Andrew – who's going to give a shit if a bit more salt goes on top?"

"The Department of Water and Environmental Regulation!"

"Yeah - and the Peoples' Front of Judea! Now bear in mind, when the system is turned on and we flood all those lakes and that causes considerable precipitation in the east and that ends the drought and saves everybody's life, we turn the system off so there will not be a constant flow of salt water onto those lakes Andrew. It will be a very temporary thing so the amount of salt dispersed onto our salt lakes with any activation will be minimal. Like I said before, a lot of people are going to be making enquiries about this, so don't worry too much about the DWER. The pollies from the east will take care of that. When they do contact you, it would be best to have that idea up your sleeve Andrew – a pipeline from Port Hedland. That will make them wonder about the possibilities."

Jack was an old timer but he certainly had some political nous.

"Now we need to get out there sometime and fit those two bore caps Andrew. I reckon I could do that today if you want me to – just spend the one night out there and be back tomorrow."

"What's the time now, eight fifteen, hmm ... if we leave within the hour, arrive mid-afternoon, complete the job by dusk and just the one night out, yeah okay but I will go with you. I don't like the idea of workers being out there alone, you know. Narelle has some take-away dishes in the fridge so if you get the ute ready with the dogs too, we'll be on our way by nine."

228

Jack went into action. Andrew organised some food for their evening dinner and morning breakfast and packed his swag. By nine o'clock they were ready to go. Rebecca came out to see them off.

"Now you boys be careful out there. See you tomorrow love."

Jack and Andrew spent the rest of the day travelling back to Lake McDonald and fitted the two bore caps that afternoon. They managed to get back to the first bore before dark and settled there for the night. There wasn't much left of old mate Rambo but as the dingoes and pigs were still hanging around Jack decided that they would camp a few kilometres to the north, as Jack didn't want to risk his dogs being in a fight with wild dogs. They set up their camp for the night.

"I wonder if our other friend will return to visit us tonight Jack."

"Old mate yowie – no chance Andrew. I think he has served his purpose."

"How's that Jack?"

"Well, what you've been doing over the last few days. I'd say he had you pegged mate. He probably even knew what you were going to do – and that is why he came to see you."

Sheep, cattle and crops!

It was bright and sunny day in Cunnamulla and Charleville, Queensland. The weather forecast was for fine weather for at least a week or more for these two towns in semi-arid outback of Bourke and the black stump. Nobody was expecting any rain and their sheep and cattle were perishing at an alarming rate. The provision of hay from other parts of the nation could not keep pace with all that was required. Much hay had been trucked into New South Wales and Queensland. Even when rain does happen, everybody knows that it will take several days for any feed to come through. They were just as cognizant, however, that if rain did happen, they could outlay more on temporary hay feed until the ground feed was established.

The temperature this day was a mild thirty nine degrees at two in the afternoon.

"Looks like a bit of cloud on the horizon Jamie. Be over the Grey Range I'd say."

"Yeah bro hope it comes this way – cool the place down a bit."

Jamie and bro went about their job for the next half hour repairing a fence line that had been damaged by desperate kangaroos seeking water and feed.

"Them clouds are gettin' closer Jamie."

"Yeah bro looks to be coming this way eh. That's good."

Jamie and bro went about their work for the next hour.

"Hey that cloud cover is nearly half-way here. Shit did you see that?"

"Yeah bro we had better take cover from that – I don't want to be hit by lightning."

"We still got time Jamie - that's at least an hour away. Better call the boss though and put him in the loop. He's been waiting for something like this."

"What do you guys want now?"

"Hey boss there's a shitload of rain coming this way. We just saw some lightning and the clouds are really getting dark out to the west."

"Bullshit! The forecasts are for hot and dry weather for the next week."

"Well I'm telling ya, we are gonna be out of here in about half an hour cos she's gonna piss down mate."

"I hope this is not some kind of a joke."

"Hey man, you're doing it tough, we don't joke about things like this. I'll shoot you a pic okay."

Bro took a pic and sent it.

"Ethel can you crank up the internet and check the weather forecast love, the boys reckon we've got rain on the way."

"Rain? Don't bloody think so."

Ethel cranked up the B.O.M. prognostic view.

"Hey where has that come from? It's red over the Grey Range Roger."

"You mean what the boys said is for real?"

"Bloody oath! Good Lord how has that happened?"

"Could be the same shit that hit the cricket yesterday love. They certainly weren't expecting that."

There was now no need for Steven Dolsen and Jane Wyatt to wonder any longer where the precipitation from this second day was heading – for the outback areas of Queensland - and one Anna Pellizzari would take a very keen interest in this substantial reprieve that some of her graziers were about to receive.

"Excuse me Ms. Premier, we have reports of violent thunderstorms out back of Cunnamulla and it seems the storms are widespread and heading toward the pastoral areas."

"True? I thought we were destined for hot, dry weather out there for the next week."

"We were, yes, but that has all changed. The weather bureau is issuing storm alerts now for Brisbane."

"This is crazy – the weather is changing all over the place. The cricket got washed out now this. Well I hope this does come about as you said Linda, God knows we need some rain out there. Could you please call Leeanne and Mark into my office, we need to talk."

The Premier's personal assistant Linda Olney called the respective Ministers for Environment and Agriculture to the Premier's office. They would want to keep a keen eye on developments here. The Premier made some phone calls to the respective shires – Paroo and Murweh.

"I will just call Barbara Kelly at Charleville to get the picture there."

"Murweh Shire good afternoon Linda Bresland speaking."

"Good afternoon this is Anna hoping to speak with Barbara please."

"I am sorry Ms. Premier Barbara is outside the office and I think she might be dancing in the rain with the rest of the town."

"Well that is good news, how is it going, when did it start?"

"Been going non-stop for about half an hour, I will let Barb know that you called."

"Thank you, Linda!"

"Paroo Shire George Tills speaking."

"Hello George, it's Anna, how's it going over there?"

"Ah, yes Ms. Pellizzari it started raining here about an hour ago and it hasn't stopped – if anything it might actually be getting heavier. We had some substantial lightning strikes too by the way."

"And George can you tell which way the storms are heading?"

"Oh I'd say they are definitely heading to the east – you people are likely to cop it in a few hours' time. Our man has just gone out to check the gauge, here he is now."

"Fifteen!"

"Fifteen millimetres of rain this last hour and we were expecting zilch Ms. Premier. I hope we do receive a lot more because this area needs at least one hundred mills of rain to drag it out of the drought as you know."

"Yes and we do believe we know why this is happening so we will try to do something substantial about it, thank you George and can you please keep my office informed about the level of rainfall throughout the rest of today."

"I will call your office before I choof off at six."

"Thank you, George."

"Well fifteen mills at Paroo already, that looks promising. Thank God this is happening now. It is strange isn't it how they have their floods out there about every ten years or so and then they can have three or four years of drought."

"Yes, the floods only occur when there's a cyclone though and, in that respect, there's nothing on the horizon at the moment."

Linda Olney knocked on the door and put her head in.

"I thought you might like to know that Blackall has received ten millimetres and Longreach and Jericho five already."

"Maybe we should thank whoever is responsible – the word is that somebody in the west stuffed up and is causing it to rain over here."

"Yes, Chris telephoned me yesterday to garner support before her Minister was going to take this up with the

Minister in the west. I'd say it's time to be onto Terri Butler and get the feds involved in this now. Thankfully we've had a change of government. Terri seems to be the proactive type. Leeanne could you please call Terri and impress upon her that our pastoralists need at least another one hundred mills of rain and whatever has happened over there in the west needs to be extended somehow. Mark you could do the same, contact the Minister for Agriculture over west and have a chat to him, let him know what has happened here but that we need more of it. I am going to call Anthony Albury so let's all meet back here in say, thirty."

"Prime Minister's Office, good afternoon, Barbara Wilkinson speaking."

"Good afternoon Barbara it's Anna Pellizzari calling to speak to Anthony please."

"Yes I will put you through. It's the Queensland Premier Anthony."

"Anna, good afternoon, now I wonder why you are calling."

"Hello Anthony, well actually you probably haven't heard yet but we are receiving substantial falls of rain here in outback Queensland and it has just started about an hour ago."

"Really? Holy shit!"

"Yes I spoke to our shire president at Paroo and they have received fifteen millimetres in just one hour and at Murweh the president was outside dancing in the rain. Apparently, the rain has reached as far north as Longreach. Now Anthony there's no official prognosis yet from the B.O.M. but we do believe that these anomalous weather conditions are all emanating from the same place in the west, so we really need to do something about this."

"Yes, my Minister has had a chat to me already and I believe she will contact the Minister for Environment in

W.A. and she is also seeking legal advice regarding an accord but, tell you what I will do, I will call Roger Brook right now."

"That's the spirit Anthony - those people in the west are being bombarded a little but that's what we need to do. Please get on to them."

"Okay leave it with me and I will call you back."

"Premier's Office, good afternoon, Kerry Hunter speaking."

"Good afternoon Kerry this is Anthony Albury calling to speak with Mark please."

"Prime Minister, good afternoon, I will put you through."

"Good afternoon Anthony."

"Afternoon Roger! Roger I've had a call just a moment ago from Anna and believe it or not they are presently receiving some quite substantial rainfall in drought-affected outback Queensland, against all weather forecasts, which seems to be in line with what occurred yesterday in Adelaide."

"Yes my man Steven Dolsen has received a call or two also, including one from the Chairperson of the EPA here who has recommended no further flooding of lakes until they conduct the appropriate environmental impact assessment, which is the usual line the EPA will take of course."

"Understood Roger - your EPA Chairperson is probably duty bound to take that approach but in view of what is happening I believe we just might need to bypass convention with this and just get some more rain out there to the farmers. It's worth a lot of money to them and to us with the cost of drought relief and foregone taxes and also to our people in the street who are paying higher prices for beef and lamb."

"Yes I do appreciate that Anthony and I think my man Steven Dolsen is just going to have to circumvent the EPA recommendation on this. It is just far too critical to be stuffing around with environmental studies that might take six weeks to complete."

"And just on that point, it might take as long to enact legislation over here but Terri Butler is consulting the Attorney General to see what legal option we might have access to, Roger. What we have in mind there is an accord between the states that will accommodate a short-term very temporary flooding of the lake system over there that caused this and only for the purpose of drought relief when the atmospheric conditions are right. By the way Roger, do you know who is responsible for this?"

"Steven briefed me this morning after his department contacted him, apparently the station owner who caused the rain at Uluru and Bourke last week wasted no time sinking a dozen bores further north at the Percival Lakes system and then, if you believe him, inadvertently left it running for nearly two days and completely flooded the Percival lakes."

"Percival lakes – I'll have to look that one up. I am familiar with Lake Disappointment of course but not heard of Percival Lakes."

"Well it's bloody huge Anthony, probably bigger than Disappointment ..."

"Bigger?"

"Yes but it is narrow compared to Disappointment and stretched out over a distance of more than three hundred kilometres so my guess is he might have made a rational, conscious decision."

"You mean he might have done this deliberately?"

"Well no doubt he set up the bores deliberately but whether he turned it on deliberately perhaps we will never know."

"Hmm ... might be time to get your Minister to phone him direct, bypass the department's heavies, Roger."

"Huh … she's after his job - she makes no bones about that."

"What's her name?"

"Jane Wyatt!"

"I've heard that name before. Is she one of ours?"

"Nope!"

"Oh well, definitely get him to bypass her – there's kudos in this for those who take action. That station man sounds interesting – just a suggestion but after your Steven has called him why don't you call him. Better still, get Bronwyn's helicopter and get up there."

"Ha-ha-ha! Good to know the job hasn't stifled your sense of satire Anthony."

"Well you could take a look first-hand at what that station owner has done. Now that will make it difficult for Ms. Wyatt to go against the flow. Perhaps take your Minister with you."

"Why don't you come over Anthony – now that will get the job done."

"Oh yes sure thing - and why don't I bring Anna and Chris over with me eh?"

"Sounds like a plan. Now that you've mentioned it Anthony, that would be a bloody good idea. Get all on board with a vested interest in this to actually fly to Percival Lakes in a show of unity. That would probably quell any dissension and make it very difficult for anybody to level objections – even the DWER."

"Has merit, but the chances of getting everybody to cooperate might be slim."

"Ask them Anthony – you're the man now. Tell them you want to fund ongoing drought relief that should sway them."

"Leave that with me Roger, I'll see what I can do. For now, perhaps have your Minister call the station owner direct and ascertain what he has done and how we would go about accessing the place if we were to take a first-hand look."

"Will do that Anthony."

"And we'll catch up for a beer while I am over there eh?"

"Look forward to that Anthony."

Roger telephoned Steven.

"Steven have you heard anything more from the EPA today?"

"No not since this morning."

"That's good, can you telephone that station owner and just sound him out as to what kind of access we could have to Percival Lakes where he sank those bores. I just might have Anthony Albury onside for a visit to the area with Anna and yourself."

"Hmm ... sounds like a plan! I do have his details here from the email that Jane Wyatt sent to me this morning. She has given him an instruction not to turn the system on again and informed him that he will be fined. His name is ... Andrew Robertson of Jennifer Downs."

"Jennifer Downs? That was old man Piper's property, old William the American owner. I met William Piper in Newman a few years ago. I wonder if this Andrew character is related, Steven."

"Don't know Roger, I will try to find out. So the plan would be to fly to Karratha and take a charter flight from there eh? Newman would be the nearest airport, but it would be a few hours from Newman by dirt road."

"Unless we can land on the lake – find out please. That way nobody is going to be too concerned about the time taken. The ladies from the east could fly direct to Karratha, walk on the lake, pose for the snaps, then fly back east the same day."

"Good thinking, Roger. I will get back to you."

Steven Dolsen telephoned Andrew Robertson.

"Good morning, Jennifer Downs station, Rebecca Robertson speaking."

"Good afternoon Ms. Robertson."

"Oh yes it is, isn't it! Time goes so quickly up here when you're busy."

"I'm sure it does. My name is Steven Dolsen and I am the state government Minister for the Environment. How are you?"

"Was feeling better a moment ago – call me Rebecca and I suppose you want to speak to my Andrew."

"Nothing to worry about I can assure you and yes, that would be wonderful."

"He's just arrived home about an hour ago after spending the night out at Lake McDonald. Andrew! There's a Mr. Dolsen on the telephone for you, he's the Minister for the Environment."

Andrew's eyes rolled upwards.

"Good morning … er … afternoon Andrew Robertson speaking."

"Andrew good afternoon, Steven Dolsen calling, I am the Minister in the state government not the federal government. Now I believe that Jane Wyatt has been in touch and I am not trying to usurp her authority, she has a role to play, but I am looking at the bigger picture here, together with some colleagues okay."

"Ah huh!"

"Now you may not be aware of this yet but we have reason to believe that your twelve bores that you sank at Percival Lakes recently has caused a substantial downpour of rain in outback Queensland, specifically in drought-affected areas."

"Really! No I wasn't aware. When did this happen?"

"About two o'clock this afternoon their time so eleven in the morning here."

"Did they get much rain?"

"Yes, quite a lot and it is still raining over there as we speak. Fortuitously, it seems that the weather conditions were conducive to carrying the precipitation in that direction rather than to Adelaide. So you've got some top brass thinking about this and the Prime Minister Anthony Albury has suggested that some of us fly to Percival Lakes and check out what you have done, with a view to further consideration."

Andrew looked at Rebecca with a beaming smile across his face as he was already starting to feel much better after the threat of a massive fine.

"Fly to the lakes? Not sure if that can be done but worth a try."

"That will be up to the charter service – they will know if that is a goer and we will be contacting them soon. Hopefully our people will fly to Karratha then straight to the lake. You must have gone in by four-wheel drive Andrew."

"Eight-wheel drive actually, but I wasn't there, my man Jack went in with the contractor."

"Oh, by the way, are you there on behalf of William Piper?"

"No, my father James took this property over from old William so we are the owners now."

"Okay thank you for that, Premier Brook did know a little of William Piper so I will let Roger know. Now, a couple of things, if a contingent of politicians, state and federal fly to the lakes, what is your availability to be there with us, you know, for the usual photographs etc.?"

"Me! Ah ... well I can be available anytime, in fact from my station we would just take a four-wheel drive up the Canning Stock Route which goes straight to the Percival Lakes, so you just give the word and Jack and myself will be there. Might take Dicko White, the contractor, in as well."

"Okay now it is subject to the availability of the others, the Prime Minister, the Federal Minister for the Environment, the Premiers of Queensland and New South Wales too. I believe Jane Wyatt spoke to you this morning and has instructed you not to turn on the system and you have agreed. Is there anything else she mentioned of note?"

"Only that the ground water supplies are finite and everybody needs access Steven, which is why my man Jack here has suggested that we pipe in seawater from Port Hedland."

"From the ocean – that would cost a bloody fortune."

"No it won't – what will cost a bloody fortune is another year or two of drought. Do you have any idea what the total overall cost is to Australia of drought that wipes out the beef and sheep industries over there?"

"Yes of course I do!"

"And if you can guarantee those industries that this project will safeguard them from drought forever and a day, by simply turning on the tap at the right time, do you think they won't be prepared to cover the cost of building the pipeline? The federal government should fund it. Minister, I suggest you check Wikipedia and read up about the Snowy Mountain Scheme - and what people can achieve if the political will is there. I read up on that scheme when I undertook my PhD in the U.S. This proposal will cost virtually – as you Aussies would say – buggar all, by comparison."

"I am fully aware of the Snowy Mountain Scheme and its benefits to Australian agriculture."

"Yes that's good because on today's values the scheme would have costs several billions of dollars – and even then, that was by engaging about a hundred thousand migrants to do the job. This pipeline proposal from the ocean at Port Hedland will probably cost no more than fifty million. The

Percival Lakes system would only require a three-hundred-millimetre pipeline, which is equal to eight seventy-five mill pipes because you could run those for a lot longer than I did with my twelve bores. That water flow could be gravity fed all the way from somewhere nearer to the coast. You would simply have to pump it to a high point somewhere with a couple of wind turbines."

"Fifty million?"

"Well probably not even that much, unless you decided to run the pipeline further south to lakes Disappointment, Burnside, Carnegie and Wells – then you would need a bigger pipeline. According to my man Jack Lambert, you would run that pipeline down the road through Marble Bar and Nullagine then inland past Jigalong. I believe your state government funded the gas pipeline all the way from Dampier to Perth and it is returning a profit."

"Yes but we sell the gas – we are not going to sell rain to the east, but that is why we would fund this federally. Food for thought I suppose."

"Yes Minister and the DWER and the EPA wouldn't be concerned about the level of the water table if we utilise seawater."

"No that's right but what you are suggesting is a medium-term proposition – we will be seeking an accord with all state governments to turn on your bore system again in these next couple of weeks to try to end the drought. So we will discuss your proposal with the others while we are there. Now hopefully we can bring this off in the next couple of days, so my staff are making enquiries with the others and, by the way, what was your area of study for your thesis?"

"I completed my study in hydrogeology Steven. The topic of my thesis was fracking."

"Hmm ... bit of a topical issue here now too. Andrew, great to touch base with you, I see you have some good ideas and don't worry, there won't be any fine okay."

"That's great, thank you Steven, I will await your call."

"So what was that all about?"

"No fine and they want to meet us up at the lake – Percival."

"Who does?"

"Sounds like everybody, including the Prime Minister Anthony Albury. Rebecca, I forgot to switch off the bores and flooded the Percival Lakes causing substantial rainfall in outback Queensland. That is going to be all over the evening news in the east tonight. It's their first rain in months and it wasn't forecast so it looks like we might end the drought. Now the pollies want all the kudos to flow in and they are going to consider a permanent setup that can be turned on at the appropriate time, possibly using seawater as Jack suggested, but for now, they just might over-ride Ms. Wyatt and turn on my bore system again. Oh and – no fine for what we did. Seems the Minister would have to sign off on something like that."

"Wow Andrew that's fantastic but what on earth made you decide to leave it on?"

"I didn't actually – decide. I did that by mistake. Turned it on to test it while the boys were there and forgot to turn it off. I ... ah ... got slightly distracted by something."

"Ha-ha-ha! Hey they might reimburse you for your outlay."

"I doubt that very much – they would be thinking they have done me a big favour by waiving any potential fine. I wouldn't expect more than that."

"So what's the next step? I heard you say you could go there by four-wheel drive."

"Yes but I need to wait until they give the word. They are looking into a charter plane to fly in from Karratha but at a time when it suits everybody. Hopefully within the next couple of days."

Steven Dolsen's staff had made some enquiries.

"Oh Steven yes there's a twelve-seater plane available from Karratha and he can take it down onto a salt pan providing it is dry."

"A twelve-seater! Yes that will suffice, I expect there will only be nine of us including the media group, unless Chris comes along, she will make it ten. Room for Jane too then."

"Huh! And who are the extras?"

"Anthony, Roger, Terri, Anna, Chris, Anthony's adviser, one security, two media, myself and Jane Wyatt. Now Anthony Albury is the main man here because it's going to need federal funding, so whenever he is ready that is when we go – the others will just have to fall in. We are not going to be stuffed around with people pontificating about their availability. They either want to be in it or they don't! As soon as Anthony and Roger are both available, we go okay. They can all fly direct to Karratha at short notice, there are plenty of flights. I really don't care if they have to stay overnight."

"Anthony can do the day after tomorrow, Roger too - I have already sounded them out."

"Okay book that charter flight please Brenda and let Anthony and Roger know that it's on. Also let the others know that they need to be there or we go without them. And email Mr. Robertson - he will need to meet us at the lake."

"What time for the flight?"

"Better make it early afternoon – give them all a fair chance to get there. Some might have to fly into Karratha that morning. We'll only be gone from Karratha for about five hours so they could get a return flight home the same day. Make sure they know that – there are plenty of flights from Karratha to Perth."

"Okay I'm onto it."

Brenda called the Prime Minister's office and delegated calls to two others to contact the Federal Minister for the Environment and the two state Premiers Beresford and Pellizzari. Surprisingly, everybody indicated that they would be available and would arrive in Karratha early that morning. It seemed that everybody was going to be there.

Karratha

It was a bright and sunny day in Karratha – as usual! The Qantas jet arrived at the usual time and there were a number of dignitaries on board. These included the Prime Minister of Australia Mr. Anthony Albury, his Minister for the Environment and Water Ms. Terri Butler, the Premier of New South Wales Mr. Chris Minehan, the Premier of Queensland Ms. Anna Pellizzari, the Premier of Western Australia Mr. Roger Brook, the Western Australian Minister for the Environment Mr. Steven Dolsen, the Prime Minister's adviser, two media people, one security officer named Tana and Ms. Jane Wyatt.

"Hell's bells who do we have here? Are all you people really taking my flight to the Percival Lakes?"

"Sure are – and you are the pilot, right? Anthony Albury, pleased to meet you."

"Hello Anthony, I am Phillip Goodwin and yes I am the pilot."

"Phillip this is Chris, Anna, Terri, Jane, Barbara, Roger, Steven, my security man Tana and our media people Janice and Craig. We are ready to go when you are. Apparently, it is a two hour flight to the lake."

"One hour and fifty minutes from take-off to touchdown sir."

"Now we have arranged to meet some people at the southern end of Lake Auld so they will be there in a four-wheel drive and that is where we need to land. It's near the southern-most bore. What we intend to do is turn on the bore, shoot some film and head back okay, because we are all booked on flights out of Karratha this evening."

"Bit of a quickie eh Anthony!"

"Yes but it will serve its purpose believe me."

Everybody boarded the plane and the pilot got the plane airborne. Once they attained altitude Anthony stood to address his entourage.

"Firstly I want to thank all of you for taking the time to make this trip. I am a little surprised that we can all be here together at such short notice, though this is very important as we all know. Who knows whether this could be a major turning point in the history of our nation. The mind boggles to think of an Australia not affected by drought because it always seems to be there. Now just for your information, I got some facts together regarding the establishment of the Snowy Mountains Scheme just after the second world war. The Commonwealth had to resort to legislation under its defence powers to initiate the scheme and to introduce the Snowy Mountains Hydro-Electric Power Act that enabled the establishment of the Snowy Mountains Hydroelectric Authority. Importantly, agreement was not reached between the Commonwealth and the States for almost another ten years. You all know that the drought is a pressing problem now, so what I am going to propose is that the Commonwealth provide the government of Western Australia with specific grants funding so that it can proceed, should we all agree, with establishing an effective infrastructure for this concept, which does seem to have a positive effect. We have already seen just these last few days that the weather can be manipulated in positive ways, providing we go about this the right way. I wouldn't call the washing out of the cricket a positive but the rainfall in New South Wales then Queensland certainly is. So the interim advice we have from the Attorney General is that we may need to establish an authority, similar to the Snowy Mountains Hydroelectric Authority, that has representation from all states and the territories."

"Including Tasmania?"

"Yes, including Tasmania because no weather experts could possibly state, unequivocally, that the changes we will be implementing could not affect Tasmania. I dare say that at times that will happen but not in any substantial way."

"What about New Zealand?"

"Well we just might have to bowl them another grubber if they think this might affect them. It was only a one day match you know."

"Ha-ha-ha-ha-ha!"

Everybody laughed – apart from the security man, Tana, who maintained his stern look.

"But seriously whatever we do will not affect New Zealand, no. Milford Sound on the west coast of the South Island gets the highest annual rainfall of any place on the planet – about twelve metres of annual rainfall."

"So today is about all of us having a first-hand look at exactly what has happened here, so that we can make some sound judgements and decisions. We might need to run the existing system again to provide instant relief to the eastern states, providing the weather is favourable, but given the limitations of the ground water system as raised by the Department of Water and Environmental Regulation here in the west, we just might need to look at some other options too."

"Any idea what type of options?"

"Look, the miners up here do dig down below the water table and they do pump water out and use it to grow hay. Phillip is going to fly us over the Nammuldi Agricultural Project near Tom Price and the Marandoo mine, where they do exactly that so we can view those projects. So one option would be to negotiate with local miners regarding the possible availability of groundwater. Apparently, it costs a lot of money to grow the hay because they need quite a lot of fertiliser and trucking costs are also quite substantial. The other possibility will be to bring water in from the ocean at Port Hedland. Minister Steven Dolsen has spoken to the station owner about this and one idea is to extend a pipeline further south to some larger lakes Carnegie and Wells."

"And Disappointment. And Burnside."

"Thank you, Steven, yes of course. Furthermore, the State Treasurer and Minister for Aboriginal Affairs Ben Wyman has suggested that if we are going to pump seawater down the Nullagine Road to Jigalong then divert it inland from there to the Percival Lakes, we could consider providing the people of Jigalong an opportunity to utilise seawater for aquaculture industries. That could possibly be with some very large dams where they could grow sea plants firstly, then fish and perhaps even lobster. The training they could receive in aquaculture industries could be more important than whatever food they might derive from that concept. That might sound like a pie in the sky at the moment but let's all keep an open mind today to the range of possibilities. Aquaculture industries are gaining considerable momentum up here."

Ben Wyman had made a return to the State Parliament after an absence of four years to resume the role of Treasurer and Minister for Aboriginal Affairs following a By-election.

"Nammuldi! Out to the right of the plane. Now if you remain in your seats please, I will do a circle over the place."

Phillip took the plane down to four hundred metres and flew the loop. Everybody got a good look at the Nammuldi Agricultural Project. Then he gave a commentary about some of the major geographical features along the way.

"Each of those pivots is about eight hundred metres in diameter. The water is extracted from the mine which goes below the water table."

About ten minutes later.

"Below us now is Mount Bruce which was considered the highest peak in W.A. until 1967 when Mount Meharry was measured at fifteen metres higher. Fairly soon we will be flying over the Karijini National Park that most of you would have heard about. It's an amazingly beautiful place."

After another forty minutes Phillip informed Anthony that he would be flying in low from the northern end of Percival Lakes to give the team an understanding of just how large the lake is.

"Yes thank you for that Phillip I do appreciate that."

"Okay people this is the start of the Percival Lakes system approaching from the northern end and flying toward the south west and then due south toward Lake Auld."

"I believe I saw one of those bores Anthony. It has left some tell-tale sediment on the lake."

"Well that's understandable – good thing it's a big lake Jane."

"There's another!"

"Well spotted Jane!"

"Okay people I see your guests waiting in the distance – we'll take her down now, seatbelts please."

The plane landed safely and Andrew, Jack and Dicko were waiting there. Everybody introduced themselves.

"Hello Mr. Albury, I am Andrew Robertson and this is my station manager Jack Lambert and Mr. Dicko White my contractor."

"Pleased to meet you all, I really am, now here we have Terri, Chris, Anna, Barbara, Jane, Roger, Steven, my film crew Janice and Craig and our security man Tana Umaga. So this is where it has all happened eh? I see we have a bore over here."

"Yes Prime Minister ..."

"Call me Anthony please. That's a mean looking truck you've got over there – I suppose you brought the equipment in with that one."

"Yes Anthony, that is a Tatra 813 ex-military from Europe that belongs to Dicko here."

"How did you snaffle that Dicko?"

"Found it on eBay, Anthony."

"Yes it's a bit of a legend up here already the Tatra. Dicko goes where no man has been before. Now Anthony, all twelve of the bores are set up exactly this way with the rock base to protect from erosion. Of course, you do get a little bit of sediment in the initial flow but then that ceases. This solenoid operated valve can be activated with the remote from anywhere and that will start all twelve bores simultaneously, as I did the other day after they had all been installed. As you know I overlooked turning the system off and caused the rainfall in Queensland."

"Yes there was a fortunate change of wind direction. Okay so you are going to give us a demonstration now is that right?"

"Yes, so I login with my password ..."

"Which is?"

"Which is 'allblacks' then I push the 'on' button like so."

Andrew pushed the button, the valve gave a slight whirring noise then water splattered out down the pipe onto the rock bed and streamed onto the lake."

"Hmm ... well apart from the password Andrew that is quite impressive."

The security man spoke up for the first time.

"That's a good password cuz!"

"So what is the flow rate like Andrew."

"From this seventy-five-millimetre pipe, about one hundred litres per minute."

"There doesn't seem to be a pump involved."

"No, up here the natural pressure from the water table is adequate to force the water to the surface."

"So at this rate it would take quite some time to cover this lake Andrew."

"Yes - about one complete day and two nights actually."

His quip brought a chuckle from most, but not from Jane.

"Correct me if I am wrong but for this system to cover the lake it would need to be running for more than say, thirty to forty hours, so we would need to work on forecasts of favourable winds, more than the present weather situation."

"Yes and also because the evaporation process will take some time too. You might need a heads up about two days before you expect the favourable winds. I think I got lucky. But the forecasters can give fairly precise prognostics several days beforehand. The B.O.M. website clearly displays that Anthony."

"Yes they can, can't they – thankfully there is nothing dubious about their science. That water sure does run out there quite well though. That's covered a substantial area already. Now you boys have seemingly been discussing the possibility of piping in seawater from Port Hedland, so I must inform you that the federal government would establish an authority to administer this project if it is to proceed. You boys would either be involved through the authority or not at all, you understand. We cannot have individual citizens dabbling with weather manipulation. If that is going to involve infrastructure from Port Hedland, the cost also would be prohibitive to private citizens. It will need to be administered by the government, especially because there will be four states agreeing to turn the system on with advice from the B.O.M."

"Oh sure we understand that."

"Now if water is piped from Hedland the pipeline would need to be substantially larger than this setup and that will take many months to install, so what I am proposing today is that you hand your controller over to the DWER and because we will utilise your existing setup in the interim period, between now and the possible construction of something more substantial.   If you do that Andrew, the Commonwealth will reimburse your costs to date okay. Our priority now is to get some type of ad hoc agreement in place between the states until we can enact federal legislation. We just might want to turn your system on again in the next few days or weeks, but that decision will need to come from the government and it will be government in control. Now I will arrange for you to provide details of costs to my staff and you need to hand the controls to the Minister here please."

"Agreed and I appreciate that gesture - thank you Anthony. I have the instructions for the remote in the ute over there."

Andrew handed the remote control to Steven Dolsen and Jack fetched the instructions.

"Now we need to leave this area soon, so our film crew will take some footage and I hope you don't mind if you three men are included because this will be one for the national archives. You never know, Australia's future generations just might want to see all of this and who was involved in ending our pervasive drought problem. It has been really great to come here and see this first-hand - we appreciate that you are a person of action Andrew and fortunately you had a good outcome on this occasion. We will keep in touch, okay?"

"Yes sir!"

Everybody stood around the bore that was flowing for the film crew to obtain footage and snapshots then they boarded the plane and prepared to take off. It had been short and sweet but Anthony knew that the actual experience of being there and seeing it all would go a very long way towards the various state authorities reaching an agreement. The Victorian and South Australian governments were not represented but the two drought affected state governments were. Chris and Anna would carry a lot of weight in their pleas with the other states even though they came from the same side of the political divide. As he was preparing for take-off the pilot Phillip spoke up.

"Anthony, it's just a thought but I could fly you down over Carnegie and Wells if you want me to. Those lakes are far larger than Percival Lakes. Apart from that you would see Disappointment and Burnside on the way. Carnegie and Wells are both about one hundred kilometres long."

"Hmm ... thank you for the suggestion Phillip but I would need to put that to the others and I don't expect them to have the time. You see we are all booked onto the same Qantas flight to leave Karratha this evening to get to Perth for the return flight to the east tonight."

"Bad idea Anthony! Those red eye flights leaving Perth about midnight are terrible – you get back there in the early hours of the morning and you haven't had sleep so then you sleep during the day. Better idea is to stay in Karratha overnight and fly back first thing in the morning after a good night of sleep."

"So to fly further south over those lakes how long would that take?"

"We would cover the entire area in about two hours and that includes time back to this point although we would take a more direct route to Karratha from Lake Wells of course, over the town of Newman. You could even fly out from Newman if you want to. Alternatively I could fly you all straight down to Perth."

"Hmm ... got a few options there Phillip. I'll see what they say. You got enough fuel to get us all the way to Perth?"

Phillip nodded his head.

"Silly question Anthony!"

"Ah ... can I have everybody's attention please. Phillip has informed me that there is a later Qantas flight that leaves Karratha about eight o'clock tonight arriving in Perth about nine thirty which would still allow time to fly east tonight. Now you will recall that on the way across Steven Dolsen mentioned the other lakes Disappointment, Burnside and Carnegie and Wells. Phillip has made a suggestion that he could fly us over those lakes then either back to Karratha for the eight o'clock flight which is probably what we were all planning – to fly from Karratha. Alternatively he could fly us to Newman where we could catch an earlier flight at either five o'clock, six thirty or seven o'clock. The final option is that Phillip could even fly us all the way back to Perth. So any thoughts please, bearing in mind that these lakes we refer to are extremely large lakes, up to one hundred kilometres in length."

"I'd like to see that!"

"Yes I would too actually!"

Chris and Anna had spoken. They were speaking from their genuine concern for their farmers and were feeling encouraged by this entire sortie. Both ladies had visited drought affected areas within their own state and Andrew's inadvertent rain had given both of them new hope.

"Thank you for that Chris and Anna and I suppose we could have enquired initially as to the prospects of this flight taking us back to Perth – just something we didn't think of. So I suppose direct to Perth would be the preferred option?"

Everybody seemed to nod in concurrence. They were all very busy people.

"Okay Phillip thank you for that – the plan is we fly south over the lakes then straight on to Perth with you mate."

"Okay fasten seatbelts please."

The plane took off from Percival Lakes. Within twenty minutes Phillip made the first announcement.

"Okay people we are about to commence the flight over Lake Disappointment – approximately fifty kilometres long and almost as wide."

Everybody was impressed. About thirty minutes later Phillip spoke up again.

"Lake Burnside is below us now."

Another twenty minutes further on.

"Okay everybody we are about to start the flight down the length of Lakes Carnegie and Wells – more than one hundred and fifty kilometres in combined length."

This made quite an impact on the state Premiers and Ministers, for they realised that with these lakes being so much larger than the Percival Lakes, the modest rainfall they had received - generated by the flooding of Percival - could be drastically enhanced if these lakes systems were flooded.

On the journey back to Perth, most of them fell asleep as was to be expected. Upon landing they all made their way back through the Qantas terminal to rebook their return flights to the east, as they had arrived in Perth earlier than expected.

"Thank you, Phillip, for that wonderful trip and for having us back in Perth so soon."

"Thank you, Anthony, any time mate."

All went their separate ways to take their respective flights – except the security man Tana Umaga. He obtained permission from the Prime Minister to remain in Perth for a few days to catch up with the odd bro and cuz.

The following day Chris telephoned Terri Butler and pointed out that, according to the B.O.M. the prevailing weather conditions were still conducive to precipitation from Andrew's system bringing rain to New South Wales. She requested that the system be activated. Terri called Anna who agreed. Terri then called the state Premiers of Victoria and South Australia. They had already been provided with a brief and that approval might be sought and both agreed. The drought was devastating and to everybody's credit, they were all prepared to trust the prognostics. Consensual forms were emailed to all concerned and returned signed before anything could happen. Terri Butler then telephoned Steven Dolsen.

"Steven, we've got approval from everybody, you need to turn on Andrew's system for twenty-four hours."

"Just twenty-four – do you think that will cut the mustard?"

"We need to be quite circumspect with this to begin with Steven so let's just tread cautiously for now, but hopefully yes."

"Okay here goes!"

Steven Dolsen flicked the switch – the panel showed the system was running.

"So I will turn this off tomorrow at midday Perth time."

"That's the plan."

The following day, Steven Dolsen made a decision to turn the system off three hours late – just as Jack had returned to restart the first bore without Andrew being aware of it. Strange thing that – about men.

"Got to give it a fair chance" he muttered to himself. "Nobody will know."

Besides, Steven was going by gut feelings that just twenty-four hours would not be sufficient and he believed that gut feelings came from heaven. He was probably right.

Now everybody knew that the system had been turned on and everybody knew that the lake would not be completely covered during the day, but they also knew that whatever water went onto that lake between midday on the day they returned to their respective offices and midday the next day, would evaporate. Even Steven Dolsen's additional three hours of water to three in the afternoon would evaporate before nightfall. What they didn't know was whether it would have any effect.

They didn't have to wait long. The following day the next group of tourists were standing at the base of Uluru.

"Red Rock Tours Natalie speaking!"

"Oh good morning Natalie this is Glenda Tyrie from Darwin I am calling to let you know that the government is trialling a weather manipulation system based on the flooding of the salt lakes in the west and that there may be a sudden change in the weather today or tomorrow. We are very closely monitoring the situation and will call you as soon as we have reason to believe that there may be some rainfall at Uluru."

"Is this to do with the same looney who caused our problem last time?"

"No the government has taken control but you must understand it is all for the good cause of providing relief to the farmers across the border. Now in the event that you do suffer a disadvantage the government will provide restitution okay."

"Hmm ... all for a good cause I suppose."

"And how are things looking there at the moment?"

Natalie looked out the window.

"Holy shit! It's pissing down over the Olgas again. Tell them the bloody thing works, I have to call Brian."

Natalie got on the phone to Brian.

"Yeah we can see it from here Nat – just like last time! We're outa here."

Twenty tourists started running around the rock as quickly as they could. A New Zealand couple led the way, of course, but not the same couple. Before the tourists got to the bus, it was pelting down. But Brian knew what to expect – once on the bus, they were all smiling!

"Apologies to you all, the rainstorm was not forecast for today but our government has found a way of tinkering with the weather and it will bring about very sudden changes. If you don't believe me and you possibly don't, all I can tell you is that our government is flooding salt lakes in Western Australia in an attempt to end the drought and it causes sudden rainfall here at Uluru. Now if anyone would like a refund, please see Natalie when we arrive back at base."

Nobody did! Glenda Tyrie of the weather bureau in Darwin got on the phone to Terri Butler.

"Hello Terri, I have just been speaking to my contact at Red Rock Tours at Uluru and you can tell everybody that rain is on the way."

"Yay!"

Terri phoned Chris and Anna to give them the good news, for another ten to twenty millimetres of rainfall was crucial in nurturing the natural feed growth. Then her telephone rang – it was the Bureau of Meteorology in Canberra with further good news.

"Terri this is Antonia Rossi from the bureau, we are expecting the prevailing conditions to continue for the next three days, hence we have decided it would be appropriate for the EPA in Perth to turn the system on again for another twenty four hours."

"Oh thank you so much for informing me that is wonderful, I will call the Minister in the west straight away, thank you again."

"Steven Dolsen good morning."

"Good morning Steven, Terri Butler calling, how are you?"

"Fine thanks, I did turn the system off yesterday afternoon ..."

"Well you can turn it on again now for another twenty-four hours Steven. I have just had a call from the bureau in Canberra, they say the present conditions will prevail for the next three days."

"Great stuff – oh by the way I have been to see the engineers at Monadelphous in Victoria Park and they are working on a feasibility study now to extract water from the ocean near Port Hedland and to pipe it all the way to Lake Wells."

"So when do they think the feasibility study will be ready?"

"They said to give them about two weeks. Apparently, they flew a team to Hedland same day for this very purpose. The engineer I spoke to mentioned that they might consider gravity feeding the water from a high point south of Hedland – a Mount Cecilia - all the way to the Percival Lakes because of its comparatively low elevation then pump it to another high point near Percival to gravity feed it to Lake Disappointment then do the same from there to gravity feed it all the way to Lake Wells. But he also stated that Jigalong is of a higher elevation so whether that can be gravity fed depends on which high point they can utilise south of Hedland nearer to Karijini or at some other point along the way."

"Hmm ... sounds like they are onto this in a big way already."

"Well I think it is all really exciting actually. It's got my blood boiling – I've been losing sleep thinking about this."

"Yes but for now let's just hope that Andrew's system can bring some relief to the east within the next few days. Wouldn't it be great if they received another fifty millimetres."

"Oh shit yeah – fingers crossed! I suppose there's a lesson in this for all of us. Sometimes you just need to get on with it, take action first, think about it later. Too much pontificating and perhaps not enough imagination. I mean why didn't somebody think of this before? Colin Barnett went to a state election proposing to build a canal from Lake Argyle all the way to Perth to supply fresh water. Makes you wonder what that water might have been utilised for along the way. It's probably the reason he lost the election too. Now there's a thought – why not fresh water from Lake Argyle down through the towns of Halls Creek and Fitzroy Crossing to the Percival Lakes? That fresh water could even flow then through Marble Bar to towns like Newman and Meekatharra and eventually to Perth or from Lake Wells to towns like Laverton, Leonora, Menzies and even on to Kalgoorlie."

"Yes and hopefully to Griffith where I am from!"

"Well some of those towns have really shitty water – Newman for one Terri, everybody there drinks bottled water."

"You're kidding me!"

"Nope! Been there many times. The tap water is highly calcified – it's within World Health Organisation limits but it tastes like shit. The only people who drink it are the Aboriginals because most of them can't afford to buy bottled water. I observed that when I went to Parnpajinya. And yet, Terri, the town of Newman is the most important iron ore town in Australia. It's worth billions to this country. So hopefully this sojourn of ours into flooding these salt lakes just might lead to something greater down the track."

"Well you West Aussies had better stick together on that. Now don't forget to turn on the system."

"Already done Terri! I have the remote right here on my desk. So seawater from Hedland itself just might be an interim measure Terri, because if this system works and prevents drought in the east, we should be raising our hands for federal funding to bring fresh water down from Lake Argyle. And due south from Lake Argyle is Lake Mackay on the border with the Territory. From there water could be piped to Alice then to Lake Eyre and Lake Torrens and even to Adelaide. We could sell fresh water from Lake Argyle to the South Australian government. The mind boggles Terri."

"Sounds like it Steven – you might be allowing too much imagination there. The crow-eaters have national parks in those areas – Lake Eyre and Lake Torrens. But as for the idea of piping water to Adelaide, yes I could mention that one to Anthony later today when I see him."

"Terri, the Snowy Mountains Scheme took about twenty five years to complete right, from 1949 to 1974. Everything I have just mentioned in the last minute could be done with today's equipment in less than two years. Now I majored in environmental science with honours and the topic of my honours thesis was about the proposal to draw water in Perth from the Yarragadee Aquifer, so yes I do have an active interest in this."

"Yarragadee ... hmm ... yes I've heard of that one, quite substantial they say."

"Substantial? There's enough water there for the whole country. It is pretty deep down though. So tell me what did you think of our trip north? I was really on quite a high the whole time, you know, with the Prime Minister, three state Premiers, yourself, Tana Umaga ..."

"Yeah Anthony had me worried when he mentioned the grubber but Andrew saved the day with his password eh – fancy that, 'allblacks' - that seemed to pacify that security man a bit."

"You do realise he did play for the All Blacks."

"Really? No I didn't know about that, wow, we had an All Black with us."

"Yes Tana was their captain in fact. He likes to keep a low profile though, so he didn't say too much. But I knew who he was."

"Well I hope to meet Tana again someday, now let's keep in touch I will let you know as soon as I hear anything from the weather bureau."

"Okay thank you Terri, goodbye."

Terri called Steven back about two hours later.

"Steven, we have rain from Charleville right down to Tamworth and they say it is heavy enough to make a difference."

"Hey, good stuff, geeze, it's all happening Terri."

"Sure is, apparently Chris and Anna are over the moon. This is going to be the main story in the evening news Steven."

"Well I hope they decide to extend the flood beyond tomorrow."

"I doubt it but that will be entirely up to the advice from the B.O.M. now."

"Well thank God for Andrew Robertson – a bloody American."

Evening news

"Good evening and welcome to the Nine News. The drought is over! The drought is officially over, with most of New South Wales and Queensland receiving substantial falls of rain this last twenty-four hours. That comes just days after the same areas received lighter falls of rain of up to twenty millimetres, but today's rain was far more widespread. Jacinta Allen reports."

"Greg I am here in outback New South Wales in the town of Bourke where, as you can see, rain is falling steadily around me and it started some time ago. Already the town of Bourke has received more than twenty millimetres of rain since nine o'clock this morning and they expect at least another ten to twenty millimetres before this rain ceases. Now that comes on top of almost twenty millimetres that this area received over a period of three days earlier in the week so, yes, I am pleased to say, the drought is officially over. Of course, it will take a few days for the ground feed to come through and provide respite to sheep and cattle stock and to thousands of kangaroos in this area too I might add, but the farmers know they will soon be able to rely on the natural vegetation and cease the provision of hay feed."

"And Jacinta there seems to be quite some jubilation in the streets of Bourke."

"Greg people here have been suffering for a long time with this drought and, of course, they still remember the effects of the six-year drought from 2006 to 2011 so everybody has been hoping this would not be a repeat of that calamity when dozens of farmers had to surrender their properties to Australia's major banks. Thankfully now Greg, that does not seem to be the case. As you can see behind me a lot of the town folk are out here in the streets talking to each other and making plans for a better future and not many of them taking shelter beneath an umbrella as I am. Earlier I spoke to one local farmer Fergus McCracken and this is what he had to say."

"We had four thousand head of sheep before the drought started and now we are down to about four hundred head. We've been feeding them with hay coming in from other parts of Australia and I know I would have lost the remaining sheep if the drought persisted much longer, because there's just not enough hay for all the farmers here. Apart from that the bank had given me just another two months to get some funds coming back in, well I am going to have to sell about a hundred of the remaining sheep to achieve that and then recommence the breeding program from there. I know I can recover completely if I get a couple of years drought-free but just one more drought in the next five years will end my life on the farm."

"Now Greg the rain has also been very widespread - we have reports that good rains have fallen as far north as Mt. Isa where they have received about ten millimetres and Charleville another twenty millimetres today on top of what they recorded just days ago so there have been good falls of rain right throughout most of Queensland which is looking quite good now too. Greg."

"Jacinta Allen with that report. Now we cross to the Bureau of Meteorology here in Sydney and our reporter Louise McMullan has some rather odd news for us. Louise."

"Yes good evening Greg, odd news for sure and certain Greg, we have just been informed by the bureau that this recent rainfall has probably come about for the same reason that the Ashes test match was washed out in Adelaide just a few days ago and that is, that a salt lake in Western Australia was flooded for almost two days with fresh underground water and the subsequent evaporation of that water from the salt lake has brought about this drastic change in the weather. Now this seems to have occurred quite by accident in the first instance but let me tell you Greg, that when rain fell on this area here just a few days ago, a delegation comprising the Prime Minister Anthony Albury, his Minister for the Environment and Water Terri Butler, the Premiers of three state governments - Chris Minehan, Anna Pellizzari and Roger Brook - plus the Minister for the Environment in W.A. Steven Dolsen all took an excursion to the actual site where all this was happening as you can see in the footage there. While they were there, Greg, they set the wheels in motion for the lakes to be flooded again and that is what has ended this drought. Of course, they could only have done this with favourable wind conditions and fortunately that is what they got so there is now hope, Greg, that this just might herald a permanent end to drought here in Australia as we know it. Greg back to you."

"Yes thank you   reporting from Sydney, quite extraordinary scenes there and here's hoping our politicians can work together to end this nation's scourge of persistent drought."

"In further news a fire broke out in a busy factory complex south of Sydney this afternoon, fire response units were quickly on the scene ...."

So the news went on. The following day there were numerous calls between the various players who had been involved in this venture of cooperation to the west – Chris called Anna and Anthony, Anna called Anthony and Terri, Anthony called Roger and Steven, Steven called Jane and Andrew. They were all ecstatic with the results they had achieved and this venture seemed to have bonded these political people closer together. The weather bureau had forecast some further favourable conditions in the week ahead, when Steven Dolsen would be able to send more rain to the east. Sure enough, in four days' time, the bureau gave the all clear and Terri Butler telephoned Steven.

"Steven good news, the B.O.M. has given the go-ahead once again, only this time they say that forty-eight hours is all go, so whenever you like you can crank it up."

Steven Dolsen gleefully flicked his switch. Surely another twenty or thirty millimetres of rain might engender sufficient weed growth to see the farmers through to the winter rains that would normally commence the following March, providing the rains did fall – even though that had not happened in this past nine months. In any event, he knew that at the first sign of a recurrence of drought, they could provide some relief at the critical time.

Several days later Steven Dolsen received a call from Monadelphous Engineering to say they had some proposals for him to consider. He invited them into his office.

"Good morning Minister Dolsen I am Georgina Burrows the chief engineer with Monadelphous and this is my assistant Greg Rintoul."

"Good morning, please come in. I hope you have some favourable news for me."

"We believe so, now we have a number of options for you to consider Minister."

"Please call me Steven."

"Thank you! We believe the best option is to extract the water from the ocean somewhere near the Pardoo Roadhouse as there is sufficient existing electrical power supply to that coastal area if you choose not to elect a wind turbine to power that part of the infrastructure. Obviously, there will be an extraction facility at the ocean with suitable screening mechanisms in place to ensure a clean intake of water without seaweed or fish and so on. The water needs to be pumped about three hundred kilometres out to the base of the Hamersley Ranges somewhere between the Auski village and Marble Bar Road, unless we find another suitable high point. Of course, the surrounding plain reaches an elevation of about two hundred and fifty metres above sea level, so the seawater would have to be pumped out to that point, then it would require a dedicated turbine or electric pumping station at the base of a hill to transfer the water to a small storage area at the top of the hill."

"So about three hundred kilometres in length with an elevation of two hundred and fifty metres."

"Yes, now there are plenty of hills along the Marble Bar Road above an elevation of five hundred metres. So option one - if we pump water to the top of one of those hills with one wind turbine that would provide sufficient gravity feed to Percival Lakes but the Carnegie-Wells system is close to four hundred and fifty metres in elevation."

"Which means the water would still flow to those lakes but very slowly?"

"Yes, it would flow but very slowly and it may not have a sufficient rate of replenishment depending on how many outlets you would have at the other end – presumably a large number."

"Once the storage area has been reached the water would gravity feed down to Percival Lakes which have an elevation of two hundred and fifty metres, quite readily."

"Why would there be a storage area? Surely once you have pumped the water to the top of the hill it will gravity feed quite freely from there."

"Ah yes it would but a small storage area would prevent air pockets, so the pipeline from the ocean would always be full. It will also provide a chance for further screening and to test the pH levels."

"Option two! Immediately to the west of Koodaideri Mine there are hills outside of the Karijini National Park with elevations above sea level of more than eight hundred metres. Now that would provide gravity feed to every lake that you are proposing to flood right throughout Western Australia. So depending upon what you want that might be the best option. A couple of wind turbines would do the trick."

"Okay we certainly need to keep that option in mind."

"Couldn't we have a large storage capacity out there somewhere near the lakes?"

"Negative! With the quantities of water that you would want to expend onto the lakes system a small storage facility would undoubtedly be exhausted very shortly after you turn on the system."

"Unless we use one of these large lakes as a storage facility."

"What do you mean?"

"Well what's the evaporation rate in this area?"

"About two metres per annum."

"So we build a wall around a large lake and maintain a level of water in that lake that will provide sufficient storage to do the job when we need it. If the evaporation rate is two metres per annum we build the wall three metres high."

"And which of these lakes would you choose?"

"Disappointment!"

"Why?"

"Because that way it won't be so disappointing. It's had everybody pissed off since the day dot. Besides from there you could gravity feed, back to the Percival Lakes at two hundred and fifty metres elevation and pump to Carnegie and Wells from a high point near Disappointment."

"Disappointment would have a circumference of two hundred kilometres. A two-hundred-kilometre wall two metres high would cost a bit."

"The Kalgoorlie pipeline is over six hundred kilometres long – they did that back in the nineteenth century. Don't tell me we've lost something! Besides, it wouldn't be a limestone wall or a brick wall it would be an earth wall – there's no dearth of rocks and dirt out there. To build that wall you could give a bloody good job to every Martu within the Pilbara for twelve months. The blokes could build a kilometre or more every day. Those mining companies build railways many times longer and they cost a hell of a lot more to build. The pastoral and agriculture industries in the east are probably worth as much to this country as the mining industry is here in the west. The bird life would love it too – especially when we bring the water in from Lake Argyle rather than the ocean. A lot of those birds only show up after its been raining and that's not very often. Let's face it – Lake Disappointment is bloody useless as it is. Why keep it that way when we can utilise it to ensure there is never another drought in Australia?"

"But are you suggesting that there be a permanent source of water out there when the system we are proposing only provides water when it is needed?"

"Not necessarily! We need to be cognizant of the environmental impact and a permanent storage facility would cause ongoing precipitation but consider that this facility could be filled just a day or two prior to the water being required."

"Hmm … call it option three if you wish but with options one and two the pipeline is always going to be full. You see when the valves at the outlets are closed the pipeline will be full of water."

"Yeah good point Greg – but geeze I do like that idea of having water in Disappointment – especially when we bring in fresh water from Lake Argyle."

"So you would be prepared to put such a plan to Cabinet?"

"Blood oath I will Georgina! So what is the timeframe for construction of the two options you have put to me so far?"

"For either we could have the system up and running in less than twelve months. That is, to provide a three-hundred-millimetre diameter water pipe for approximately one thousand kilometres with wind turbines and the necessary electrical turbines. Our costings are included in the submission. Oh and I hasten to point out that back in 1984 and 1985 the former State Energy Commission of Western Australia constructed the Dampier to Bunbury gas pipeline in less than two years, on time and below budget, welding one hundred and twenty seven thousand sections of twelve metre length pipe together – and that was six hundred and sixty millimetre diametre pipe. The total length of the pipeline exceeds fifteen hundred kilometres."

"That's very interesting. So the cost of your immediate proposal is?"

"One hundred and seventy million dollars. That is excluding your idea of an earth wall around Lake Disappointment."

"Yes of course but you could cost that for us too could you not – before I send this to Canberra? This project is for the benefit of the whole country so Canberra is going to fund this."

"Can do within a couple of days. Now we understand that the Argyle option is a long-term concept and you will give consideration to that in a few years' time is that correct?"

"Well ... our immediate priority is to replace the setup that this pastoralist has handed us that draws on the groundwater resources, with the present idea of seawater from Hedland, then perhaps after water starts to flow, we will look at the Lake Argyle option. I personally am in favour of that because of the advantages of fresh water over seawater and also because of other uses for fresh water right down through the goldfields but I'd say that could be up to two years away. Unless the Federal Government decides to fund that too. If the Feds save a lot of money with us ending the drought in Australia it just might do that. How much is the cost of this feasibility study?"

"One hundred and forty thousand."

"Okay, I am going to bite the bullet here - I am going to authorise you, in writing today, to commence the feasibility study of piping water from Lake Argyle, through Halls Creek and Fitzroy Crossing, to Newman then through Punmu, Parnngurr and Jigalong, to replace this seawater option with fresh water, then to continue that supply through Leinster, Laverton, Leonora and Menzies to Kalgoorlie, okay."

Georgina and Greg looked at each other.

"Was that a snap decision?"

"You talked me into it! You guys will probably be the main contractor so you can farm this work out to other sub-contractors as you see fit, to get the first section of seawater to the Percival Lakes completed in six months, not twelve months, okay?"

"That's a tall order."

"I don't care if you sub-contract the bloody Australian Army, I want this done. This project will save lives! I honestly don't think there has been any engineering project as big as this since the Snowy Mountains Scheme."

"Perhaps the Opera House?"

"Very smart! So is a six month construction timeframe plausible?"

"Yes I believe so if we coordinate a concerted effort utilising all available sub-contractors. We can start working on the feasibility study but the cost of that would be several times the cost of this present feasibility study. You would be looking at a cost in excess of five hundred thousand dollars for the Lake Argyle to Kalbloodygoorlie feasibility proposal."

"Don't worry that's about what we have outlaid already sending hay to the eastern states just in the last twelve months. We were expecting that to continue for the next few months or a lot longer - and with what we have achieved recently we now have far more leverage with the federal government. Ending the drought is worth billions to the Feds."

"Then at some point of time in the future we look at an off-shoot from Fitzroy Crossing across to the coast at Broome, take it back to Derby, down the coast to Port Hedland, on to Karratha then to Carnarvon, Geraldton and possibly to Perth again. Give ourselves a second stream of fresh water to benefit all towns along the way."

"Why would you pipe water to Kalgoorlie - they already have water from Mundaring?"

"Well we just might be able to reverse the flow and provide water back to Perth City. Perth doesn't receive the rainfall that it used to so Mundaring Weir gets pretty low at times."

"Now, fresh water from Lake Argyle would be a constant flow to those numerous towns and you would draw on that for the evaporation system as required right?'

"Yes Georgina - and that water would be permanently available for the evaporation system at the lakes."

"You're gonna need a bigger pipe!"

"True, but please factor in the cost of a suitable diameter pipe in the initial instance to provide water to the evaporation system and the towns as far as Lake Wells - so Halls Creek, Fitzroy Crossing, Newman and Jigalong, then from there out through the lakes system. Then once that is in place, we can add a larger pipeline along the exact same route, before we extend the system down further south to the mining towns I mentioned. Then one day, who knows when, we add an even larger pipeline again to provide water to Perth, okay, so imagine pipeline one is our three-hundred-millimetre job, pipeline two is six-hundred-millimetres and pipeline three is nine-hundred-millimetres. From there we can always add additional pipelines as required. A constant flow from a nine-hundred-millimetre pipeline into Mundaring Weir is going to keep that weir chocka. In a few years from now there could be four or five nine hundred millimetre pipelines along the same route."

"Why don't you pipe it to South Australia they've got shit water over there? You could run that via the Trans Continental railway line."

"Yes, that's got considerable merit and our Minister for Water is going to mention that possibility to the Prime Minister, so we would sell the water to South Australia and we license them to on-sell to Victoria and to New South Wales and Queensland adding their own margin. Of course, it's a bloody long way to the border from Kalgoorlie so we would probably consider running such a pipeline from Lake Argyle down through Alice Springs to Adelaide."

"That would be far more direct!"

"Yes it would and, you know, when I was in year ten, I read up about how the Western Australian government sealed the Eyre Highway all the way to the border back in the sixties. South Australia didn't come to the party because they didn't want people from the east going through S.A. to the west – they wanted those people from the east to stay in S.A. That didn't change until the Whitlam government sealed the highway in 1975. My father told me he drove across on the dirt road from the border to Penong in S.A. in his old Ford Falcon and the dirt road was just over four hundred kilometres long. So there was some very backward thinking at that time by state and federal governments prior to Whitlam's considering the interstate freight transport factor also. And that road to the border that W.A. sealed in the sixties would have cost a lot more, in real terms, that constructing a water pipe to the border."

274

"Yes it certainly would – road construction is far more expensive. A pipeline would be comparatively cheap in fact. As I recall also it wasn't all that long ago when a blight hit Melbourne's water supply system – I think it was caused by a fire that contaminated the dam – and the most stringent restrictions were put into place. My rellies in Melbourne said they weren't even able to have a shower every day."

"You'd want to be in good with your mates at work eh!"

"Ha-ha-ha! Nice one Greg."

"Just on that point you've made there, Georgina, consider also that a similar blight could affect Melbourne again in the future – they seem to be so reliant on that main source don't they?"

"Yes a comprehensive water strategy should become part of a national project to safeguard water resources to ensure that all Australians have ample access to a range of water resources.   Apart from that, consider how much money Australians spend every year on bottled water."

"Good point there Georgie - and that shit costs more than Coca Cola."

"I wouldn't call bottled water 'shit' Greg!"

"You drink water – I drink Coke. The best idea though would surely be to pipe that water down from Lake Argyle through Alice and into Adelaide rather than taking the long road to grandma's house through Kalgoorlie. I mean, look what Australia has spent on the NBN – I think the initial estimate was about fifty billion dollars and it might have blown out since then. A pipeline to all major centres of Australia would cost a lot less."

"Yes and surely water is just as important!"

"No – water is more important Georgina – we could survive without the internet but not without water."

"Good point Steven!"

"So you Monadelphies are into this kind of thinking too eh! I am pleased to hear that. I thought I might be the only oddball around here!"

"Well we do have the ulterior motive Steven. If a national water supply project was undertaken, we would pick up quite a bit of the work."

"Yes, point taken!"

"And don't forget also that water and gas can be transferred in the one pipeline then separated at the other end. Sell the bastards gas as well!"

"I wouldn't call our fellow Australians bastards Greg, they ..."

"Well you're the one who raised the issue of the road Steven."

"Yes, but they must be regarded by all of us as potential customers okay, of our water resources and our gas reserves."

"And oil!"

"Ah yes ... that oil strike off the coast of Carnarvon ... that could be a big one for us too."

"And Rio's copper strike east of Broome! Bigger than Mount Isa they say."

"Yet to be confirmed Georgina but here's hoping. Now you two have given me a good idea. We really do need a national think tank on all this stuff, don't we? I mean we do have the national infrastructure mob but they just seem to lack imagination and, for mine, they seem to overlook factoring in the foregone aspects of a concept – like you mentioned before Georgina about the cost of bottled water. I would be totally surprised if any of our infrastructure organisations have taken that into account at all."

"Yeah why is that Steven?"

"In a word Greg – complacency! They really just don't have the plight of the people at heart, the way that Labor governments do. Conservatives in this country are more concerned about preserving their negative gearing tax minimisation and forcing their latest application for another high-rise apartment block through their local council by paying people off, than they are about providing Aussies with drinking water."

"Is that what they are up to?"

"Yes Greg! I mean, consider what we have done here in the west with Tonkin Highway for example. Sure the boffins who costed the project came up with what the dollar outlay would be to build the upgrade, but it is saving the people a lot of money and time too – companies who employ truck drivers are saving a tremendous amount of time and money – they used to line up down the highway waiting to get through the traffic lights at Horrie Miller Drive to gain access to their warehouse. But you will find there are no costings for the benefits in any of the equations – the only benefits expressed are in terms of traffic flow. The fact that we did not undertake that project ten years earlier probably cost the people of this state far more than it cost to build the bloody thing ten years later. So that is the way we normally go about things – because most of our politicians and bureaucrats are either inappropriately educated, too short-sighted, too complacent or too motivated by good old self-interest to do what they should be doing. Anyway, that's my rendition for the day."

"You should be our Prime Minister Steven! Why did they give you this portfolio anyway?"

"Environment? So I can keep a close eye on our errant-minded woodchippers Georgie."

"Okay so we had better choof off and get some more of these costings done for you. So you will send an authority to cost the pipeline through Halls Head, Newman etc. ..."

"Halls Creek!"

"Oh yes Halls Creek - and the fresh water pipeline from Lake Argyle to Halls Creek also."

"Yes you will receive my authority on that today."

"Great to see someone prepared to take action for a change Steven."

"Yes well I might have learnt something myself from that Robertson character recently. But paramount in my mind is the fact that what has happened is going to save Australian governments both federal and state, a hell of a lot of money, so we need to make some outlays with those savings, that will benefit all future Australians."

"Okay we will be in touch - and your department will refer all of this to the EPA right?"

"Yes of course!"

Jane Wyatt

"Oh Mr. Dolsen Jane Wyatt is here to see you."

"Please send her in."

"Good morning Jane."

"Morning Minister."

"To what do I owe the pleasure this morning?"

"To my advice that all of this water activity in the east Pilbara needs to stop, you see Steven, the EPA has not had an opportunity to conduct any Environmental Impact Assessments whatsoever, as you would undoubtedly know. That Robertson guy did not even obtain approval from the Water Corporation to sink his bores."

"Yes, of course I realise this has not followed normal protocol Jane, but this is a time of peril for thousands of farming families in the eastern states. You have seen the outcome for yourself. What that man Robertson did was initiate rainfall that would not have occurred naturally. There's absolutely no doubt about that – all of the boffins from the Bureau of Meteorology agree on that. The changes in the weather perpetrated by Mr. Robertson were totally unexpected, extremely sudden and quite profound. He has virtually already saved hundreds of farmers from either going under, losing their farms or experiencing enormous trauma, so the occasion needs everybody to be realistic and to cut some slack."

"Cut slack or cut corners Steven?"

"Haven't you been watching the news this last week?"

"Yes of course, I have seen the outcome of what Mr. Robertson did. I was there at the lakes the other day when everybody was so delighted with what he had done and the effect it had. But that doesn't mean we should simply circumvent all pre-existing requirements under the

Environmental Protection Act. The law is the law Steven, so I have referred this entire project to the EPA for an Environmental Impact Assessment."

"Don't you think I would have done that if it were deemed as necessary Jane?"

"But you didn't Steven, so I felt compelled to act."

"You do want my job!"

"I might consider standing at the next state election, yes. And obviously if I was elected and my party won the election, I should think that I would be the prime candidate for the Ministry, yes."

"This Ministry?"

"I would think so, yes."

"Do you think I wouldn't make it known to people in your electorate that you are the person who tried to delay the saving of a few thousand farmers?"

"A moment ago you said hundreds."

"Don't quibble with me – could be hundreds, could be thousands. Who the hell knows!"

"I would expect the people in my electorate to uphold my view, Steven, that the law is the law."

"If somebody is running red lights, bashing elderly women or breaking into houses, yes, but invoking the letter of the law for its own sake and ruining Australian families in the process just might be regarded by real Australian people in your electorate, as officiously pedantic and grossly obtuse."

"Well we will see! Regardless, I have referred the matter to the EPA."

"Well it's a good thing for everybody concerned that the Environmental Protection Authority advises the Minister – it doesn't make decisions. And it takes the social impact of its assessments into consideration when it does conduct its assessments Jane, so I have reason to believe that you are on a losing streak."

"Only time will tell Steven!"

"Besides, unbeknown to you Jane, the federal government has taken care of that and the project will proceed with haste – federally funded in every conceivable way. I had a call from Anthony just an hour ago – it has all been decided – including the larger pipelines from Lake Argyle to Adelaide and probably into regional New South Wales also."

"How so?"

"Under the Defence Act! The Federal Government invoked the Defence Act to commence work on the Snowy Mountains Scheme way back in 1949. As alluded to by Anthony when we were on the plane, the specific legislation for the project wasn't enacted for about ten years."

"And how, pray-tell does defence have anything whatsoever to do with this? What we are dealing with here is literally an act of environmental vandalism that was not referred to the EPA for an assessment by the errant protagonist. He just went ahead and did his own thing, flooding huge salt lakes with bore water that normally only receive fresh water from rainfall."

"Jane, the Thomson Dam in Victoria was contaminated in December 2006 by ash from a bushfire and it wasn't just the Collingwood football fans who couldn't take a shower it was the entire Melbourne population. Apparently, the subsequent prevailing redolence was more overbearing than the local D'Orsogna Brothers salami production plant. Even the Carlton players' wives were unable to wash their Toorak Road tractors for a couple of weeks."

"I don't follow your meaning there Steven."

"Well I'm not surprised but consider that until then the people of Melbourne had never experienced anything like

281

that - they had always assumed they would have an abundance of drinking water. But that fire and the contamination it caused made everybody cogently aware of the importance of our water resources. Now without stating the obvious and putting malicious thoughts into anyone's mind, we believe that a comprehensively diversified water supply infrastructure is absolutely critical to Australia's defence needs. Anything short of that will leave us susceptible and the full bench of the High Court would certainly endorse that in any challenge – I mean, there is legal precedent from 1949 Jane. So it has been decided that construction on the pipelines from Lake Argyle will commence immediately and from Fitzroy Crossing will diverge to both Broome and to Newman – then onwards from there toward the coastal towns and Kalgoorlie toward Perth City. I will have people here in my office from Monadelphous, John Holland and Leighton this afternoon for a briefing. I have also asked them for a feasibility study to pipe Lake Argyle water down through Alice and into South Australia. That will not proceed unless and until we have completed the first pipeline from Port Hedland to Lakes Carnegie and Wells, but once that water starts to flow and brings a permanent end to the drought, we will definitely be starting the pipeline down through central Australia."

"That seems rather precipitant!"

"It's an absolute imperative Jane and it will happen in the very first term of this Albury Federal Government. Chris Minehan has requested a feasibility study to pipe water from Lake Argyle to the Presbury Weir on the Barwon River and to construct a second weir nearby, to enable periodic flushing of the Darling River. It's a catastrophe over there and it's a national disgrace what has happened to the Darling River. We will do something about it."

"And I suppose your government is going to run up a massive budget deficit paying for all of this. You do realise don't you that this will cost billions of dollars."

"Yes and we are doing the costings now – but don't worry Jane this will be fully funded without any budget blowout."

"As if!"

"Believe me Jane - your cohorts will fund this by increased taxation revenues brought about by the abolition of all of the factitious mechanisms that top-end accounting firms provide your supporters with, to minimise their taxation liability and their contribution to the national purse."

"So you mean to abolish negative gearing of private residences?"

"No! This will be fully funded by the abolition of family trust perks. That blatant abuse of the tax system to benefit the wealthy in this country has gone on for too long. So your friends will start to contribute their fair share soon Jane – we are working on next May's federal budget already. By the way, don't be surprised if there is a federal Royal Commission into the taxation system and how artificial mechanisms have caused our national deficit. We will also be looking at ways of dragging back some of what was lost over the last thirty or forty years."

"You can't introduce retrospective taxation legislation!"

"No but we can increase state government land taxes and intervene in the commercial property market with state owned property – you know, to keep the rents reasonable and ensure that your mates don't pass on the extra taxes to their tenants."

"You bastard!"

Jane's family owned considerable commercial property in the Karratha business district.

"Don't make it so personal Jane – it's only politics! Just stick to your guns with your own policies – whatever they are! Most Liberal people don't actually understand why they support the Liberal Party – apart from those who stand to gain personally of course."

"So, you are going to forge ahead with feasibility studies for three pipelines already. Probably a few votes in that lot for you Steven."

"Don't worry we will not waste a moment on this one. The other seawater pipeline from Port Hedland will commence also, due to the fact that it will be several hundreds of kilometres shorter and completed at least six months sooner than the longer fresh water pipelines. We need the ability to utilise those salt pans as soon as possible in case this prolonged drought goes into next winter as well – or the winter after for that matter. Apart from that, it will provide seawater for aquaculture ventures at the communities and if needs be, we can always convert it to fresh water once the Argyle pipeline reaches Hedland. In fact, it could virtually run hot or cold as we wish."

"Hot or cold?"

"Yes – run seawater through the pipeline to Punmu, Parnngurr, Kunawarritji and Jigalong for their envisaged aquaculture ventures before it goes to the salt lakes, then if we need fresh water, we turn on the fresh water and simply run brackish water out to waste. Then we can switch back to seawater when we want to and run brackish to waste again and so on."

"And where would that brackish water be run to, Steven?"

"That would be run onto a salt pan somewhere whether it is seawater, fresh water or brackish Jane. In reality that won't make a skerrick of difference to any salt pan – as you probably know yourself."

"It has to make some kind of a difference simply because it is different – that's a fundamental tenet of social science theory Steven and you know that. As I said, Steven, those salt lakes normally only have fresh rainwater running onto them – now you are proposing to have either seawater or water from Argyle run onto those lakes, so it has to make a difference."

"Well whether the water comes from rainfall or the ocean Jane, salt is salt – the lakes are covered with salt that has risen from beneath the topsoil. Salt from the oceans will not be so vastly different – and water from Argyle came down into the Argyle drainage basin from rain Jane, so that was rainfall at one time."

"A wide variety of birds use those salt lakes when the lakes are inundated with rain Steven."

"Well I'm sure those birds will greatly appreciate being able to take a swim more often. So you go ahead and make your submission to the EPA Jane and I will do the same. By the way, if you don't mind me asking, which seat will you be contesting at the next state election?"

"I am registered on the electoral roll in Karratha, Steven – that is my home town."

"So you will be directly up against me for a seat in the Legislative Council?"

"Or the seat of Pilbara in the Legislative Assembly, so yes Steven, I will see you there if not before."

"Probably see you tomorrow Jane – I mean, you do work here. By the way, as a public servant you cannot stand as a candidate for the state election unless you either ..."

"Resign, Steven – okay? Prior to nominations being received. Goodbye Minister!"

Grand plan

"Roger Brook's office good morning, Kerry Hunter speaking."

"Oh good morning Kerry it's Steven Dolsen calling for Roger please."

"Good morning Steven, yes Roger is available, I will put you through."

"Steven good morning."

"Hello Roger – you were right, that witch is after my job."

"Ha-ha-ha tell me about it."

"Well she's submitted an application to the EPA for an environmental impact assessment, so I got her a bit riled up by disclosing some details of the master plan and she became somewhat aggressive and threatened to resign to contest the next state election, hoping to become the Minister herself."

"Huh! Good luck to her Steven - she's going to need it. The public will be onside with us on this in a huge way. This proposal has the potential to entrench Labor governments in power both here and Canberra for at least two or three terms. I expect that the feasibility studies will provide some forecasts of labour requirements and that's not simply to construct the pipeline – we will need some roads concomitant with that for some sections at least."

"Yes, and I have briefed the engineering contractors to insist that construction commence at several points along the proposed Port Hedland to Percival Lakes route – I basically told them to get as many sub-contractors as possible out there, that will exhaust their resources. I call it the Chinese approach – don't waste time with one contractor building ten bridges – get ten contractors to build one each.

If the benefits flow sooner, it actually saves money. You follow?"

"Makes sense!"

"The way I see it Roger, sub-contractors to Monadelphous can commence from every town or vantage point along the route, so obviously there will be a contractor commencing from Port Hedland another commencing from Newman and both of those or alternatively a different contractor could be commencing work along the Great Northern Highway from Auski or anywhere in between where they can establish a camp. Apart from that a contractor can be working from the Percival Lakes area also. I just want as many teams out there that they are capable of providing – even if that means bringing in construction teams from the east. That might get up the nose of some West Australians, Roger, but we are all Australians first."

"Oh don't worry Steven I fully concur with your view on that."

"Now, the pipeline from Lake Argyle will only commence providing the Hedland pipeline is fully resourced with construction teams. Monadelphous initially said we were looking at twelve months for the Hedland pipeline, so I queried them on just how many teams that plan involved and it seemed to me the entire process could be expedited by engaging more bases and teams along the way, so now we are looking at six months not twelve. I believe it is absolutely imperative to have that seawater flowing as soon as possible to guard against any drought next winter."

"Oh, absolutely Steven."

Once the Hedland line is completed to Percival Lakes, we then swing all teams to the Lake Argyle to Fitzroy Crossing section. Again, it will only be once that line is completed, at least to Broome or Port Hedland, that we commence the pipeline through the centre to Alice."

"Why only to Broome or Port Hedland – the plan is to take water all the way to Kalgoorlie and Perth?"

"Yes, but the people of Kalgoorlie and Perth and all towns in between do have good quality water and the central system to Alice then on to Adelaide is a more pressing priority because we are going to sell the water to generate cash flows."

"Hmm … good point!"

"So the Monadelphous teams are revising their feasibility plans for us to put to the Feds and this is the logical strategy that we need to pursue with Anthony and Tanya to take to Cabinet, Roger. This plan will provide seawater to the Percival Lakes within six months, during which time we utilise Mr. Robertson's bore water if we need to – then we will have the option of both fresh water and seawater within twelve months, before we commence the Alice pipeline. That pipeline really needs to be completed to generate cash flow before we commence further options in Western Australia."

"Hmm … sounds like you've done your homework on this Steven. I'm surprised Monadelphous didn't see it this way to begin with."

"They were taking the conventional approach – we are going to let contracts out for the various stages as soon as subbies become free Roger."

"Hmm … good strategy Steven – I like it!"

"So how did you fare with Jane in the end? I knew she was angling at an entry into politics - she made a crass remark last year to me at the Christmas party that she might be the Minister one day."

"She came up with the usual stuff – Labor spending money we don't have, running up a deficit etcetera, so I put her in the loop about the critical role of previous Liberal politics and how that has contributed to Australian government deficits and, to some extent, how our grand plan

288

would be funded through additional taxation revenues by clipping the wings of some of her support base."

"Do you mean through abolishing negative gearing and family trust perks?"

"Yes and the additional state land taxes on commercial property."

"Hmm ... you need to keep that one to yourself until after the next state election Steven – we don't want the other mob scare-mongering people about a hike in commercial rents. The plan to attenuate or restrain any such tendency for rent increases is a medium to long term plan. We will need time to either construct or purchase property to keep a competitive lid on commercial rents."

"Okay I will do, I will be rather more prudent in anything I say to Jane or anybody else from now. You have my commitment on that Roger."

"Thank you, Steven, but just on that point, when we do establish our working party to examine the proposals to purchase properties, I want you to be involved in a big way – I want you to be the convenor and chair of the working party, okay?"

"Well certainly, but why me if I may ask?"

"Your disclosure to Jane about this means you do have conviction in the cause Steven, that is why. When this idea was first touted to me by Tanya Parkinson, who is a fairly long way left of centre as you know, I took it with a grain of salt myself but I did take the trouble to mention the concept to my Cabinet colleagues individually and it just didn't seem to gel with them as being something of significance. You are the first of my Cabinet colleagues to mention it since, so it seems to me that you do think there is something in that."

"Well I do believe it has considerable merit Roger – we all know that during the last resources boom commercial rents in Perth City went through the roof. We all know there are market forces at work but profiteering to the point of bankrupting law firms indicates it all goes too far when times are good."

"Yes those lawyers fell victim to the forces dictated by the oil and gas sector – willing to pay more than the asking price for central Perth office accommodation. Now look at it – there's a glut of vacant space. There certainly needs to be a moderating influence, but the retail sector is just as important – tenants are being ripped off everywhere Steven. It's as if they factor in a pre-determined level of destruction when they adjust their rents to the so-called 'market value' upon expiration of ten year leases. But that is all in the medium to long term Steven - I don't expect we will look at purchasing domestic properties for commercial redevelopment until after our next term in office."

"That means at least another six years Roger."

"Yes I think we will have our hands full with these water projects during our next term of government."

"Unless Jane's mob wins?"

"Highly unlikely – the way we are leading in the polls - and this water project will entrench us even further. So where do we go from here?"

"I have been informed by Monadelphous that their revised feasibility study will be completed within a week and I intend to put the contracts out to tender immediately. I expect the Buckeridge Group will lodge bids but we won't give all four of them a lot of time to submit. We must get the ball rolling on this as soon as possible. Once the contracts have been gazetted and allocated, I expect work to commence within just a matter of weeks."

Just three days later the Monadelphous CEO telephoned to advise that his teams had been working feverishly on redeveloping the feasibility and were ready to meet the Minister. Fortunately, all engineers and on-site inspection teams that had gone north were back in Perth City to work on it.

"Minister Dolsen the Monadelphous team is here."

"Ah please show them to the conference room Gail. I will be there in a flash."

"Hello Georgina, Greg!"

"Hello Minister and allow me to introduce our CEO Mr. Glen Carbon."

"Very pleased to meet you. Please take a seat and let me know what you have."

"In view of your request to have this project completed within six months we have identified eleven sections of the route between Port Hedland and Newman where construction could commence virtually simultaneously, whether it goes via the Great Northern Highway or the Nullagine Road through Marble Bar. That will necessitate utilising three or four major sub-contractors as you have insisted. The contractors will need to establish their camps on Crown land and get moving on transporting their plant and materials to site as soon as they gain their part of the contract. Fortunately, there is presently an abundance of transportable accommodation in the Pilbara region due to a number of construction projects being completed and that will pretty well cover administration, dining and ablution requirements also. However, there is only sufficient twelve metre length pipe in storage here in the west to get them all started, so replacement production needs to commence immediately."

"Obviously, the best way to transport the sections of pipe to site will be by sea to Port Hedland then triple road train from there – the road from Hedland to Newman being just four hundred and fifty odd kilometres compared to almost twelve hundred from Perth to Newman. Each triple will be able to haul one hundred and forty four sections of three hundred millimetre pipe with each section being twelve metres in length. Hence each triple road train will carry sufficient pipe to complete a section of pipeline seventeen hundred metres long, which means you will require almost three hundred road train trips just for the Hedland to Newman section, so costing about three million dollars in haulage fees for that section. I am pointing that out to you Minister so you can conceptualise what the comparative will be for the Newman to Percival Lakes section will be."

"Yes I appreciate that, please continue."

"Oh, you might want to talk turkey with BHP as to whether they would be prepared to transport half of the pipe to Newman on an empty ore train. They would be stacked on pallets that a crane would lift and drop straight into their Bradken cars. They could quite easily fit half of the pipe onto one train which has about two hundred and thirty cars, which would drastically reduce road cartage costs. The train could be unloaded somewhere near Eastern Ridge just outside of Newman."

"Hmm ... food for thought – I do have contacts within BHP and they are a good corporate citizen. I will run that past them today."

"Today?"

"Yes, today!"

"Yesterday?"

"No not yesterday – I said yes ... today!"

"Okay I'll leave that one with you for now Minister. Now for the section from either Telfer or Newman to the lakes you might need to upgrade the road – at least to be a suitable gravel road. The Punmu Track or the Talawana Track may not accommodate triple road trains and we are looking at a section of dirt road some five hundred kilometres in length from either Marble Bar or Newman to the lakes. The one saving grace is that the triples will not be comparatively heavy, just bulky because it's only poly pipe. By the way, the PVC will be heat-protected from the sun with some type of a woollen cover. It's something new. The shorter option to the Percival Lakes would be via the Marble Bar road through Telfer to the lakes. That section of track is shorter by at least one hundred kilometres and it is sealed all the way to Telfer, but it would pass through the Karlamilyi National Park and very close to the Punmu Community – save for a deviation road."

"Another advantage of the Marble Bar road is that it doesn't negotiate those considerably steep sections of gorge in the Hamersley Ranges Minister."

"Yes of course, they are substantial aren't they!"

So if the roads do require an upgrade your Minister for Aboriginal Affairs will need to negotiate an expeditious agreement with the Martu people of Punmu or Parnngurr or both."

"Ben! Yes, well fortunately he is also the state Treasurer and Minister for Finance so hopefully he can appease them expeditiously as you say. I am sure Ben will incorporate some benefits for the local communities into this somehow. Let's not overlook the aquaculture concepts along the way."

"Hopefully, yes, now the transporting of aggregate to those areas can be done from the Holcim quarry at Big Rock just ten kilometres north of Newman. We have consulted Holcim and they can provide suitable aggregate in the quantities that will be required so that is a bonus with the quarry being so local."

"And the cost of that will be?"

"They will be utilising quad side tippers and each train will provide sufficient aggregate for just four hundred metres, so the haulage cost is considerably more for this than it is to transport the pipes from Hedland to site. Apart from that you may need a capping layer and a sub-base layer so

293

two quad tippers for every four hundred metre section. If that is the case the total cost will be in excess of six million dollars, but relying on Holcim's advice, one layer of aggregate will cost three million dollars.

Then of course once the road has been upgraded the pipes need to be transported in for that section – again from Hedland – unless BHP comes to the party with the train option. With that extra distance and assuming it is all by road from Port Hedland you are looking at eleven million dollars. I mean each return trip for a triple will be up to eighteen hundred kilometres from Hedland to Percival Lakes. So total transport costs could be around the twenty million dollar mark. Once they reach the lake surface, they can drive on that providing it has not been raining, which it does for about seven days per month in summer and considerably less in winter."

"Now factor in the cost of the pipe and the cost of the aggregate and we are looking at up to an additional nine million dollars. Over and above that – the construction costs. So if Monadelphous was to do the total job alone our quote would be for approximately eighty million dollars Minister. Allocating sections of the pipeline to our competitors also, you would expect the cost to blow out by at least five to ten million. Hence the total cost will be around the one hundred and thirty million dollar mark including the shipping costs – Minister."

"Okay well let's get cracking!"

The three people in the room looked slightly sideways at each other, for the Minister seemed to be in haste with this.

"I will authorise my department to place orders with the suppliers of the pipe and the road aggregate to ensure that they are getting on with production and the contracts will be advertised in the gazette this week. I will present your study to cabinet tomorrow morning. Now the section from Argyle to Fitzroy Crossing and to Hedland to integrate with the seawater pipeline?"

"Yes we have costed that also Minister and it will come in at approximately twice as much – so around the two hundred and fifty million mark for a thirty centimetre pipeline. And you need to hold commencement of that back until some of the construction teams on the Hedland to Newman section have completed their work and become available."

"So any idea how long that will take?"

"Yes approximately three months – then they could divert resources to Kununurra, Halls Creek or to Fitzroy Crossing depending upon which part of the contract they have been assigned – and as you realise completion of that section will take more than eighteen months."

"So for three hundred and eighty million we will have our pipeline in place to provide seawater or fresh water to Percival Lakes via Punmu or Parnngurr but not Jigalong, then we turn our attention to upgrading the track via the Canning Stock Route to Lake Disappointment."

"Well it's not that bad actually, if you flood Percival Lakes from the Telfer Road access, you then run that pipeline to Lake Disappointment which is about another one hundred kilometres. Of course, to disperse that water onto Percival Lakes you will require a smaller gauge pipeline to run the length of the lakes. But you would want to run this first three hundred millimetre pipeline all the way along Lake Disappointment too, though it will not carry sufficient quantities to flood all of Percival Lakes and Lake Disappointment within one twenty four hour period. That is likely to take thirty six hours to disperse just a fifty millimetre coverage and, of course, most of that will evaporate before it covers the lake. But that is what you want isn't it – once you turn the system on and the water hits the lake the evaporation process will commence immediately any time after about eight in the morning! Of course, you could gain coverage if the system is turned on in the evening, but it will still be the same result – whatever you dispense onto that lake system in a thirty six hour period will have evaporated within forty eight hours."

"Yes, that is certainly the object of the project for sure, yes."

As a politician Steven would always have positive electoral fortune in the back of his mind also.

"Of course, once this initial pipeline is up and running you would want to replicate it or even install a wider pipeline down the same route for the purpose of completing the project to Lake Wells, if you intend to take it further south to Lake Burnside then to Carnegie and Wells."

"Yes, thank you for that Greg. That will be the plan. What gauge would you envisage for that part of the project."

"Well as Georgina stated earlier, you are going to need the bigger pipe, so we would be looking at a six hundred millimetre pipeline to Lake Burnside then Carnegie and Wells. Transport costs will be significantly higher because a triple cannot fit forty eight sections onto a trailer, just twenty sections – you only fit five across a trailer not eight and only four high not six."

"Do you believe that will suffice?"

"Yes, the rainfall that Mr. Robertson was responsible for that covered much of Queensland and New South Wales all came from Percival Lakes after just a thirty six hour coverage, but he got lucky ... we got lucky ... with the air stream the way it was that facilitated that. The window of opportunity may not always be that favourable, so we have factored in what level of coverage you will need if you have just a twenty four hour conducive wind factor."

"Hmm ... makes sense!"

"But you would be looking at a third pipeline, long term, if you want to extend it to Kalgoorlie through Laverton, Menzies etcetera. For that reason, you might consider a nine hundred millimetre pipeline from Argyle to Fitzroy Crossing then two six hundred millimetre pipes on to Newman and Broome."

"Or a sixty to Newman and a ninety to Broome if you want to run that further south towards Perth through Karratha, Carnarvon, Geraldton and so on."

"Yes thank you Glen. Not to forget Derby too of course!"

"Now as for the section from either the Great Northern Highway or Marble Bar road to the Percival Lakes and Lake Disappointment, we have identified eight sections that could be commenced simultaneously providing the road has been upgraded to accommodate the road trains transporting the pipe. So your road contractor needs to have the road ready after just four months."

"So the contract with the Martu at Punmu or Parnngurr becomes the critical aspect to get the ball rolling. We need to get Ben out there with some interpreters and a contract of consent for their elders to sign. I like that idea of the aquaculture industry being developed, especially if it means they can grow marron or even lobster. We could utilise bore water to begin with to establish some gilgie or marron farms."

"I would suggest that if the Punmu community did not want the road that goes direct to their settlement upgraded with triple road trains running through it, you consider a bypass option to the north and external to the Karlamilyi National Park. You still need their consent for the rest of the track to there and also from the Kunawarritji community which is about sixty kilometres beyond Percival Lakes."

"Apart from that Greg, you might have to consider, Minister, upgrading that sixty kilometres of road to the

Kunawarritji settlement as part of the deal. They do have their four-wheel drive vehicles so to have the road upgraded from red dirt to gravel might have quite some appeal to them."

"Hmm ... food for thought, yes!"

"All of which means that Mr. Robertson went ahead and sank his twelve bores at Percival Lakes without any consultation or agreement from the communities. But if he hadn't done so we wouldn't be sitting here discussing this now."

"Yes, Glen he did, didn't he – and that is true isn't it – that if that man had not done what he did we would not be giving consideration to any of this. The results actually vindicate what he did."

"I would suggest that your man Ben keep quite a few additional benefits up his sleeve to negotiate with – one that comes to mind would be a grader, so the communities can keep the gravel road maintained and also to provide training to a few people out there on how to maintain the road. "Once the fresh water flows, they might like to utilise that for drinking and possibly a pool for their community, again with appropriate training to maintain the pool. I am sure the children out there would love that."

"Yes, some reasonably good ideas there, Glen! A golf course too, perhaps?"

"Now don't be silly, but a vegetable garden would be a great idea for them. Apparently, you can grow anything out there if you have enough water."

"Yes, well that might be more myth than fact. Now I will forward your feasibility study to our state Premier and to the Prime Minister. I believe my first step as Minister now is to liaise with the Premier and Minister for Aboriginal Affairs to seek consent from the communities as soon as possible. I believe they do have title already so there won't be an issue there – fortunately they are empowered to make decisions regarding their land as Indigenous Protected Areas."

"Do you think they might object to what Andrew Robertson has done? He didn't consult them."

"Possibly but Jennifer Downs is in good with them. Perhaps as a contingency plan we might exclude Percival Lakes from the project and run the pipeline straight to Lake Disappointment then on to Burnside and Carnegie from there."

"You would still require consent from the Talawana Martu and the three communities are all part of the same broader community, so if one community objects don't expect the others to accede. A further contingency plan might be to construct a new track from Newman straight across the Tropic of Capricorn due east to Lake Disappointment, depending upon where the community's title and IPA's extend to."

"Nah that might confuse a few workers regarding their tax concessions for working north of the twenty sixth!"

"Ha-ha-ha-ha-ha! Yeah they'd be working right on it!"

"Perhaps one steel capped boot could be claimed but not the other one!"

"At least they could stock up on all food and drink requirements etcetera from the Cappy Roadhouse."

"And pizza!"

"Okay enough banter, I'm pleased that the seriousness of your work doesn't nullify your sense of humour. Thank you for coming in and providing your presentation. Now I assume that you people will draft all of the specifications for each section during the next two weeks while the contracts are being gazetted – we need to provide those specs to the bidders."

"Yes Minister the specs will be ready within two weeks as usual."

"Thank you, Glen. I will go to see Premier Brook and Treasurer Ben Wyman today."

"Goodbye Minister Dolsen."

The Ministers

"Ben thank you for coming in. Steven and I have some serious considerations regarding the construction of the pipeline through Martu land to Percival Lakes or Lake Disappointment. I will let Steven put you in the picture."

"Ben, I had my meeting with Monadelphous this morning and they have provided their feasibility study which will be forwarded to the Prime Minister for the funding. Now we need to firstly construct a seawater pipeline from Port Hedland to either the Percival Lakes or to Lake Disappointment depending on whether or not we can procure consent from the Martu communities to possibly upgrade the road, but in any event to run triple road trains down the track from Telfer through Punmu to the Percival lakes, or via the Talawana Track to either Percival Lakes or Lake Disappointment. The former is the preferred option because it is shorter and will cost less. The Talawana Track involves the Parnngurr Community, but both are part of the wider Martu community."

"Yes I understand that!"

"We know that the communities welcome visitors along the Canning Stock Route and there is apparently a large 'Welcome' sign at ... ah ... is it Kulawarritji?

"Kunawarritji!"

"Yes Kunawarritji, so they do get a good share of traffic from various directions Ben, but triple road trains carrying the pipe could possibly meet some objection. Of course, it is imperative that we commence soon as so we need to procure their consent and we know that you have been there and met all of the elders."

"I was there just three months ago Steven."

"So, Ben we urgently need your department to draft an agreement of consent and for you to take it out there and see if you can get them to agree. Offer them whatever they want."

"From my last visit, Roger, I know they want to have their solar hot water systems replaced because every few years they clog up with calcium from the treated ground water that they are forced to drink. The installation of a water purifier would be the way to go, together with training of a few people on how to operate and maintain it. That way they would have better drinking water and their hot water systems would last a lot longer."

"Okay that seems like a good start – so what else can we offer them? Steven was thinking of utilising the seawater for aquaculture somehow, to cultivate crab or lobster? Bearing in mind that we expect fresh water to flow within eighteen months of the completion of the pipeline, which will open the door to other benefits also."

"Offer them a solar power supply. They are presently drawing off the grid from Whaleback."

"Well it doesn't cost them anything – BHP covers that but they know where it comes from and at times the power does fail, so, yes solar power."

"That's a good start now once the fresh water gets flowing, we can look at establishing some crops, especially vegetables and fruit and once again, some training in how to maintain any crops."

"Yes Roger, with anything we decide to offer I am keen to provide concomitant training, for the young people in particular. We need to be cognizant about providing transferrable skills."

"Pardon my ignorance but with fresh water and solar power I don't suppose evaporative air conditioning would be a consideration Ben."

"No it won't Steven – the indigenous people will not have air conditioning."

"Is there a reason for that?"

"Yes, it's not part of their link with the land – the land is hot and it's their church!"

"Point taken! I don't suppose a swimming pool would be considered then?"

"That they would consider, yes, but only for the benefit of the young ones. They would make good use of that and might learn better in school if they know they can take a swim afterwards. Again I reiterate, training for some local people to manage the pool would be necessary."

"So seawater to start with to grow crab, presumably in large ponds to be constructed below ground level, a solar power farm followed by vegetable crops and a pool when freshwater flows within eighteen months. If there is anything else you can think of please do – we cannot be averse to providing considerable benefit to secure this consent. The construction teams need to get cracking on this."

"So Ben how soon do you think your department can draft the contract?"

"Seems pretty straightforward – they already have fuel and other supply trucks going down that road so they should be okay with it if there's something we are offering. Give me a couple of days and I will have that drafted. I suppose you boys want me to go up there to get this done?"

"How soon can you Ben?"

"Ah ... we have a couple of Winnebago stationed at Newman so I could take two staff up there with me next week – fly to Newman, buy some supplies and head out there."

"Ben you are a champion, now if you do reach consent could you call me to let me know – my staff will issue a purchase order for additional PVC piping to be manufactured. Apparently, stocks are quite low for a project of this magnitude – over one thousand kilometres of three hundred millimetre pipe just for phase one. I expect my department to sign off on contracts within four weeks, but I don't have a timeframe for the manufacture of that amount of PVC and we are hoping to complete this phase within six months."

"Yes, I will give you a call Steven."

"And Ben, the Feds are going to fund this to end Australia's drought problem, so don't be afraid to offer the Martu whatever they need, okay."

"Might have to throw in a mini-bus and a troop carrier Roger. They could use a couple of new Hilux utes."

"Ben, ending the drought is worth billions so don't leave without a sale okay, whatever they need. Now I am going to call Anthony Albury and put the Feds in the loop. I'm sure they will be pleased that we are acting on this already. Steven, well done! Ben, that was a really good decision of yours to head north a couple of months back, well done."

Premier Brook shook hands with his two Ministers and they went their respective ways. Minister Dolsen instructed his department to draft the contracts according to the recommendations in the Monadelphous report and the State Treasurer and Minister for Aboriginal Affairs Ben Wyman prepared to meet his department's lawyers to draft an agreement. He would leave for Newman with the consent documents just three days later.

"Prime Minister's office Barbara Wilkinson speaking, how may I help you?"

"Good afternoon Barbara this is Roger Brook, could you ask Anthony to call me as soon as he is free please."

"Hello Roger, yes I will but he won't be free until tomorrow, he is at a conference with the CFMEU this evening over the scandal in the building materials standards. He doesn't expect that to be completed until midnight, you know, with what has happened with the apartment towers collapsing."

"Okay tomorrow morning will be fine, but can you let him know we are already making good progress with the water project and I am about to email a copy of the feasibility report to him."

"Okay I will thank you Roger, good to hear, I know that is very dear to Anthony and he really enjoyed going to the location I can tell you. He was telling everybody all about it and isn't it so wonderful to have ended the drought the way you people have, it's amazing."

"Don't know that we have ended the drought yet, but it seems we are heading in that direction, thank you Barbara."

The next day.

"Roger this is Anthony, how's it going over there?"

"Morning Anthony, going a lot faster than I expected – my man Dolsen is pushing it along fast as. He has the feasibility study report from Monadelphous and as soon as Ben Wyman can procure consent from the Martu, we can proceed with allocating the construction contracts. They have a few options depending on what transpires there but, in any event, construction will commence from the Port Hedland end within weeks Anthony."

"Yes I saw that the feasibility report came through – I haven't had time to read it yet but will do sometime today."

"How was the conference last night Anthony?"

"Really good thanks Roger, we are going to implement some stringent monitoring programs for all building materials brought into Australia and if they are not compliant, they will be returned at cost to the suppliers. I've had enough of this shit coming in from China mate."

"You and me both Anthony – we had that fiasco with our new children's hospital."

"Yes, that wasn't good was it? Seems to be happening everywhere now."

"So we are looking at about one hundred and thirty million for this first phase of seawater to Percival Lakes and Lake Disappointment, then another two hundred and fifty million to bring fresh water into the system from Lake Argyle in the Kimberley Anthony. That will give us coverage all the way to Lake Wells through Carnegie, Burnside and Disappointment."

"Does Ben envisage any problem with the consent."

"No, he is in good with them and was up there just a few months ago and, apart from that, he has a few cherries up his sleeve ... ah ... a water filtration system, solar power, some aquaculture projects, a mini-bus and once the fresh water flows, a pool, vege' farms and so on. So we should have that secured okay."

"Yeah, good work Roger, let's hope we can bring this to fruition in the timeframe mentioned – the long range weather forecast isn't looking good. Apparently the National Oceanic and Atmospheric Administration has detected El Nino conditions in the east Pacific again so it looks like being a dry winter next year. That will devastate thousands of people and completely demoralise small business in the bush. Very hard to put a value on business confidence Roger. It will also cost us a fortune, you understand."

"Billions, Anthony!"

"Yes, on the other hand, avert a drought and reap some good harvest and cattle and sheep production the nation will make billions and revitalise business confidence."

"It's absolutely critical, this project, Anthony."

"Why haven't we trialled this idea before, Roger? Why haven't we?"

"I've heard things like this suggested before Anthony, by ordinary Australian people but, we just seem to be dismissive, don't we? We seem to have a thought ensconced within our minds – 'what the hell would they know'?"

"Time to listen to the people, Roger."

"Yes and time to calculate the cost of opportunity and production foregone. What do you think drought has cost Australia just in the last twenty years Anthony?"

"That picks up the six year drought and probably one before that so I could say, probably, at least fifty billion dollars but probably much more than that."

"So it would make sense to invest whatever into our project to avert further losses Anthony. Three hundred and eighty million is small fry by comparison."

"Yes, I would go along with that, Roger."

"But you need to start thinking about that Argyle water being piped into Adelaide so they can sell it to your people in Melbourne Anthony. Just remember the Thomson Dam fiasco."

"Oh shit I do don't worry. We were all limited to a five minute shower. My wife couldn't wash her Ford Territory."

"Do you live in Toorak Road Anthony?"

"Very funny! Okay Roger, thanks for calling and please keep me up to speed on everything okay. I won't mind if you call me daily on this."

"Will do, thanks Anthony."

On the second day after the meeting of the Ministers, Ben Wyman had received the contract of consent from his department, which had been sanctioned by the Attorney General's office. There were four copies to be signed. Ben's staff booked their flights to Newman for the following morning. By eight in the morning they had arrived at the Martumili Art Centre where their Winnebago were garaged. Ben had two staff with him from the Department of

Aboriginal Affairs – Fiona who was Martu and Natalie who was Wongi. Both young women had completed Bachelor of Arts degrees at Curtin University majoring in Aboriginal Anthropology and Political Sociology and had worked for the department for five and six years respectively. Fiona had retained her fluency in the Martu language. The girls would share a Winnebago for the next three days, or so it seemed, while they visited Parnngurr, Punmu and Kunawarritji. They drove into Newman and did some shopping at the new IGA supermarket and left Newman by nine thirty in the morning. Prior to leaving, they stopped at the Dome café for a cappuccino where they had a discussion about their purpose.

"Now Fiona, I have virtually been given an open cheque book to provide these communities with whatever they need okay, so our role here is to ask them - and then ask them again okay. We are not here to throw money away, but we can provide them with anything they need so don't be skittish in pressing them a little. This project is worth a lot of money to the entire country. Future drought will cost this country billions, okay."

"Understood Ben – I haven't been here for about eight years but if things are still much the same, they will need a decent water system for drinking water. The water up here is shit Ben. According to the Monadelphous report the fresh water won't be here for about two years so we need to do something different for them in the interim. The other thing that always goes kaput up here is the solar hot water because the pipes get chocka with calcium so that will be a priority. A water purifier will solve that one too Ben."

"Okay so the word is – whatever they ask for they are going to be given, so we really need to get these agreements signed and sealed before we return to Perth okay."

"Yep!"

That is when Fiona's telephone rang.

"Yep! Oh thank goodness, that's great Kayleen, thank you for letting me know. Okay so tomorrow morning at ten o'clock Parnngurr. Might see you sooner than we expected … okay bye."

"So what's the good news from Kayleen?"

"Now I haven't told you this before now because you were busy and I didn't want to give you false hope, but yesterday I made some telephone calls to Kunawarritji, Punmu and Parnngurr, okay, and Kayleen has just called me to say that all the elders would meet us at Parnngurr tomorrow morning. So we only need to go to Parnngurr Ben."

"Shit! That's bloody fantastic Fiona – thank you for arranging that. That means if we can get an agreement and get these documents signed, I can call Steven Dolsen with the go ahead tomorrow afternoon."

"Well done Fiona!"

"Thanks Nat! Make my hubby happy if I'm back a day or two sooner."

"Ha-ha-ha!"

"How is Eugene making out with the job Natalie?"

"Yeah good Ben, they've got him onto a digger now up there at Solomon. He's bringing home some big bucks. Good thing he's off swing at the moment though – he's looking after the kids."

"So there's now no such urgency to head off to Parnngurr – I wouldn't mind calling in to see the general manager at Whaleback. We could go to the gatehouse and they could call him."

"He won't be expecting you!"

"No but I am one who gives him the good news or bad about the level of royalties they have to pay when the current contract expires. And it ain't good!"

"You going to tell him?"

"No not on this occasion – we'll go through the motions of negotiation when the time arises and disclose the result then, next year. But I am sure he will want to see me – he'll probably think he can butter me up a little. But we do have a couple of apprentices there from Carnarvon at the M.E.W. so it might be good for them if we can go see them for ten minutes. You know – show some interest, provide some encouragement. They do have a few hurdles to jump as Yamatji people working in a place like that. If they do well it will open a very wide door for others."

"They related to you Ben?"

"No but I do know their families. My father was close to them. Those two boys would be in their third year by now so getting really close to becoming tradies. They both attended Aquinas College like I did and I believe they have younger brothers at Newman College in Churchlands who might follow them down the same road as apprentices."

"You and Roger planning a big increase in royalties Ben?"

"An increase yes Nat, after all, things are really cranking up. Our trade delegation to India to examine prospects for infrastructure development there is starting to pay off. They need a China type of infrastructure revolution over there, which means they will need a lot more iron ore than they can provide locally or purchase from Vale. That could be huge and additional output means we can negotiate a higher royalty, which is what W.A. needs right now."

"Sounds like you boys are onto it."

"Fortunately, I do expect to be State Treasurer for quite some time and I expect one of you young ladies to be the next State Minister for Aboriginal Affairs. I believe you girls are both at the same branch of the party."

"Yes, the Scarborough branch! I live in Doubleview and Natalie is in Wembley Downs Ben. But Dylan and I are contemplating a move to North Fremantle and Natalie and

Keith will be moving to Busselton so we would join the local branches there."

"Hmm ... that means you could contest Cottesloe and Vasse – both held by the Libs Fiona. We'll have to work on that okay."

"Sounds like a plan! Minister for Aboriginal Affairs eh, yeah I like that."

"Over my dead body – that's going to be my job."

"Ha-ha-ha-ha-ha!"

"You girls like another cappuccino? It's going to be a long day and I wouldn't expect to get out of Whaleback until after midday."

"Yep, sounds good."

After another twenty minutes the three headed for the Whaleback mine, arriving at the gatehouse. They parked up outside and entered the gatehouse.

"Well look who's here! Mr. Ben Wyman of all people."

"Good morning Brendan, this is Natalie and this is Fiona. We are here unannounced and were not planning to visit but we've had a fortunate change of plans so we have some time to spare. Can you please contact the mine manager for me, I would really like to visit the two Yamatji apprentices at the M.E.W.?"

"Dale and Derek – named after those Kickett footballers! Yep sure thing, just give me a moment and I will contact the mine manager."

"Good morning Janice it's Brendan at the gate ... ah ... we actually have the State Treasurer and Minister for Aboriginal Affairs, Ben Wyman, here unexpectedly. Can you tell me if your manager is available to see Ben."

"I'm afraid not he is in an international conference with Singapore and Vale so he doesn't expect to be available until early afternoon."

"Okay no worries I will ask the liaison officer to come out and take Ben, Natalie and Fiona in to the M.E.W. okay.'

"All good this end. Leave that with me I will send the liaison officer out straight away."

"Thanks Janice!"

"The mine manager is in telephone conference with head office in Singapore and with Vale from Brazil so he cannot see you until after midday but a liaison officer will escort you into the M.E.W. and Janice will let the superintendent know that you are on your way. Now we need you to provide a breath sample, sign in and take a visitor's pass please."

"You girls been drinking?"

"No Ben, have you?"

"No not till tomorrow night eh!"

"Good idea!"

"You guys staying in town for a while?"

"No, we will be flying out tomorrow night Brendan. Going out to Parnngurr today for a meeting in the morning."

The liaison officer arrived in just five minutes and escorted Ben, Natalie and Fiona into the M.E.W. workshop where they met with the superintendent first then with Dale and Derek. The boys were pleased to have visitors and chatted for twenty minutes. On the way out, Ben mentioned to the liaison officer that Minister Dolsen would be in touch to request that a returning train might bring some PVC pipe back from Port Hedland for the water project. The liaison officer offered to raise the matter with the mine manager and Ben agreed. Then it was off toward Parnngurr for the trio.

The drive to Parnngurr went quite smoothly with the two Winnebago in convoy – Ben following the girls. Upon arriving just after five o'clock they parked up in the visitors' caravan park and went to the community centre to see some of the locals. Fiona had made it known that they would be arriving about that time. The local elders were pleased to see Ben again and even more pleased to see Fiona as it had been a while since her previous visit. They introduced Natalie as a Wongi woman. Out of deference to the elders from Punmu and Kunawarritji there was no talk at this time of the business they were there for – save for Ben telling them he had heard that their water tasted like shit. They did agree on that. As dusk was approaching, they turned in for the night with the girls and Ben cooking up their dinner on the community's barbeque.

The following day the meeting took place at ten o'clock in the community centre and apart from the senior elders from all three communities there was a large contingent of younger men and women there also, who were fluent in Martu languages and English. Ben Wyman asked Fiona to explain the reason for their visit and the importance of the project to the Australian nation. As she went through her rendition, she allowed time for each statement to be translated to the senior elders in their own dialect. She explained that Ben had documents where their requests would be recorded and that it was up to them what they bargained for. After Fiona had completed her talk, they agreed that the local people would spend a period of time to draft their requests while Ben and the girls waited outside. A young lad named Buddy – named after a footballer - offered to walk them around the settlement and explain what everything was, so they accepted. That little mini tour took almost an hour and Natalie was quick to notice that the school room had a very small air conditioning unit, which she mentioned to Fiona and Ben.

"Surely that would affect the attendance at school – if the classroom had better air conditioning the attendance rate would improve in summer months, surely."

"That is a significant problem alright."

Buddy showed them the chook house. There were only six chickens in the chook house.

"Do the chickens all lay eggs?"

"Yeah we get about four eggs every day."

"So why do you only have six chickens Buddy?"

"We used to have more but some foxes got the others."

"How many did you have Buddy?"

"Nineteen!"

"You know with a bigger and more secure chook house and more chickens you could have one egg every day for each person here Buddy."

"Yeah that would be cool."

"I see you have quite a few rabbits."

"Yeah the foxes couldn't get in there – just the chook house. We like to eat rabbit and they breed like rabbits."

"Ha-ha-ha."

"You've got one nasty looking female redback on the fence join there, Buddy."

"Yeah they're everywhere up here but we don't get bitten very much."

"Well they breed even faster than rabbits Buddy. So what do you do if someone is bitten?"

"We treat the bite mark with ice for a day and give them pain killers."

"Yeah, some decent first aid there. Perhaps we can fumigate the place for you. We know they have a place in the natural environment Buddy, but they do coalesce or get together, in big numbers wherever people are, so there are far more redback spiders here than there should be. See, there's two more over here Buddy. I wouldn't like to see young children get bitten."

"Yeah a girl was a couple of weeks ago. We put ice on the bite but she cried a lot."

"You got goats eh?"

314

"Yeah fourteen goats at the moment but sometimes more come in and sometimes some of ours go. They are pretty free to come and go. The women do milk them to make cheese. It tastes really good."

"You don't have a pool here Buddy."

"No we don't! It would be really cool to have a pool."

"Is there any kind of children's playground here, I mean, for the really young ones?"

"What like the one at McDonalds in Karratha?"

"Yes something like that."

"No we ain't got nothing like that. If we had a pool we could have a water slide eh!"

"Yes top idea that one Buddy. That football oval looks pretty hard and dry."

"Sure is! We get hurt when we fall over."

"Fresh water Ben! Cover the oval with a soft grass."

"You could cover the entire community with grass."

The trio continued their walk with Buddy until the elders were ready to bargain. They entered the community centre and listened intently as the list of priorities was read by a young elder woman. There were no surprises on the list and some of the items they had talked about were covered – save for the fumigation, the grassing of the oval, the provision of a decent chook house to keep foxes out. They had listed the solar power system upgrade, the water filtration system, the pool, the vegetable garden, the mini-bus, the upgrade of the roads and a local arts centre for the women to paint before going into Martumili in Newman. Then Ben informed them of some of the plans he had for the communities, the seawater aquaculture ponds, the freshwater aquaculture ponds, the playground and a troop carrier. Ben asked them if they were aware that there would be big triple trucks coming through the area with water pipe and that they understood the nearby lakes would occasionally be flooded but the sun would evaporate the water within a day or two. Ben then asked them if they were prepared to list everything on the documents for each settlement to sign and they agreed.

Within two hours there were four signed copies of an agreement of consent and a copy was given to the respective elders. It was now almost two in the afternoon, so the trio thanked everybody and said goodbye as they had a plane to catch. As they were leaving the building, some elder women were outside doing a traditional dance for them as they walked by toward their vehicles. Fiona explained.

"It's the dance of the rainbow serpent – only women's business really so we are quite privileged. They really are paying us great respect with this."

The three of them stopped to observe as the women completed their dance.

"The dance said they have been waiting the return of the rainbow serpent and now he is coming. They really like you Ben."

"Hmm ... please thank them for me from the depth of my spirit – for I am bungarra."

Fiona did so, then all of the women started clapping – which took everybody by surprise. When Ben got to his Winnebago he made a call to Steven Dolsen.

"Ben how did it go?"

"All signed Steven – you can give the orders to proceed with gazetting and purchase orders."

"Ben, Ben, Ben thank you so much for this ... I almost can't believe it mate. Just three days after we met in Roger's office, I really can't believe this. I will get on the blower straight away. I have people from John Holland, BGC and Leighton waiting to hear from me. Catch you when you get back."

The two Winnebago left the community for the return trip to Newman so that the girls and Ben could make it for the last flight from Newman back to Perth.

Gazetted

"Yes Steven?"

"Roger, I have heard back from Ben, they have the consent documents and he and the girls are on their way back to Newman from Parnngurr. Apparently, they met with all of the elders there."

"How did they swing that?"

"I don't know but I wanted to let you know that I have authorised the gazette notices for this Thursday and I have made calls to all prospective contractors to start preparations."

"So you are confident that they will all get a piece of the action?"

"Yes, these projects are too big for any one or two of them to commence within the specified timeframe so Monadelphous will secure the main contract and sub-let to the others. Monadelphous have given us a work schedule that could see as many as nineteen construction teams all working concurrently so it might just need all four to six contractors. Besides a lot of the preliminary preparation is maintenance work on their plant and equipment so that won't go astray. Monadelphous should have all the specs available next week so, I expect work to commence within a month or so."

"So your timeframe of six months just might become a reality Steven."

"Actually I didn't believe it at first but thought I would give it a shot. That Robertson character said something to me about Parkinson's Law, which I had never heard of."

"Oh yes, Parkinson's Law ... something like 'work expands to fit the time allocated to it' I believe."

"Something like that, so it got me into thinking just how quickly I could push people along with this."

"Rather than dragging their feet like they usually do eh? Good for you Steven, because Anthony mentioned to me this morning that El Nino is probably going to give this continent a long, hot and dry winter next year. If we are going to beat the drought, we will need this to be completed a.s.a.p. There is no way that we can rely on Mr. Robertson's bores at Percival Lakes to do the job every time."

"Okay that gives me more detail to push those contractors Roger. By the way Roger, did I hear a whisper that the runway at Newman is going to be extended to accommodate the seven six seven?"

"Yes possibly, the seven six seven – direct from the east. The equivalent Airbus too of course. But we expect the same will happen at Paraburdoo, Coondewanna, Punurunha, Brockman and Koodaideri, Steven."

"Don't they think we will have sufficient labour here in the west?"

"They certainly didn't last time – there were people flying in from New Zealand direct to Perth every two, three or four weeks for their swing. So it is in response to a request from the mining companies. They will fly their FIFO staff direct from Brisbane, Sydney, Melbourne and Adelaide. Apparently, the big miners are already taking enquiries from India now and out trade delegation is presently in Djakarta, Steven. They are placing a huge emphasis on upgrading the local infrastructure to modernise the economy, following the example set by the Chinese government, which requires copious amounts of steel. It's going to be raised in Cabinet next week."

"Okay, sounds good! Well for now I will keep on the tail of these contractors for the water project, get them up and running as quickly as possible and keep you informed, Roger."

The following day Ben Wyman and his delegation came back into the office and met with the Premier and the Minister for the Environment.

"Ben, Fiona, Natalie come in please and tell us all about it. How was the trip?"

"Bloody fantastic! Had a great time."

"Yeah it was good! I hadn't been to the Pilbara before so for me the scenery was awesome."

"Especially for me too, because I hadn't been there to that community for a few years and there were my people from Parnngurr and Kunawarritji too."

"Sounds great, so let's go through it Ben and tell us what they have come up with."

"Right, nothing too extravagant considering that the project could be worth billions of dollars to this nation and a lot of this was totally predictable – due to the appalling conditions they live in out there in the desert. They virtually require the same for all four communities."

"Four?"

"Yes - this includes the Jigalong community, south-east of Newman. Now consider all of this from the perspective that they have plenty of land and abundant sunshine okay."

"And heat!"

"Yes abundant heat but a dearth of fresh water! First cab off the rank – a swimming pool – one for each community! They see that as critical in making life bearable for their kids, but they will only have the pool available outside of school hours during school terms. Now with every one of these initiatives they have requested that residents be trained into the operation and maintenance of the infrastructure, okay. They have agreed to provide the necessary chemicals for the pools from their community account and they have accepted

320

that this will have to wait for the fresh water to be available. Secondly, replacement of the hot water systems as a priority – they haven't been replaced for more than four years so they are overdue."

"Wouldn't it be better if that is done after the better fresh water is available."

"Better for you but not for them! No, the fresh water should be available within eighteen months so if the existing hot water systems are replaced pronto, they should hang in there for at least another ten years. Some of them do not have hot water at present."

"Next!"

"Fish ponds – to be constructed for seawater first since that should be available within six months then for the ponds to be converted to fresh water as it becomes available. That will allow them to grow ocean species such as herring, schnapper, dhufish, whiting etcetera and to do some fishing – which the kids out there would love to do every day. Of course, with the advent of fresh water they will grow different species, including marron."

"Marron?"

"Yes, some of them have been marron fishing down south and they have a farm where there is a ramp into a dam and the marron come up onto the ramp to feed on baits then they are scooped up with a net, so the kids really want that."

"Sounds like fun! What's next?"

"They want to go really big on growing vegetables and fruit, so they want extensive greenhouses large enough to grow all of the fruit and vegetables that they will ever need. Again, the training of residents into knowledge and procedures pertaining to every type of vegetable and fruit that can grow there at different times of the year. But the greenhouses will ensure that the local fauna don't damage crops or trees."

"So what types of vege's and fruit are they hoping for?"

"Everything that is capable of growing out there – obviously the usual – tomato, lettuce, cabbage, cauliflower, broccoli, corn, potato, asparagus, onion, sweet peas, oranges, apples, mandarin and peach. All that stuff!"

"You left out kiwi fruit!"

"Whatever they want to try is all the go okay, I'm sure they can get some good advice from horticulturalists somewhere."

"Next?"

"They want to get into animal husbandry in a big way, so they are requesting a number of fenced areas where a pivot control system can deliver fresh water to grow pasture where they can raise whatever animals they want to. That will include kangaroo, emu, sheep, cattle, goats, horses, pigs, ducks, geese and chickens, okay? The pasture areas will need to be shaded in part, to provide relief for the stock from the sun."

"Sounds interesting!"

"It is! Each community could have up to ten different areas with appropriate fencing so that the different animals can be isolated from others. The sheep and goats could be together with cattle and horses and so on but, obviously, you wouldn't put all of them in the same pasture. They might want to keep the horses away from emus for example or keep the chickens separate to all others. Again, they will take some good advice on board."

"Could get David Attenborough to come out here eh"

"Ha-ha-ha-ha-ha! Not a silly idea at all Nat."

"David Attenborough, right, he's now on my to do list. So the pivot system would ensure good pasture growth and an abundance of feed for all species. Some of the stock will provide food so they will need a slaughter shed and again, suitable training in slaughter procedures. The elders are

322

keen to have the young people trained into everything that might provide opportunities for them to integrate into the wider community. They will also require a milking shed to obtain fresh milk from dairy cattle and goats. They are keen to continue making goats cheese too."

"So what size are they thinking of for the pivot control systems?"

"Large! There's no reason to be small minded about this – they have plenty of land and plenty of sunshine, so they are thinking of about a one hundred metre diameter pasture for each one."

"Yeah that is certainly achievable – I am sure that ADP can do that or larger, no problem."

"Yes, they actually do up to eight hundred diametre at Nammuldi. As I said, sections need to be shielded from the sun to provide respite for the stock and that needs to be both total cover and shaded cover."

"So, the idea is they can run sheep, cattle, horses – all of those stock you mentioned and move them from one area to another depending on the growth rate of the pasture."

"Exactly, they want to keep the stock safe from dingo and wild boar and be able to move them as they see fit then utilise them for whatever purpose they need. They will cull animals for food, ride horses, milk cattle, get fresh eggs from chicken etcetera. Basically they want ... need ... to be able to raise any type of useful animal. Including bungarra!"

"Bungarra?"

"Yes, more-so for the cultural aspects of raising bungarra for food. Their children need to be taught those skills. Also bush turkey for the same reason."

"The bustard?"

"Yes the Australian Bustard. Not sure how they will go with people but certainly worth a try. Hopefully they can succeed with that and cultivate some for release back into the wild. So some huge plans there for animal husbandry and I suspect more will develop from that as time progresses. They are hoping to become as self-sufficient as possible with a lot of this."

"Sounds great!"

"I'm really excited for them! I have lived through the conditions there, you know. Poor water quality, hot dusty conditions, no pool for respite from the hot sun, relying on vege's and fruit that has to come in from Newman, no animals for the kids to learn with."

"Me too Fiona!"

"Yes it does sound quite fantastic, doesn't it? There's more to come though?"

"Sure is! They need a workshop with tools and equipment, so they can teach their young people some transferrable skills that might encourage them to seek employment in the mining industry - so mechanical repair and servicing equipment, welding gear, spray painting and panel beating gear etcetera."

"Great idea!"

"They want a picture theatre!"

"Picture theatre?"

"Yes, of course, let's face it they have buggar all out there for entertainment so with a theatre they can download all the latest from Netflix and keep their kids happy. The theatre needs to be air conditioned, of course and large enough to accommodate about sixty or so people at a time."

"Yeah that's a good idea."

"And the theatre will have a kitchen and dining area as an adjunct where they can gather for food and a cappuccino after the movie to socialise. The elders are intent on regulating the hours so as to not interfere with the kids' sleep and preparing for school. They think they might run a movie just two or three times per week. They do want the mini-bus and a new Hilux plus a few trail bikes for all three communities. The swimming pools must have shaded areas, grassed areas and seating so protection from the sun and ... oh ... a diving board at the deep end of the pool too."

"Okay so the pool must be full on!"

"Yes and they all want their own art workshop and a display gallery so they can develop their artistic skills and educate their young people into artwork. They can then take their work to the Martumili centre in Newman or display their artwork locally to tourists and visitors who traverse the Canning Stock Route. So that covers the main items, but I have told them to let me know if there are any additional items as time go by."

"Great work Ben – sounds like they have some good plans there."

"Yes they do but as part of the community I wonder why a lot of this has not been provided until now Steven. Let's face it – successive governments have failed these people – especially from the perspective of encouraging their young people to feel content within their community and to learn the skills they will pick up from this."

"Yes as Premier, Ben, I must admit we have failed them abysmally and when the time comes, perhaps at the opening of the water flow, we need to apologise for virtually forcing them to live in such squalid conditions. Those young people, in particular, could have had so much more done for them in the past, you know, to develop transferrable skills to improve their life prospects."

"That would be a good idea, Roger. Now I will get this down to the Attorney General's office for registration under the agreement."

"Well done! Now Steven, we need to discuss the progress of this project here with Ben and myself virtually every day to make sure it progresses as planned."

"Don't worry Roger, I will push those contractors along as quickly as I can. Ben that really is exciting what you have come up with there with those communities, well done mate. Fiona, Nat – well done!"

The three Ministers of the Crown then returned to their normal business. The applications for sub-contracts were lodged on cue and allocated by the major contractor, Monadelphous, within two weeks, with all sub-contractors receiving a piece of the pipe pie. Monadelphous lodged the sole application for the role of major contractor. Then the Minister received some good news from Monadelphous.

"Minister we have Mr. Glen Carbon from Monadelphous on the line for you."

"Glen this is Steven Dolsen, how are you?"

"I'm very well thank you Steven and we do have some positive news for you this morning – Holcim have informed us that there are only some minor sections of the Telfer to Punmu Track that will require an upgrade and they expect to complete those works within four weeks."

"That's fantastic! That means the track won't hold up construction, virtually at all Glen – it's going to take at least four weeks before most of the contractors can commence work. They need to get all their logistical plant and equipment in place and establish their camps."

"Apart from the seawater extraction facility north west of the Pardoo Roadhouse, they can get cracking on that virtually straight away – that small team of workers could stay at the roadhouse accommodation each night, either for the eight weeks it will take them to construct that facility or until that contractor provides dongas. It might take a week or two for the machinery to arrive, but they can commence ground works for the building within a few days."

"Is the equipment for the extraction facility readily available?"

"Yes that can be procured virtually off the shelf from the manufacturer that supplied the plant and equipment for the desalination plants south of Perth. It's pretty much the same setup except that we don't need to extract those great quantities, so a smaller plant will suffice."

"So that team could be the first to start?"

"The ground surveyors will be the first people on the job Minister. As for the word from Holcim, yes, it is good news - it seems the East Pilbara Shire does maintain the track reasonably well for the sake of the communities. They do have articulated vehicles using the track to provide for the Punmu community, including fuel trucks. The shire will maintain the grade of the track for the duration of the project, after all, it is their responsibility."

"So apart from the extraction facility will there be any other sections that can kick off straight away without having to wait for the establishment of a suitable camp?"

"Yes ... well any sections where workers have reasonable access to accommodation facilities and can drive in-drive out. So from Port Hedland and Newman no problem - they could make a start on groundworks without having any concrete bases or pipeline to install, as soon as the surveyors have pegged the plots. Apart from that the suppliers of materials too can get cracking. BGC is going to fabricate the concrete bases for all sections so that will commence immediately and, by the way, our specs stipulate that all concrete bases from Marble Bar to Lake Wells must be formed to accommodate future six hundred and nine hundred millimetre pipelines. That way a future addition won't require the manufacture of concrete bases. The same goes for the Argyle to Fitzroy Crossing section – the concrete bases must accommodate the three hundred, six hundred and a nine hundred millimetre fresh water pipeline. Of course from Fitzroy Crossing to Broome it will just be a six hundred then nine hundred millimetre job so that is in our specs also."

"And we are going with the three hundred millimetre pipe first rather than just starting with the six hundred because ..."

"To get the water to the lakes as quickly as possible – the transportation of the six hundred millimetre pipe will take a lot longer and you may not be able to drain the groundwater for that long with the existing bores."

"Good thinking!"

"Obviously the manufacturers of the PVC can make a start – they simply need to increase their output - operate twenty four seven if they need to. There are a number of suppliers we can draw from for pipe - there's no paucity of them in Western Australia. So all contractors have been issued with their specifications and the specs include all details of groundworks, support infrastructure and the required timeframe. The supports being supplied by BGC include metal attachments, to be fabricated by Civcon, that will be affixed to existing bridges where the rivers would otherwise preclude installation of the pipeline."

"Yes I was wondering about that. We certainly do have some doozy rivers up there. So it sounds as though most things are coming together and various contractors are gearing up to get started Glen."

"Yes and some of the construction contractors will undertake their section working twenty-four seven at times. It's a lot cooler in the nights up there. So as the major contractor we will be monitoring progress along the way and keep you informed of how everything is going. You will see some real action within the next two weeks Minister."

"Thank you, Glen - and good luck."

Steven Dolsen called in to see Roger Brook.

"Yes Steven, come in please?"

"Roger, I have just had a call from Monadelphous. It seems everything is ready to rock and roll with the project. The surveyors are on their way to Pardoo to make a start on the extraction facility as we speak and BGC Concrete in Canning Vale has commenced manufacturing the concrete bases to support the pipelines. The PVC manufacturers are onto it also and we need only minor upgrading to the road to Punmu, so it's all systems go already. Roger, I am more confident than ever now that this first component of the project can be completed within the six months that we specified."

"That's wonderful Steven! I am pleased that you are keeping on top of everything the way you are. Now I have had a call from Terri Butler and the Bureau of Meteorology has forecast favourable conditions for the end of next week for us to start Mr. Robertson's bore system. So they are going to monitor that very closely and keep us informed during the week for a possible start-up in six or seven days from now."

"So obviously the rainfall they have received isn't sufficient?"

"No that was probably about ten percent of their annual average and will simply get the ground feed shooting but to achieve proper growth for their cattle and sheep they will need just as much in the next week or two. Then hopefully they get rain in the winter, but the El Nino effect looks like cutting in big time. I suspect we will be saving the day at least five or six times in the next six months."

"So that will be completely reliant on Robertson's infrastructure - shit, bloody good job he did what he did eh Roger? The result will certainly vindicate his actions."

"The man's a life saver Steven. There are lessons in this for us – just get on with it – whatever has to be done. Cut the crap and do things!"

329

"I can now fully concur with that, Roger. No place for complacency in the future Australia."

I mean, let's think about this for a moment Steven. Why didn't we do this ourselves? Why didn't we do this last year when the drought was already in full swing? What is it about us – we politicians and bureaucrats that seems to prevent us from doing things like this that need to be done? You mentioned the word 'complacent' there a moment ago, but are all of us complacent, really? I've noticed the change in you over this Steven Dolsen."

"Yeah I guess I have changed a little. I don't think I was up to this six weeks ago, before we found out what Robertson had done. I was cruising! Perhaps with the drought being over there and not here one could become somewhat complacent about it. You know - when it doesn't affect yourself and the people around you personally."

"True but I think it goes deeper than that Steven. We allow ourselves to become straight-jacketed by the system we live in – you know, so much of what we do now is subject to red tape, bureaucratic requirements, permits, legislation, steering committees, parliamentary enquiries, reviews and consultation and all the pressure from lobby groups and their henchmen. It seems to be impossible now to just decide to do something – which Robertson did."

"He didn't consult anybody!"

"No and probably just as well. I mean, where do you think this would be now if Mr. Robertson had contacted your department and floated his idea to flood the Percival Lakes to end the drought in the eastern states?"

"Probably on Jane Wyatt's desk."

"Exactly! She would probably have been afraid to refer the enquiry on to the EPA for an assessment – probably would have scoffed at the idea as an absurdity. And I am not specifically mentioning Jane in that, I think almost anybody of similar ilk would have done the same."

"So we have lost something in our compilation of administrative law or even in our quest for democratic rule, Roger."

"We've lost the derring-do to do! A friend of mine once said to me that the best form of government was benevolent dictatorship. That one man taking the action he did has given us a chance Steven – a chance to save people's lives and an industry worth billions of dollars. Let's face it Steven, that proposal would not have got up if it had been referred to the EPA. For starters, you wouldn't gain a consensus between the so-called experts regarding the likely outcome. Many would be too reticent about putting their name to something like this for fear of professional ridicule. Too many would say it's not going to work and people would argue about something like this being a waste of money – without being prepared to even trial it."

"But putting a couple of hundred million dollars on the line with a new idea that could save billions, Roger – a lot of Australians would say 'have a go' wouldn't they?"

"Yes exactly Steven – but they are not politicians nor bureaucrats. We allow ourselves to get caught up in all this stuff. So I am thinking about how to solve this type of problem and the only way I can think of achieving this is with legislation that allows Ministers of the Crown to have greater discretion."

"Hmm ... that could be dangerous!"

"I mean, look at what happens in Parliamentary debate. It is a succession of digression and a parade of people pushing their own barrow Steven. They stand up there and mouth off on behalf of people with ulterior motives who stuff electoral funds into their member's pockets."

"Would there be any safety mechanism in this utopia of yours, Roger?"

"The Minister would have to answer to the Parliament – and to their electorate. Perhaps a decision of no confidence that requires a two thirds majority from the house. That way if a Minister did run awry, a vote of no confidence would probably require at least some from their own party to vote against them. On that we would all be subject to scrutiny. Yep! I think I like that idea."

"How would you get that through the Parliament?"

"By convincing everybody that when their shot at government does come about – and it always does – they will have far greater Ministerial autonomy without having to enact legislation. Or perhaps an Act that accommodates Ministerial discretion with all decisions then being subjected to a no confidence vote. The Snowy Mountains Scheme eventually required an Act of Parliament to completely formalise it Steven. But why should it have? Everybody wanted the scheme to succeed."

"Hmm ... everybody wants this scheme to work too I reckon."

"Yes of course they do, but it took one person to take the action that was required – no committees, no collective decision making, Steven – just action!

"So thanks for the update and keep me informed."

Construction

On cue, the surveyors were in Port Hedland the next morning and drove out to the coast north of Pardoo Roadhouse – the nearest point from which seawater could be drawn for the pipeline through Marble Bar. Within four months the extraction building and some sections of the pipeline were complete, though yet to be joined to sections being completed by neighbouring contractors, which would be a formality. Contractors who had completed their section were then engaged to commence work on the section from Fitzroy Crossing toward Halls Creek, with other contractors to commence from Argyle. Closer to Marble Bar, two wind turbines were being constructed at the base of hills within forty kilometres of Marble Bar that would pump water to a reservoir being constructed at an elevation of four hundred metres due east of the Meentheena Conservation Park and just eight kilometres off the Rippon Hills road. This would allow for gravity feeding to the outlets on the Percival Lakes and Lake Disappointment. The eventual construction of the pipeline to Lake Carnegie and Lake Wells would require two additional turbines to pump water to an elevated position above those lakes.

The first extremely important phase of this project, to provide seawater to the Percival Lakes system and to Lake Disappointment to substitute Andrew Robertson's groundwater, that would placate any aggrieved pastoralists, was on cue to be finalised within the six month period.

Construction of the extraction facility with appropriate screening mechanisms and pumping equipment was completed by Monadelphous in nine weeks. Monadelphous also completed the first section of pipe to Marble Bar utilising concrete bases fabricated by BGC Concrete. Bridge structures fabricated by Civcon were attached as adjuncts to all bridges along the route. John Holland had been constructing the two wind turbines near Marble Bar that would pump water to the top of the hill due east of Meentheena to the reservoir constructed by Leighton who also laid the pipe to the Punmu community. Leighton also constructed the first concrete ponds that would be utilised to accommodate ocean fish species until fresh water became available. These ponds would eventually be used to accommodate freshwater species, as the communities had requested a number of water-based initiatives. The Monadelphous crew picked up the pipe construction from Punmu to the Percival Lakes, where the BGC crew had been laying pipe the length of the lakes system along Percival Lakes – some two hundred kilometres and more and utilising Dicko White's bore locations plus just as many more. Leighton then completed the pipeline to Lake Disappointment and established outlets along the western perimeter of the lake.

As each major contractors' crew completed their sections, they were engaged on work for the six hundred millimetre seawater pipeline which would cover the same route then be extended from Lake Disappointment to Lake Burnside and Lakes Carnegie and Wells. These lakes too, would initially be flooded with seawater to provide more comprehensive relief to drought affected areas in the east. The fresh water pipeline from Lake Argyle would take at least eighteen months to be completed to Punmu then to Parnngurr and Kunawarritji, being a nine hundred millimetre pipeline. This pipeline would also provide fresh water to the people at the Jigalong community via a three hundred millimetre spur line to a storage tank.

Meanwhile, back at the station, life had been going on as normal on a cattle station, with old Jack Lambert taking

Andrew through all aspects of management. Then one morning, life took a turn in a new direction.

"Are you okay love – you look a bit pale?"

"Andrew, I have just been sick in the lavatory and I am feeling really nauseous. I have reason to believe that I might be pregnant."

"Wow, that's great, wow Bec, let's hope so Bec!" as Andrew gave his wife a huge hug.

"Well it is what we've been hoping for. I don't have a pregnancy kit though, you know, to test if I am pregnant."

"And is this the very first day you have been feeling nauseous?"

"Yes, just since this morning."

"Okay, wow ... ah ... why don't we just head off this morning into Newman to buy a kit and perhaps you could see a doctor while we are there. I could call now to make an appointment for this afternoon love."

"Yeah okay, can you do that for me please – I feel like I might be sick again soon so I had better go back to the bathroom."

"Perhaps you had better lay down until we are ready to leave Bec. I will make the call now."

Rebecca went to the bathroom and Andrew picked up his phone to dial a doctor. The phone rang several times.

"Thank you for calling the Eastern Las Vegas Medical Centre. We are unable to take your ..."

"Shit ... wrong number! Better get that updated ... ah ... let's see, Google, doctor, Newman ..."

"Good morning Kinetic Medical Newman."

"Yes good morning I would like to book an appointment for my wife for this afternoon if possible, please. We have reason to believe she might be pregnant."

"We do have one appointment time left at four o'clock - would you like to come in then?"

"That will be fine thank you - her name is Rebecca Robertson."

"Rebecca Robertson booked in for four o'clock, thank you."

Andrew and Rebecca left the homestead for their quick trip to Newman, which confirmed that Rebecca was indeed pregnant. Her child would be born on the second day of October - the same day of the year as old Jack Lambert and a day he shared with Mohandas Ghandi - just two months after the water from the extraction facility near the Pardoo Roadhouse began to flow through Punmu to the Percival Lakes in August 2025.

"Good morning Premier Brook I have Mr. Glen Carbon of Monadelphous on the telephone for you."

"Glen good morning how is everything going?"

"Mister Premier, your pipeline will be completed and ready to launch in four days from now. Of course, it will take a day or so for the water to reach the Punmu Community so that gives you a little more time to plan but I expect you might want to be there to open the valve to the fish pond."

"Yes and Anthony Albury wishes to be there also with his Minister Terri Butler so thank you for letting me know Glen and I will contact Anthony now to check on their availability. I think it would be most appropriate for the official opening to be at the Punmu Community rather than at the Pardoo extraction facility, after all, we do want the local people to be involved in the opening ceremony. Ben Watts tells me they will do a corroboree dance of the Wagyl. Now there might be a slight delay depending on the Prime Minister's availability, so will get back to you shortly Glen."

The Premier of Western Australia Mr. Roger Brook telephoned the Prime Minister of Australia Mr. Anthony Albury.

"Good morning Anthony, Roger Brook calling."

"Hello Roger, how are things in the west?"

"Excellent! I have just had a call from Monadelphous Anthony. The seawater pipeline from Pardoo to Punmu is almost ready, in fact it will be ready to flow at Punmu this Saturday."

"Saturday, yes that works in well with me so pencil me in for that. I will have my staff make the arrangements, now as time is tight Roger, perhaps that pilot could fly us direct to the lake at Punmu then back to Perth. That would save a lot of travelling time and I am midway through negotiating with some top former bankers to establish a new government owned bank, Roger."

"You don't mean as the Commonwealth Bank used to be Anthony?"

"That's exactly what I mean, Roger. So much for a government owed corporation being privatised for efficiency – what the other bastards have done has cost the Australian people billions."

"Shit that's pretty bloody radical Anthony – the banks won't take this lying down."

"Well the banks don't run the bloody country, Roger – I do! They've had their chances and had it far too good for too long, so they need some honest, tempering competition now."

"And I thought you were a moderate Anthony!"

"I was!"

"You swinging around a little Anthony?"

"This was Tanya's idea and yes, I suppose she is having a bit of an influence on me. It's made me so bloody irate Roger, what the banks have been doing to blatantly rort the Australian people. So a one day trip to Punmu would be the go for myself and Terri okay. We can arrive in Perth about eight-thirty in the morning to be at Punmu by eleven o'clock, then leave there say three o'clock back to Perth by five and

Canberra by eight, Perth time, so ten o'clock our time – that's good."

"Okay Anthony, leave the organising of the function up to us I can assure you it will be all set for Saturday. Oh, and the seawater will initially fill some ponds that will be used for ocean fish but be switched to fresh water when that becomes available."

"Sounds good, Roger – look forward to seeing you guys on Saturday morning."

All arrangements were made by the Premier's Department and Phillip the pilot was in Perth to take the contingent to Punmu. Approval had been granted for the jet to land onto Lake Auld at Punmu – part of the Percival Lakes system. On the way north, Anthony Albury and Roger Brook had some interesting discussions.

"Hopefully this opening of the system today will result in some rainfall where it is needed Anthony."

"The bureau believes it will, but we are still a long way from ending the drought problem. What happened in recent weeks has only just initiated the germination process of the grasslands and they will need this follow up rain very soon to keep that process going. Those pastoral areas usually receive over two hundred millimetres of rain per annum Roger, so we will desperately need the pipeline extended to the southern lakes as soon as possible."

"To Carnegie and Wells?"

"Yes, the bureau has been going back through old records and data to determine the frequency of favourable wind systems and it seems that next winter we could be utilising the system seven or eight times during the next few months from February. As I said on the phone, Roger, the forecasting is not good due to the El Nino effect so I am keen to extend this concept to other lakes in Western Australia and to the Territory and South Australia too if it seems to work well."

"Yes, we have a Lake Mackay and a Lake Macdonald several hundred kilometres south of Lake Argyle and near the border with the Northern Territory and if you are going to consider the possible pipeline from Lake Argyle down through the centre of Australia to Adelaide, those two lakes could definitely come into consideration."

"The Northern Territory and South Australia have dozens of large lakes that could be brought into the system too - excluding Lake Eyre, Lake Gairdner and Lake Torrens of course because they are within national parks. Lake Amadeus in the Territory is over one hundred and eighty kilometres long and about ten k's wide, so we will have to give some thought to that as a possible route for a pipeline. Having more lakes set up with reticulation systems will provide greater options for the different wind systems that arise. The word seems to be getting around that there could be a pipeline project down through the centre because we are getting enquiries from people who want to mine the salt and potash if we construct any kind of road system. Apparently, that is the only thing that is holding them back – the lack of road infrastructure."

"That may be Anthony, but surely you wouldn't outlay the cost of sealing all roads along the pipeline?"

"Roger – there's sometimes just no way of telling what providing such infrastructure may give rise to, that realises previously unforeseeable benefits. Okay some people do come up with wacky ideas – like the one who wants to build a golf course that circumscribes Uluru – but imagine the tourism benefits of something like that. Perhaps it's not crazy until it's proven to be, providing it isn't so close as to upset the local indigenous people."

"The Pitjantjatjara!"

"I mean, people would fly to Uluru from all over the world to play on such a golf course, Roger. Everybody knows of Uluru – it is *the* Australian icon and it gets a fair share of publicity."

"Anthony, you would need to build three golf courses to circumscribe Uluru – and that would require a lot of water."

"That's an even better idea, Roger – build three golf courses around Uluru. There'd be quite a few jobs in that for the local Pitjantjatjara people. It would have to be designed to their approval, of course, so as to not impinge upon any sites of significance. So what might seem like a wacky idea to begin with just might solve some very significant social problems too. What opportunities do the young Pitjantjatjara people have to develop a career? You see what I mean! So the sealed road to the lakes could give rise to increased efficiencies for mining companies, Roger."

"I would like to play golf at Uluru Anthony."

"But getting back to the subject, apparently there's a shitload of salt and potash out there on some of those lakes that might be worth mining if the road infrastructure can keep the transport costs down. Presently that's not the case! That's not even taking into account the benefits of additional mineral exploration that such infrastructure would create. I mean, imagine if somebody found Lasseter's Reef, Roger."

"Wouldn't that be something, but yes, we do realise that mineral exploration is somewhat stymied by the lack of infrastructure so perhaps developing the pipeline to Adelaide could pay for itself in the long run in various ways."

"Apart from that Roger, we do have an enormous problem with the Darling River being choked by algae that kills millions of fish, so we need additional rainfall for that problem also. People are becoming really perturbed about that and it is a national tragedy itself."

"Well we do have several other large lakes here in Western Australia Anthony, in our Mid-west region, particularly in the shires of Sandstone and Leonora. Lake Barlee is the second largest lake in Western Australia Anthony – it's about one hundred kilometres by eighty. Lake Moore is over one hundred kilometres long and not too far from there is Mongers Lake and lakes Ballard and Marmion. We envisage the pipeline from Lake Wells being constructed to Kalgoorlie through the towns of Leinster, Laverton, Leonora then Menzies and spur pipelines could be run to all of those lakes. So you may not need to look outside of Western Australia for the evaporation concept. Conceivably the pipeline from Lake Wells could be extended to those lake systems, or there could be a spur pipeline to those lakes with the main pipeline flowing on to Kalgoorlie."

"Kalgoorlie! I believe somebody spoke of the possibility of reversing the flow back to ... where is it?"

"Mundaring Weir."

"Yes, Mundaring Weir – now wouldn't that have some historical significance for the state of Western Australia. That water has been flowing east to Kalgoorlie for a long time, Roger."

"More than one hundred and twenty years Anthony – and it provides drinking water to more than one hundred thousand people in our state. Correct me if I am wrong Anthony, but what I hear you saying that would be a watershed moment in the history of our state. The symbolic significance would be that now we go forward in a new direction, eh Anthony."

"Yeah, something like that, Roger."

"Except that this time we could manufacture the pipe ourselves here in the west – the pipe for the goldfields line was manufactured overseas – and the entire project only took about five years to complete."

341

"Without all of the machinery that we have available today, Roger. How far is that exactly, to Kalgoorlie?"

"About six hundred kilometres."

"Shit, that far! And they did that in just five years over a century ago. Puts us to shame really doesn't it?"

"Afraid so! And the Snowy Scheme took twenty five years Anthony."

"Yes! So from Lake Argyle to Adelaide would be about five times that distance from Kalgoorlie to Mundaring."

"Yeah pretty close to that."

"Yes, plenty of food for thought there, Roger – seems we will need a task force to consider all of the pros and cons of several options."

"I like that idea Anthony – a task force to thrash it all out. You would need some economic geographers involved in that. One of my lecturers at the University of Queensland was a West Aussie who completed his doctorate thesis on the subject of the economic impact that the deviation of the Great Eastern Highway in Victoria Park had on local businesses. That is the type of discipline we would be looking at eh."

"Yep, good point, Roger! We would certainly need people from a multitude of disciplines involved in that project. It's also something that could be developed on an ongoing basis – provide a nine hundred millimetre pipeline to Adelaide to begin with, then duplicate it or deviate additional lines to a wide range of areas throughout Australia. Shit – everybody needs good quality water."

"Yes, it's time we got on with it eh?"

"Yes, you know how I said that Tanya came up with the idea of another government owned bank."

"Yes, very interesting, that one."

"Well she's full of good ideas Roger, in fact, once I have led the party to the next election, I think I would stand aside for her, perhaps even mid-term, to be our next Prime Minister, Roger."

"Good ideas eh?"

"Yes, consider this, Roger. This water project could cost a lot of money ,right?"

"Right – a few billion if you took it to the 'nth' degree."

"So if it has the prospect of realising financial benefits for the Federal Government in the long run, why not – and this is Tanya's idea – why not put it to the Australian people that they can invest their superannuation funds into an infrastructure development fund that provides them with a government guaranteed annual return that exceeds the consumer price index by a factor of three or four, depending on mid-term rolling returns?"

"Hmm ..."

"I mean, consider this Roger, that would be tantamount to a capital guaranteed fund that would probably exceed what the open market would return through its capital guaranteed funds, hence the incentive, but would be stable and transparent so that everybody could see exactly what the fund is returning and what infrastructure projects the capital is invested into. And the guaranteed return would be set to allow your average citizen to be completely financially independent in retirement – and I mean long-term retirement."

"So no need for welfare pension payments from the government?"

"Exactly – an enormous saving to the government when we are going to have a problem already with our baby boomers retiring."

"Interesting Anthony! And this fund would be used for projects like the pipeline?"

"Yes! So no outlays from general revenue, Roger – the funds would come through superannuation savings."

343

"I like it already! What else has she come up with?"

"Using the same to fund super-fast trains all around Australia's capital cities."

"You're kidding me!"

"No! We have an enormous problem with congestion now, especially in Sydney, Melbourne and now Brisbane. Perth isn't too bad as you know because you guys electrified the train system when the Libs couldn't ..."

"Well not only that Anthony, they closed the train line to Fremantle and proposed to build bus lanes down the centre of the freeways rather than trains. I mean, imagine how many buses and bus drivers we would have needed. Shit – one of our long trains can carry over one thousand people."

"Yes Roger, but the system is already starting to become overloaded is it not?"

"Well – yeah!"

"So Tanya's idea is to build terminals for very fast trains on the outskirts of the capital cities – and I mean outskirts Roger, say, between thirty to sixty kilometres out – and have people travel by either car, bus, pushbike or light rail away from the capital city to a major transport terminal, where they catch the very fast train into the city via a network of tunnels, that has no stops along the way or perhaps just one or two stops at major centres like universities or commercial precincts."

"Shit! That sounds a bit out there."

"It is, but think of it this way, the infrastructure to transport people to the outposted terminal is comprehensive and efficient so it doesn't take forever to get to the major terminal – perhaps ten to twenty minutes for most people – and we do this while we still have sufficient space to create the transport corridors that go away from the cities. Then they board the VFT which gets them to the city in just ten to twenty minutes.   It would travel at over two hundred

344

kilometres per hour, so even a fifty kilometre journey would be covered in just fifteen minutes. Problem solved, Roger!"

"Sounds like a plan! Hopefully nothing could go wrong."

"Bullet-proof safety systems would be the go, Roger – including Tanya's idea of a scout vehicle leading the way ahead of the train, that would detect any problems. One at each end, of course."

"We should be doing that already! I recall that very substantial derailment years ago when a train took a corner too quickly near the Blue Mountains. A scout vehicle would have alerted the train drivers to their problem."

"Yes! But just imagine if most of those people trying to drive into the cities on congested highways and freeways are actually driving away from the cities, Roger – and on roads that are totally efficient while we still have the space to create them. Or they go to those terminals via a light rail system rather than driving their cars."

"You could be right about Tanya, Anthony - a true visionary eh!"

"Yes, but that's not all she has come up with, Roger. Now you need to keep this to yourself okay."

"Mum's the word Anthony."

"Tanya has proposed the formation of Labor Corporation, Roger."

"Labor Corporation? What for?"

"Again, encouraging Australian workers to invest their superannuation funds to become virtual shareholders, the Labor Corporation would surreptitiously purchase a majority shareholding in one of Australia's major banks and then replace the board with a Labor oriented board, with somebody like Paul or Julia as the new chairperson or CEO."

"Paul?"

"Keating! It would then reduce interest rates across the board for all workers who would virtually be shareholders through their superannuation investment, to literally compete the other banks into following suit. It would still be able to provide investors with a good annual return without all of the greed factor that our existing banks are so notorious for."

"So an annual return similar to the proposed infrastructure fund, Anthony."

"Yes, wealth accumulation over a prolonged period is really all about having a net return that exceeds the Consumer Price Index by threefold or fourfold, Roger. The downward pressure on interest rates emanating from our bank would also keep the CPI in check – keep it down below one or two percent."

"So if the CPI is two percent, a net return to the superannuation fund of seven or eight percent would suffice."

"Yes, especially in a long-term super fund, Roger. Most of our problems emanate from the fact that our ruling class wants an annual net return of ten percent minimum – with all costs passed off to the consumer. And look at the destruction that causes, Roger – half the people working for our major banks in debt and credit card collection would not be required if the interest rates on credit cards were capped at fifteen percent. The additional five percent interest causes most of the self-perpetuating default problems."

"Hmm … wouldn't those shareholders you are referring to want their ten percent?"

"Not your bog-stock Aussie fair-minded citizen, Roger – he or she will settle for the eight percent guaranteed via bank shares, if they knew that the CPI would be one percent and if it would also lead to cheaper finance for themselves. So much of our capitalist economy is based on greed, Roger. You know that is why we become members of the Labor Party – to correct that through government."

"Yes, I have to say I share your sentiments about the bog-stock Aussie and us actually."

"But that's not all, Roger! Apart from reduced interest rates provided to superannuation shareholders, Tanya has also proposed that even lower interest rates are offered to those who are also union members. That's going to encourage a lot of Aussie workers to take advantage of lower interest rates on offer – especially on credit card finance – by joining a trade union."

"Hmm ... now that is a radical move, but it sure would encourage a lot more people to become members and to reap the benefits eh?"

"Exactly! And as you know the major banks have offered lower interest rates to high income earners for several decades now – the doctors, the lawyers ..."

"The shopping centre shareholders!"

"Yes them too! The other thing Tanya is pushing for is a Royal Commission into the history of the tax minimisation industry in Australia – and she means taking it back to the sixties when all this bullshit started, you know, family trust structures and all that crap. We need to do something about that, Roger."

"But we had the Henry review not long ago."

"Reviews are just another way of coming up with same cake different icing, Roger. Most government funded reviews do exactly that just to justify why we funded them. Tanya is talking real change – like abolition of negative gearing and family trusts that we have been advocating, but also to account for the historical cost of those artificial mechanisms to the Australian people and how to recoup some of that."

"And how does she propose to achieve that Anthony?"

"Once the truth can be clearly demonstrated through her Royal Commission – and keep this to yourself too, Roger ..."

347

"My mother is still my mother Anthony!"

"Through a wealth tax, Roger!"

"A wealth tax?"

"Yes, a wealth tax that will apply only to people with assets that exceed fifty million dollars. So a national assets register and a totally comprehensive review via the Australian Taxation Office of the extent to which people who have accumulated considerable wealth, have done so through negative gearing and family trust minimisation and the levying of a wealth tax upon them. That would also pick up a lot of the wealth that people have gained by mining our resources, Roger. There should always have been limitations on how much wealth individual people could exact from the discovery of resources. As Julia once said to the mining industry, Roger – 'you do not own the resources'."

"You're gonna need a bigger tax office!"

"Your attention please, this is the captain speaking, we are about to commence our descent so can all passengers please fasten your safety belts. We should touch down in approximately ten minutes."

"Yes, and Tanya's got that covered too. Those outposted transport terminals I mentioned for the super-fast trains – the first major tenant in the concomitant commercial precinct will be the new ATO offices – at least two in every capital city, employing at least an additional ten thousand people to administer the legislation. Obviously, the commercial precincts will be the centre of substantial housing estates and we will attract other commercial industries like banks and law firms to those centres with government owned property offering realistic rents."

"Sounds like our Joondalup and Ellenbrook concepts Anthony, which have been extraordinarily successful. Also sounds quite radical Anthony, but the tax reforms are long overdue, providing they target the right people."

348

"Yes, they will, Roger – the assets register would only apply to people with net worth that presently exceeds fifty million dollars and that will pick up both residential and commercial investment properties and equities – including all shareholdings in ASIC listed companies."

"Won't they simply pass on their tax liability to the tenant as they always do? You know the saying Anthony – 'you can't make the rich pay taxes' eh!"

"That's why the future Labor Corporation will also be investing in commercial property, Roger – to keep the rents down to realistic levels. And that includes retail property too, Roger."

"Tell me about it – when we were going through our resources boom period the mining companies were so willing to pay exorbitant rents in the CBD that even some law firms went broke having to keep up with their rent increases."

"Yes I became aware of that. That is why all future state governments will own commercial towers in capital cities, Roger."

"Won't future Liberal governments simply sell them off – privatise them?"

"Not if Labor adopts a set of resumptions policies that will apply upon its return to office, Roger. Who would want to buy it - that property? No one! So we use that property to temper the omnipresent threat of future rent increases in good times."

"Tanya also wants Australia to lead an international accord on corporate tax rates – so that transnational corporations do not play off one country against another the way they have been doing and drag corporate tax rates down to rock bottom in the process. We need established bottom line corporate tax limits that nations cannot transgress and an exchange of financial information between governments with centralised monitoring, so that will need to be done through the United Nations. All of our fiscal problems are caused by wealthy people not paying their fair share of tax revenues, Roger."

"So all corporate tax treatment out in the open eh!"

"Yes and Tanya also wants a government foray into retail property, Roger, in a way that will bring downward pressure on retail rents. Virtually every tenant in major retail centres have responded saying they operate with skeleton staffing levels and they know they need more staff, but the rents and other overheads are so high they have to skate through with absolute minimal staffing levels. So property developers in retailing have virtually converted monies that were formerly paid to employees in the form of wages, into higher rents and property values, Roger. So Tanya has come up with a master plan to ameliorate that problem too – that all future major retail developments are on state government and local government owned property. Then finally, once the takeover of the bank has been finalised to benefit all Australians, the Labor Corporation targets BHP in the same way. You know, BHP exports as much work as it can to offshore cheap labour, Roger - and in taking control of BHP we restore the respect to workers that they deserve rather than all of this capricious and flippant dismissal they currently preside over, you know, guys being sacked over buggar all and losing their homes and their marriages then topping themselves."

"Yes I am aware of some cases where that very tragic outcome has occurred for that very reason."

"We would also ensure that our big Australian pays its fair share of taxes – and that goes for Rio as well. As Julia said to them, 'if you mine the dirt here you pay the tax here'."

"Yes she was quite a visionary herself wasn't she!"

"So we basically use collective worker wealth to circumvent the political institution – we use the capitalist system and work from within it to benefit Aussie workers. If we are not elected to govern to achieve our goals through politics, we use the corporate sector to achieve the same. You know Roger, very soon the collective value of all superannuation funds held for Aussie workers will exceed three trillion dollars. And I'm talking about our real workers – your truck drivers and checkout operators and factory workers, Roger – I'm not talking about those blood-sucking managers of retail super funds here!"

"There's some very heady Labor concepts there Anthony. Could be something for your second or even your third term in office – you know what happened to Gough when he went up with too many radical ideas too soon."

"God bless him! Yes, our beloved ruling class brought him down. I was just twelve years old then but I still remember a lot of things my father had to say about it. He was in tears when Gough was dismissed. Yes, I think I might actually leave all that up to our future Prime Minister Parkinson to implement. After all, they are her ideas."

"I'll have to give you more detail about the retail plan on the way back, Roger – we'll be landing soon."

He didn't get the chance to divulge Tanya's retail plan, as everybody was so tired on the return journey they all fell asleep on the plane, but it was also something the Prime Minister preferred to be a little coy about. It would definitely be a third term Labor government initiative – after every bog-stock Aussie had derived some benefits from this Labor government – apart from the wealthy.

The plane landed smoothly on lake Auld and the contingent were welcomed by the local elders. Everybody gathered for the official opening of the valve that allowed the first water from the ocean north-west of Pardoo to flow into the fish pond. The state Minister Steven Dolsen had the honours to cut to ribbon and to announce the project had officially started.

"This is truly a great occasion for the Martu people and for the people of Australia. Congratulations and thank you to all contractors involved in bringing this together within the very short time frame that I specified - you have all done a remarkable job. This project has been undertaken in a spirit of total cooperation, for the sake of our fellow Australians in the eastern states who are suffering this prolonged drought that we now seem to be capable of ending. I thank the Martu people of Punmu, Parnngurr and Kunawarritji for granting permission for us to utilise the salt lakes as evaporation ponds. It pleases us immensely to be able to provide some benefits in return and on that note, I will hand over to our state Premier Mr. Roger Brook who has a special message for the Martu people."

"Thank you Minister Dolsen, I will be brief, on behalf of the people of Western Australia I also wish to thank the Martu people for allowing this very special project to be completed – you will save the lives of hundreds of desperate farmers in the eastern states and I also now extend our sincere apology to the Martu people for the blatant neglect of the needs of your communities that this project has brought out into the open. I am pleased that you did make all of the requests that you have done and we will provide anything you might need in the future to make your quality of life more bearable in this very harsh and arid region of our state. I will admit that we could have done a lot more much sooner and I do feel quite some shame that successive state governments have neglected the communities here so flagrantly for such a long time. We hope your young people, in particular, will now feel they enjoy a better quality of life with the initiatives that this Wagyl project will provide – the ability to raise animals, to grow vegetables and fruit, to do some fishing and swim in the pool, to be artistic and to learn a plethora of new skills in the process in the workshops. Once again thank you to all of the Martu people. Now a word of thanks from the Prime Minister."

"Thank you Premier, Roger Brook. I too wish to thank all of you good Martu people here on behalf of all Australian people for allowing this project to be undertaken. I see the effects of the drought every day in Victoria where I come from and also in areas close to Canberra and the devastation it causes is horrific, so hopefully your cooperation in this will bring enormous benefit to all Australians, so for that we will be forever grateful. I also want to personally thank Mr. Andrew Robertson and Mr. Jack Lambert who are here with us today for taking the action they did, even though they did so without approval from the Water Corporation or the Environmental Protection Authority. I think we have all learned something from your proclivity to just get on with things and to take action when it is required, so thank you both. I don't mind telling you that I, myself, will endeavour to emulate you on that in my own way. There are tens of thousands of Australian families in the east who have suffered enormously from the prolonged drought and the bushfires that causes because so much of our natural vegetation perishes and the land becomes a virtual tinderbox just waiting for fires to occur. It has been unspeakable horror to see so much of our beloved country blown away by these natural phenomena.

Apart from that, we now see a new hope for the Darling River and the Murray River into which the Darling flows to be restored to natural health once the fresh water pipeline is completed to Walgett in New South Wales. There are thousands of families too, involved in agriculture who are going to benefit from having a secure source of fresh water and who will be able to grow more crop than they have ever

353

done before. This project really does give the entire nation of Australia a new hope for a brighter future. So I pledge to you good Martu people here today that we will do everything we can to provide you with benefits to improve your quality of life. My department is already in some negotiations with major stakeholders to come up with a plan of action that will provide real employment and career opportunities for all people in this part of Australia. So without any further to do I will ask the Minister for the Environment to open the pipeline."

Minister Steven Dolsen then proceeded to cut the ribbon.

"As Minister for the Environment in Western Australia and acting on behalf of the Minister for Water Mr. Ned Kelly and the Minister for Regional Development and the Minister for Agriculture and Food Ms. Alannah McKenzie, I hereby declare the Wagyl pipeline officially open."

Everybody clapped and cheered as the water flowed from the pipeline into the first fish pond, which had been constructed beneath a structure that would provide shade for the aquatic life for most of the day. This first pond of approximately thirty metres square would take almost a day to fill before the second much larger pond would be filled. The communities would endeavour to raise various types of ocean marine life including species that thrive in brackish water – such as barramundi - until the fresh water became available. If they succeeded with ocean species, they would retain the seawater facility permanently in one of their ponds. Once the water started to flow, the Monadelphous head engineer Mr. Glen Carbon, called his team at the pipeline junction to open the valve to send water on toward the Percival Lakes. Over several days the water would flow to all of the outlets that had been constructed around the Percival Lakes and Lake Disappointment, ready to be opened at a time when air streams were conducive to providing

rainfall to the drought affected areas - as determined by the
Bureau   of   Meteorology   in   Canberra.

Rain!

They didn't have to wait long. The following day the Bureau of Meteorology in Canberra was on the phone to the Federal Minister for the Environment and Water Terri Butler.

"Good morning Minister this is Brendan Denham from the bureau ... ah ... can you please advise us just how soon they can open the evaporation system to have water flow onto the lakes in the west, because we believe there will be favourable prevailing winds from tomorrow evening."

"Brendan, I believe the water has reached some of the outlets at Percival Lakes this morning so they can open the system at any time now. It won't reach all of them yet because the most remote outlets are more than two hundred kilometres from the nearest outlets, nor will it have reached Lake Disappointment. That should happen sometime today. But the water is flowing as we speak, so there would be no reason not to open the valves to disperse water onto the lakes if you believe the time is right."

"Yes please give them the go ahead and hopefully we will see some rainfall within the next two days."

They did! The valves were opened, the seawater started to flow onto the Percival Lakes and during that same day it started to evaporate as soon as it hit the extremely hot salt surface of the Percival Lakes. Two days later, the rain came down between Cunnamulla in Queensland and Dubbo in New South Wales – not a very extensive area but only part of the lakes system had been flooded that first day. Twenty four hours later, the rain fell in the entire area from Mount Isa in Queensland to Orange in New South Wales – only about five millimetres but that was enough to provide some further grass growth – and some additional hope. The system was up and running and it was working the way it was meant to. The following day water started to evaporate from the upper reaches of the Percival Lakes and the lower reaches of Lake Disappointment. A further ten millimetres of rainfall was recorded throughout most of the target area over the next two days, with some areas receiving up to twenty millimetres of rainfall.

The Federal Treasurer immediately contacted Treasury officials to commence revision of the federal budget, for there would be a significantly less requirement for drought relief funds - and significantly higher revenues from this profound farming and grazing sector.

Now that the concept had proven itself, everybody concerned was more positive and confident about proceeding with other parts of the plan. This initial success allayed any concerns over the ongoing construction of the nine hundred millimetre pipeline from Lake Argyle through Halls Creek and Fitzroy Crossing, as the use of seawater was considered an interim measure only – save for the communities continuing to utilise seawater to grow ocean fish species. The salt pans would be utilised with fresh water as soon as it became available from further raising of the dam wall at the Ord River.

The positive effects on the federal budget also allayed any concerns over the cost of constructing the pipeline to other parts of Australia. The Prime Minister immediately ordered construction to commence on the first nine hundred millimetre pipelines to Adelaide through Alice Springs, to Mount Isa in Queensland through Tennant Creek in the Northern Territory and then to Walgett in New South Wales. Chris Minehan and the Premiers of both Victoria and South Australia had lobbied for this and for the construction of a reservoir to store water, to replenish the Darling River, which had periodically been choked by algae. The poor health of the Darling River could adversely affect the Murray River in western Victoria and in South Australia.

From the southern reaches of Lake Argyle, the water would first be pumped to a reservoir constructed on the summit of Mount Pitt - a high point due south of Lake Argyle that had an elevation above four hundred and fifty metres. From there the water would be gravity fed all the way to Tennant Creek, Mt Isa and Walgett, all of which were of lower elevations. The section to Walgett was completed with this first pipeline as the Darling River urgently required a substantial influx of fresh water to replenish the health of this waterway. The reservoir on the Darling River would be constructed between Walgett and Bourke so that, apart from a constant flow into the river, a substantial flush of the river system could be released at any time. Subsequent and parallel pipelines would then be constructed to provide water to towns in outback New South Wales. The Great Dividing Range precluded any consideration of this water flowing into Sydney, but it was urgently needed in outback New South Wales – somewhere back of Bourke.

The Western Australian pipeline was constructed as planned by Premier, Roger Brook, through the towns of Newman, Meekatharra and Mount Magnet to Dalwallinu and then to other towns in the extremely vital wheatbelt. Some wheatbelt farmers constructed pivot watering systems to grow certain crops and vegetables and fruit, emulating the projects of the Martu communities.

The eventual provision of fresh water from the Kimberley within two years created immense opportunity for ongoing meaningful employment for the local indigenous people. The largest iron ore mining companies – including BHP, Rio Tinto and Roy Hill – funded the construction of an international class golf resort, complete with its dedicated airstrip, in the very scenic area to the east of the Karlamilyi

National Park with views of the Fingoon Range and the Connaughton Hills. The resort boasted five-star accommodation and an adjacent wildlife sanctuary where kangaroo and emu would graze at will. Tourists from Japan, South Korea and China flocked to the area through the international airport at Port Hedland. The local indigenous people from the Parnngurr community were employed in the hospitality resort, in maintaining the golf course, attending the fauna in the sanctuary and providing four-wheel drive tours through the Karlamilyi National Parks.

The success of this initial resort project inspired a decision by the big four miners to construct similar resorts due east of the Kunawarritji community, taking in the undulations surrounding Kidson Bluff and also to the east of the Jigalong Community Reserve. The people from Kunawarritji and Jigalong, too, were to be gainfully employed in a wide range of traineeship careers. With the abundance of fresh water being available from Lake Argyle, similar resorts were also constructed near Leinster, Leonora and Laverton within five years, for at last the people and government of Western Australia had realised the potential for such resorts to provide for the needs of remote indigenous communities.

The coastal pipeline would supply all towns from Derby to Geraldton. The goldfields pipeline would flow from Lake Wells through the towns of Leinster, Laverton, Leonora and Menzies to Kalgoorlie. This project would take more than two years to complete, but once it was completed, the flow of water between Kalgoorlie and the Mundaring Weir was reversed and water from Lake Argyle flowed into towns between Kalgoorlie and Mundaring Weir and into parts of suburban Perth between Sawyers Valley and Midland. From the Mundaring Weir, water flowed into the Helena River and then onwards into the Swan River at the town of Guildford.

The Wagyl would return to his natural home.

Back to the bush

Following the opening ceremony Andrew and Jack proceeded to return to Jennifer Downs via Newman and Jigalong, taking a few Jigalong locals with them. While in Newman they went to see the doctor at Kinetic once again as a check on Rebecca's pregnancy. Then they did some shopping at the IGA supermarket and the Newman Hardware store. They stopped at Jigalong for two hours to discuss some business with the local people and to gain an update on how the construction works were progressing there. It would take several weeks before the water would flow at Jigalong but construction of their swimming pool and fish ponds were on cue. As was the case at Punmu, Parnngurr and Kunawarritji, the kids would not be averse to swimming in the seawater pond before fresh water became available.

Rebecca Robertson would give birth to two children on 2nd October 2025 – a birthdate they would share with old Jack Lambert - first a girl and then a boy. Both of her children would become lawyers and enter politics through the Australian Labor Party, following the footsteps of old Jack Lambert. One of her twin children, endowed with the spirit of the Wagyl, would become the very first President of Australia, appointed so by King William V of England, in the year 2060.

Once back at the station, Jimmy informed Andrew and Jack that he had been out bush and another bore cap had been spilling, so Andrew and Jack prepared for a sortie to the small Lake McDonald the next day. They took the dogs with them again, fixed the bore cap and set up a campfire for the night.

"You haven't told me very much about yourself Jack – you know, your past, wives, jobs etc."

Jack paused for several seconds.

"Had a wife for twenty years Andrew. Was very happy for about five years, had a good sizeable deposit for our house where we lived that we were about to buy from her parents. Then her brother came down to Perth from Kalgoorlie and they got into talking about buying a business to provide him with a good income. He had suffered an accident in the mining industry and was unable to work again. So based on her prior experience with owning food businesses, they purchased a café in a shopping centre from four Italian men."

"Good business?"

Jack shook his head.

"Those blokes turned out to be the Perth mafia. That business wasn't making any money – just losing a fortune. The only thing those men ever cooked properly was the books. To cut a long story short, we lost everything."

"Wouldn't that be against the law, I mean, basically – fraud?"

"Huh! Yes, we went to the police and they did a cursory kind of investigation before backing away – told us the blokes had paid tax on the profit. Turns out they hadn't."

"How did you find that out?"

"We sued them in the Supreme Court. They were losing more money than we lost."

"So did you have a win?"

"No! That's when our lawyers stuffed it up, by preparing a claim that did not allow them to interrogate the main protagonist – the manager of the business. So we lost even more by suing the bastards."

"So did you sue the lawyers?"

"Yep – that's when we learned of advocates immunity Andrew. In Australia, lawyers cannot successfully be sued if they stuff up in court – something that has changed almost everywhere else, even in New Zealand. So we lost more money by suing the lawyers. We might have won against the lawyers but couldn't take it as far as the High Court to determine if advocate's immunity applied to our case. Some lawyers said it would and others said it wouldn't."

"Was there some type of moot aspect about that?"

"Yes, because the original case did not proceed to trial. We were forced to settle out of court at a substantial loss through fear of losing the case."

"Which would have meant that you would have been required to pay the other party's legal costs."

"Yes! As far as we are concerned, that moot point should have been sorted by the legal profession, the courts and the politicians too before it jumped up to destroy us. But since then we found out that the police were possibly corrupt too Andrew. That was intimated by two police officers during the Royal Commission into the police force, that police in the fraud squad were possibly on the take - graft payments from the fraudsters. A donation to the police boys club to back away from levelling charges!"

"Shit, that is sinister!"

"It's love for money Andrew. Rather than give us our lives back by prosecuting those evil men, they put their hand out for, who knows, a quick five thousand or ten thousand bucks."

"That reminds me of what the good Lord said Jack – 'no man can have two masters, he will love one and despise the other - you cannot serve God and money'. That's what the good Lord said."

"Well, I'll stick to serving the good Lord, Andrew."

"You no longer with your wife then Jack?"

363

Once again Jack paused for several seconds.

"She died! The stress killed her! And as far as I am concerned Andrew, those lawyers and those police have blood on their hands, but they couldn't give a damn about that. But I'd rather be in my shoes than theirs. They seem to work from an assumption that there is no God in heaven Andrew. Seems to me that a lot of people would sell their soul for love of money."

"Well I am really sorry to hear that Jack, what happened to you, I really am. You've been through some pretty heavy stuff there. I had no idea, nobody has said anything."

"Nobody up here knows, that's why"

"So what are you going to do about it Jack?"

"Well, your water project, Andrew, has emphasised to me just how pervasive political complacency is. This could have been done fifty years ago Andrew. So I just might have a crack at the old politics myself. Based on my experience I have a few good ideas."

"Yes, you should Jack Lambert – politics needs good people like you. Tell me Jack, what would your most important single policy be?"

"The formation of an Australian Justice Commission! One that has a charter to care for the little people – people who are crushed by the wrongdoing of others – crushed by big banks or fraudsters or negligent lawyers or corrupt police or franchisors or retail property developers. Our legal system doesn't provide justice Andrew. The Justice Commission would have powers beyond the Australian Securities and Investments Commission and the A.C.C.C. – and not suffer from the same complacency but will be proactive. It would fund cases of national interest, especially where determinations are required from the High Court. So that is an example, Andrew, of where a Justice Commission could play a role. Apart from that, I believe all statements of claim need to be scrutinised by independent counsel prior to the courts exposing them as inadequate, which is what happened to us."

"You know, you have some really good ideas there, Jack Lambert - and you just might bring about some substantial goodness from your own adversity Jack. Reminds me of a verse from Saint Paul's letter to the Romans."

"Oh yeah! And what was that?"

"Chapter eight verse twenty-eight – 'all things work together for good with those who love God'. Your prolonged adversity Jack Lambert, just might bring about some significant change to this entire nation."

"I doubt it!"

"Have you stopped to think that perhaps somebody's mistake - or deception - in providing us with just two cracked bore caps has resulted in the end to this prolonged drought in Australia Jack?"

"Well only because you did the right thing – or the wrong thing! And not only this drought Andrew, but hopefully all drought."

"I reckon it was your man yowie who made me do that Jack. You got me thinking out there, Jack Lambert, about the most significant thing that has ever happened to me in my life."

"And that was – the demise of your mother?"

"Yeah, maybe – to that point of time. But I do recall thinking, Jack, based on what you said to me, that I hope the most significant thing that ever happens in my life is still ahead of me. We probably would not have washed out that cricket match if you had not flooded the second lake Jack and kept those bores flowing for as long as you did. And I am convinced that I would not have sunk those extra twelve bores at the Percival Lakes had it not been for your yowie, Jack."

"Well, Andrew, all I can say is - I hope he enjoyed the rabbit!"

Other books by this author

"World of Words 500"

Advanced English vocabulary to professional level, five hundred of the most important words in the English language. Compulsive reading for all school students aged twelve and above. Highly conducive to superior essay writing for university or college. Average reading time between four and six hours.

"The Visitation Eternal"

An unidentifiable flying object arrives in New York City and this historically monumental event immediately raises questions regarding our belief in the existence of God.

Futuristic fiction pertaining to the future of the human race and a reconciliation between religious belief systems and the probable existence of intelligent extra-terrestrial life.

Yes, we are unique and alone in the universe and we do survive and prosper.

"All good people go to heaven!"